Call Us Americans

Call Us Americans

Edited by Dorothy A. Chernoff

Illustrated by Jack Wolf

Doubleday & Company, Inc., Garden City, New York

Grateful acknowledgment is made for the use of the following copyrighted material:

"Neighbor Rosicky" by Willa Cather. Copyright 1930 by the Crowell Publishing Company; copyright renewed, 1958, by the executor of the estate of Willa Cather. From *Obscure Destinies* by Willa Cather. Reprinted by permission of Alfred A. Knopf, Inc.

"The Decline and Fall of Augie Sheean" by Joe Coogan. Copyright 1954 by Joe Coogan. From *To The Rear, March* by Joe Coogan. Reprinted by permission of Doubleday & Company, Inc.

"The Odyssey of a Wop" by John Fante from *Dago Red*. Copyright © 1940 by John Fante. Copyright renewed, 1968, by the author. Reprinted by permission of McIntosh and Otis, Inc.

"Mama and the Occasion" from *Mama's Bank Account* by Kathryn Forbes. Copyright, 1943, by Kathryn Forbes. Reprinted by permission of Harcourt, Brace & World, Inc.

"American Me" from *American Me* by Beatrice Winston Griffith. Copyright 1947 and 1948 by Beatrice Winston Griffith. Reprinted by permission of Houghton Mifflin Company.

"The Circus Cat of Prickly Orange" by MacKinlay Kantor. Copyright 1938 by the Curtis Publishing Company, Inc. Reprinted by permission of Paul R. Reynolds, Inc.

"Rosebud Was Her Name" from *It Might Be You* by Ruth Adams Knight. Copyright 1949 by Ruth Adams Knight. Reprinted by permission of Doubleday & Company, Inc.

"Chinatown Family" from *Chinatown Family* by Lin Yutang. Copyright 1948 by the John Day Company. Reprinted by permission of the author.

"Young Man Axelbrod" by Sinclair Lewis. Copyright 1917 by the Century Company; copyright 1945 by Sinclair Lewis. From *Selected Short Stories of Sinclair Lewis*. Reprinted by permission of Ernst, Cane, Berner & Gitlin.

"The Ambassador" by Edward Newhouse. Copr. © The New Yorker Magazine, Inc. Reprinted by permission of the New Yorker Magazine, Inc.

"Yes, Your Honesty" from *Anything Can Happen* by George and Helen Waite Papashvily. Copyright 1944 by George and Helen Waite Papashvily. Reprinted by permission of Harper & Row, Publishers.

"Mr. Kaplan the Magnificent" from *The Education of Hyman Kaplan* by Leonard Q. Ross. Copyright, 1937, by Harcourt, Brace & World, Inc.; copyright, 1965, by Leo Rosten. Reprinted by permission of the publisher.

"The Man From Far Away" by Jack Schaefer. Copyright 1954 by Jack Schaefer. Reprinted by permission of the Harold Matson Company, Inc.

"Uncle Bosko" from *A Long Way Home and Other Stories* by Vern Sneider. Copyright 1956 by Vern Sneider. Reprinted by permission of A. L. Fierst.

"Brudie's Pickle" by Booth Tarkington. Copyright 1916 by Booth Tarkington. From *Harlequine and Columbine and Other Stories* by Booth Tarkington. Reprinted by permission of Brandt & Brandt.

"Every Other Thursday" by Edna Ferber. Copyright 1926 by Edna Ferber. Reprinted with the kind permission of the author.

FOREWORD

"We are a nation of immigrants." These words, spoken by the late President Kennedy, echo back from the air around us. The clatter and the faces and the smells of our city streets tell us. The earth, first tamed and turned to furrows by foreign hands, bears witness. The records of immigration officials document our history; rambling districts of our cities have grown with surges of immigrants, first from one country, then another. Many groups or individuals are still easily identifiable with the land they or their people left. Others have blended quickly into the world around them. Out of all these immigrants we Americans have grown, and all of us together *are* America, the bearers and the builders of all she has.

This collection of stories about immigrants to the United States has been selected for young adults. The stories have been chosen because they are good stories, because they offer insight as well as information, and because as a group they may lend new understanding of the blending of differences that has made America what she is today. This book makes no attempt to relate the history of what has come to be called the immigrant movement. Nor does it preach a moral or attempt to evaluate the contributions made by one particular group or another. Rather, I hope that it will provide a glimpse of the many who have come and give us a new perspective on ourselves. America is a nation of immigrants; if we forget this, we forget who we are.

D.A.C.

CONTENTS

Call Us Americans

MR. K*A*P*L*A*N

THE MAGNIFICENT

LEO ROSTEN

Mr. Parkhill had decided that perhaps it might be wise for the class to attempt more *practical* exercises. On a happy thought, he had taken up the subject of letter writing. He had lectured the students on the general structure of the personal letter: shown them where to put the address, city, date; explained the salutation; talked about the body of the letter; described the final greeting. And now the fruits of Mr. Parkhill's labors were being demonstrated. Five students had written the assignment, "A Letter to a Friend," on the blackboard.

On the whole Mr. Parkhill was satisfied. Miss Mitnick had a straightforward and accurate letter—as might be expected—inviting her friend Sylvia to a surprise party. Mr. Norman Bloom had written to someone named Fishbein, describing an exciting day at Coney Island. Miss Rochelle Goldberg had told "Molly" about a "Bŏs ride on a bŏs on 5 av." Mrs. Moskowitz, simple soul, had indulged her fantasies by pretending she was on vacation in "Miame, Floridal," and had written her husband Oscar to be sure "the pussy should get each morning milk." (Apparently Mrs. Moskowitz was deeply attached to "the pussy," for she merely repeated the admonition in several ways all through her epistle, leaving no room for comment on the beauties of "Miame, Floridal.") And Mr. Hyman Kaplan—Mr. Parkhill frowned as he examined the last letter written on the blackboard.

"It's to mine brodder in Varsaw," said Mr. Kaplan, smiling in happy anticipation.

Mr. Parkhill nodded, rather absently; his eyes were fixed on the board.

"Maybe it vould be easier I should readink de ladder alod," suggested Mr. Kaplan delicately.

"'Letter,' Mr. Kaplan," said Mr. Parkhill, ever the pedagogue. "Not 'ladder.'"

"Maybe I should readink de latter?" repeated Mr. Kaplan.

"Er—no—no," said Mr. Parkhill hastily. "We—er—we haven't much time left this evening. It is getting late." He tried to put it as gently as possible, knowing what this harsh deprivation might mean to Mr. Kaplan's soul.

Mr. Kaplan sighed philosophically, bowing to the tyranny of time.

"The class will study the letter for a few minutes, please," said Mr. Parkhill. "Then I shall call for corrections."

The class fell into that half-stupor which indicated concentration. Miss Mitnick studied the blackboard with a determined glint in her eye. Mr. Pinsky stared at Mr. Kaplan's letter with a critical air, saying "Tchk! Tchk!" several times, quite professionally.

Mrs. Moskowitz gazed ceilingward with an exhausted expression. Apparently the vicarious excitements of the class session had been too much for poor Mrs. Moskowitz: an invitation to a surprise party, a thrilling day at Coney Island, a Fifth Avenue bus ride, and her own trip to Florida. That was quite a night for Mrs. Moskowitz.

And Mr. Kaplan sat with his joyous smile unmarred, a study in obvious pride and simulated modesty, like a god to whom mortals were paying homage. First he watched the faces of the students as they wrestled with his handiwork, and found them pleasing. Then he concentrated his gaze on Mr. Parkhill. He saw anxious little lines creep around Mr. Parkhill's eyes as he read that letter; then a frown —a strange frown, bewildered and incredulous; then a nervous clearing of the throat. Any other student might have been plunged into melancholy by these dark omens, but they only added a transcendental quality to Mr. Kaplan's smile.

This was the letter Mr. Kaplan had written:

459 E 3 Str
N.Y.
New York
Octo. 10

HELLO MAX!!!

I should telling about mine progriss. In school I am fine. Making som mistakes, netcheral. Also however doing the hardest xrcises, like the best students the same. Som students is Mitnick, Blum, Moskowitz —no relation Moskowitz in Warsaw. Max! You should absolutel coming to N.Y. and belonging in mine school!

It was at this point, visualizing too vividly *another* Mr. Kaplan in the class, that anxious little lines had crept around Mr. Parkhill's eyes.

Do you feeling fine? I suppose. Is all ok? You should begin right now learning about ok. Here you got to say ok all the time. ok the wether, ok the potatos, ok the prazident Roosevelt.

At this point the frown—a strange frown, bewildered and incredulous—had marched onto Mr. Parkhill's face.

How is darling Fanny? Long should she leave. So long.

With all kinds entusiasm

Your animated brother

H * Y * M * I * E

Mr. Kaplan simply could not resist the aesthetic impulse to embellish his signature with those stars; they had almost become an integral part of the name itself.

Mr. Parkhill cleared his throat. He felt vaguely distressed.

"Has everyone finished reading?" he asked. Heads nodded in halfhearted assent. "Well, let us begin. Corrections, please."

Mrs. Tomasic's hand went up. "Should be 'N.Y.' after 'New York' and 'New York' should be on top of."

"Correct," said Mr. Parkhill, explaining the difference and making the change on the board.

"In all places is 'mine' wrong," said Mr. Feigenbaum. "It should be 'my.'"

Mr. Parkhill nodded, happy that someone had caught that most common of Mr. Kaplan's errors.

The onslaught went on: the spelling of words, the abbreviation of "October" and "street," the tenses of the verbs.

"Mr. Kaplan got so many mistakes," began Mr. Bloom with hauteur. Mr. Bloom was still annoyed because Mr. Kaplan had rashly offered to correct the spelling of Coney Island, in Mr. Bloom's letter, to "'Corney Island,' like is pernonced." "He spelled wrong 'progress,' 'some,' 'natural.' He means 'Long should she *live*' —not 'Long should she *leave*.' That means going away. He even spelled wrong my name!" It was clear from Mr. Bloom's indignant tone that this was by far the most serious of Mr. Kaplan's many errors. "Is double 'o,' not 'u.' I ain't like *som* Blooms!"

With this jealous defence of the honor of the House of Bloom, Mr. Bloom looked at Mr. Kaplan coolly. If he had thought to see Mr. Kaplan chagrined by the barrage of corrections, he did not know the real mettle of the man. Mr. Kaplan was beaming with delight.

"Honist to Gott, Bloom," said Mr. Kaplan with admiration, "you soitinly improvink in your English to seeink all dese mistakes!"

There was a fine charity in this accolade. It had, however, the subtle purpose of shifting attention from Mr. Kaplan's errors to Mr. Bloom's progress.

Mr. Bloom did not know whether to be pleased or suspicious, whether this was a glowing tribute or the most insidious irony.

"Thenks, Kaplan," he said finally, acknowledging the compliment with a nod, and considered the injuries of "Corney Island" and "Blum" expiated.

"I see more mistakes," said Miss Mitnick, intruding an unwelcome note into the happy Kaplan-Bloom rapport. Mr. Kaplan's eyes gleamed when he heard Miss Mitnick's voice. Here was a foe of a caliber quite different from that of Norman Bloom. "'Absolutel' should be 'absolutely.' 'Potatoes' has an 'e.' 'Prazident' is wrong; it should be 'e' and 's' and a capital." Miss Mitnick went on and on making corrections. Mr. Parkhill transcribed them to the board as swiftly as he could, until his wrist began to ache. "'ok' is wrong, should be 'O.K.'—with *capitals* and *periods*—because it's abbreviation."

All through the Mitnick attack Mr. Kaplan sat quiet, alert but smiling. There was a supreme confidence in that smile, as if he were waiting for some secret opportunity to send the whole structure that Miss Mitnick was rearing so carefully crashing down upon her head. Miss Mitnick rushed on to the abyss.

"Last," she said, slowing up to emphasize the blow, "*three* exclamation points after 'Max' is wrong. Too many."

"Aha!" cried Mr. Kaplan. It was The Opportunity. "Podden me, Mitnick. De odder corractinks you makink is fine, foist-class—even Hau Kay, an' I minn Hau Kay mit *capitals* an' *periods*," he added sententiously. "But batter takink back abot de tree haxclimation points!"

Miss Mitnick blushed, looking to Mr. Parkhill for succor.

"Mr. Kaplan," said Mr. Parkhill with caution, sensing some hidden logic in Mr. Kaplan's tone. "A colon is the proper punctuation for the salutation, or a comma. If you *must* use an—er—exclamation point"—he was guarding himself on all fronts—"then, as Miss Mitnick says, *three* are too many."

"For de vay *I'm* fillink abot mine *brodder?*" asked Mr. Kaplan promptly. In that question, sublime in its simplicity, Mr. Kaplan inferentially accused his detractor of (1) familial ingratitude, (2) trying to come between the strong love of two brothers.

"But, Kaplan," broke in Mr. Bloom, jumping into the fray on the side of Miss Mitnick, "*three* exclama—"

"Also he's mine *faworite* brodder!" said Mr. Kaplan. "For mine *faworite* brodder you eskink *vun—leetle—haxclimation point?*" It was an invincible position. "Ha! Dat I give to *strengers!*"

Mr. Bloom retired from the field, annihilated. One could hardly expect a man of Mr. Kaplan's exquisite sensitivity to give equal deference and love to *strangers* and his favorite brother. Mr. Parkhill paused to mobilize his forces.

"How's about 'entusiasm'?" said Miss Mitnick, determined to recover face. "Is spelled wrong—should be 'th.' And 'With all kinds enthusiasm' is bad for ending a letter."

"Aha!" Mr. Kaplan gave his battle call again. "Maybe *is* de spallink wronk. But not de vay I'm *usink* 'antusiasm,' becawss"—he injected a trenchant quality into his voice to let the class get the deepest meaning of his next remark—"becawss *I* write to *mine* brodder in Varsaw *mit real antusiasm!*"

The implication was clear: Miss Mitnick was one of those who, corrupted by the gaudy whirl of the New World, let her brothers starve, indifferently, overseas.

Miss Mitnick bit her lip. Mr. Parkhill, trying to look judicious, avoided her eyes.

"Well," began Miss Mitnick yet a third time, desperately, "'animated' is wrong. 'Your *animated* brother, Hymie?' *That's* wrong."

She looked at Mr. Parkhill with a plea that was poignant. She dared not look at Mr. Kaplan, whose smile had advanced to a new dimension.

"Yes," said Mr. Parkhill. "'Animated' is quite out of place in the final greeting."

Mr. Kaplan sighed. "I looked op de void 'enimated' *spacial.* It's minnink 'full of life,' no? Vell, I falt *planty* full of life ven I vas wridink de ladder."

Miss Mitnick dropped her eyes, the rout complete.

"Mr. Kaplan!" Mr. Parkhill was left to fight the good fight alone. "You may say 'She had an animated expression' or 'The music has an animated refrain.' But one doesn't say 'animated' about one's *self*."

The appeal to propriety proved successful. Mr. Kaplan confessed that perhaps he had overreached himself with "Your animated brother."

"Suppose we try another word," suggested Mr. Parkhill. "How about 'fond'? 'Your *fond* brother—er—Hyman?'" (He couldn't quite essay "Hymie.")

Mr. Kaplan half-closed his eyes, gazed into space, and meditated on this moot point. "'Fond,' 'fond,'" he whispered to himself. He was like a man who had retreated into a secret world, searching for his Muse. "'Your fond brodder, Hymie.'" He shook his head. "Podden me," he said apologetically. "It don' have de *fillink*."

"What about 'dear'?" offered Mr. Parkhill quickly. "'Your *dear* brother,' and so on?"

Once more Mr. Kaplan went through the process of testing, judgment, and consultation with his evasive Muse. "'Dear,' 'dear,' 'Your dear brodder, Hymie.' Also no." He sighed. "'Dear,' it's too *common*."

"What about—"

"Aha!" cried Mr. Kaplan suddenly, as the Muse kissed him. His smile was as the sun. "I got him! Fine! Poifick! Soch a void!"

The class, to whom Mr. Kaplan had communicated some of his own excitement, waited breathlessly. Mr. Parkhill himself, it might be said, was possessed of a queer eagerness.

"Yes, Mr. Kaplan. What word would you suggest?"

"'Megnificent!'" cried Mr. Kaplan.

Admiration and silence fell upon the class like a benediction. "Your magnificent brother, Hymie." It was a *coup de maître*, no less. Mr. K * A * P * L * A * N the Magnificent.

As if in a trance, the beginners' grade waited for Mr. Parkhill's verdict.

And when Mr. Parkhill spoke, it was slowly, sadly, aware that he was breaking a magic spell. "N-no, Mr. Kaplan. I'm afraid not. 'Magnificent' isn't really—er—appropriate."

The bell rang in the corridors, as if it had withheld its signal until the last possible moment. The class moved into life and toward the door. Mr. Norman Bloom went out with Mr. Kaplan. Mr. Parkhill could hear the last words of their conversation.

"Kaplan," said Mr. Bloom enviously, "*how* you fond soch a beautiful woid?"

"'Megnificent,' 'megnificent,'" Mr. Kaplan murmured to himself wistfully. "Ach! Dat *vas* a beauriful void, ha, Bloom?"

"Believe me!" said Mr. Bloom. "*How* you fond soch a woid?"

"By *dip* tinking," said Mr. Kaplan.

He strode out like a hero.

THE DECLINE AND FALL
OF AUGIE SHEEAN

JOE COOGAN

I was thirteen years old on the day that Augie Sheean sold his
soul to the devil. Augie, a short, stocky boy with a round, cheerful
face was an eighth-grade classmate of mine, who lived four doors
away from me in an old two-story row house on Eighteenth Street
in Philadelphia. He was a newcomer to our neighborhood. At just
about the time the new school term was beginning, Augie and
his widowed mother arrived from Tinahely, a small Irish village,

and moved into the house left vacant by the death of old Matt
Harvey, a bachelor who had lived in the old house on Eighteenth
Street for twenty years. It seems that the Sheeans were cousins of
his, and old Matt—who had been a saving and fairly prosperous
plumber—used to send money to them when he was alive; when
he died, he left them the house and a small legacy.

"It's a mystery to me," my mother said, "why he didn't send for
them long ago. Rattling around by himself in that big house when
he could have had a fine woman to take care of it for him."

The mystery was cleared up when we got to know Margaret
Sheean. A tall, heavy-set woman with an air of brisk, determined
piety, she was, in her rather breezy way, what my father called a
"great frowner." One of the things she frowned on was America.
"A land of flappers, gangsters, bootleggers and drunkards," she
called it. Old Matt would have had no living with her. Matt drank.

Augie was a year older than I and had graduated from school
in Tinahely, but it was decided that he'd have to repeat the
eighth grade at St. Anselm's grammar school to qualify for ad-
mittance to the Catholic high school. St. Anselm's school was a
squat, brick building which huddled self-consciously against the
stone, majestically sprawling church. It was only about five blocks
down the street from our house, so I was commissioned to take
Augie there on the first few mornings and see that he got to know
everybody.

As I came out of the house on the first day of class, Augie was
standing on his front doorstep waiting for me. He was dressed in
a dark-blue coat and knickers, high black shoes and stockings. I
was wearing what everyone wore that year—brown corduroy knickers and knee-length boots with a penknife jammed in the top of
them. Augie pointed to my boots.

"Is it hunting you're going?"

I decided to dislike him. "These are lumberjack boots. I'm going
to be a lumberjack in Canada. A bunch of us are."

"They're lovely things."

I decided to like him. "Maybe you can get a pair and come
along. Canada needs good men."

"It's not for me. I'm going to be a priest."

I stared at him in awe. He looked a little like a priest at that, with his large Irish face and dark clothes. "You've got a vocation?"

"My mother's been praying for it. Everything my mother prays for comes true." He crossed the index and middle fingers of his right hand. "She and Saint Joseph are just like that!"

"Don't you *want* to be a priest?"

"Ah, I suppose so. But a fellow has no say in it. The saint has never refused her a thing in his life. She lights the candle every morning, and whatever she wants she gets. It's hard to believe."

It was. It was especially hard for me to believe that Mrs. Sheean could get prompt, efficient service from such a busy, high-level, heavenly executive. Although Joseph was my patron saint, I rarely prayed to him. I was then working on the theory that if you really wanted anything done you should go to someone who had, as it were, less paperwork. I had great devotion, that year, to Saint Polycarp.

I was about to mention this to Augie, when Mrs. Sheean loomed up in front of us.

"Hello, me buckos." Mrs. Sheean had a deep booming voice and a figure like an uptilted dirigible. She stared at my boots. "Did you join up with the Army?" she asked me.

"They're lumberjack boots."

"A small, skinny thing like you a lumberjack? With a fine name like Joseph, it's a priest you should be. I'll say a few prayers for you."

"No, don't!" I said quickly.

"Well, you needn't shout, lad. If I can't help your soul, perhaps I can perform a corporal work of mercy. Drop by with Augustine after school, and I may find a little something to fatten you up." She waved cheerily and floated up the street.

"Augie," I said when she left, "if your mother likes Saint Joseph so much, how come she christened you Augustine?"

Augie scratched his head. "'Tisn't too sure I am, but I think at one time she was very fond of Saint Augustine. Then she found out a few things about him she didn't like and turned pretty cool. You know, those are lovely things, those boots."

After school, Augie reminded me of his mother's invitation. We found Mrs. Sheean in the kitchen, cutting a large chocolate cake.

"Sit down and eat up, boy," she said. "Don't stint yourself. You're not Jerry Clarke, praise God." Jerry Clarke, Mrs. Sheean went on to explain, was a miserly atheist who lived near her when she was a girl.

"Scrawny and mean he was. Came to a bad end. Said he'd prove there was no God. Ran into the chapel during Mass one morning, and let loose a string of blasphemies." She smiled. "He burst into flame."

"Was he hurt?" I asked.

"Ran screaming from the church and collapsed on the steps, burnt to a crisp. When they stirred the ashes the one thing left of him was a small pool of melted gold. It was the only good thing the little blackguard ever did—God rest his soul. There was enough gold there to repair the steps. Have another piece of cake."

I ate a good bit of Mrs. Sheean's cake in the next month or so and heard a good many of her stories. The cake was always chocolate and delicious; the stories were always bloodcurdling and moralistic. I became quite fond of Mrs. Sheean.

I became fond of Augie too. Everybody did. He was a friendly, easygoing kid and within a few weeks he was one of the most popular boys in the neighborhood.

Mrs. Sheean's reception was more mixed. No doubt, everyone agreed, she had her good points. She was very nice to Augie (she bought him the boots right off) and she was always cruising forth to nurse at a sickbed or mourn at a wake. Yet she dispensed this spiritual largess with an irritating, hearty aloofness. She may have had good cause for her exalted attitude. It turned out to be amazingly true that every prayer Margaret Sheean made was immediately answered. For didn't Annie Brophy, whom the doctors had given up for dead, recover when Mrs. Sheean gave the nod to Saint Joseph? And when she predicted that Corny Hughes (who hadn't seen a sober day in fifteen years) would lay off the hooch, didn't he come down with a liver complaint and have to give up the bottle entirely? Mrs. Sheean had only to mutter a request as she lit her morning candle and the thing was as good as done. Corny Hughes never forgave her for it.

As a matter of fact, Mrs. Sheean's morning devotion became something of a parish scandal. The vigil lights in front of the statue of Saint Joseph were placed in diminishing rows, like racked billiard balls, in an ascending brass triangle. The red one at the apex of the triangle was Mrs. Sheean's. Every morning after eight-o'clock Mass she'd kneel for a few minutes at the *prie-dieu*, then light the candle. If it had been already lit by some lesser suppliant, Mrs. Sheean would pinch it out before relighting it, then light the usurper's candle farther down the line. This caused a great deal of talk, but nobody tried to do anything about it.

Augie's piety was a little less manifest. He regarded his ordination as a *fait accompli* and, like any good priest, he was in church more often than most of us, refused to listen to the mildly irreverent stories that sometimes made the rounds, and had a tendency to spot virtue in everything. It was when he began to spot the virtue in Doris Clooney that all the trouble started.

Doris Clooney, another Eighteenth-Streeter, was the Clara Bow of the eighth grade. A plump, flirtatious girl, she wore longer hair and shorter skirts than any other girl in the class, and there were occasional rumors of cloakroom kisses with Lindy Geoghegan, her steady boy friend. Lindy, a tall, slow-spoken kid who was in the eighth grade for the second time, always wore a black imitation-leather flier's helmet. He was mad about Doris Clooney, and although he lived in the opposite direction he carried her books up Eighteenth Street every day.

Augie and I frequently walked behind them, and when we did it was hard to get a sensible word out of him. He looked like a man walking underwater; he inched along with his eyes blurred and his lips contorted into a large, rubbery smirk. Then one day Doris smirked back.

I don't know exactly how it happened, but pretty soon Augie and I started walking home with Doris and Lindy. Lindy and I never said much, but Doris—who, it appeared, had developed quite an interest in religion—kept chattering to Augie about sacramentals and church ceremonies and what a noble life priests lead. What he saw in her was beyond me. I thought Doris Clooney was fat and dumb.

It wasn't a completely compatible quartet, and it broke up on the last day of our October retreat.

Sister Mary Rita had just told us about a Belgian peasant girl who was possessed by the devil. When the devil took over, this girl would turn black, float twelve feet in the air and tell off-color stories in Ancient Assyrian. She became the talk of the eighth grade.

"I'd call it," Doris Clooney said as we walked up the street, "a truly awe-inspiring story." That's what sister had called it.

Augie was about to answer when Lindy cut him off: "I'd call it a lot of junk."

"Lindy Geoghegan, that's blasphemous!" Doris said.

"Twelve feet in the air? I don't believe a word of it."

I decided to come to Christianity's rescue. "I jumped from a twelve-foot diving board last summer," I said. "Twelve feet isn't so high."

"It's not bad for such a short take-off," Lindy said.

Doris giggled; Augie frowned; Doris turned prim.

"Come on, Augie," she said, pulling him ahead, "let's not associate with these heathens."

From then on, Augie and Doris walked home alone together. Or rather, Doris walked Augie home. He and Doris would stop and chat when they reached Augie's house; then, as I approached (I always followed a block behind) Doris would smile, blow him a kiss and saunter up Eighteenth Street.

I was a little hurt about all this. I couldn't understand why she should be sore at me. She wasn't, Augie explained; but a wonderful thing had happened. Doris had discovered that she, too, had a vocation; she wanted to be a nun, but she was constantly bothered by worldly thoughts. It did her good to tell Augie about them.

Doris started calling Augie her "dear, dear friend," and wouldn't so much as pass the time of day with poor Lindy Geoghegan.

Augie's spiritual work of mercy came to an abrupt end on a snowy day in mid-November. When I started up Eighteenth Street, I was surprised to see Augie and Doris still standing in front of his house. Mrs. Sheean, who suddenly appeared on the front steps, was even more surprised than I. I couldn't hear what she said, but I saw her right arm come up and make a slow rigid arc until it pointed due north. And I saw Doris bundle her books under her arm and flee into the storm. As I came closer, the thunder of Mrs. Sheean's voice rumbled around my head, and the compasslike arm swung in my direction.

"You're to come in here, too, young man. It's time you learned about things."

I walked up the steps. She put one arm around me, the other around Augie, and pushed us ahead of her into the kitchen. Mrs. Sheean stood in the center of the room, flushed, silent and swaying violently. Then suddenly:

"What's her name?" she bellowed.

"Doris Clooney," Augie muttered.

Mrs. Sheean stopped swaying. She stood stock-still, dropped both hands to her sides and threw back her head.

"I'll tell you a few things about your friend Miss Clooney. I know her type well, and a bad type it is. All satin and Satan and hanging around in low dens with gangsters and sailors with their slick patent-leather hair." (*Lindy's helmet?* I thought.) "Oh, sure, she'll say to you, 'Come on, it won't matter. What difference will it make?'" Mrs. Sheean imitated what she thought was Doris' voice. It came out a kind of mincing boom. "'Sure it can't make any difference, dearie. Who'll see us?'" Her fist banged on the table. "I'll tell you who will see you. There's the cherubim'll see you, and the seraphim, and all the saints in heaven, and God, and the good Saint Joseph himself." Unperturbed by this unorthodox billing, Mrs. Sheean went on. "But, no! She'll tell you it won't matter."

Just *what* wouldn't matter wasn't very clear to either Augie or me.

"I don't know about the young narrowback here," Mrs. Sheean continued, "but as for you, Augustine, you have a mother's curse if you come near that flapper again. It'll be part of me general intention when I talk to the good saint tomorrow."

That was enough for Augie. After that, he might have been deaf and dumb for all the attention he paid to Doris Clooney. Doris didn't seem to mind, though. She and Lindy Geoghegan became chummier than ever.

I thought when Augie found out Doris didn't have a real vocation after all, he'd feel relieved. He didn't; when I mentioned it he called me a "meddlesome little prattler" and told me to stop bothering him. And he took to going to church more often than ever.

As I came from the confessional one Saturday afternoon, I saw Augie kneeling before the statue of Saint Joseph. The burning vigil lights sent bright flashes of colored fire flickering across his fore-head. His lips moved rapidly and his face had the desperately cordial look of one who is doggedly and unsuccessfully trying to get a word in edgewise.

I waited on the church steps until he came out. "Guess what?" I said. "We decided that the first thing we'll do when we get to the woods is clear out a space for the chapel." Augie was supposed to be the lumber camp's chaplain.

"God of Virtues!" he said. "Will I never hear the end of your silly, childish brillabralla?"

"I just wanted to tell you."

"You told me. Now must you be forever tagging after me? Sure I'm sick of listening to you and your plans. I'd appreciate it if you didn't come near me again."

This was the beginning of a lonely time for me. I got so mad at Augie that I almost didn't invite him to my birthday party.

The birthday parties that my mother threw for me came fairly close to being a racket. I was born on the twenty-sixth of December and although the party was the only gift I got from the family, I usually wound up with a fair share of the neighborhood Christmas loot.

I didn't see Augie from the afternoon school closed for the holi-days until two days before Christmas, when I went down to learn if he could come to the party. I found him and his mother in the kitchen. Augie was eating a piece of chocolate cake and his mother was telling him something about the specter of a bad priest that had to say Mass every night in the middle of a great bog. She stopped short when she caught sight of me. Augie didn't even look up.

"Och, boy," she said. "Did somebody steal the bell from the door?" Mrs. Sheean wasn't too friendly with me these days either.

"I'm going to be thirteen on the day after Christmas. I'm having a party and I wonder if Augie could come?"

"Well, now, he might," Mrs. Sheean said in what she thought was a sweet voice. "Who all will be there?"

"Oh, the whole gang."

"And will Miss Clooney be making her appearance?"

"I don't know. Maybe. I guess so."

"Then I'm sure Augustine has no desire to be there. Do you, aroon?"

Augie didn't answer.

"If he did," Mrs. Sheean said, "he'd call down the wrath of the angels, and the devil himself would surely take possession of his soul." It seemed unlikely that Augie would attend.

He did, though. The party had been going on for about an hour when I had to leave a game of Pin the Tail on the Donkey to answer the doorbell. It was Augie.

"I stopped by to say hello," he said.

"Could you come in for a minute?"

"Well, I'm not dressed at all." He had on the boots and knickers he wore to school.

"As much as I am," I said, pointing to the shiny new boots that were my favorite Christmas present.

"But I have no gift. I'm sorry about that. And about other things."

"Forget it," I said. "I'm glad you could make it. I never thought your mother would let you."

"She didn't. I told her I was going to church to visit the crèche."

"You lied to her?"

"She believed me. The woman has never been crossed."

It wouldn't have surprised me at all to see him turn black and float twelve feet in the air. It was a terrible price to pay for a bit of ice cream and cake.

But Augie not only managed to keep his footing, he appeared to be having the time of his life. After winning first prize in the treasure hunt (a fifty-cent piece which he gave me as a present) he did a funny jig, sang a few Irish songs, and was, in general, the life of the party. Not once, however, did he speak to Doris Clooney, and she acted as if she weren't in the same room with him.

Then, as usual, just when the party was getting good, some girl interrupted the fun by suggesting a game of Post Office. I started to object, but my older sister, Kathleen, grouped the boys and girls at opposite ends of the room and began giving out the numbers.

"You won't like this," I told Augie. "It's a kissing game."

He took it philosophically. "No matter. It'll be over soon, and we may as well be polite about it."

Kathleen had finished with the girls and came over to us. Just as she was telling Augie his number, Doris Clooney popped up out of nowhere.

"I'm sorry," she said, "but I can't seem to remember mine."

"Thirty-two," Kathleen said.

Lindy Geoghegan must have overheard, for he called out "Thirty-two" the first time he was up. Doris walked over to him, turned her face and let him kiss her on the cheek. Lindy returned to his place looking a little disappointed.

Doris stood in the center of the room smiling at Augie. "Thirteen," she purred. It was Augie's number.

Doris half closed her eyes, leaned back her head and moistened her lips with the tip of her small pink tongue. Seeing her waiting there like that, I felt a warm, sweet cloud filling my chest as if my heart were dissolving in a mist of honey. For the first time in my life, the game made sense to me.

Augie stood up. He was having a terrible time trying to be polite. He stumbled awkwardly toward Doris; then, just as he was a shadow's breadth away from her, he let a wild, unearthly shriek out of him, wheeled around and raced out the front door.

Doris Clooney jumped back, and everybody laughed and yelled. I grabbed my coat and took off after him.

When I reached the street he was a block away from me, running like a man possessed. I would never have caught up with him if he hadn't turned up the steps of the church.

When I arrived, panting, at the church vestibule, I could see Augie kneeling before the statue of Saint Joseph with his bent head cupped in his hands. As I debated whether to leave or stay, Augie stood up, leaned forward and blew out the top vigil light. I could have sworn that every light in the church went out, and a fierce, joyous terror surged up in me. Augie strode toward me and would have passed by if I hadn't reached out and grabbed his shoulder.

"Augie," I whispered, "you'd better go back and light it."

"Not a bit of it," he growled. "Those two have made life miserable for me long enough."

I said a quick prayer to Saint Polycarp. Augie marched out and I followed slowly.

"Come on," he shouted, "let's get back to the party." He walked ahead a few steps and waited for me to catch up to him. "By the way," he said, "that number Geoghegan called. It was thirty-two, wasn't it?"

"It was twenty-three," I said.

"That's odd. I could have sworn—" He broke off when he saw the smirk on my face. "Why, you sly little rogue! You wanted to keep it for yourself?" He laughed and gave me a playful punch on the arm.

Then suddenly, for no reason at all, we ran madly up Eighteenth Street, laughing like lunatics, our boots clacking against the brick pavement like the sound of cloven hoofs.

NEIGHBOR ROSICKY

WILLA CATHER

One

When Doctor Burleigh told neighbor Rosicky he had a bad heart, Rosicky protested.

"So? No, I guess my heart was always pretty good. I got a little asthma, maybe. Just a awful short breath when I was pitchin' hay last summer, dat's all."

"Well now, Rosicky, if you know more about it than I do, what did you come to me for? It's your heart that makes you short of breath, I tell you. You're sixty-five years old, and you've always worked hard, and your heart's tired. You've got to be careful from now on, and you can't do heavy work any more. You've got five boys at home to do it for you."

The old farmer looked up at the doctor with a gleam of amusement in his queer triangular-shaped eyes. His eyes were large and lively, but the lids were caught up in the middle in a curious way, so that they formed a triangle. He did not look like a sick man. His brown face was creased but not wrinkled, he had a ruddy color in his smooth-shaven cheeks and in his lips, under his long brown mustache. His hair was thin and ragged around his ears, but very little gray. His forehead, naturally high and crossed by deep parallel lines, now ran all the way up to his pointed crown. Rosicky's face had the habit of looking interested—suggested a contented disposition and a reflective quality that was gay rather than grave. This gave him a certain detachment, the easy manner of an onlooker and observer.

"Well, I guess you ain't got no pills fur a bad heart, Doctor Ed. I guess the only thing is fur me to git me a new one."

Doctor Burleigh swung round in his desk chair and frowned at the old farmer. "I think if I were you I'd take a little care of the old one, Rosicky."

Rosicky shrugged. "Maybe I don't know how. I expect you mean fur me not to drink my coffee no more."

"I wouldn't, in your place. But you'll do as you choose about that. I've never yet been able to separate a Bohemian from his coffee or his pipe. I've quit trying. But the sure thing is you've got to cut out farm work. You can feed the stock and do chores about the barn, but you can't do anything in the fields that makes you short of breath."

"How about shelling corn?"

"Of course not!"

Rosicky considered with puckered brows.

"I can't make my heart go no longer'n it wants to, can I, Doctor Ed?"

"I think it's good for five or six years yet, maybe more, if you'll take the strain off it. Sit around the house and help Mary. If I had a good wife like yours, I'd want to stay around the house."

His patient chuckled. "It ain't no place fur a man. I don't like no old man hanging round the kitchen too much. An' my wife, she's a awful hard worker her own self."

"That's it; you can help her a little. My Lord, Rosicky, you are one of the few men I know who has a family he can get some comfort out of; happy dispositions, never quarrel among themselves, and they treat you right. I want to see you live a few years and enjoy them."

"Oh, they're good kids, all right," Rosicky assented.

The doctor wrote him a prescription and asked him how his oldest son, Rudolph, who had married in the spring, was getting on. Rudolph had struck out for himself, on rented land. "And how's Polly? I was afraid Mary mightn't like an American daughter-in-law, but it seems to be working out all right."

"Yes, she's a fine girl. Dat widder woman bring her daughters up very nice. Polly got lots of spunk, an' she got some style, too. Da's nice, for young folks to have some style." Rosicky inclined his head gallantly. His voice and his twinkly smile were an affectionate compliment to his daughter-in-law.

"It looks like a storm, and you'd better be getting home before it comes. In town in the car?" Doctor Burleigh rose.

"No, I'm in de wagon. When you got five boys, you ain't got much chance to ride round in de Ford. I ain't much for cars, noway."

"Well, it's a good road out to your place; but I don't want you bumping around in a wagon much. And never again on a hayrack, remember!"

Rosicky placed the doctor's fee delicately behind the desk telephone, looking the other way, as if this were an absent-minded gesture. He put on his plush cap and his corduroy jacket with a sheepskin collar, and went out.

The doctor picked up his stethoscope and frowned at it as if he were seriously annoyed with the instrument. He wished it had been telling tales about some other man's heart, some old man who didn't look the doctor in the eye so knowingly, or hold out such a warm brown hand when he said good-bye. Doctor Burleigh had been a poor boy in the country before he went away to medical school; he had known Rosicky almost ever since he could remember, and he had a deep affection for Mrs. Rosicky.

Only last winter he had had such a good breakfast at Rosicky's, and that when he needed it. He had been out all night on a long, hard confinement case at Tom Marshall's—a big rich farm where there was plenty of stock and plenty of feed and a great deal of expensive farm machinery of the newest model, and no comfort whatever. The woman had too many children and too much work, and she was no manager. When the baby was born at last, and handed over to the assisting neighbor woman, and the mother was properly attended to, Burleigh refused any breakfast in that slovenly house, and drove his buggy—the snow was too deep for a car —eight miles to Anton Rosicky's place. He didn't know another farmhouse where a man could get such a warm welcome, and such good strong coffee with rich cream. No wonder the old chap didn't want to give up his coffee!

He had driven in just when the boys had come back from the barn and were washing up for breakfast. The long table, covered with a bright oilcloth, was set out with dishes waiting for them, and the warm kitchen was full of the smell of coffee and hot biscuit and sausage. Five big handsome boys, running from twenty to twelve, all with what Burleigh called natural good manners—they hadn't a bit of the painful self-consciousness he himself had to struggle with when he was a lad. One ran to put his horse away, another helped him off with his fur coat and hung it up, and Josephine, the youngest child and the only daughter, quickly set another place under her mother's direction.

With Mary, to feed creatures was the natural expression of affection—her chickens, the calves, her big hungry boys. It was a rare pleasure to feed a young man whom she seldom saw and of whom she was as proud as if he belonged to her. Some country housekeepers would have stopped to spread a white cloth over the oilcloth, to change the thick cups and plates for their best china, and the wooden-handled knives for plated ones. But not Mary.

"You must take us as you find us, Doctor Ed. I'd be glad to put out my good things for you if you was expected, but I'm glad to get you any way at all."

He knew she was glad—she threw back her head and spoke out as if she were announcing him to the whole prairie. Rosicky hadn't said anything at all; he merely smiled his twinkling smile, put some more coal on the fire, and went into his own room to pour the doctor a little drink in a medicine glass. When they were all seated, he watched his wife's face from his end of the table and spoke to her in Czech. Then, with the instinct of politeness which seldom failed him, he turned to the doctor and said slyly: "I was just tellin' her not to ask you no questions about Mrs. Marshall till you eat some breakfast. My wife, she's terrible fur to ask questions."

The boys laughed, and so did Mary. She watched the doctor devour her biscuit and sausage, too much excited to eat anything herself. She drank her coffee and sat taking in everything about her visitor. She had known him when he was a poor country boy, and was boastfully proud of his success, always saying: "What do people go to Omaha for, to see a doctor, when we got the best one in the state right here?" If Mary liked people at all, she felt physical pleasure in the sight of them, personal exultation in any good fortune that came to them. Burleigh didn't know many women like that, but he knew she was like that.

When his hunger was satisfied, he did, of course, have to tell them about Mrs. Marshall, and he noticed what a friendly interest the boys took in the matter.

Rudolph, the oldest one (he was still living at home then) said: "The last time I was over there, she was lifting them big heavy milk cans, and I knew she oughtn't to be doing it."

"Yes, Rudolph told me about that when he came home, and I said it wasn't right," Mary put in warmly. "It was all right for me to do them things up to the last, for I was terrible strong, but that woman's weakly. And do you think she'll be able to nurse it, Ed?" She sometimes forgot to give him the title she was so proud of. "And to think of your being up all night and then not able to get a decent breakfast! I don't know what's the matter with such people."

"Why, Mother," said one of the boys, "if Doctor Ed had got breakfast there, we wouldn't have him here. So you ought to be glad."

"He knows I'm glad to have him, John, any time. But I'm sorry for that poor woman, how bad she'll feel the doctor had to go away in the cold without his breakfast."

"I wish I'd been in practice when these were getting born." The doctor looked down the row of close-clipped heads. "I missed some good breakfasts by not being."

The boys began to laugh at their mother because she flushed so red, but she stood her ground and threw up her head. "I don't care, you wouldn't have got away from this house without breakfast. No doctor ever did. I'd have had something ready fixed that Anton could warm up for you."

The boys laughed harder than ever, and exclaimed at her: "I'll bet you would!" "She would, that!"

"Father, did you get breakfast for the doctor when we were born?"

"Yes, and he used to bring me my breakfast, too, mighty nice. I was always awful hungry!" Mary admitted with a guilty laugh.

While the boys were getting the doctor's horse, he went to the window to examine the house plants. "What do you do to your geraniums to keep them blooming all winter, Mary? I never pass this house that from the road I don't see your windows full of flowers."

She snapped off a dark red one, and a ruffled new green leaf, and put them in his buttonhole. "There, that looks better. You look too solemn for a young man, Ed. Why don't you git married? I'm worried about you. Settin' at breakfast, I looked at you real hard, and I see you've got some gray hairs already."

"Oh, yes! They're coming. Maybe they'd come faster if I married."

"Don't talk so. You'll ruin your health eating at the hotel. I could send your wife a nice loaf of nut bread, if you only had one. I don't like to see a young man getting gray. I'll tell you something, Ed; you make some strong black tea and keep it handy in a bowl, and every morning just brush it into your hair, an' it'll keep the gray from showin' much. That's the way I do!"

Sometimes the doctor heard the gossipers in the drugstore wondering why Rosicky didn't get on faster. He was industrious, and so were his boys, but they were rather free and easy, weren't pushers, and they didn't always show good judgment. They were comfortable, they were out of debt, but they didn't get much ahead.

Maybe, Doctor Burleigh reflected, people as generous and warm-hearted and affectionate as the Rosickys never got ahead much; maybe you couldn't enjoy your life and put it into the bank, too.

Two

When Rosicky left Doctor Burleigh's office he went into the farm-implement store to light his pipe and put on his glasses and read over the list Mary had given him. Then he went into the general merchandise place next door and stood about until the pretty girl with the plucked eyebrows, who always waited on him, was free. Those eyebrows, two thin India-ink strokes, amused him, because he remembered how they used to be. Rosicky always prolonged his shopping by a little joking; the girl knew the old fellow admired her, and she liked to chaff with him.

"Seems to me about every other week you buy ticking, Mr. Rosicky, and always the best quality," she remarked as she measured off the heavy bolt with red stripes.

"You see, my wife is always makin' goose-fedder pillows, an' de thin stuff don't hold in dem little down-fedders."

"You must have lots of pillows at your house."

"Sure. She makes quilts of dem, too. We sleeps easy. Now she's makin' a fedder quilt for my son's wife. You know Polly, that married my Rudolph. How much my bill, Miss Pearl?"

"Eight eighty-five."

"Chust make it nine, and put in some candy fur de women."

"As usual. I never did see a man buy so much candy for his wife. First thing you know, she'll be getting too fat."

"I'd like dat. I ain't much fur all dem slim women like what de style is now."

"That's one for me, I suppose, Mr. Bohunk!" Pearl sniffed and elevated her India-ink strokes.

When Rosicky went out to his wagon, it was beginning to snow —the first snow of the season, and he was glad to see it. He rattled out of town and along the highway through a wonderfully rich stretch of country, the finest farms in the county. He admired this High Prairie, as it was called, and always liked to drive through it.

His own place lay in a rougher territory, where there was some clay in the soil and it was not so productive. When he bought his land, he hadn't the money to buy on High Prairie; so he told his boys, when they grumbled, that if their land hadn't some clay in it, they wouldn't own it at all. All the same, he enjoyed looking at these fine farms, as he enjoyed looking at a prize bull.

After he had gone eight miles, he came to the graveyard, which lay just at the edge of his own hay-land. There he stopped his horses and sat still on his wagon seat, looking about at the snow-fall. Over yonder on the hill he could see his own house, crouching low, with the clump of orchard behind and the windmill before, and all down the gentle hillslope the rows of pale gold cornstalks stood out against the white field. The snow was falling over the cornfield and the pasture and the hay-land, steadily, with very little wind—a nice dry snow. The graveyard had only a light wire fence about it and was all overgrown with long red grass. The fine snow, settling into this red grass and upon the few little evergreens and the headstones looked very pretty.

It was a nice graveyard, Rosicky reflected, sort of snug and home-like, not cramped or mournful—a big sweep all round it. A man could lie down in the long grass and see the complete arch of the sky over him, hear the wagons go by; in summer the mowing machine rattled right up to the wire fence. And it was so near home. Over there across the cornstalks his own roof and windmill looked so good to him that he promised himself to mind the doctor and take care of himself. He was awful fond of his place, he admitted. He wasn't anxious to leave it. And it was a comfort to think that he would never have to go farther than the edge of his own hay-field. The snow, falling over his barnyard and the graveyard, seemed to draw things together like. And they were all old neighbors in the graveyard, most of them friends; there was nothing to feel awkward or embarrassed about. Embarrassment was the most disagreeable feeling Rosicky knew. He didn't often have it—only with certain people whom he didn't understand at all.

Well, it was a nice snowstorm; a fine sight to see the snow falling so quietly and graciously over so much open country. On his cap and shoulders, on the horses' backs and manes, light, delicate, mysterious it fell; and with it a dry cool fragrance was released into the air. It meant rest for vegetation and men and beasts, for the ground itself; a season of long nights for sleep, leisurely breakfasts, peace by the fire. This and much more went through Rosicky's mind, but he merely told himself that winter was coming, clucked to his horses, and drove on.

When he reached home, John, the youngest boy, ran out to put away his team for him, and he met Mary coming up from the outside cellar with her apron full of carrots. They went into the house together. On the table, covered with oilcloth figured with clusters of blue grapes, a place was set, and he smelled hot coffeecake of some kind. Anton never lunched in town; he thought that extravagant, and anyhow he didn't like the food. So Mary always had something ready for him when he got home.

After he was settled in his chair, stirring his coffee in a big cup, Mary took out of the oven a pan of *kolache* stuffed with apricots, examined them anxiously to see whether they had got too dry, put them beside his plate, and then sat down opposite him.

Rosicky asked her in Czech if she wasn't going to have any coffee.

She replied in English, as being somehow the right language for transacting business: "Now what did Doctor Ed say, Anton? You tell me just what."

"He said I was to tell you some compliments, but I forgot 'em." Rosicky's eyes twinkled.

"About you, I mean. What did he say about your asthma?"

"He says I ain't got no asthma." Rosicky took one of the little rolls in his broad brown fingers. The thickened nail of his right thumb told the story of his past.

"Well, what is the matter? And don't try to put me off."

"He don't say nothing much, only I'm a little older, and my heart ain't so good like it used to be."

Mary started and brushed her hair back from her temples with both hands as if she were a little out of her mind. From the way she glared, she might have been in a rage with him.

"He says there's something the matter with your heart? Doctor Ed says so?"

"Now don't yell at me like I was a hog in de garden, Mary. You know I always did like to hear a woman talk soft. He didn't say anything de matter wid my heart, only it ain't so young like it used to be, an' he tell me not to pitch hay or run de corn sheller."

Mary wanted to jump up, but she sat still. She admired the way he never under any circumstances raised his voice or spoke roughly. He was city-bred, and she was country-bred; she often said she wanted her boys to have their papa's nice ways.

"You never have no pain there, do you? It's your breathing and your stomach that's been wrong. I wouldn't believe nobody but Doctor Ed about it. I guess I'll go see him myself. Didn't he give you no advice?"

"Chust to take it easy like, an' stay round de house dis winter. I guess you got some carpenter work for me to do. I kin make some new shelves for you, and I want dis long time to build a closet in de boys' room and make dem two little fellers keep dere clo'es hung up."

Rosicky drank his coffee from time to time, while he considered. His mustache was of the soft long variety and came down over his mouth like the teeth of a buggy-rake over a bundle of hay. Each time he put down his cup, he ran his blue handkerchief over his lips. When he took a drink of water, he managed very neatly with the back of his hand.

Mary sat watching him intently, trying to find any change in his face. It is hard to see anyone who has become like your own body to you. Yes, his hair had got thin, and his high forehead had deep lines running from left to right. But his neck, always clean shaved except in the busiest seasons, was not loose or baggy. It was burned a dark reddish brown, and there were deep creases in it, but it looked firm and full of blood. His cheeks had a good color. On either side of his mouth there was a half-moon down the length of his cheeks, not wrinkles, but two lines that had come there from his habitual expression. He was shorter and broader than when she married him; his back had grown broad and curved, a good deal like the shell of an old turtle, and his arms and legs were short.

He was fifteen years older than Mary, but she had hardly ever thought about it before. He was her man, and the kind of man she liked. She was rough, and he was gentle—city-bred, as she always said. They had been shipmates on a rough voyage and had stood by each other in trying times. Life had gone well with them because, at bottom, they had the same ideas about life. They agreed, without discussion, as to what was most important and what was secondary. They didn't often exchange opinions, even in Czech—it was as if they had thought the same thought together. A good deal had to be sacrificed and thrown overboard in a hard life like theirs, and they had never disagreed as to the things that could go. It had been a hard life, and a soft life, too. There wasn't anything brutal in the short, broad-backed man with the three-cornered eyes and the forehead that went on to the top of his skull. He was a city man, a gentle man, and though he had married a rough farm girl, he had never touched her without gentleness.

They had been at one accord not to hurry through life, not to be always skimping and saving. They saw their neighbors buy more land and feed more stock than they did, without discontent. Once when the creamery agent came to the Rosickys to persuade them to sell him their cream, he told them how much money the Fasslers, their nearest neighbors, had made on their cream last year.

"Yes," said Mary, "and look at them Fassler children! Pale, pinched little things, they look like skimmed milk. I'd rather put some color into my children's faces than put money into the bank."

The agent shrugged and turned to Anton.

"I guess we'll do like she says," said Rosicky.

Three

Mary very soon got into town to see Doctor Ed, and then she had a talk with her boys and set a guard over Rosicky. Even John, the youngest, had his father on his mind. If Rosicky went to throw hay down from the loft, one of the boys ran up the ladder and took the fork from him. He sometimes complained that though he was getting to be an old man, he wasn't an old woman yet.

That winter he stayed in the house in the afternoons and carpentered, or sat in the chair between the window full of plants and the wooden bench where the two pails of drinking water stood. This spot was called "Father's corner," though it was not a corner at all. He had a shelf there, where he kept his Bohemian papers and his pipes and tobacco, and his shears and needles and thread and tailor's thimble. Having been a tailor in his youth, he couldn't bear to see a woman patching at his clothes, or at the boys'. He liked tailoring, and always patched all the overalls and jackets and work shirts. Occasionally he made over a pair of pants one of the older boys had outgrown, for the little fellow.

While he sewed, he let his mind run back over his life. He had a good deal to remember, really; life in three countries. The only part of his youth he didn't like to remember was the two years he had spent in London, in Cheapside, working for a German tailor who was wretchedly poor. Those days, when he was nearly always hungry, when his clothes were dropping off him for dirt, and the sound of a strange language kept him in continual bewilderment, had left a sore spot in his mind that wouldn't bear touching.

He was twenty when he landed at Castle Garden in New York, and he had a protector who got him work in a tailor shop in Vesey Street, down near the Washington Market. He looked upon that part of his life as very happy. He became a good workman, he was industrious, and his wages were increased from time to time. He minded his own business and envied nobody's good fortune. He went to night school and learned to read English. He often did overtime work and was well paid for it, but somehow he never saved anything. He couldn't refuse a loan to a friend, and he was self-indulgent. He liked a good dinner, and a little went for beer, a little for tobacco; a good deal went to the girls. He often stood through an opera on Saturday nights; he could get standing room for a dollar. Those were the great days of opera in New York, and it gave a fellow something to think about for the rest of the week. Rosicky had a quick ear, and a childish love of all the stage splendor; the scenery, the costumes, the ballet. He usually went with a chum, and after the performance they had beer and maybe some oysters somewhere. It was a fine life; for the first five years or so it satisfied him completely. He was never hungry or cold or dirty, and everything amused him: a fire, a dog fight, a parade, a storm, a ferry ride. He thought New York the finest, richest, friendliest city in the world.

Moreover, he had what he called a happy home life. Very near the tailor shop was a small furniture factory, where an old Austrian, Loeffler, employed a few skilled men and made unusual furniture, most of it to order, for the rich German housewives uptown. The top floor of Loeffler's five-story factory was a loft, where he kept his choice lumber and stored the odd pieces of furniture left on his hands. One of the young workmen he employed was a Czech, and he and Rosicky became fast friends. They persuaded Loeffler to let them have a sleeping room in one corner of the loft. They bought good beds and bedding and had their pick of the furniture kept up there. The loft was low-pitched, but light and airy, full of windows, and good-smelling by reason of the fine lumber put up there to season. Old Loeffler used to go down to the docks and buy wood from South America and the East from the sea captains. The young men were as foolish about their house as a bridal pair. Zichec, the young cabinetmaker, devised every sort of convenience, and Rosicky kept their clothes in order. At night and on Sundays, when the quiver of machinery underneath was still, it was the quietest place in the world, and on summer nights all the sea winds blew in. Zichec often practiced on his flute in the evening. They were both fond of music and went to the opera together. Rosicky thought he wanted to live like that forever.

But as the years passed, all alike, he began to get a little restless. When spring came round, he would begin to feel fretted, and he got to drinking. He was likely to drink too much of a Saturday night. On Sunday he was languid and heavy, getting over his spree. On Monday he plunged into work again. So he never had time to figure out what ailed him, though he knew something did. When the grass turned green in Park Place, and the lilac hedge at the back of Trinity churchyard put out its blossoms, he was tormented by a longing to run away. That was why he drank too much; to get a temporary illusion of freedom and wide horizons.

Rosicky, the old Rosicky, could remember as if it were yesterday the day when the young Rosicky found out what was the matter with him. It was on a Fourth of July afternoon, and he was sitting in Park Place in the sun. The lower part of New York was empty. Wall Street, Liberty Street, Broadway, all empty. So much stone and asphalt with nothing going on, so many empty windows. The emptiness was intense, like the stillness in a great factory when the machinery stops and the belts and bands cease running. It was too great a change, it took all the strength out of one. Those blank buildings, without the stream of life pouring through them, were like empty jails. It struck young Rosicky that this was the trouble with big cities; they built you in from the earth itself, cemented you away from any contact with the ground. You lived in an unnatural world, like the fish in an aquarium, who were probably much more comfortable than they ever were in the sea.

On that very day he began to think seriously about the articles he had read in the Bohemian papers, describing prosperous Czech farming communities in the West. He believed he would like to go out there as a farm hand; it was hardly possible that he could ever have land of his own. His people had always been workmen; his father and grandfather had worked in shops. His mother's parents had lived in the country, but they rented their farm and had a hard time to get along. Nobody in his family had ever owned any land—that belonged to a different station of life altogether. Anton's mother died when he was little, and he was sent into the country to her parents. He stayed with them until he was twelve, and formed those ties with the earth and the farm animals and growing things which are never made at all unless they are made early. After his grandfather died, he went back to live with his father and stepmother, but she was very hard on him, and his father helped him to get passage to London.

After that Fourth of July day in Park Place, the desire to return to the country never left him. To work on another man's farm would be all he asked; to see the sun rise and set and to plant things and watch them grow. He was a very simple man. He was like a tree that has not many roots, but one taproot that goes down deep. He subscribed for a Bohemian paper printed in Chicago, then for one printed in Omaha. His mind got farther and farther west. He began to save a little money to buy his liberty. When he was thirty-five, there was a great meeting in New York of Bohemian athletic societies, and Rosicky left the tailor shop and went home with the Omaha delegates to try his fortune in another part of the world.

Four

Perhaps the fact that his own youth was well over before he began to have a family was one reason why Rosicky was so fond of his boys. He had almost a grandfather's indulgence for them. He had never had to worry about any of them—except, just now, a little about Rudolph.

On Saturday night the boys always piled into the Ford, took little Josephine, and went to town to the moving-picture show. One Saturday morning they were talking at the breakfast table about starting early that evening, so that they would have an hour or so to see the Christmas things in the stores before the show began. Rosicky looked down the table.

"I hope you boys ain't disappointed, but I want you to let me have de car tonight. Maybe some of you can go in with de neighbors."

Their faces fell. They worked hard all week, and they were still like children. A new jackknife or a box of candy pleased the older ones as much as the little fellow.

"If you and Mother are going to town," Frank said, "maybe you could take a couple of us along with you, anyway."

"No, I want to take de car down to Rudolph's, and let him an' Polly go in to de show. She don't git into town enough, an' I'm afraid she's gettin' lonesome, an' he can't afford no car yet."

That settled it. The boys were a good deal dashed. Their father took another piece of apple cake and went on: "Maybe next Saturday night de two little fellers can go along wid dem."

"Oh, is Rudolph going to have the car every Saturday night?"

Rosicky did not reply at once; then he began to speak seriously: "Listen, boys; Polly ain't lookin' so good. I don't like to see nobody lookin' sad. It comes hard fur a town girl to be a farmer's wife. I don't want no trouble to start in Rudolph's family. When it starts, it ain't so easy to stop. An American girl don't git used to our ways all at once. I like to tell Polly she and Rudolph can have the car every Saturday night till after New Year's, if it's all right with you boys."

"Sure it's all right, Papa," Mary cut in. "And it's good you thought about that. Town girls is used to more than country girls. I lay awake nights, scared she'll make Rudolph discontented with the farm."

The boys put as good a face on it as they could. They surely looked forward to their Saturday nights in town. That evening Rosicky drove the car the half-mile down to Rudolph's new, bare little house.

Polly was in a short-sleeved gingham dress, clearing away the supper dishes. She was a trim, slim little thing, with blue eyes and shingled yellow hair, and her eyebrows were reduced to a mere brush-stroke, like Miss Pearl's.

"Good evening, Mr. Rosicky. Rudolph's at the barn, I guess." She never called him father, or Mary mother. She was sensitive about having married a foreigner. She never in the world would have done it if Rudolph hadn't been such a handsome, persuasive fellow and such a gallant lover. He had graduated in her class in the high school in town, and their friendship began in the ninth grade.

Rosicky went in, though he wasn't exactly asked. "My boys ain't goin' to town tonight, an' I brought de car over fur you two to go in to de picture show."

Polly, carrying dishes to the sink, looked over her shoulder at him. "Thank you. But I'm late with my work tonight, and pretty tired. Maybe Rudolph would like to go in with you."

"Oh, I don't go to de shows! I'm too old-fashioned. You won't feel so tired after you ride in de air a ways. It's a nice clear night, an' it ain't cold. You go an' fix yourself up, Polly, an' I'll wash de dishes an' leave everything nice fur you."

Polly blushed and tossed her bob. "I couldn't let you do that, Mr. Rosicky. I wouldn't think of it."

Rosicky said nothing. He found a bib apron on a nail behind the kitchen door. He slipped it over his head and then took Polly by her two elbows and pushed her gently toward the door of her own room. "I washed up de kitchen many times for my wife, when de babies was sick or somethin'. You go an' make yourself look nice. I like you to look prettier'n any of dem town girls when you go in. De young folks must have some fun, an' I'm goin' to look out fur you, Polly."

That kind, reassuring grip on her elbows, the old man's funny bright eyes, made Polly want to drop her head on his shoulder for a second. She restrained herself, but she lingered in his grasp at the door of her room, murmuring tearfully: "You always lived in the city when you were young, didn't you? Don't you ever get lonesome out here?"

As she turned round to him, her hand fell naturally into his, and he stood holding it and smiling into her face with his peculiar, knowing, indulgent smile without a shadow of reproach in it. "Dem big cities is all right fur de rich, but dey is terrible hard fur de poor."

"I don't know. Sometimes I think I'd like to take a chance. You lived in New York, didn't you?"

"An' London. Da's bigger still. I learned my trade dere. Here's Rudolph comin', you better hurry."

"Will you tell me about London sometime?"

"Maybe. Only I ain't no talker, Polly. Run an' dress yourself up."

The bedroom door closed behind her, and Rudolph came in from the outside, looking anxious. He had seen the car and was sorry any of his family should come just then. Supper hadn't been a very pleasant occasion. Halting in the doorway, he saw his father in a kitchen apron, carrying dishes to the sink. He flushed crimson and something flashed in his eye. Rosicky held up a warning finger.

"I brought de car over fur you an' Polly to go to de picture show, an' I made her let me finish here so you won't be late. You go put on a clean shirt, quick!"

"But don't the boys want the car, Father?"

"Not tonight dey don't." Rosicky fumbled under his apron and found his pants pocket. He took out a silver dollar and said in a hurried whisper: "You go an' buy dat girl some ice cream an' candy tonight, like you was courtin'. She's awful good friends wid me."

Rudolph was very short of cash, but he took the money as if it hurt him. There had been a crop failure all over the county. He had more than once been sorry he'd married this year.

In a few minutes the young people came out, looking clean

and a little stiff. Rosicky hurried them off, and then he took his own time with the dishes. He scoured the pots and pans and put away the milk and swept the kitchen. He put some coal in the stove and shut off the draughts, so the place would be warm for them when they got home late at night. Then he sat down and had a pipe and listened to the clock tick.

Generally speaking, marrying an American girl was certainly a risk. A Czech should marry a Czech. It was lucky that Polly was the daughter of a poor widow woman; Rudolph was proud, and if she had a prosperous family to throw up at him, they could never make it go. Polly was one of four sisters, and they all worked; one was bookkeeper in the bank, one taught music, and Polly and her younger sister had been clerks, like Miss Pearl. All four of them were musical, had pretty voices, and sang in the Methodist choir, which the eldest sister directed.

Polly missed the sociability of a store position. She missed the choir, and the company of her sisters. She didn't dislike housework, but she disliked so much of it. Rosicky was a little anxious about this pair. He was afraid Polly would grow so discontented that Rudy would quit the farm and take a factory job in Omaha. He had worked for a winter up there, two years ago, to get money to marry on. He had done very well, and they would always take him back at the stockyards. But to Rosicky that meant the end of everything for his son. To be a landless man was to be a wage-earner, a slave, all your life; to have nothing, to be nothing.

Rosicky thought he would come over and do a little carpentering for Polly after the New Year. He guessed she needed jollying. Rudolph was a serious sort of chap, serious in love and serious about his work.

Rosicky shook out his pipe and walked home across the fields. Ahead of him the lamplight shone from his kitchen windows. Suppose he were still in a tailor shop on Vesey Street, with a bunch of pale, narrow-chested sons working on machines, all coming home tired and sullen to eat supper in a kitchen that was a parlor also; with another crowded, angry family quarrelling just across the dumb-waiter shaft, and squeaking pulleys at the windows where dirty washings hung on dirty lines above a court full of old brooms and mops and ash cans. . . .

He stopped by the windmill to look up at the frosty winter stars and draw a long breath before he went inside. That kitchen with the shining windows was dear to him; but the sleeping fields and bright stars and the noble darkness were dearer still.

Five

On the day before Christmas the weather set in very cold; no snow, but a bitter, biting wind that whistled and sang over the flat land and lashed one's face like fine wires. There was baking going on in the Rosicky kitchen all day, and Rosicky sat inside, making over a coat that Albert had outgrown into an overcoat for John. Mary had a big red geranium in bloom for Christmas, and a row of Jerusalem cherry trees, full of berries. It was the first year she had ever grown these; Doctor Ed brought her the seeds from Omaha when he went to some medical convention. They reminded Rosicky of plants he had seen in England; and all afternoon, as he stitched, he sat thinking about those two years in London, which his mind usually shrank from even after all this while.

He was a lad of eighteen when he dropped down into London, with no money and no connections except the address of a cousin who was supposed to be working at a confectioner's. When he went to the pastry shop, however, he found that the cousin had gone to America. Anton tramped the streets for several days, sleeping in doorways and on the Embankment, until he was in utter despair. He knew no English, and the sound of the strange language all about him confused him. By chance he met a poor German tailor who had learned his trade in Vienna, and could speak a little Czech. This tailor, Lifschnitz, kept a repair shop in a Cheapside basement, underneath a cobbler. He didn't much need an apprentice, but he was sorry for the boy and took him in for no wages but his keep and what he could pick up. The pickings were supposed to be coppers given you when you took work home to a customer. But most of the customers called for their clothes themselves, and the coppers that came Anton's way were very few. He had, however, a place to sleep. The tailor's family lived upstairs in three rooms; a kitchen, a bedroom, where Lifschnitz and his wife and five children slept, and a living room. Two corners of this living room were curtained off for lodgers; in one Rosicky slept on an old horsehair sofa, with a feather quilt to wrap himself in. The other corner was rented to a wretched, dirty boy, who was studying the violin. He actually practiced there. Rosicky was dirty, too. There was no way to be anything else. Mrs. Lifschnitz got the water she cooked and washed with from a pump in a brick court, four flights down. There were bugs in the place, and multitudes of fleas, though the poor woman did the best she could. Rosicky knew she often went empty to give another potato or a spoonful of dripping to the two hungry, sad-eyed boys who lodged with her. He used to think he would never get out of there, never get a clean shirt to his back again. What would he do, he wondered, when his clothes actually dropped to pieces and the worn cloth wouldn't hold patches any longer?

It was still early when the old farmer put aside his sewing and his recollections. The sky had been a dark gray all day, with not a gleam of sun, and the light failed at four o'clock. He went to shave and change his shirt while the turkey was roasting. Rudolph and Polly were coming over for supper.

After supper they sat round in the kitchen, and the younger boys were saying how sorry they were it hadn't snowed. Everybody was sorry. They wanted a deep snow that would lie long and keep the wheat warm, and leave the ground soaked when it melted.

"Yes, sir!" Rudolph broke out fiercely, "if we have another dry year like last year, there's going to be hard times in this country."

Rosicky filled his pipe. "You boys don't know what hard times is. You don't owe nobody, you got plenty to eat an' keep warm, an' plenty water to keep clean. When you got them, you can't have it very hard."

Rudolph frowned, opened and shut his big right hand, and dropped it clenched upon his knee. "I've got to have a good deal more than that, Father, or I'll quit this farming gamble. I can always make good wages railroading, or at the packing house, and be sure of my money."

"Maybe so," his father answered dryly.

Mary, who had just come in from the pantry and was wiping her hands on the roller towel, thought Rudy and his father were getting too serious. She brought her darning basket and sat down in the middle of the group.

"I ain't much afraid of hard times, Rudy," she said heartily. "We've had a plenty, but we've always come through. Your father wouldn't never take nothing very hard, not even hard times. I got a mind to tell you a story on him. Maybe you boys can't hardly remember the year we had that terrible hot wind, that burned everything up on the Fourth of July? All the corn an' the gardens. An' that was in the days when we didn't have alfalfa yet—I guess it wasn't invented.

"Well, that very day your father was out cultivatin' corn, and I was here in the kitchen makin' plum preserves. We had bushels of plums that year. I noticed it was terrible hot, but it's always hot in the kitchen when you're preservin', an' I was too busy with my plums to mind. Anton come in from the field about three o'clock, an' I asked him what was the matter.

"'Nothin',' he says, 'but it's pretty hot, an' I think I won't work no more today.' He stood round for a few minutes, an' then he says: 'Ain't you near through? I want you should git up a nice supper for us tonight. It's Fourth of July.'

"I told him to git along, that I was right in the middle of preservin', but the plums would taste good on hot biscuit. 'I'm goin' to have fried chicken, too,' he says, and he went off an' killed a couple. You three oldest boys was little fellers, playin' round outside, real hot an' sweaty, an' your father took you to the horse tank down by the windmill an' took off your clothes an' put you in. Them two box-elder trees was little then, but they made shade over the tank. Then he took off all his own clothes, an' got in with you. While he was playin' in the water with you, the Methodist preacher drove into our place to say how all the neighbors was goin' to meet at the schoolhouse that night, to pray for rain. He drove right to the windmill, of course, and there was your father and you three with no clothes on. I was in the kitchen door, an' I had to laugh, for the preacher acted like he ain't never seen a naked man before. He surely was embarrassed, an' your father couldn't git to his clothes; they was all hangin' up on the windmill to let the sweat dry out of 'em. So he laid in the tank where he was, an' put one of you boys on top of him to cover him up a little, an' talked to the preacher.

"When you got through playin' in the water, he put clean clothes on you and a clean shirt on himself, an' by that time I'd begun to get supper. He says: 'It's too hot in here to eat comfortable. Let's have a picnic in the orchard. We'll eat our supper behind the mulberry hedge, under them linden trees.'

"So he carried our supper down, an' a bottle of my wild-grape wine, an' everything tasted good, I can tell you. The wind got cooler as the sun was goin' down, and it turned out pleasant, only I noticed how the leaves was curled up on the linden trees. That made me think, an' I asked your father if that hot wind all day hadn't been terrible hard on the gardens an' the corn.

"'Corn,' he says, 'there ain't no corn.'

"'What you talkin' about?' I said. 'Ain't we got forty acres?'

"'We ain't got an ear,' he says, 'nor nobody else ain't got none. All the corn in this country was cooked by three o'clock today, like you'd roasted it in an oven.'

"'You mean you won't get no crop at all?' I asked him. I couldn't believe it, after he'd worked so hard.

"'No crop this year,' he says. 'That's why we're havin' a picnic. We might as well enjoy what we got.'

"An' that's how your father behaved, when all the neighbors was so discouraged they couldn't look you in the face. An' we enjoyed ourselves that year, poor as we was, an' our neighbors wasn't a bit better off for bein' miserable. Some of 'em grieved till they got poor digestions and couldn't relish what they did have."

The younger boys said they thought their father had the best of it. But Rudolph was thinking that, all the same, the neighbors had managed to get ahead more, in the fifteen years since that time. There must be something wrong about his father's way of doing things. He wished he knew what was going on in the back of Polly's mind. He knew she liked his father, but he knew, too, that she was afraid of something. When his mother sent over coffeecake or prune tarts or a loaf of fresh bread, Polly seemed to regard them with a certain suspicion. When she observed to him that his brothers had nice manners, her tone implied that it was remarkable they should have. With his mother she was stiff and on her guard. Mary's hearty frankness and gusts of good humor irritated her. Polly was afraid of being unusual or conspicuous in any way, of being "ordinary," as she said!

When Mary had finished her story, Rosicky laid aside his pipe.

"You boys like me to tell you about some of dem hard times I been through in London?" Warmly encouraged, he sat rubbing his forehead along the deep creases. It was bothersome to tell a long story in English (he nearly always talked to the boys in Czech), but he wanted Polly to hear this one.

"Well, you know about dat tailor shop I worked in London? I had one Christmas dere I ain't never forgot. Times was awful bad before Christmas; de boss ain't got much work, an' have it awful hard to pay his rent. It ain't so much fun, bein' poor in a big city like London, I'll say! All de windows is full of good t'ings to eat, an' all de pushcarts in de streets is full, an' you smell 'em all de time, an' you ain't got no money—not a damn bit. I didn't mind de cold so much, though I didn't have no overcoat, chust a short jacket I'd outgrowed so it wouldn't meet on me, an' my hands was chapped raw. But I always had a good appetite, like you all know, an' de sight of dem pork pies in de windows was awful fur me!

"Day before Christmas was terrible foggy dat year, an' dat fog gits into your bones and makes you all damp like. Mrs. Lifschnitz didn't give us nothin' but a little bread an' drippin' for supper, because she was savin' to try for to give us a good dinner on Christmas Day. After supper de boss say I can go an' enjoy myself, so I went into de streets to listen to de Christmas singers. Dey sing old songs an' make very nice music, an' I run round after dem a good ways, till I got awful hungry. I t'ink maybe if I go home, I can sleep till morning an' forgit my belly.

"I went into my corner real quiet, and roll up in my fedder quilt. But I ain't got my head down, till I smell somet'ing good. Seem like it git stronger an' stronger, an' I can't git to sleep noway. I can't understand dat smell. Dere was a gas light in a hall across de court, dat always shine in at my window a little. I got up an' look

round. I got a little wooden box in my corner fur a stool, 'cause I
I ain't got no chair. I picks up dat box, and under it dere is a roast
goose on a platter! I can't believe my eyes. I carry it to de window
where de light comes in, an' touch it and smell it to find out, an' den
I taste it to be sure. I say, I will eat chust one little bite of dat goose,
so I can go to sleep, and tomorrow I won't eat none at all. But I tell
you, boys, when I stop, one half of dat goose was gone!"

The narrator bowed his head, and the boys shouted. But little
Josephine slipped behind his chair and kissed him on the neck
beneath his ear.

"Poor little Papa, I don't want him to be hungry!"

"Da's long ago, child. I ain't never been hungry since I had your
mudder to cook fur me."

"Go on and tell us the rest, please," said Polly.

"Well, when I come to realize what I done, of course, I felt terrible. I felt better in de stomach, but very bad in de heart. I set on
my bed wid dat platter on my knees, an' it all come to me; how
hard dat poor woman save to buy dat goose, and how she get some
neighbor to cook it dat got more fire, an' how she put it in my corner
to keep it away from dem hungry children. Dey was a old carpet
hung up to shut my corner off, an' de children wasn't allowed to
go in dere. An' I know she put it in my corner because she trust me
more'n she did de violin boy. I can't stand it to face her after I
spoil de Christmas. So I put on my shoes and go out into de city.
I tell myself I better throw myself in de river; but I guess I ain't dat
kind of a boy.

"It was after twelve o'cock, an' terrible cold, an' I start out to
walk about London all night. I walk along de river awhile, but dey
was lots of drunks all along; men, and women too. I chust move
along to keep away from de police. I git onto de Strand, an' den
over to New Oxford Street, where dere was a big German restaurant on de ground floor, wid big windows all fixed up fine, an' I
could see de people havin' parties inside. While I was lookin' in,
two men and two ladies come out, laughin' and talkin' and feelin'
happy about all dey been eatin' an' drinkin', and dey was speakin'
Czech—not like de Austrians, but like de home folks talk it.

"I guess I went crazy, an' I done what I ain't never done

before nor since. I went right up to dem gay people an' begun to beg dem: 'Fellow-countrymen, for God's sake give me money enough to buy a goose!'

"Dey laugh, of course, but de ladies speak awful kind to me, an' dey take me back into de restaurant and give me hot coffee and cakes, an' make me tell all about how I happened to come to London, an' what I was doin' dere. Dey take my name and where I work down on paper, an' both of dem ladies give me ten shillings.

"De big market at Covent Garden ain't very far away, an' by dat time it was open. I go dere an' buy a big goose an' some pork pies, an' potatoes and onions, an' cakes an' oranges fur de children—all I could carry! When I git home, everybody is still asleep. I pile all I bought on de kitchen table, an' go in an' lay down on my bed, an' I ain't waken up till I hear dat woman scream when she come out into her kitchen. My goodness, but she was surprise! She laugh an' cry at de same time, an' hug me and waken all de children. She ain't stop fur no breakfast; she git de Christmas dinner ready dat morning, and we all sit down an' eat all we can hold. I ain't never seen dat violin boy have all he can hold before.

"Two three days after dat, de two men come to hunt me up, an' dey ask my boss, and he give me a good report an' tell dem I was a steady boy all right. One of dem Bohemians was very smart an' run a Bohemian newspaper in New York, an' de odder was a rich man, in de importing business, an' dey been traveling togedder. Dey told me how t'ings was easier in New York, an' offered to pay my passage when dey was goin' home soon on a boat. My boss say to me: 'You go. You ain't got no chance here, an' I like to see you git ahead, fur you always been a good boy to my woman, and fur dat fine Christmas dinner you give us all.' An' da's how I got to New York."

That night when Rudolph and Polly, arm in arm, were running home across the fields with the bitter wind at their backs, his heart leaped for joy when she said she thought they might have his family come over for supper on New Year's Eve. "Let's get up a nice supper, and not let your mother help at all; make her be company for once."

"That would be lovely of you, Polly," he said humbly. He was a very simple, modest boy, and he, too, felt vaguely that Polly and her sisters were more experienced and worldly than his people.

Six

The winter turned out badly for farmers. It was bitterly cold, and
after the first light snows before Christmas there was no snow at all
—and no rain. March was as bitter as February. On those days when
the wind fairly punished the country, Rosicky sat by his window.
In the fall he and the boys had put in a big wheat planting, and now
the seed had frozen in the ground. All that land would have to be
plowed up and planted over again, planted in corn. It had happened before, but he was younger then, and he never worried
about what had to be. He was sure of himself and of Mary; he
knew they could bear what they had to bear, that they would always pull through somehow. But he was not so sure about the
young ones, and he felt troubled because Rudolph and Polly were
having such a hard start.

Sitting beside his flowering window while the panes rattled and
the wind blew in under the door, Rosicky gave himself to reflection
as he had not done since those Sundays in the loft of the furniture
factory in New York, long ago. Then he was trying to find what he
wanted in life for himself; now he was trying to find what he
wanted for his boys, and why it was he so hungered to feel sure
they would be here, working this very land, after he was gone.

They would have to work hard on the farm, and probably they
would never do much more than make a living. But if he could
think of them as staying here on the land, he wouldn't have to fear
any great unkindness for them. Hardships, certainly; it was a hard-
ship to have the wheat freeze in the ground when seed was so high;
and to have to sell your stock because you had no feed. But there
would be other years when everything came along right, and you
caught up. And what you had was your own. You didn't have to
choose between bosses and strikers, and go wrong either way. You
didn't have to do with dishonest and cruel people. They were the
only things in his experience he had found terrifying and horrible;
the look in the eyes of a dishonest and crafty man, of a scheming and
rapacious woman.

In the country, if you had a mean neighbor, you could keep off his land and make him keep off yours. But in the city, all the foulness and misery and brutality of your neighbors was part of your life. The worst things he had come upon in his journey through the world were human—depraved and poisonous specimens of man. To this day he could recall certain terrible faces in the London streets. There were mean people everywhere, to be sure, even in their own country town here. But they weren't tempered, hardened, sharpened, like the treacherous people in cities who live by grinding or cheating or poisoning their fellow men. He had helped to bury two of his fellow workmen in the tailoring trade, and he was distrustful of the organized industries that see one out of the world in big cities. Here, if you were sick, you had Doctor Ed to look after you; and if you died, fat Mr. Haycock, the kindest man in the world, buried you.

It seemed to Rosicky that for good, honest boys like his, the worst they could do on the farm was better than the best they would be likely to do in the city. If he'd had a mean boy, now, one who was crooked and sharp and tried to put anything over on his brothers, then town would be the place for him. But he had no such boy. As for Rudolph, the discontented one, he would give the shirt off his back to anyone who touched his heart. What Rosicky really hoped for his boys was that they could get through the world without ever knowing much about the cruelty of human beings. "Their mother and me ain't prepared them for that," he sometimes said to himself.

These thoughts brought him back to a grateful consideration of his own case. What an escape he had had, to be sure! He, too, in his time, had had to take money for repair work from the hand of a hungry child who let it go so wistfully; because it was money due his boss. And now, in all these years, he had never had to take a cent from any one in bitter need—never had to look at the face of a woman become like a wolf's from struggle and famine. When he thought of these things, Rosicky would put on his cap and jacket and slip down to the barn and give his work horses a little extra oats, letting them eat it out of his hand in their slobbery fashion. It was his way of expressing what he felt, and made him chuckle with pleasure.

The spring came warm, with blue skies—but dry, dry as a bone.

The boys began plowing up the wheat-fields to plant them over in corn. Rosicky would stand at the fence corner and watch them, and the earth was so dry it blew up in clouds of brown dust that hid the horses and the sulky plow and the driver. It was a bad outlook.

The big alfalfa field that lay between the home place and Rudolph's came up green, but Rosicky was worried because during that open windy winter a great many Russian thistle plants had blown in there and lodged. He kept asking the boys to rake them out; he was afraid their seed would root and "take the alfalfa." Rudolph said that was nonsense. The boys were working so hard planting corn, their father felt he couldn't insist about the thistles, but he set great store by that big alfalfa field. It was a feed you could depend on—and there was some deeper reason, vague, but strong. The peculiar green of that clover woke early memories in old Rosicky, went back to something in his childhood in the old world. When he was a little boy, he had played in fields of that strong blue-green color.

One morning, when Rudolph had gone to town in the car, leaving a work team idle in his barn, Rosicky went over to his son's place, put the horses to the buggy-rake, and set about quietly raking up those thistles. He behaved with guilty caution, and rather enjoyed stealing a march on Doctor Ed, who was just then taking his first vacation in seven years of practice and was attending a clinic in Chicago. Rosicky got the thistles raked up, but did not stop to burn them. That would take some time, and his breath was pretty short, so he thought he had better get the horses back to the barn.

He got them into the barn and to their stalls, but the pain had come on so sharp in his chest that he didn't try to take the harness off. He started for the house, bending lower with every step. The cramp in his chest was shutting him up like a jackknife. When he reached the windmill, he swayed and caught at the ladder. He saw Polly coming down the hill, running with the swiftness of a slim greyhound. In a flash she had her shoulder under his armpit.

"Lean on me, Father, hard! Don't be afraid. We can get to the house all right."

Somehow they did, though Rosicky became blind with pain; he could keep on his legs, but he couldn't steer his course. The next thing he was conscious of was lying on Polly's bed, and Polly bending over him wringing out bath towels in hot water and putting them on his chest. She stopped only to throw coal into the stove, and she kept the tea kettle and the black pot going. She put these hot applications on him for nearly an hour, she told him afterwards, and all that time he was drawn up stiff and blue, with the sweat pouring off him.

As the pain gradually loosed its grip, the stiffness went out of his jaws, the black circles round his eyes disappeared, and a little of his natural color came back. When his daughter-in-law buttoned his shirt over his chest at last, he sighed.

"Da's fine, de way I feel now, Polly. It was a awful bad spell, an' I was so sorry it all come on you like it did."

Polly was flushed and excited. "Is the pain really gone? Can I leave you long enough to telephone over to your place?"

Rosicky's eyelids fluttered. "Don't telephone, Polly. It ain't no use to scare my wife. It's nice and quiet here, an' if I ain't too much trouble to you, just let me lay still till I feel like myself. I ain't got no pain now. It's nice here."

Polly bent over him and wiped the moisture from his face. "Oh, I'm so glad it's over!" she broke out impulsively. "It just broke my heart to see you suffer so, Father."

Rosicky motioned her to sit down on the chair where the tea kettle had been, and looked up at her with that lively affectionate gleam in his eyes. "You was awful good to me, I won't never forget dat. I hate it to be sick on you like dis. Down at de barn I say to myself, dat young girl ain't had much experience in sickness, I don't want to scare her, an' maybe she's got a baby comin' or somet'ing."

Polly took his hand. He was looking at her so intently and affectionately and confidingly; his eyes seemed to caress her face, to regard it with pleasure. She frowned with her funny streaks of eyebrows, and then smiled back at him.

"I guess maybe there is something of that kind going to happen. But I haven't told anyone yet, not my mother or Rudolph. You'll be the first to know."

His hand pressed hers. She noticed that it was warm again. The twinkle in his yellow-brown eyes seemed to come nearer.

"I like mighty well to see dat little child, Polly," was all he said.

Then he closed his eyes and lay half-smiling. But Polly sat still, thinking hard. She had a sudden feeling that nobody in the world, not her mother, not Rudolph, or anyone, really loved her as much as old Rosicky did. It perplexed her. She sat frowning and trying to puzzle it out. It was as if Rosicky had a special gift for loving people, something that was like an ear for music or an eye for color. It was quiet, unobtrusive; it was merely there. You saw it in his eyes—perhaps that was why they were merry. You felt it in his hands, too. After he dropped off to sleep, she sat holding his warm, broad, flexible brown hand. She had never seen another in the least like it. She wondered if it wasn't a kind of gypsy hand, it was so alive and quick and light in its communications—very strange in a farmer. Nearly all the farmers she knew had huge lumps of fists, like mauls, or they were knotty and bony and uncomfortable-looking, with stiff fingers. But Rosicky's was like quicksilver, flexible, muscular, about the color of a pale cigar, with deep, deep creases across the palm. It wasn't nervous, it wasn't a stupid lump; it was a warm brown human hand, with some cleverness in it, a great deal of generosity, and something else which Polly could only call "gypsy-like"—something nimble and lively and sure, in the way that animals are.

Polly remembered that hour long afterwards; it had been like an awakening to her. It seemed to her that she had never learned so much about life from anything as from old Rosicky's hand. It brought her to herself; it communicated some direct and untranslatable message.

When she heard Rudolph coming in the car, she ran out to meet him.

"Oh, Rudy, your father's been awful sick! He raked up those thistles he's been worrying about, and afterwards he could hardly get to the house. He suffered so I was afraid he was going to die."

Rudolph jumped to the ground. "Where is he now?"

"On the bed. He's asleep. I was terribly scared, because, you know, I'm so fond of your father." She slipped her arm through his and they went into the house. That afternoon they took Rosicky home and put him to bed, though he protested that he was quite well again.

The next morning he got up and dressed and sat down to breakfast with his family. He told Mary that his coffee tasted better than usual to him, and he warned the boys not to bear any tales to Doctor Ed when he got home. After breakfast he sat down by his window to do some patching and asked Mary to thread several needles for him before she went to feed her chickens—her eyes were better than his, and her hands steadier. He lit his pipe and took up John's overalls. Mary had been watching him anxiously all morning, and as she went out of the door with her bucket of scraps, she saw that he was smiling. He was thinking, indeed, about Polly, and how he might never have known what a tender heart she had if he hadn't got sick over there. Girls nowadays didn't wear their heart on their sleeve. But now he knew Polly would make a fine woman after the foolishness wore off. Either a woman had that sweetness at her heart or she hadn't. You couldn't always tell by the look of them; but if they had that, everything came out right in the end.

After he had taken a few stitches, the cramp began in his chest, like yesterday. He put his pipe cautiously down on the windowsill and bent over to ease the pull. No use—he had better try to get to his bed if he could. He rose and groped his way across the familiar floor, which was rising and falling like the deck of a ship. At the door he fell. When Mary came in, she found him lying there, and the moment she touched him she knew that he was gone.

Doctor Ed was away when Rosicky died, and for the first few weeks after he got home he was hard driven. Every day he said to himself that he must get out to see that family that had lost their father. One soft, warm moonlight night in early summer he started for the farm. His mind was on other things, and not until his road ran by the graveyard did he realize that Rosicky wasn't over there on the hill where the red lamplight shone, but here, in the moonlight. He stopped his car, shut off the engine, and sat there for a while.

A sudden hush had fallen on his soul. Everything here seemed strangely moving and significant, though signifying what, he did not know. Close by the wire fence stood Rosicky's mowing machine, where one of the boys had been cutting hay that afternoon; his own work horses had been going up and down there. The new-cut hay perfumed all the night air. The moonlight silvered the long, billowy grass that grew over the graves and hid the fence; the few little evergreens stood out black in it, like shadows in a pool. The sky was very blue and soft, the stars rather faint because the moon was full.

For the first time it struck Doctor Ed that this was really a beautiful graveyard. He thought of city cemeteries; acres of shrubbery and heavy stone, so arranged and lonely and unlike anything in the living world. Cities of the dead, indeed; cities of the forgotten, of the "put away." But this was open and free, this little square of long grass which the wind forever stirred. Nothing but the sky overhead, and the many-colored fields running on until they met that sky. The horses worked here in summer; the neighbors passed on their way to town; and over yonder, in the cornfield, Rosicky's own cattle would be eating fodder as winter came on. Nothing could be more undeathlike than this place; nothing could be more right for a man who had helped to do the work of great cities and had always longed for the open country and had got to it at last. Rosicky's life seemed to him complete and beautiful.

AMERICAN ME

BEATRICE GRIFFITH

We go every July from Los Angeles to pick the fruits in the summer hills of Hanford. We lived in tents and would get up early in the gray morning when it was cold. Then we all ate outdoors over a little fire. Everybody getting up from their tents and talking and calling to each other and cooking the beans. Then we go to work and stand on our feet from seven in the morning until six at night. Gee, man, I would get so tired. You know, in the fruits you dream, sleep, walk, breathe, and talk apricots—yellow and big and soft all around you. You pick 'em, you dump 'em, you squash 'em, you peel 'em, you cut 'em, you count 'em. Everything is apricots. How many you pick? How many you peel? How much buckets or trays? Always it is to eat and smell apricots. Cause apricots is pennies and some-times they are silver dollars after you pick them a long time. Now we get lots more money in the fruits cause there is a war, and now we can go to the carnival with rich money like the boss of the ranch.

This day I tell you the boss came and paid the checks. Man, it was great. To all the working people and kids he paid them. My father and mother and me and my brother gots a hundred dollars for working three weeks, would you believe it? When I saw that check I told my mother she was fooling. The boss was just playing a game. But she said it was real money, and when I heard that I jumped up crazy I guess. I told her that check was a lot of school dresses. She said that in that check was a couch that made a bed at night for my father and brother who are tired to sleep on the little iron bed by the washing machine. And it was clothes for my brother and my father, and in it was a car. Would you believe it? A little broken car was in that check? And sure it was. Oh I tell you all was happy that night for getting money and lots clothes and food and stuff in that check.

At this camp was my new boy friend, Mokey. He was clean and handsome, not too tall—just right for me with a big smile and a handsome nose. He always looks like a movie actor in his Levis. And he walks with a swing real sure, like the Negro baseball player at school who never hurries, just reaches out and grabs the ball so slow he count the stitches on them. It was Mokey who helped Freddie and my cousin Ramón fix a good shower for us when we got to camp. They took some rubber hose and put it up high, then spread branches to spray from the water. Then they made it private with boards, and we had a shower. Sure, there was a little hole down by our legs and the boys used to look in and sing and yell:

> *Shakes like a Devil*
> *Waves like a frog*
> *When she makes love to me*
> *Oh hot dog!*

She's fine . . . . she's fine,
Fine and mellow.

That's what they sing. But we had a shower, the only ones.

This night of getting paid was excitement, *Jijola!* All the kids call from the tents about going to the carnival near Fresno. My old aunt who remembers the little jamaicas in Mexico, and who is with a young heart still, comes to our fire to talk over the war, and her boy who is a prisoner in Bataan, and the long fights and revolutions of the Mexicans, with my father. My aunt is a very beautiful woman with smooth brown skin and a proud face. She knows everything, all things in the heart of a girl. She had eight with five in the grave behind the adobe house on the hill. It is like all those dead girls were making her heart sweet with their wants of living in their dark graves. She brought my father a little bottle of her old old wine this night, and he goes with her and my mother to sit by the fire, where others from the fields are sitting and eating under the trees in the night.

My cousin Ramón from Hanford has a little truck that's green and cute named Benito, that will take us to town. To get to this truck and Ramón, Mokey and me walk through the fields to the long dusty road. In the fields was sometimes little rabbits and birds, and there was always haystacks all bunched to jump on real quick and run. With Mokey, he loved those rabbits and sometimes would catch one and rub it soft on his face. Always it was like that. Sometimes he look at a little black fly, so careful how his wings is made, and his head put on by God. And he looks so long at the plants to see their little veins and how is a leaf put on that his sister tell him, "What you see in that plant, a picture of a pretty girl, a blondie maybe?" Then Mokey tell her to go lay an egg—and a big one.

Walking across the fields into the dark hills far away with Mokey was keen. He took my hand and said, "I wish Felix and Frankie could see this sky. Man, they knew this country, they worked this country."

"Mokey, you know lots, what makes wars anyway? All my brothers too are gone to war and they weren't mad at anybody—except the cops." I looked at him but he only shake his head.

"Lucy, I don't know. Sister at church says wars is from all the people's sins. But my mother says it's the big heads make 'em, and the little people slave 'em. I tell her, wars just don't happen. It's from the people bumping and pushing and getting mad at each other, I guess. Maybe they're afraid." He stopped and cut two sunflowers, then he stuck each the one in my braids. "Now let's run, I'll race you to the truck," and so we did.

Inside the truck without much paint was lots kids already. Everybody was happy and singing and calling to everybody, pushing and laughing. All the kids sit tight in the truck cause it goes to pieces lots of times and the sides all fall down. You always hit hard when you drive cause the tires go flat sometimes. Then Ramón and the boys stuff rags into the tires when they go flat so we ride lots of hitting together. Manuel he's my cousin they call Jitterbug Sanchez, cause he's a good dancer and his picture is in the paper for the prize fight, well Manuel brings his good guitar to sing some ranchero songs and some songs for love. All sing "Soldatos Razos," and are happy for smiling and yelling, cause all are happy for living, I guess.

It used to be that when I wanted to make a boy run after me I would give him a pretty little smile, now I throw my head and give him a dirty look—and boy do they run, then I run! But with Mokey it is to sit down, and he puts his arm down and holds my hand tight for fun. I like Mokey lots. Adelita was there too, with ribbons and braids done up on her head like she was going for a dance. Adelita is always throwing looks at the boys, but man they like it, so she just toss her braids and look to see they not run for the flirty Chavella from Fresno. Adelita and me wear cute little brassières with soft in them so they don't hurt, and the boys can't see so much, but we don't wear pillows in them to make them stick up. I wear my God skin and no cheating.

When we come onto the long highway that goes to Hanford this night I tell you about, two policemen in their white car stopped the truck because they see us Mexicans inside. But my cousin Ramón, who's been to high school and who is smart knowing all about maps and what means a filibuster and the United States Congress, says to that cop, "This is a free country ain't it? We can sing in this little truck if we want can't we? Who says Mexicans can't sing for breaking the law in this truck doesn't know his country."

So the cops, seeing my cousin was smart said, "Oh, wise guy, huh? Okay, let's see your draft cards. All of you."

But only my cousin had a card from the draft, only he was eighteen. The cops look hard at his draft card and then tells us, "Okay, cholos, go on."

And so we go down the long bright highway into the streets of the town. Lots of people and kids were holding hands and walking down the streets. Little cars from the ranches and fruit camps passed us, some fast with only one light, some honking horns, but everybody was laughing and calling. Mokey waves his arms and says some dirty words to the car in back of us that gives us a big bump. The boys all pile out to look, then pile in again when they see it was nothing.

Pretty soon we come to the carnival. You know it's the place before you get there cause the music comes right through the trees and houses and into our truck. And you can see high up in the pink sky the ferris wheel going swing around the stars. And the voice of the ticket man you can hear a little, just like the radio from the boss's house in the night on the ranch. Only sometimes you cannot hear it with the crickets, like it went around the posts and cars and barns to get to us who were listening.

At the carnival everything was excitement, and all the kids pile out. First thing I see is my cousin Danny. My cousin Danny, I tell you, was fun like Cantinflas in the Mexican movies. Gee, man, he is so dirty it's a ten-to-one shot the dirt grows from one week on his face, and his pants and shirt gots a big tore in them, and he never never take a bathe. But always he is laughing, and for giving money, and always I tell you he is singing. And Danny is the only kid I know who can make rich money out of poor money.

The popcorn man saw Danny and called him, "Peanuts, popcorn, five cents, only five cents . . . peanuts, popcorn . . . *piñones.*"

But what the popcorn man don't know is that Danny only had some poor money this night, five pennies he had. Danny called him with a smile and say, "How much fifteen bags of popcorn with butter coming through the sack?"

So the popcorn man get his pencil from under his apron and write the figures on a pink striped sack. "Seventy-five cents for fifteen sacks with the butter coming through," he tells Danny.

So my cousin tells him thanks he wasn't good for arithmetic in school, only he always wanted to know how much fifteen bags of popcorn was. Then he laugh and say, "Keep the bags. I'll be back and make you rich, old man." But the man was mad and spilled the popcorn white from the sack on the ground.

The flying baskets with skirts and legs swinging in the sky stopped, and Mokey and me got in a gold basket. Adelita and Manuel sit in a red one, and soon the music begin and we are whizzing in the sky with all the stars falling around and down down to the ground. Then we jerked up high almost to a pink cloud, and Mokey held me tight, with the air whirring around us like a dive bomber. There was little screams coming from around like they was whistles that got stuck, but it was only the girls liking the hugging I think.

When we got out from the gold basket Mokey and me was still hugging like in the movies. All the peoples and tents and music and little screams was going around dancing in my head like a jitterbug. Up the streets some kids was riding on the merry-go-round and yelling and laughing to catch the gold ring from the horses and lions. Mokey and me watched Felix showing how strong he was from working and getting hard muscles in the hay fields that summer. He hit the wood block bang with the big hammer, and hit it so hard the little bell at the top in the dark would ring. The other guys was laughing and making fun of him showing off big for Theresa, him that didn't know she was going steady with two marines.

The tin woman in the next show was laughing too, but always she is laughing. Whenever you walk or ride in that carnival, or down the near streets, you hear her big laugh, in the night or day, you always hear it.

Across the carnival street, behind the wire fence, was the place where the little green and yellow and red automobiles go bump and crash around the big floor with music and fun. In one of the automobiles was an old man with red hair waving his arms and bumping the other autos like a borrachito. He had a white duck he won in the carnival and waved that duck over his head like a flag I think.

Pretty soon down the carnival street come all the kids singing and laughing and shouting. All their arms was around each other like a chain. In the middle was Danny with his arms full of Kewpie dolls. He had Kewpie feathers in his dirty green shirt and over his ears.

His pants was falling down from the string that was a belt. There was some Kewpies in his belt too. Around his neck was a clock he won. Danny was happy like nobody I ever seen in my life. He was like Flip Corkin. Everybody loved him and wanted to be his friend. But he only laugh and say he was taking all the Kewpies home for the Virgin Mary who stands on the little wooden shelf by his bed. All the girls love him and he throws them a big look, but is not caring for nothing but to laugh and sing.

Danny was always like the miracle man in the circus. Always he could go to a carnival with nothing but poor money, some pennies and nickels, and come home with hams and ducks and alarm clocks and Kewpies. Only never before tonight was there so many Kewpies.

He gave a Kewpie to Mokey for some tickets to ride the little automobiles. Then he yelled us, "Come on, let's have a race!"

We all piled in the cars, red, green, yellow—all the cars that was empty gots full. Danny put all his Kewpie dolls around him and piled some more in the other cars. Then the race began. *Qué suave!* Man it was swell. My heart was pumping up and down like some jumping beans. I got scared bumping so many cars and my heart went black and my ears go clank . . . clank, but it was fun.

Danny banged my car, Mokey hit him, then Manuel and Adelita and Ramón and Rosie all was banging cars and yelling. Everybody got bumped, nobody got hurt and the music was loud like in the circus. The American kid bumped Mokey and laughed, and Mokey bumped him back. Then they was bumping, laughing and pushing, each car a little faster and a little harder. Pretty soon then the American guy looked away, and Mokey gave him a hard bump. Then they was getting mad for reals. The American kid called him, "Dirty Mexican, I'll fix you!"

Mokey tell him, "Who do you think you are, calling me dirty Mexican?"

The guy banged him hard and say, "Well, I'm me American me. That's who I am!"

So Mokey banged him hard on the head with a pink Kewpie and yell him, "Yeah? Well I'm American me too. American inside, but Mexican on top!"

Danny throws a Kewpie to Mokey who jumps high in his car to catch it. Then all the kids begin to make trouble for purpose, all bunching and popping out of the cars to fight and hit. Danny throws us all his Kewpies, and the fight was on hard. The Kewpies was going over the cars hitting kids, busting on the floor with broken pieces getting smashed and run over. Everybody was mad with anger falling down and busting like a bomb in that place. The Kewpies was going zoom like big bullets. The cars was driving hard and spinning and bumping. Adelita's car she whirled in a circle, round and round. The air was thick and hot with kids. Some stand up in their cars the better to hit. The cars all jammed up in bunches. Everybody was all mixed up and tangled, hitting hard, zam the next one to him.

The manager or somebody cut off the electricity. Ramón yells, "Cops coming!"

Then it was a fight to get out that door with everybody running and tripping and getting socked. The American kids beat it out first, running through all the carnival people to where their cars was parked. We got in our truck, but before Ramón got the engine started everything was all mixed up again, with the American kids and us all yelling and hitting and pulling hair and getting socked. But we finally got going and drove bumping down the street by the popcorn man and the carnival people. Some of those kids was hanging on the truck but we banged their hands and they let go.

Ramón drove fast going down that big road in our truck. Danny turned off the lights so the cops wouldn't see our truck and we rode into the very night across the fields to the highway. Like Danny, Mokey's hands was bloody and his clothes was torn, and his breath was breathing hard—but he put his arms tight around me in that little ride.

It was quiet in the dark with the trees and fields and hills. Only could we hear the kids whispering and the car going fast like the wind, and the loud crazy laughing of the tin woman at the carnival following us down the road into the mist to our tents across the black fields.

Soon we would be in bed in our tents by the camp in the fruits, and I would put my head from under the tent and Mokey put his from his tent in the dark and stars, and we would talk and talk so long, our heads by the dark ground. All swell, until our mothers say, "Quit your talking and long gossip." And then we would go to sleep in the warm tent for morning to wake us to move on to pick the prunes.

But now, this little minute, I was sitting tight close to Mokey. I ask him, "Mokey, knowing about pushing and bumping and hating and all that, doesn't keep people from getting mad, huh?"

Mokey hugs me tighter. Then he kissed me soft soft, the first kiss. For Mokey knows that to be a gentleman means always please the lady for what she wants.

MAMA AND THE

OCCASION

KATHRYN FORBES

There was excitement at school.

Winford, it was whispered, was to have an exceedingly distinguished visitor.

Miss Grimes, our Principal, called a special assembly to confirm the news. "We are to be honored," she announced, "by a visit from Mrs. Reed Winford, that gr-eat lady." Miss Grimes rolled her words like our minister did when he preached Damnation.

"Mrs. Winford is," she continued, "the widow of that gr-eat and no-ble educator for whom our school is named. She will be with us on Chuesday week."

Mrs. Reed Winford, we learned, was famous as an educator in her own right, and had been Dean of Women these many years in an important Eastern university.

Now, since Mrs. Winford intended to spend her sabbatical year in the Far East, she would stop over in San Francisco just long enough to greet the upper-grade pupils and the teaching staff of the school that was a monument to her husband.

Genteel excitement ran high among the teachers, but our eighth grade was not particularly interested until Miss Grimes gave us complete charge of the refreshments for the reception.

Miss Scanlon twittered with delight and appointed Hester Prinn the chairman. Hester took elocution lessons and knew how to speak pieces. She never blushed or seemed ill at ease when she had to stand up in front of the class.

Now she said: "Let us all work together, girls, to make this a never-to-be-forgotten *Occasion*. Wouldn't it be nice if several of us brought some special little tidbit from home? Made this a real fancy tea?"

Miss Scanlon smiled and nodded. Hester nodded back graciously and held her hands together, very ladylike. "I," she said condescendingly, "shall be glad to bring our Silver Tea Service and our Sterling Silver Cake Plate from home for the Occasion. And the tea."

The girls clapped politely. And for one awful moment I hated Hester Prinn more than anything else in the world. I envied her her assurance and aplomb; I had never in my life seen a Silver Tea Service, much less owned one—and I hadn't the slightest idea what a "tidbit" was.

"Now won't someone else," Hester begged prettily, "also volunteer?"

"My mother makes lovely currant cake," Madeline said.

"Splendid."

"And *mine* makes fancy little cucumber sandwiches when *she* has a tea. I know she will let me bring some." Thyra Marin smiled primly at the rest of us.

"Fine!" Hester said heartily. "Someone else?"

"Cookies?" Mary Weston offered shyly.

"Are they—fancy cookies?"

"Oh, yes. Frosted, and all in different shapes."

"Then by all means, cookies."

Carmelita raised her hand. "I'll bring something, I don't know what. I'll have to ask my mother."

Now I loved Carmelita dearly, but it was unthinkable that she be allowed to get ahead of me.

"I, too, will bring something," I announced loudly. I had no idea what it would be, and to forestall questions, I added hastily, "a tidbit—a special tidbit."

"Thank you all so very much," Hester said. "I appoint the girls who are contributing to be the serving committee."

Before school was dismissed that afternoon, I sneaked a glance in the big dictionary on Miss Scanlon's desk. "Tidbit," it said, "a choice morsel of food."

I breathed a sigh of relief.

When I got home from school, I found Aunt Jenny in the kitchen, visiting with Mama. I told them about the distinguished visitor that was coming to Winford and bragged about being appointed to the serving committee.

"Mama," I asked, "what do you cook specially well? A—a choice morsel?"

"I just cook plain," Mama said.

Aunt Jenny snorted. "You are too modest," she said. "I just wish I had your knack with pastry, with *lutefisk*." She closed her eyes. "And your *kjödboller*," she said dreamily, "in the cream sauce. Why, they melt in a person's mouth."

Mama blushed at Aunt Jenny's praise. "Perhaps," she conceded, "perhaps I do make the good *kjödboller*—the meatballs."

"Oh, Mama," I begged, "would you make some for me to take to the reception for Mrs. Winford?"

Mama did not think that meatballs were quite the appropriate dish for an Occasion. "Why not a cake?" she suggested.

"One of the girls already offered to bring a cake."

"Cookies, then? I will make *kringler*."

"No. Mary Weston's bringing cookies. And Thyra's mother is going to make cucumber sandwiches."

Aunt Jenny was shocked. Cucumbers? Didn't people know that fresh cucumbers were poisonous? Sandwiches, to her way of thinking, were a waste of time. "Give them something to eat," she said heartily, "something they can smack their lips over."

Mama looked uncertain. Had we forgotten that *kjödboller* must be served hot?

But Aunt Jenny and I disposed of Mama's gentle arguments, one after the other. I was obsessed with the idea of showing the "clique" what a wonderful cook my mother was; of bringing some "tidbit" that would so outshine the other contributions that the Occasion would stand out in their memories forever. The girls could not *help* liking me—wanting to be my friends—if I made the Occasion a big success.

And Aunt Jenny was determined that the poor teachers, "thin as sticks, every one of them," should, for once in their lives, taste real food.

Keeping the meatballs hot? Easy. One of Aunt Jenny's neighbors had a contraption called a chafing dish that was guaranteed to keep food hot. And if Katrin would promise to be very careful of it—

"Oh, I *will*, Aunt Jenny."

Aunt Jenny planned it all out, very capably. The meatballs must be prepared in the morning, and I could come home for lunch on the day of the reception and take them back to school with me. Aunt Jenny would instruct me how to light the alcohol lamp under the contraption, and there you were. What was wrong with that idea?

Mama had to admit that it sounded all right.

Since Carmelita hadn't told the girls what she was going to bring, I decided not to tell about my wonderful contribution either.

"Wait and see," I told Hester when she asked me. "And will you be surprised!"

Hester and Madeline and Thyra were almost nice to me during the days we waited for the Occasion. Once they let me play in their jacks game, and twice they walked clear across the schoolyard with me during recess.

I was quietly happy. After the reception, I dreamed, after the teachers and Mrs. Reed Winford had smacked their lips over Mama's delicious meatballs, the girls would notice me even more.

"I simply *must* have the recipe," I could hear Miss Grimes say.

And Mrs. Winford would ask to meet the girl whose mother cooked so wonderfully. "Quite the nicest tidbit," she would say, "of this whole reception."

And the girls would smile and nod at me. They might even clap. And I wouldn't blush a bit.

"Chuesday week" finally arrived, and I rushed home at lunch time to get the Tidbit.

Mama was flushed, but happy. "Never," she told me, "have I had such good luck with the *kjödboller*. Just taste."

I tasted, and assured her that she had indeed outdone herself. Flaky, tender, swimming in the creamy sauce, the meatballs looked like a picture out of a magazine.

Carefully, we transferred them to the chafing dish. And with many warnings, Mama gave me the tiny bottle of alcohol and a block of matches. Mama had a great fear of things blowing up.

It started to rain when I got to the corner, but I was too excited to go back home for my raincoat and umbrella. Shielding the precious burden as best I could, I raced the two blocks to school.

When I got there, Miss Scanlon sent me down to the furnace room to dry my shoes. On my way, I tiptoed into the auditorium and deposited the chafing dish on the long, white-clothed table that held Hester's gleaming Silver Tea Service. I wasn't even jealous; the chafing dish looked every bit as nice.

When I got to the furnace room, the janitress was sitting on an upturned soap box, talking to herself.

"Reception," she was muttering. "*Reception*."

She looked at me sternly. "Don't I always keep this school clean?"

I nodded timidly and moved closer to the furnace.

"Better," she declared, "than any other janitress ever did. Ask anyone. Ask the Board of Education. They'll tell you that Mrs. Kronever, she takes pride in her work."

"Ha!" she continued. "Ha. Reception!" She rocked back and forth and glared at me. "Who," she demanded, "who works hardest at this Winford school? Tell me that."

"I guess you do, Mrs. Kronever."

She made her eyes small. "Then why am I not asked to the Reception, too?"

"I—I don't know."

"Ha!" she said again. "All right, all right. Let them have their old Reception. Without me!"

I stood up. Wet shoes or not, I'd better get back to the classroom. This, I decided, was what Miss Scanlon meant when she said that Mrs. Kronever was temperamental. I made my escape, leaving the janitress to her dark mutterings.

The afternoon session dragged by. A cold and driving rain had darkened the day, and we shivered. Three times Miss Scanlon had to send girls down to Mrs. Kronever with requests for more heat, without tangible results.

Dismissal bell finally rang, and the lower grades were sent home. We favored ones in the eighth congregated in the hall outside the auditorium, waiting with the teachers for Miss Grimes and the Distinguished Visitor.

For the first time, I noticed that Carmelita held a long, paper-wrapped package.

"What did you bring?" I whispered, hoping anxiously that it would not be something to compete with the delectable meatballs.

"A bottle of fine wine," she whispered back, and tore off a piece of the paper to show me the bottle, cased in straw.

I shuddered. A faint doubt entered my mind. Were we doing the right thing, Carmelita and I? Of course, meatballs were different from *wine*—but—

"What will Miss Grimes say?" I asked anxiously.

Carmelita shrugged. "The wine," she said, "is very good for the stommack."

I remembered the lecture Miss Grimes had given us on the evils of rum. Had she mentioned wine? I was torn between two loyalties; I did not want to hurt my friend's feelings, nor did I want her held up to the ridicule of the school.

"Wrap it up again," I implored her. "Let me think."

"Is good for the stommack," Carmelita persisted, and tore off the rest of the wrapping.

Miss Grimes came bustling down the hall then, followed by a tall gray-haired lady in a black fitted suit. We stood back bashfully and Miss Grimes opened the auditorium door with a flourish, and bade our Distinguished Visitor enter.

We trooped after her, I to my chosen place by the chafing dish, along with the other members of the serving committee; the rest of the class and the teachers to chairs placed in front of the platform.

The pungent odor of meatballs greeted us, and I sniffed appreciatively as I lighted the lamp under the chafing dish. Miss Grimes looked uncomfortable and wrinkled her nose a little, but she gave a wonderful introduction to the Distinguished Visitor.

Mrs. Winford was a beautiful lady. She stood up and told us how happy she was to be with us; how she had looked forward to meeting us all—I lost the rest of the speech because Hester was motioning to Miss Scanlon from the doorway, and I was curious.

I began to notice how cold it was in the auditorium and wondered why someone didn't turn on the lights. Then Miss Scanlon rushed in and whispered something to Miss Grimes and Miss Grimes rushed out the door.

Mrs. Winford finished talking and we clapped politely. She stood there on the platform until Miss Grimes came rushing back again. Miss Grimes's face had turned awful red.

"*Most* unfortunate," she announced, "but we are unable to find our janitress. She—she forgot to turn on the heat. And, stupidly enough, she has also gone off with the key to the domestic science room and the girls cannot get in to use the stove to boil the water for tea.

"But if you will just be patient," she promised, "we will have everything under way very shortly. I know we are all anxious for our tea."

Mrs. Winford looked as if she could do with a cup of hot tea. But she just smiled graciously and held her coat more tightly around herself. Miss Scanlon sneezed, twice, and Miss Grimes glared at her. The teachers went on vain expeditions for the missing janitress.

Miss Grimes and the teachers sat in a group by the platform

and made valiant conversation with our shivering guest, while the nerves of the serving committee became increasingly edgy. We watched the dainty little cucumber sandwiches become soggy and limp. Madeline tried to cut the currant cake with the cake server, and it fell into crumbs. Hester made futile little dashes from the tea table to the hall.

"It's getting late," Hester fretted, "and colder. Miss Lyons thinks she may have a key to the domestic science room at her home. She's gone to see. If we stand around much longer, we'll freeze." She noticed Carmelita. "What in the world," Hester asked crossly, "are you holding?"

"Wine."

"Wine? *Wine?* Don't you know that all teachers are W.C.T.U.?"

I didn't know what W.C.T.U. was, but Carmelita was my Best Friend. "It is good," I parroted, "for the stommack."

"They'll probably *expel* you!" Hester hissed.

Carmelita gulped, but held tightly to the wine.

"And what are *you* being so mysterious about?" Hester asked me impatiently. "What have you got in that old chafing dish?"

Reverently, I lifted the cover. "Meatballs," I breathed. "In cream sauce."

It was the signal for laughter. Harsh and highpitched laughter, vainly smothered by crammed handkerchiefs. Hester and Madeline and Thyra giggled and sputtered; then held tightly to one another and kept repeating "Meatballs!" "To a fancy tea she brings *meatballs!*"

From her seat by the platform, Miss Grimes frowned at the unseemly noise and signaled us to be quiet.

The girls wiped streaming eyes—looked at me—and collapsed into one another's arms again.

"Meatballs!" Hester grimaced. "*Poor* people eat meatballs."

"For *dinner*, if ever," Madeline hiccuped, "not at a tea."

My cheeks burned. My eyes smarted. But I dared not let the tears fall. Nobody liked my lovely, lovely surprise. Soon, now, Miss Grimes and Mrs. Winford would discover my stupidity. And the teachers. And everyone would laugh and laugh. And never, now, would my classmates be friendly.

Through the haze of unshed tears I saw my sister Christine.

She was standing by the tea table, holding out my raincoat and rubbers. "Mama sent me back with them," she said matter-of-factly. "It's pouring out."

"Go home!" I whispered fiercely. "Go home!"

Her calm gaze went to the table—to the girls. "I heard—" she began.

"Go home!" I clutched her arm, pulled her out of earshot of the still giggling girls. "If you dare tell Mama—"

Christine shook off my hand. "You and Carmelita should have known better," she said reasonably. "Mama should have known better."

"But her feelings will be hurt, Christine," I pleaded. "Please don't ever tell." Quickly I explained about the janitress. Christine shrugged, and with a cool look at the girls standing by the table, she moved away.

And I watched her go—envying her from the bottom of my aching heart. Christine *would* have known better. Christine had been born knowing the proper things. She was never impulsive, headstrong. Never did foolish, stupid things. Christine moved calmly and clearly through life, serene and—invulnerable.

Miss Grimes mounted the platform to announce that since it was getting late, and stormier, all but the girls on the serving committee would be dismissed.

Those of us left stood awkwardly about the tea table. Madeline and Hester would look at the chafing dish and then make silly faces at each other. I examined the tips of my shoes with infinite care. Carmelita moved closer to me, as if for comfort.

It got darker and colder.

One by one, the teachers made their excuses and escaped.

At last, only the serving committee, the Distinguished Visitor, and Miss Grimes were left.

"Miss Lyons should certainly be here with the key soon," Miss Grimes fretted. "Hark! I hear someone coming along the hall."

We watched the doorway hopefully.

And Mama came in!

In her arms she carried two bulky newspaper-wrapped packages.

I rushed over to her, words tumbling from my lips.

"Christine already brought my rain things, Mama."

Silently, desperately, I prayed: Please, oh, please, let Mama go back home before she finds out. If Christine had told! If the girls dared to laugh at my mother—

Mama smiled at me and walked right over to Miss Grimes and Mrs. Winford.

"You will catch cold," she scolded gently. "You need the good hot coffee to warm you up."

Mrs. Winford laughed ruefully. "What wouldn't I give," she sighed, "for a cup of hot coffee!"

Miss Grimes sneezed violently.

Mama clucked sympathetically. "See now what I have brought. Wrapped in the newspaper to keep the warmth." She herded us down to the tea table, smiled at Hester, Thyra, Mary, Madeline, and Carmelita.

She set her packages down. "In this one—the hot coffee." Mama brought forth our copper pitcher, fragrant steam escaping from it. "And in this one," she unwrapped the other package, "is the hot chocolate for Katrin's friends."

Within a few minutes, Mama had us all comfortably seated about the tea table. Mrs. Winford and Miss Grimes drank great, loud draughts of the steaming coffee. The girls and I were just as greedy with the blessedly hot chocolate.

Mama was always good at making folks comfortable. Now she passed the fancy cookies and the crumbs of currant cake. She said that Mary's cookies were about the nicest she had ever tasted, and she complimented Madeline on the delicious cake. She also commiserated with Thyra about the collapse of the cucumber sandwiches, and wholeheartedly admired Hester's tea set.

Warm and relaxed, we finally drained the last drop of coffee and of chocolate. Miss Grimes thanked Mama so sincerely that she seemed like a different person from the austere Principal we were so used to. She thanked the serving committee too, and said that she was proud of us. She said that although we had been confronted with a trying situation, the cold—and the long wait—we had acted like Little Ladies throughout.

Mrs. Winford complimented us, too. And when she was leaving, she took Mama's hands in both of hers, and they spoke together for a long time.

After Miss Grimes and the visitor had gone, we began to clear the table. Mama worked with us. Hester started to speak several times. Finally she blurted: "I would—excuse me, but—I would like to taste the—meatballs."

I gulped indignantly and started to say something, but Mama shook her head at me. Serenely, she took a clean saucer, heaped it with *kjödboller*, and passed it to Hester. Hester tasted bravely. "Why," she said wonderingly, "why, they're delicious."

And as the rest of us passed our saucers to Mama for portions, she spoke of other Norwegian dishes. Of *svisker gröd*, of the festive *Yule kage*, and *pannkaka med lingon*. The girls seemed interested.

"You must bring your friends to our home, Katrin," Mama said to me. "I will make for you the *Norske kroner*—the Norvegian cookies."

I didn't, couldn't, answer.

"Perhaps," Mama continued quietly, "the girls would like to see the baby Kaaren."

Hester's face got pink. "A baby? Have you a baby at your house?"

Mama nodded and smiled.

"We had a baby once," Hester said softly. "My little brother. We —we lost him."

"Kathryn has a big attic, too!" Carmelita bragged loudly.

"An attic all your very own?" Madeline asked.

I looked at the girls. Their faces were friendly.

"Next Wednesday," Mama said. "Come next Wednesday after school. We will make of it a party, yes?"

The girls said they would come. We locked the auditorium door and went out into the schoolyard. Hester, Madeline, Thyra, and Mary not only smiled as they left but waved, too, and said "Last look!"

Carmelita and I trudged after Mama.

"The wine," I remembered suddenly. "What of the wine?"

"Under the table your Mama put it," Carmelita said succinctly. "For Mrs. Kronever, maybe."

"It will be good," I joked, "for her stommack."

And Carmelita and I giggled happily all the way home.

THE CIRCUS CAT
OF PRICKLY ORANGE

MACKINLAY KANTOR

And now I will tell about the most remarkable cat ever seen in our neck of the woods, and what happened after it came. Maybe the cat wasn't as big as a wolf, but it was broad-shouldered and muscular of frame. Before it got through, folks had heard about its wonders clear past Sabine and down to the flat country at Winstone.

Fittingly enough, Phelps Lackey was the first to discover the cat's presence in our midst. On a fine spring morning Phelps was walking toward the Songer place to fetch back a clevis-pin which was his property, and which Ed Songer had loaned off of him and never returned. At the top of the grade by the big sycamore tree, Phelps came opposite the old Hooper house.

In usual times all one could see of the old Hooper house were roof-trees and chimneys, for the bushes had grown fair in front of it. The apple trees had become gnarly and witchlike in those years since the Hoopers went away. Nobody lived there but wood mice and wrens, and likely there wasn't even a ghost to bear them company.

Odell Hooper was the last to go. He departed in the summer of 'Sixty-one bold enough, but he never came back to Prickly Orange Hill after the war. Instead he chose to roam the world, and various ancient Hoopers lay in the burying ground and were granted their peace by mankind.

On this spring day Phelps Lackey stopped in his tracks, when he saw something move in the underbrush that choked the old path. It wasn't the kind of motion made by a snake or a weasel, but a whisk of colored cloth such as might occur if a youngun played there. And the next minute there hopped up on the fence, and sat eying him, a shape that glued Phelps Lackey flat-footed in the road.

It was a cat. Nobody raised that kind of cats in the Prickly Orange country. It had a green coat with brass buttons, and a little soldier cap on the back of its head, fastened tight with an India-rubber band. Phelps said afterward that he felt his knees shiver, and he couldn't get his breath, despite his horse-strength and his six-foot frame.

The cat's coat was shiny and bright and its soldier cap was red, and when it looked at Phelps, he swore that it shook its head mighty disdainful. But at that moment, to rescue his saneness, a woman's voice hollered, "John! John, where are you?" and there was another flash of color in the bushes; the woman herself appeared and stood inside the fence agazing at Phelps.

She was young, and cornstalk slim. Her hair was the color of cornsilks when they turn ruddy dark in the fall; her eyes were reddish-brown as well, and they looked fearfully out of her small face; then, in the same instant, she smiled and said Howdy.

Phelps Lackey, although amiable at heart, had a stern and sober nature, and he believed it to be indecent for cats to go around like Calathumpians. He unbent a forefinger from his big fist and pointed at the critter on the fence. "Lady," he said, "is that your property?"

Her smile was gone, and her little jaw got hard and tight. "John is my cat," she said. But she didn't pronounce the word "John" like civilized folks pronounce it, for a J wasn't just a J to her: it had Z and Y and some other sounds mixed up in it, and Phelps reckoned that he was confronted by a foreigner.

"Listen to me, lady," said Phelps. The woman had an orange-colored ribbon around her hair, and gypsies weren't popular in those parts. "Who gave you leave to move into the Hooper place?"

The woman laughed again, and it wasn't the kind of laugh that accompanies a smile. "You are a funny man," she said. "So big! But I think you are a little boy. I think you are a savage, no? I am Ernestine Hooper. This house belongs to me and to my kitty John," and she poked her finger at that idiotic animal, and the cat hauled off and boxed with her.

Phelps sort of teetered there in the road, with his jaw falling half-way to his knees, whilst she went on talking. She spoke rapidly and excitedly, and threw her pronunciations all over a ten-acre lot, as is the custom with foreigners, so that Phelps couldn't understand half of what she said.

But in the half which he could understand, came the news that she was Odell Hooper's widow. She was born across the water, she said, and her father was a lion-tamer, and she said that she was raised with seven bears, and one of the bears was named Fritz, and he was the biggest one.

And she said that Odell Hooper had traveled with Dan Rice's Circus; and later he became manager of Dupray Montgomery's Colossal and Gigantic One-Ring Show. That was where he met this girl half his age, and wedded her. And that was where he died, from going to bed with an elephant after he had treated himself at a tavern in Covington, Kentucky; because the elephant turned over in the night, but Odell Hooper didn't.

So his widow sold out her circus interest, and now she wanted to lead a peaceful life, and she had kept only one of her trained cats. Back she traveled to her husband's home which she had never seen, and she said that the forest sounds scared her out of her wits all night long, and she would have to spend almighty sums to make that house habitable.

Whilst Phelps Lackey stood bug-eyed and disbelieving, Lennie Fossett came toiling up the hollow road with his uncle's mule team. Lennie had boxes and barrels in the wagon, and there was a hair trunk painted all over with stars and bedazzled with signs about the circus: surely these were the woman's possessions, fresh-come from the steam cars at Winstone.

Matters might have progressed plumb neighborly and contented, only for Choctaw. Choctaw was Phelps Lackey's big brindled dog, with a nose like a hound and ears like a mastiff, and not much tail at all. He was known far and wide as a cat-killer of parts, and one time he had mighty nigh pulled the leg off a creditor of old Joe Lackey; and he had even tangled with three skunks. Now he hankered to accompany his master, and he came atearing up Phelps's trail, dirty and drooling and noisy as a herd of cattle.

He was five jumps away, when he spied that cat setting calm and insolent on the low fence; he changed his course on the fourth jump. The woman screamed, but anybody could have told her there was no use screaming when Choctaw got started on a cat: it was just grab and shake and go-out-to-the-barn-for-a-spade. Phelps sighed and stepped back; he didn't bear the cat any real grudge. He just didn't like its green coat nor its soldier hat, and he didn't admire to see any cat strut so pridefully.

On the third jump, Choctaw left the ground like a flying squirrel, and soared toward the top rail. There was a new yell—a most horrible one—and Phelps closed his eyes because he couldn't abide seeing Choctaw murder a cat wantonly. But he opened his eyes right smart, for the yell came from Choctaw.

That dog defied all laws of nature. He walked in the air. He flopped backward about ten flops, and then his hindquarters hit the ground, and he bounced. His nose had been slit from between his eyes down to the top of his muzzle, and the cat was kind of leaning on one elbow awatching him.

All this time Mrs. Ernestine Hooper was living up to the name her departed husband had given her, and Lennie Fossett's gray mules were weaving on their hind legs. It looked as if trunks and barrels would be spread halfway to Winstone in the next instant.

But no matter how mean that Choctaw dog might be, he had a fighting heart, and he had his reputation to sustain. He shagged around in the dust, shaking his head and bristling his shoulders, and then he made another dive for the fence. There was a smother of green and red and white: the green was John's soldier jacket, and the red was John's cap, and the white was John's native fur. It was like a spinning top, Phelps said, with green and red and white on the peak of it. Brindled brown whirled underneath, and the brindled brown was Choctaw; the dust went six feet high, though it had rained only two days before.

Then Choctaw cut for home. The only trouble about this was that the cat John had suffered a change of heart. He seemed to desire Choctaw's company, and didn't want to part with him no way. He sat astride the dog, close upon his shoulders, and he ripped away with two sets of claws. They say you could hear Choctaw halfway to Desolate River, and Phelps's brother-in-law was up there a-hunting, and he said the very rocks shivered at the sound.

Down the road toward the Lackey place, after the dust was settled from its disturbance, there appeared a little figure in a green coat. It was the cat, and Phelps fully expected to see him walking on his hind legs, though he didn't. Still, he kind of sauntered on his path; when he got to his own yard fence, he jumped to the rail without a word and gave his mistress a swipe with his paw.

"John," cried the woman, "you are killed!" She rubbed the tears out of her eyes, and they were blazing as she faced Phelps with that fatfaced, grinning cat clutched against her breast. "What a dog," she said, "and what a man! What a savage dog for such a cruel, savage man to have!"

Lackey heard himself saying, kind of weak: "See here, ma'am, you can't keep that cat around here. I reckon he's more dangerous than a panther!"

And Lennie Fossett sung out, hanging onto his mules' bits with both hands: "A cat like that ain't human! My mules act like they was poison drunk, and I don't blame them."

Widow Hooper began to spout more fireworks than a Democratic candidate at a rally. She said that she was sorry she had moved to those parts, and that beside such people and such dogs, the lions and tigers in the circus seemed like a gang of preachers. She said there were bricks toppling out of the chimney in the Hooper house, and she'd keep a pile of them handy, and if any such ornery dogs or folks came nigh, she'd let fly at them.

All this she said with her pronunciations splintering all over the landscape, and saying foreign words too, and there was a might of brimstone in every sound she uttered. Lennie Fossett didn't linger long after he had unloaded her paraphernalia, but he laid on gad, and took those mules back to Sabine in two shakes. Before that night, half the county heard how the circus woman had moved onto the Hooper place with a couple of trained elephants; and some said that she pulled down her chimney brick by brick, and threw the bricks at Phelps Lackey and his innocent dog.

As for Phelps, he forgot about the clevis-pin. He went home to see if he couldn't doctor Choctaw somewhat, so that eventually he'd grow into a whole dog again. But it took him six hours to persuade Choctaw out from under the corncrib; and even then he had to take old Tige, his father's tomcat, and shut him in a closet, or Choctaw wouldn't have come. The Lackeys gathered and heard the news, and there was plenty of head-shaking and cussing about this circus woman and her trained cat, though the younguns kind of relished the idea.

And Sunday morning was full of astonishments, as well, for the Campbellite structure was only half a mile distant from the Hooper place. Preacher Carrington hadn't even started to say how thankful we should be for such a pleasurable Sabbath, when the circus woman herself came in.

She walked as proud and earnest as if church-going was half her existence, and as if she had never been mired in the sins of circuses. Trim and beautiful she looked, for she had left off the orange ribbon from her hair, and she had donned a shawl like any other woman might wear. She sat herself down on the first bench where there was room, and cast up her eyes, and was Christian and humble.

Preacher Carrington sort of swallowed over his introductions; he went to reading the Scriptures. He read Judges, Fourteenth Chapter, and luck would have it that in those verses Samson should desire a wife of the Philistines.

You could watch Phelps Lackey's ears getting red all this time.

"Then his father and his mother said unto him, Is there never a woman among the daughters of thy brethren or among all thy people? . . . And Samson said unto his father, Get her for me, for she pleaseth me well."

Folks had no right to look at Phelps Lackey the way they were doing, nor to speculate on how red his ears were becoming, for he had barely talked to the Widow Hooper; and his dog had been wounded ferociously by her cat, and that doesn't make for love in anybody's language.

Still, she was a mighty pretty woman, and Phelps was the biggest and handsomest of all the Lackeys, though the only one that had never taken him a wife. You could feel that all of Prickly Orange was wondering what would happen if this woman went on living there amongst them, and I reckon old Joe Lackey wondered the hardest of all. Joe didn't approve of circuses no way, and he used to scalp his younguns every time they snuck off to them.

Maybe there were those who half expected to see the circus woman climb up on her bench and perform acrobatics; but she was as prim as any widow that ever wore a bonnet to a burying. Her slim little hands were folded under her shawl, and the womenfolks admitted thereafter that they felt charitable and motherly toward her. And over on the men's side, the looks leveled in her direction were no way nigh as hostile as they might have been.

The sermon was said and the long prayer too, and responses and Amens were bespoken firm and honest. Then a hymn was tuned up; on a sudden, the Campbellites nearest the door felt that competition was approaching down the hill of Prickly Orange.

It was the kind of sound that creeps upon you unawares when you haven't expected to hear it, and then you swear you've been listening to it for an hour. It was just the same two notes, over and over; and by the time it reached the churchyard, it rose high and shrill above the ordinary scuffling of mules, and the bird warbles that filled the region.

Sweetly over hill and valley
Sounded far a voice of old,
Like a strain of angel music,
Floating down from gates of gold.

And that was in the song, too—at least, the one the folks were
singing. I reckon it may have been exaggeration to believe that
the voice of John Cat was like a strain of angel music. But it wasn't
like any music ever heard in our neck of the woods, and probably
his voice had been trained as well as his paws and habits.

Straight up to the door he came—but minus his costume—and in
he marched, and his outcry didn't ring true with the voices of the
women. They sang on—how the tender lambs should be gathered
from the world's dark ways of sin—but a blind man could have told
that they didn't approve of gathering that cat into the church, with
the smell of behemoths and anacondas still about him.

Widow Hooper swung around on her bench and picked up the
critter, and he grinned from ear to ear. She was consternated by his
presence. First it seemed that she would make a rush for the door
with John on her arm; and then you could feel that she reasoned it
would be unsightly to leave in such fashion. So she wrapped John
up in a fold of her shawl; naturally he had ceased his caterwauling
when he found the mistress he sought, and she just sat on, whilst
the song was fought through to the end.

Then everybody choked, and Preacher Carrington picked up his
Bible and laid it down again. Custom called for a second tune before dismissal, and the woman who was the striker-up of hymns was
dumb and frigid, staring at the spectacle before her. Old Joe Lackey
it was who got the second hymn agoing. It was "Fall In!" and you
could hear Joe Lackey's voice screeching above all others; there
was no doubt about whom he meant, the way he was glaring.

Satan comes with mighty hosts
And desolates the land—

Mrs. Ernestine Hooper didn't need further hint. She scooted for
the door, and it was misfortune that Phelps Lackey scooted at the
same instance. They collided and jammed, and the cat fell out of
her arms and dove away down the path with his tail pointing high.

If Phelps's ears were red before, they were beet-brown now, and so were the rest of his visible parts.

"Tell them," the Widow Hooper was heard to say, "tell these people I am so sorry. I put John in the kitchen, but the window was not there!" Anybody with half an eye in his head, could have told that she was lamenting her angry words of the previous day, and wishing that she could become friendly with the nearby people, and with Phelps himself. "Tell them, please!" she said again, and then she caught up her skirts and ran fast on the homeward path where the cat was leading her.

Tongues were unloosed, and a storm of talk spouted up inside the church-house and around it. The younguns were tearing down the road to see if they could get another look at that animal, and the women all got in bunches and clacked like sparrows. At first the men were more silent and self-contained, and then they began to sneak little remarks to one another, and nod their heads in the direction of Phelps, and go off to chuckle on the off-sides of their teams. Phelps took it in patient fashion for a while, though I reckon his soul was unsteadied.

He went down to the fence corner to talk with his neighbors. And then it was that Ed Songer mentioned how a circus life had always appealed to him. Ed said that it was plumb delightful to consider sleeping in a tent, and setting down to feed with camels and clowns; he reckoned that if a man was to take up the circus business seriously, he'd find that even monkeys had their good points.

Phelps didn't say anything to that. He just knocked Ed Songer across two rocks and into some blackberry brush, and people had to bring water from the creek and throw it on Ed's face. Phelps went home, pursuing a roundabout way, not daring to take the road the Widow Hooper had traveled.

He said out loud to his family that very evening, that he was glad their own Tige wasn't a circus cat, and he surprised his mother by rubbing Tige's fur and swinging him up in the air, the way he hadn't done since Tige was a kitten; and Tige went under the bed to think about it.

Tige was known in the neighborhood as a plaid cat on account of the yellow-and-gray mixture which adorned him. He wasn't calico in the ordinary sense of the word, but he seemed to possess a regular pattern, like the tartan that old Andrew Drummond fetched with him all the way from Scotland, and still wrapped around his knees on cold days in the wagon.

I reckon Tige didn't hold any real aversion to the circus cat, though he was set above others of his species by being the only cat which heretofore Choctaw wouldn't assault with full intent to kill. And right away he scraped a friendship with John, the circus cat, and they went hunting together, for I saw them myself.

Phelps Lackey was a victim of fate, because now he had the whole countryside looking at him askance, and speculating on whether he held an abiding interest in the circus woman. As for high-toned ladies of the region, they swore they wouldn't be caught dead on that woman's doorstep. Circuses and menagerie morals couldn't mix righteously in their minds, no matter how many times Mrs. Ernestine Hooper sat amongst the Campbellites. Thereafter she took care to imprison John so that he couldn't follow after and create scandal, and she had a good voice for hymns; finally the congregation looked upon her with reasonable kindness, but from a distance.

Curiosity ruled the neighborhood younguns, who used to roost on the Hooper front fence and watch Widow Hooper put John through his paces. She did it every day so that he wouldn't become forgetful and like ordinary cats. Though growing fat as a shoat, he could jump, and turn somersaults, and he could march after a fashion, and carry a little wooden gun. Mrs. Hooper was proud of these tricks, and friendly toward the children who came to witness them. But the more she carved down the weeds and bushes that had worked ruin in the Hooper dooryard, and the more she tacked white curtains at the windows and prettied the house, the darker she burrowed into her solitude. She was choked with mournfulness because the people of Prickly Orange couldn't claim her as their own.

Phelps Lackey hankered after seeing more of her than he saw, but his father was a hellion. Old Joe swore that none of the Lackeys had ever betokened interest in circuses before this, and now was no time to begin. Though Phelps was man-grown he was silent in his nature, and generally so uncomplaining that the old man found it easy to lead Phelps around as if he had a ring in his nose. The cornfield which bounded Widow Hooper's place was just the spot where old Joe would work his own self, and far down the ridge was the spot he chose for Phelps's endeavors.

May went on and June approached, and one evening some horse traders visited the neighborhood. At least they made out to be horse traders, but they only had one spavined nag led on behind the wagon. There were two of them—scraggly and dirty looking— and when you saw them, you figured you'd best go home and bolt the cellar door before you went to your rest, and keep the shotgun handy, too.

They encamped in a patch of brush above the Hooper place, and at suppertime old Joe Lackey found Phelps walking up and down and refusing to eat.

"Phelps," said the old man, "come nigh the table and get yourself busy with your vittles," and Phelps tried, but he made sad work of it.

"He's plagued by those horse traders," said Mam Lackey, from beside the stove.

Old Joe speared himself a mess of greens. "I'd never hold worry for them," he said. "They're not horse traders no way, but plain ordinary tramps."

And while they ate, it got darker and darker, and the woods outside seemed evil and deplorable, and fit to hide a variety of misfortunes.

"I'd best go yonder and spy them out," said Phelps. "The weasels have took enough of our chickens already. We can't spare none to wanderers of that sort."

Old Joe laid down his knife. "If it's the circus woman that's worrying you," he said, kind of sarcastic, "I reckon you can save your grief. Don't I recollect that she threatened to heave bricks at anybody who came nigh?"

But Phelps declared that he wasn't thinking about the Widow Hooper, but just his own family hen roost.

"Choctaw's underneath the house," old Joe told him. "He'd cry out in wrath if anybody came prowling."

Well, the story goes that they went to bed after discussing it a mite further, but Phelps rolled and tossed in his hot little room under the eaves, and several times he went out to the front gate in his shirt and listened. In another hour he couldn't stand the state of his own mind, but pulled on his breeches and boots. He wasn't halfway to the Hooper place before he heard a commotion, and he heard the widow scream.

The story came later from Phelps himself by slow degrees; and from the circus woman, with her queer pronunciations. But none of it came from the horse traders, for they up and left the country that very night.

Phelps went through those bushes like a rock rolled off a hill. By the time he got to the Hooper house, the varmints had broke down the door, and the widow was crying for help. Phelps Lackey had no weapon upon him, and no reptile of those men's breed ever went unarmed.

He roared through the doorway spry enough and waded in. The first one, he picked up by the seat of his breeches and flung him clean through the new window. The second one had his knife out, by that time. It was nip and tuck for several minutes. Then the knife went into the fireplace, and the scalawag went through the door, to land on his head, and groan.

Phelps stood leaning heavily, with one hand on the leg of the upset table.

"Mr. Lackey," said Ernestine Hooper, "you are killed!"

Phelps said No. But he hung onto his side, and it seemed to be growing heavier every minute, as if it were filling up with sand. "No," he said. "He just lacerated me a mite, that's all."

Then he got ferocious again, and picked up a poker and went hunting horse traders. But they had crept off, and later on, when Joe Lackey and the rest approached the camp with their guns ready, the strangers had vanished astride their team, although they left their wagon and tent and old nag behind.

Phelps was taken home; he could walk the first ten rods; after that he had to be toted. Mam Lackey put him to bed and called in the nearest granny, who had a way with wounds since the earliest times, and a neighbor boy was sent on a colt to Sabine to fetch Doctor Lester. And all the way the neighbor boy wondered how Mrs. Ernestine Hooper felt; for old Joe Lackey swore that it was all her fault, and that if she had only stayed with the clowns and

zebras where she belonged, this outrage would never have oc-
curred, and his son would not be lying stabbed nigh unto death.

And the neighbor boy hoped that old Joe and the people at large
wouldn't blame the poor young widow too much. I know he did;
I remember; for still I recall how black and frightening the woods
appeared.

When those horse traders came storming into the Widow
Hooper's house, they broke down much more than her front door.
They broke down the high spite-fence of unfriendliness which
Prickly Orange had erected around her, and more than one neighbor woman walked up there the next day. They said: "You poor
thing!" and "I vow I would have been scairt half to death!" and
they saw to it that their menfolks repaired her front door at an early
hour.

But the Lackeys were of a different breed. At least old Joe was.
He never ceased reciting the tribulations which the pretty woman
had brought upon him and his, as people came to peek at Phelps
and query him, and tell him he ought to be grateful that he hadn't
been slain.

Doctor Lester looked mighty grave when first he saw the wound.
On the second day Phelps became plumb feverish, and once he
didn't even know who was beside his bed. Then at last he was on
the mend; the misery in his side became less hurtful, and a week
after his battle he was setting up with goose-feather pillows behind
him, areading the Bible and the doctor-book and the Winstone
Democrat, and the few picture papers that kind folks had left to
soothe him.

Then at last the Widow Hooper appeared on the stoop; she stood
there pale-lipped and shaky-kneed, confronted by old Joe Lackey's
sour glances. She said that she had come to call on Phelps. I reckon
she was scared to come before this, but day by day she had got her
dander up; a dozen old Joe Lackeys couldn't have kept her, in the
end, from bespeaking her gratitude to Phelps Lackey.

And she had brought him something to eat made with her own
hands. Phelps spooned it up, every drop, whilst she sat stiff on the
edge of the rocker and watched him. It was white potato soup,
but unlike any white potato soup ever cooked up on Prickly Orange

Hill before that time. It was thick and kind of blank and sweetish by taste; the top was dressed with green onion sprouts cut up as fine as pepper; and instead of being hot, it was as cold as the tomb, for the widow had chilled it deep down in her well.

Phelps had a kink between his brows, the while he ate, but at last he put down the dish, and said, "That's mighty tasty, ma'am. I'm grateful to you."

"Grateful to me?" said the Widow Hooper, in a weak voice. "How is it you can be grateful to me, Mr. Lackey? It is you who saved me. I owe so much to you, my neighbor."

Phelps became rosy, despite his natural miseries and paleness, and then he looked past the foot of his bed and saw his father.

Joe Lackey hadn't stirred foot from the room, and he had watched it all: the fetching of the soup and the eating of it by Phelps. He had daggers in his eyes, and his chin was as tough as an old soda biscuit, but he didn't speak his mind. He just looked.

And Phelps swished around a little under the covers. The color petered out of his face.

"I must go home," said Ernestine Hooper, still in that distant voice. "I see I am not welcome in this house."

Phelps Lackey cried out, "You are welcome, ma'am!" But old Joe spoke no word, nor lifted a hand to halt her departure.

"You come again," Phelps cried. "Lady, we've never turned a soul from this door who chose to come in friendly fashion!"

But the widow was in the doorway as he spoke, and she shook her head.

"If you have need," said Phelps, with his breath coming short and hurting him, "never be reluctant to call upon me, day or night."

And the Widow Hooper promised, for she knew that Phelps Lackey meant those words he said. Then she went away without looking back, and her cat came to meet her in the road.

From his window Joe Lackey spoke disgust at any manner of life that permitted cats to be dressed in mortal clothes—that permitted women to wear the kind of earrings such as decorated Mrs. Hooper's ears. He told his son tale after tale about the cruelties and wickedness of circus people, and how they stunted the growth of their own sons to make midgets out of them, and how they kept the lowest company, and danced and reveled on the day of the Lord.

But Phelps just set there in bed and heard him out, and never said Boo.

Another week passed by, and one besides that. Phelps Lackey was up in his ordinary clothes. He couldn't yet take his place in the fields, but he set for hours on the front stoop amending harness, and tinkering at other chores of like nature. He began to grow brown and hearty again, with the rent in his side nearly mended, and the sunshine sinking through his bones, to tighten them up again.

Sometimes he'd go to the gate and look up the road, and he'd pass the time of day with travelers who journeyed along. Come Friday afternoon, he even swung a scythe for an hour. And his pappy thanked the Lord that his tallest son was whole; he hoped that no more evil newcomers, and foreigners at that, and females into the bargain, would come cluttering up those hills and making it possible for his children to lay at death's door.

It was late that night, ten at least, and the old folks were abed, and Phelps was feeling that way himself—when he heard Choctaw yip and bray, and the boards squeaked outside the door. Phelps opened up without a challenge, with the tin lamp high in his hand, and there stood the Widow Hooper.

It had been raining that evening. The tiny drops twinkled on her dark hair and made it a thousand times blacker than it really was.

"Ma'am," he whispered. In that moment he heard his pappy in the next room, fumbling around for his breeches.

"I have come," the woman told him, "because I am in need."

Phelps said, still standing there like a dummy with the lamp aloft, "If there's aught I can do—"

"Help me find John," cried the widow, plumb desperate.

The door of the chamber opened, and out came Joe. Phelps Lackey, he stood for a long minute, saying never a word. Then with one hand he placed the lamp upon the table, and with the other he caught his hat from its peg. "Pap," he said, without turning around, "where's the lantern?"

"The lantern ain't filled," said the old man. "And if it was, I vow you shouldn't carry it on a foolish errand."

The woman whispered, "It is to find my John. It is to hunt for my kitty!"

Joe Lackey grinned, mean and stubborn behind his beard. "If that plagued critter is lost," he declared, "I hope it's lost for good and all. I shouldn't wonder but that Satan himself came to fetch it away." And then his wrath popped up like hot grease from a skillet: "Hear me, Phelps! You're not to wander the brush aseeking circus cats!"

Phelps had found the lantern. He listened in studious fashion to the swish of its oil. "There's oil enough to lighten the woods for a spell," he said, half to himself. "Wait till I strike a flare, ma'am, and I'll accompany you."

Old Joe shouted so loud that he brought Mam Lackey from the bed behind him. "I say you're not to go! You went to her aid once before, and a knife laid you low. I don't make denial that a woman in need is a woman in need, but circus cats will have to take their chance in the woods on Prickly Orange. And I ought to add circus women to that!"

Phelps lighted his lantern and went to the door and stood there, dark and somber beside the little woman in her shawl. Then he turned around and spoke firm enough, but with no anger in his heart.

"What's acceptable to the rest of mankind, is acceptable to me. Every soul in this region has crossed this lady's threshold with Christian intent. I reckon even Preacher Carrington has become her friend, and I hate like poison to see you be the last."

He pointed to the big Bible above the fireplace, and he said: "If you read that Book for a spell tonight, it won't do you no harm. I read it by the hour, when I was abed, and I found no mention whatsoever of circuses, of the people that live with them, nor even of trained cats. But it warns a powerful lot about folks being brotherly, and courteous to strangers, no matter where they hail from. And I do begrudge you every stripe you took out of my hide, when I was a youngun and ran off to Sabine to see the elephant."

Old Joe sort of staggered, he was so astounded. For a long minute nobody broke the silence, and then it was Mam Lackey who spoke. "Phelps," she said, "I do admire your spunk at last! I'd begun to think you didn't have none, but I reckoned it wasn't for me to tell you. Go along," she said to her befuddled husband, "and read the Scriptures like your son tells you."

Phelps closed the door, and he and the woman stood in the night with the little lantern between them.

There is no need to detail their wanderings and their callings, for it didn't occupy them long. There is no need to relate how the woman cried, and said that she had been desolated in her heart since the night before, when John up and took French leave.

"Just resign it to me," said Phelps. "I'm kind of weak on my pins yet, but with the lantern we can search every thicket. I reckon that cat hasn't gone far."

Sure enough, he spoke the literal truth. They had reached the tangles due east of Ernestine Hooper's back fence, when they heard a "Mew, mew," and John himself crept up into the dim light. That cat had retreated into the hollow of a basswood tree which had been broke half off in an ancient storm, and there John had made a nest.

They lifted the lantern high; they held it over the hole, while John cuffed contentedly at the Widow Hooper. Down in that hole there was other fur and other mewings, though mighty puny ones. There were six kittens, and when Ernestine Hooper saw the color of their plumage, she put her hands on her hips and looked ferocious, and said, "Plaid kittens. Your Tige!"

"But, ma'am," cried Phelps Lackey in bewilderment, and trying to be strict and formal as if he didn't know that his hand was half around the woman's waist. "I don't rightly understand this. I thought that cat's name was John!"

The widow laughed, and then she replied, "But this *is* John," saying Z and Y, and making the whole sound of the name in her foreign fashion. And for the first time Phelps learned that the French have got a lady's name that sounds pretty much like John, but isn't spelt the same way. So that was the first foreign word she taught him.

ROSEBUD WAS HER NAME

RUTH ADAMS KNIGHT

The Yusukis were home again, and Rosebud Yusuki's heart was almost bursting, she was so happy.

It was true their place didn't look much the way it had when they'd left it. The people who had lived in it while they were gone had been war workers, and had had no time for other things. The wagon trail that led to it from the highway had almost disappeared. The gardens hadn't been touched and weeds had flourished. The house itself needed repairs; the door was sagging on its hinges and a board was missing on the back porch and the paint was so weatherbeaten you couldn't tell what its color was supposed to be. But all these details would yield quickly to her father's energetic attack, Rosebud was sure, the way the interior had to her mother's scrub brush and broom.

They would all pitch in and help, even Joe. Joe was at home to stay now. His hospital pallor was gradually disappearing. And while there was something Rosebud still couldn't think about without crying, at least he was with them. And if they were patient, the doctors had said, one day he'd be almost the way he'd been before he went away, before they'd all gone away. They'd all laugh and chatter again then, as though none of it had happened. Since it couldn't be changed, it must be forgotten.

And it all couldn't be forgotten too soon for Rosebud. Precious time had been lost, she knew, even though she hadn't minded the relocation camp so much as some of the other girls had. But she had been a small girl when it had begun, and now she felt quite grown up. She was a pretty child, sturdily built in spite of her name, but with shining dark eyes and a shy little face that had kept a cherry-blossom delicacy about it. She had the look of having stepped from an exquisite Japanese print. She had looked that way even in the little red dress and sports shoes she had worn to school before the seventh of a certain December. And she had gone on giving the same impression in the queer new world she had found herself in after that significant date.

They had lived until then in the hot San Joaquin Valley on their small truck farm. Rosebud's father was an expert gardener and the green vegetables he could grow in a little space had made everyone marvel. In the center of his land was the house, and neat rows of lettuce and tomatoes ran right up to the door of rooms equally neat. Their windows shone, the curtains were always crisp and fresh, the floors scrubbed, and the furniture, though there was not a great deal of it, was carefully placed. There had been only four rooms in the house. Rosebud had had to share her grandmother's bed and her brother Joe had slept on a couch in the living room. But the minute Joe was up the bedcovers had been folded and put away and when the family sat down at the little table for breakfast the room looked like a regular dining room. At night, after dinner, the table was pushed against the wall and a lamp

put on it, and the room was the living room. They all thought it a
fine house and were very happy when they came back to it at
the end of the day.

They were a busy family. Joe didn't want to be a gardener.
He'd worked in a big factory. But he helped his father after he
got home. They'd stand outside the back door, usually speaking
Japanese, which Rosebud didn't understand too well. But Joe kept
putting in English words because he said their father and mother
ought to use them, too, to be really American. They both tried,
and their father could carry on his business conversations now with
no trouble. But for their mother it was harder. And for their
grandmother—the only American word Joe had been able to teach
her to say was "nuts!" The old lady hadn't a notion what it meant,
but Joe had explained that it was what people exclaimed when
they were disgusted, and it was very funny to hear her sometimes,
when the silks with which she did fine embroidery work got in
a tangle, repeating over and over in her cracked, high-pitched little
voice, "Nuts! Nuts! *Nuts!*" Rosebud didn't think Joe should have
taught it to her. At school her teacher had said it was slang and
vulgar. But Joe just laughed. He was a gay, strong boy, always
smiling, and everybody loved him. Nobody scolded Joe much no
matter what he did.

Joe had many friends in the neighborhood and so had Rosebud.
Rosebud had gone to the same little school from the time she
started. The girls in her class all belonged to a club and they had
regular meetings and served refreshments and even had pins with
the letters O.C., meaning Our Club, to show they were members.

Looking back on it while she was in relocation camp, Rosebud
had sometimes felt it had been too good to be true. Maybe, she'd
thought wistfully, that was why it hadn't lasted. The end of it had
been so swift and sudden it seemed a bad dream. It had been
on a Sunday afternoon and Rosebud had been reading a book and
Joe had been listening to his little radio in the living room. And
then, all at once, a man's voice had broken into the program talking in a queer, solemn tone. He hadn't spoken long, only a few
sentences. But Joe had let out a shout, "Jeepers!" and when she
ran to see what had happened he'd had the queerest expression on

his face and was twisting the dial from station to station, as if he
was trying to find something.

"What was it, Joe?" Rosebud had demanded. "I didn't hear what
the man said."

Joe's black eyes had looked straight into hers.

"He said the Japanese had attacked Pearl Harbor," he told her.
"Boy, are we in it now!"

The whole family had sat around the radio the rest of the afternoon, waiting for more news, Joe still looking strange, their father
excited and unhappy, and their mother only bewildered. At first
they didn't tell Rosebud's grandmother anything about it. It would
only frighten her, Mother said. But she sensed something was
wrong and began such an insistent cackling that Joe finally tried
to explain it to her. But he might better have saved his breath.

"She thinks it's a joke," Joe told Rosebud, when the old lady
finally went indignantly into her own room and shut the door. "She
believes I'm fooling her. She says it's impossible. Japanese and
Americans are friends. Japanese like us *are* Americans."

"It does seem that way," Rosebud said soberly. "Could it be a
mistake, Joe?"

"You heard what they're saying on all the radio stations. It
sounded as if they had the real stuff."

"*But, Joe—*" They stared at each other as if the end of the world
had come, feeling that in some ways the end of theirs had. At
last Rosebud whispered, "Joe—then—there'll be *war*—war between
America and Japan?"

From his corner by the radio her father let out a stream of
shrill exclamations and beat his fists on his knees. "No," he protested. "No. No war."

"But that's the way it is," Joe said slowly. "War," he repeated.
"*War.*"

After a while he went away, to town, driving their rickety old
car. When Rosebud saw him next he had on a uniform.

The days that followed were a kind of blur to her. There were
many rumors about what was going to happen. For the first time
in Rosebud's life there seemed to be a dividing line at school between the girls who were Japanese and those who weren't. The
Japanese girls, most of them, were worried about what was going

to happen to them now and they huddled together, reporting on what went on at home, what their parents said, what their brothers were going to do.

"What do you think of your old emperor now?" Sally Hayes, a little blond girl with a pug nose, shot at them all one day at recess when they were consulting as usual. "Letting Japan do a thing like that!"

"*My* emperor?" said Rosebud who was nearest. She looked completely bewildered. "He isn't my emperor. *I'm an American.*"

But if he wasn't her emperor he was her grandmother's. Finally convinced of what had happened, the old lady broke into voluble Japanese based upon her lifelong conviction that the Emperor could do no wrong. If Pearl Harbor had been attacked, it must have deserved it, she declared. Joe, listening, gave a rueful grin.

"It's a good thing most folks around here don't understand Japanese," he observed grimly. "Those aren't ideas that ought to be aired in a one-hundred-percent American family. Not to a guy in an American uniform. Grandmother's too old to understand or to change, I suppose. But you're going to have to make her hold her tongue."

His confused and loyal parents did what they could. The pain of what had happened was almost more than they themselves could bear and certainly more than they could understand. Japan was long ago and far away and loyalty to her superseded by a much newer and deeper devotion to the wonderful land of their adoption. But its memory still stirred their affection. As long as possible they fought acceptance of the conflict. But when they saw Joe in uniform the die was cast. No matter what they had been, they tried to explain to the angry grandmother, they were American now. What America required them to do to prove that fact they must do willingly. Grandmother might think what she pleased. But before them she must never say another disloyal word.

What America required them to do became clear very quickly. The presence on the West coast of any Japanese constituted a danger to themselves and their country, they were told. They must leave at once; pack up and be gone. They must go with hundreds of others to a place provided for them called a relocation camp. It would be dismal and uncomfortable—a place of mud roads and rude barracks—but there they must stay until the war was over. When Rosebud's father, his face white with desperation, asked how long that would be, a wearied official could only shake his head and cast his eyes upward. Only Heaven knew that, he told them.

They hadn't been able to take much with them. Clothes, bedding, pots, and pans, the few things they could carry to make the grandmother more comfortable. With everything in her the old lady fought the indignity that was being thrust upon her—the hasty packing, the confusion, the mounting uncertainty that was almost fear, the endless questions and reports. Papers to be signed, credentials to be secured threw her into panic. For years now she had lived comfortably in the new land while her heart remained firmly planted in the old. She was far too aged to change, but her attitude was a complication Rosebud found difficult to meet.

Because Rosebud had no memories, she was one hundred percent American. And her country was at war.

Rapidly as her family was forced to go, the rally to war work was faster. When she left, the sock she was knitting at school was half finished and already she had become adept in making the corners of a surgical dressing. She had thrown herself into it all with an intensity that shook her. The country was her country, all soldiers were her brother. She felt prepared for any sacrifice.

She found plenty was required of her. The first night in relocation camp was sheer horror to her young mind. Cold, in a pouring rain that had turned the roadways into a sea of mud, the little family searched in vain for a long time for the cubicle they were to call their home. When, finally, they found it, stilled the grandmother's shrill protests and huddled, miserable, frightened, and bewildered on the bare planks of the shelter, Rosebud looking at her parents' faces found her pain too deep for words.

"No one questions your patriotism," they'd been told over and over again as they went through the endless official procedures. "We know you are loyal. This is as difficult for us as for you. But this is *war*. You are Japanese. These rulings must be complied with."

But if no one questioned their loyalty why were they here?

After the first difficult days Rosebud figured out the answer. Even while she stood endless hours in line to get supplies, or carried heavy buckets of water from the distant faucet, or tried to make presentable a room that could never be other than bleak and hopeless, she knew. Since there was a war to fight, everyone would have to fight it, though each in a different way. This was hers. Her father and mother had wanted to be Americans. They'd come to this land and found what they'd hoped for. Rosebud had been born here. It was her own country, and she'd enjoyed its good things. Now the time had come to pay for what they'd had. The thing she was asked to do was difficult. But the worse it was the more it made her a part of it all. If she was brave and worked long enough, one day it would be over. They would be at home again, at home more than ever before because they had earned it.

But it wasn't easy, no matter what she told herself. Her father and mother worked hard, as they had always done, but the joy was out of it now. When Joe came, as he did on his infrequent furloughs, they brightened, for he was like sun at midday, livelier and sturdier than ever, full of wisecracks and funny stories about life in an army camp, loud with G.I. gripes, and yet giving them a sense of security that warmed them long after he went whistling down the muddy road. But Mr. Yusuki labored in the big celery beds now from duty not desire, and Mrs. Yusuki could not find any sense of home in the rough boards of her new dwelling place. Even the school held little joy for Rosebud. Everyone was home-sick no matter how they tried to conceal it. There was a great deal of good sportsmanship, but sometimes Rosebud thought it might have been easier if they'd done what Joe referred to as "grip-ing." Nobody pretended he liked being in the Army, he said frankly. But there was a job that needed doing. It got done.

It was when Joe stopped coming that things grew really bad. He hadn't told his father and mother the furlough was his last but there had been something in his manner that had warned Rose-bud. He had been more than usually gay, teasing his grand-mother for whom he'd brought an extra blanket because she complained so of the cold; telling more than his customary number of stories about his loud-mouthed sergeant and the tricks he had played on him. He'd mentioned casually at the last that they were going on maneuvers. He might not be out again for some time but they mustn't worry. And inside Rosebud's head something said, suddenly and clearly, "Joe's going overseas. He doesn't want to tell them, but he's scheduled to go."

When he left she walked down the road with him a way. And she put it into words, even though she knew he'd rather she hadn't. "You've heard something, Joe. You've got orders?"

"There's talk. Probably nothing to it. But don't fuss if I don't show up for a while."

"Where'll you be?"

He only grinned.

"You'll write?"

"Soon as I can."

He bent and kissed her. "Hey," he said, "don't look that way. Keep 'em smiling. We'll all be back home again before you know it."

He didn't believe a word of it, Rosebud thought as she ran back in the darkness. She had to stop before she went in to wipe away the stinging tears. Joe didn't want them to know—he wanted to be over there before they realized he had gone. She'd help all she could. She would work hard and be bright and cheerful and not even think of the danger—the ship making its slow way across the great gray ocean; the planes that could appear suddenly, circling, circling with their bombs; the submarine that could strike before anyone even suspected it was near.

Fear came up in her throat and choked her. Oh, don't let anything happen to Joe—gay, warm, funny Joe.

It was a long while before they found out where he was. By then her mother had ceased to smile at all. And after that the gray days were all alike. By the time Cassino was a household word and the Battle of the Bulge was over with and VJ and VE Days were things of the past, Rosebud had begun to feel that any life before this one in the great bare barracks was a dream. By the time unconditional surrender was fact and not a demand in the hearts of the democracies Rosebud wasn't a child any longer. Her bright giggle still broke out occasionally, but for the most part she was grave beyond her years. There were weeks when she didn't smile at all, either—those weeks when Joe was reported missing.

They hadn't told that to her grandmother. The old lady sat all day as it was, muttering to herself, shaking her head—a tiny, wrinkled lost soul in a world too frightful for her to contemplate. Joe, her beloved grandson, was fighting against his own people, against his *emperor*. He would be punished for his sin, of that there could be no question. Her head shook when she spoke of it; her old hands shook, too, and her voice rose almost to a scream. Her woe was enough; they would not add to it by telling her Joe had been missing for weeks. But a thoughtless neighbor, stopping in to chat, blurted out a question in front of her, and she got its impact.

"Your son? Have you had any word about him at all? Or have you given him up?"

They had to tell her then. Oblivious as she sometimes seemed to the world, she had an uncanny alertness when they least expected it. They told her all they knew, which was almost nothing. Just that they'd had a telegram—missing in action.

All night she mourned loudly, sobbing and muttering to herself so that no one near could sleep, and there were many complaints. In the morning she did not rise from her bed, or the next morning or any morning. Yet it did not seem to Rosebud she died, but rather dried up from her grief, so that in the end she was like a little brown leaf and not much heavier than one when they put her in the rough coffin and took her away. She had been very old, and Rosebud could not feel unhappy so much at her going as at what had been in her mind as she died. By everything she had been taught her grandmother had been right in all she believed— her ancestors and her emperor had been her gods. Yet in her old age she had had to see the grandson she loved fighting against them. She had died mouthing words that were treachery to the America Rosebud loved. Why should such things be? Rosebud wondered. Why couldn't people agree, or at least be kind about other ways than their own? But no one, not her parents, or her teachers, gave her a satisfactory answer. Different races had different beliefs was all they told her. Joe might have known the answer. But Joe was dead on some faraway battlefield, dead for the things *he* had believed in. She could guess what he would have said though.

"Forget the worrying, kid," he'd have told her. "You're American now, and that's the best."

Yes. Her grandmother, the only link with the past, was gone. Her brother had given his life for America. The Yusukis were Americans now.

And then one night the news came. He wasn't dead. *Joe wasn't dead at all!* He'd been terribly wounded and unidentified for weeks. He had lost a leg, but he was alive. And he was coming back to them eventually. He'd be in hospitals in this country for quite a while, even after he was able to get about, because he had to learn to use his new artificial leg. But that didn't matter. Nothing mattered but the wonderful fact he was alive.

At first they couldn't believe it, the Yusukis. They sat, the three of them, holding hands and not saying much of anything except "Joe isn't dead." "He's alive." "Joe's coming home." "He'll be lame, but maybe not very. Teacher said the new artificial limbs they use are wonderful." He'd be able to walk so well nobody would even know he'd been wounded, except for the medal he'd be wearing on his coat, she told her parents.

So after a while they were at home again—Rosebud and her father and mother and Joe. And after the house was scrubbed from the front door to the back and the rubbish taken away from the yard and the paths raked it all seemed much as it had before. It was strange to Rosebud to be back in her room without Grandmother, especially at night. But there was so much to do and she got so tired that she fell asleep at once, with no time to think. Her mother wasn't too well, she had developed rheumatism in her hands at the relocation camp, and Rosebud had to take over a lot of the housework. And her father was older and more silent. As for Joe— Joe didn't look like the same boy. But he was the same boy—her wonderful big brother. They were a family again. Not people set apart any longer, suspected. They were an American family. They'd proved it.

Now they would have their reward.

Joe got around pretty well. He helped his father some. He couldn't go back to his old job in the factory, of course, because he couldn't stand all those hours every day. But he didn't complain. He didn't wear his medal, though, the way Rosebud had imagined he would. He kept it in his dresser drawer and at first he hadn't even wanted to show it.

"It wasn't anything," he kept saying, but finally he brought it out.

"Tell us just what you did," his mother had asked, but he'd only shrugged his shoulders.

"Just my job," he'd said. "Just what any soldier would do."

At first Rosebud had thought that was a terrible way to feel, as though losing your leg for the sake of your country wasn't anything special. But after a while she saw it was part of what made Joe really an American—this feeling he had that you did your duty as a matter of course. He'd gone into battle that way even; not screaming a wild battle cry, the way his ancestors had, but calmly, determinedly, one of a tiny group who had taken an important enemy position with quiet daring.

The most wonderful thing of all about being home was going back to school. Rosebud had been afraid that perhaps the schoolwork she had done in camp wouldn't qualify her to go on with her old class. But everything seemed to be all right and when school opened she found herself in the same group, and at first she thought it was going to be as though she had never been away.

But almost at once she realized there was a difference. What it was she couldn't be too sure. Maybe just the awkwardness that came of having been away from the group for so long. They had done so many things together she didn't know anything about. When they talked about their war work, she tried to tell of the things they'd done in camp, where she'd rolled bandages by the hour. But nobody seemed much interested. When they talked about their entertainments, she was reminded of the parties they'd tried to have in the big barrackslike buildings nothing could make festive. She wanted to make it all sound very funny. But nobody laughed. After a while she got a little cross at Sally Hayes, who was taller than she had been, but just as blond and just as snippy in her manner. Sally talked all the time about *her* brother, who had been a lieutenant in the Air Force and been shot down in the Pacific. He'd been rescued and got home all right and now he had a job in the bank. But Sally went on telling about him as though he was still swimming around in the cold blue water of the Pacific.

Rosebud had planned to do the very same thing about her brother. She'd even asked Joe if she couldn't take his Silver Star medal to school to show. But he'd given her such a look of scorn that she realized at once she had made an awful mistake.

Because the better Joe got the less he wanted either his heroism or his injury mentioned. He was impatient now about the little services he'd accepted from her at first. He wanted to do everything for himself, as though he hadn't been hurt at all. He wouldn't talk about the war any more, and when any reference was made to his part in it he changed the subject at once. Joe, Rosebud realized more clearly every day, was determined to take the whole experience in stride. His patriotism went so deep now, she thought, he not only wouldn't brag about it, it was second nature.

She let Sally talk.

But as the days passed she realized there was something really wrong. In class she was one of the good students and everything went smoothly under the eyes of her teacher. But at recess and after school it wasn't the way it had been before at all. Myrtle Bates, who had been her best friend, hadn't seemed nearly so glad to see Rosebud as Rosebud had been to see her. She always appeared busy and preoccupied. After school she never had time any more to walk home with Rosebud. She wouldn't come over in the evening so they could study together. Not once was Rosebud invited to Marie Palmer's to swim, as she once had been, and Selma Barker hadn't stopped to pick her up on the way to school. Before she went away Rosebud had been president of her class. This year she wasn't even mentioned for an office.

Gradually understanding came to her that for some reason she was being left outside the group where she had once been an active member. As she walked home alone one afternoon along the dusty road she went over in her mind what had happened that day and knew it all couldn't have been accidental. At noon, when she had looked about for someone to have lunch with, the group to which she had been in the habit of attaching herself seemed to have completely disappeared. It wasn't until the hour was almost over that she found them behind the big rock where they had spread their lunch. But when she'd said, "No wonder I couldn't find you. You're almost hidden. Tomorrow I'll know where to look for you," nobody said anything for a moment, and then Sally had snickered and Marie had murmured, "We won't be here tomorrow."

"Where will you be then?" Rosebud had asked. But nobody had answered her. Everyone had appeared to be very busy picking up her things and getting ready to go back to the schoolroom.

And then, after school, they had all gone down the walk together. But when she had paused a moment, waiting to see who would walk with her, the four girls who went her way had linked arms and gone off in the opposite direction. And when she'd called, "Where are you going? Aren't you walking home?" nobody had turned a head or had answered her.

Myrtle hadn't written her a single note since she got back, she remembered suddenly. And she'd written her a dozen. She'd thought at first maybe it was because Myrtle was afraid of being caught. But now she wondered. Could it be because Myrtle had nothing to say to her? Because she didn't want to have anything to say to her?

Rosebud had been too busy and too happy when she first came home to realize. She had taken the resumption of her life here for granted, and it hadn't crossed her mind that any snubbing could be more than accidental. But all at once she felt alone and very solitary. What could they all have been doing, going off like that without even saying where they were headed for? Somehow they'd looked very secret and queer.

Suddenly Rosebud felt strange and sick inside. She realized that not one of her close friendships had been resumed since she'd returned, though she felt her heart running over with friendliness. What was wrong? Had she said something, done something? It shouldn't be like this with girls she cared about. Why, they'd been together since first grade—they'd founded a club. O.C.—Our Club. And pledged eternal friendship with chubby hands.

What had happened to Our Club? she wondered suddenly. She hadn't heard it mentioned since she got back. It had been fun, though it was an awfully kid sort of an affair. But the idea had been good. And if they'd outgrown that, they ought to have another one to take its place.

That was a good idea, she thought. Maybe she hadn't made it clear how glad she was to be back, or how much she'd missed everybody. She had had a lot on her mind, helping out at home and with all her worries about Joe. She'd make it so clear now everybody would understand, she decided. Tomorrow she'd speak about the club and suggest they start another one, with the same members they'd had before, the same kind of a club, too, a friendship club.

She lay awake late that night planning it. Before she went to bed she'd hunted around in the little box in which she kept her treasures and found the O.C. pin, a little tarnished now, and pinned it on her nightgown. It made her feel a lot better, as if she really belonged. And, after all, she did. The pin proved it.

She'd suggest the new club at recess tomorrow, she decided. Wherever they all got together to eat lunch she'd join them. She'd say, "What ever happened to our old O.C. and why don't we have another—a friendship club?" They could have meetings once a week, and she'd see if her mother wouldn't let her have the very first one. Maybe even with cookies and lemonade for refreshments.

She had it so carefully planned that she couldn't understand why, when the recess bell rang, she suddenly felt scared, as though something really awful was about to happen, something as awful as December the seventh. There wasn't a thing to be afraid of, except that she wanted the club so badly. But she made herself be calm and slow, so slow that when she came out of the door with her lunch box in her hand the girls all had disappeared again.

But she knew they couldn't be very far away. She wandered about, looking for them. But she'd visited every possible place she could think of before she found them huddled together in the school basement. They giggled when they saw her and then looked defiant, but she pretended not to notice.

"Oh, here you are," she said. "What a funny place to eat lunch."

"We're all through," Myrtle said loudly. "We were just leaving."

"Well, I don't need to eat now anyhow," Rosebud said. "I just wanted to find you to ask whatever became of Our Club."

Sally shrugged her small shoulders.

"That old thing," she said. "We were just little kids. It all broke up."

"I know we were little then. But it was a good idea." Rosebud's voice shook with her eagerness. "We ought to have another one. Can't we start one now—all of us here—a friendship club?"

Nobody said anything. Rosebud stared at them, but their eyes went every way but toward her. It seemed suddenly very still, and the shouts of the boys on the playground rang in her ears.

"I want to start it," she said. "I want to start it right away. I'll have the first meeting at my house tomorrow. How many of you can come?"

She looked at Myrtle first.

"I can't," said Myrtle. "I've got a music lesson."

"My mother's going to take me shopping," Marie said.

"The next day then?" Rosebud asked in her soft little voice. "That would be just as good."

There was another period of stillness. Rosebud saw them looking at one another now and their looks said something, but it was a thing she did not understand. And then suddenly Sally's shrill voice came out with "Oh, what's the use? If she's too thick to get it, let's tell her."

There *was* something wrong then—something she'd said or done. Something that had to be fixed. Well, she was glad she could get it into the open—

"Yes. Please tell me. Is there something bad?"

Sally laughed. Marie laughed, too.

"Something bad!" Sally said. "She wants to belong to a club with us—she says is there anything wrong!"

"I want to start a club," Rosebud began.

"Well, you don't need to start one for this crowd. We've *got* a club. We've had one for a long time. And everybody that was in O.C. is in it but you."

Rosebud's eyes went from one face to another.

"Then—then—you don't want me—"

"No," Sally said. "We don't want you—not in our club. It's bad enough your going to our school."

"But what did I do?"

"You started a war—that's what you did."

"My father says we were silly ever to have trusted you people," Marie was saying now. "I don't suppose it's actually your fault, Rosebud. But it was a wicked, treacherous thing—"

Your people. Her father and mother—leaving everything behind —working and waiting so patiently in the dismal relocation camp. Her brother, half his body torn away, face downward in the mud, but saying, "You take it in stride, kid."

"I don't see why our government doesn't send you all back to your own country where you belong," Sally was saying scornfully.

But this was her own country. She said it out loud.

"This *is* my country."

"It isn't. It can't be. *You're a Jap.*"

Rosebud started to explain, to protest. But then she looked at the angry faces in front of her and saw it wasn't any use. What they wanted wasn't the truth. What they felt hadn't anything to do with facts. To people like them she knew a Japanese would be a Jap forever and forever.

She turned and walked away. For just a moment she looked her name, a frail and almost broken flower. But by the time she reached the schoolhouse her face was blank, her black eyes as expressionless as shoe buttons. Before she opened the door she turned and threw something from her. She threw hard and with great accuracy. Without even a rustle the O.C. pin disappeared into a pile of rubbish waiting to be hauled away from the school-yard driveway.

THE MAN FROM

FAR AWAY

JACK SCHAEFER

In America, people said, there was work for anyone willing to work. A man with a trade could make his way there and freedom would be a real thing freshening the air he breathed.

Four years Hugo Kertchak saved for the passage money. He had the few coins that remained from his mother's burial fund and the small amount that had been left to him by his father. He had the smaller amount that had come to him with his wife. He had the gold piece given to him by his uncle at the birth of the first child because it was a son and would bear the uncle's name. He had these and he saved in many ways. He saved, though he had work only about one week in three. He put away his pipe, out of sight and out of mind. He drank only one mug of beer, and that only on Sunday, and after a time none at all. He fed himself and his family on bread and potatoes and occasional green vegetables. The money that would have bought meat joined the rest in the old purse that had been his father's.

After four years and two months he had enough. He sold the few pieces of furniture in the rented cottage that were his. He led the way for his family. Under his left arm he carried the long narrow toolbox that had been his father's and his grandfather's. His right hand held the small hand of his seven-year-old son. Behind him came his wife. On her left shoulder she carried the bundle of extra clothing wrapped in a blanket with a strap around it. Her right hand held the small hand of their five-year-old daughter. They walked the nine miles to the station, where they waited for the train that took them west across Europe to the port and to the ship that took them west across the Atlantic.

Hugo Kertchak walked the streets of New York. He left his wife and children in the boardinghouse run by a man from the old country, and walked the streets of the strange city. He knew fifty-three words of English, useful words learned the last days of the crossing from another steerage passenger on the ship. He could not learn them as fast as his wife, for she was quick at such things, but he was learning more each day, learning them slowly and thoroughly, so that he would never lose them and so that he could pronounce them clearly. He walked the streets and times were hard. There was no work.

There was plenty of work in the new lands, people said, in the new settlements westward with the afternoon sun. A country was growing and a man could grow with it, even a man in his middle thirties.

Hugo Kertchak talked to the boardinghouse man. He talked to a patient man at the railroad station, using the words he had learned and had difficulty arranging in right order. He counted what was left of the money. It was enough.

Hugo Kertchak and his wife and two children rode upright on stiff railroad-coach cushions west to Chicago. All one day and one night they rode. They walked across the sprawling city to the other station. They carried the toolbox and the bundle and they walked, asking directions. They rode upright on other slat-backed seats west across Iowa into Nebraska. They leaned against each other and slept in snatches as the train jolted through the darkness of night. The sun rose and they sat up straighter and divided and ate the last loaf of the bread and the last piece of the cheese bought in Chicago. They looked out the train windows and saw the wide miles reach and run past them. It was a new and a strange and a big country. But in the side pocket of Hugo Kertchak's jacket was a letter from the boardinghouse man addressed to a friend out in this new and strange and big country.

The train stopped at the town. Hugo Kertchak and wife and two children stepped down into the dust of the road that was the town's one street, flanked on one side by the single line of track, on the other by a brief row of false-fronted frame buildings. The train moved on and the sun beat down and the wind blew and they were alone in the road dust. The few sparse buildings of the town seemed lost in a circling immensity. Distance stretched outward and on and beyond grasp of the eyes in every direction. They walked through the swirling dust across the road and up the two steps to the platform along the front of the building whose sign said STORE & POST OFFICE. Hugo Kertchak set the toolbox down and went into the building.

At the rear of the store two men sat hunched on stools playing checkers on the squared-off top of a barrel. They raised their heads and looked at him. Behind a counter at the right another man was leaning back in an old chair with his feet up on the counter, reading a newspaper. This one lowered the paper and looked over it at him like the others. Hugo Kertchak took the letter from his pocket. He went to the counter and held the letter out so that the name on it could be seen.

"You know?" he said.

The man behind the counter raised his feet and set them carefully down on the floor. He folded the newspaper and laid it carefully on the counter. He leaned forward and took the letter and read the name. He handed the letter back.

"Sure I know," he said. "Or aiming it a mite better, I'd offer I used to know. That there particular person ain't inhabiting these parts any more."

Hugo Kertchak frowned in the effort to understand. "You say what?"

The man behind the counter smacked a hand down upon it. "I say hightailed out of the country. Skedaddled. He's gone."

Hugo Kertchak understood the final words. "You say where?"

The man behind the counter shouted a question at the men who were playing checkers.

"Back East somewheres," one of them said. "Didn't name a place."

The man behind the counter shrugged his shoulders. "Reckon that's that. Anything else, stranger?"

Hugo Kertchak shook his head. He could think of nothing else, only the fact that confronted him. Slowly he turned and went out again to the front platform. He tore the letter into many small pieces and let these fall fluttering around his feet. Slowly he sat down on the platform edge with his feet on the lower step, and his head sank forward. In the old leather purse in his pocket there was thirty-seven cents of the strange American money. And a woman and two children were staring at him in silence.

The tireless wind of the wide country blew upon him, hot and dry. The wind brought with it a sound, the sound of a hammer driving a nail.

Hugo Kertchak's head rose. He stood, erect on the step. He reached and took the toolbox. "Anna," he said to his wife, "here you wait."

Hugo Kertchak walked along the road through the swirling dust. The sound led him to the last building westward. Around the far side out of sight before, a man was constructing a small shed. The framework was already up, the rafters in place. There was a pile of lumber on the ground with a small keg of nails beside it. The man had cut several side lengths of board and was nailing them to the corner posts. He stopped and turned to look at Hugo Kertchak. He seemed glad of an excuse to stop.

"Am carpenter," Hugo Kertchak said. That was wrong. He made the correction. "I am carpenter."

"Be hanged if I am," the man said. "This beswoggled hammer has a mind of its own. Likes my thumb better'n the nails."

Hugo Kertchak was not certain what all the words meant. But here was work, the work he knew. "I show," he said. He laid down the toolbox and opened it. He took out the hammer with the new handle that he had whittled and sanded long hours on the journey until the balance was exactly right for his broad, square hand. He dropped some nails from the keg into his jacket pocket. He lifted the next side board and set it in position. He swung the hammer in smooth, steady strokes. It was good to be using a good tool again. But the framework was not solid. The whole skeletal structure quivered under the strokes.

Hugo Kertchak forgot the man watching him. He was intent upon the problem before him. He walked around the framework, examining it from each side. The joints were not well fitted. They did not lap each other so that they would share and subdue the strains. The braces were in the wrong places.

Hugo Kertchak took his wooden rule from the toolbox and unsnapped it to full length. He made his measurements. He selected several boards and marked them off, using a nail to scratch the lines. The saw was in his hands—the saw that had been his father's and that he had filed and refiled on the long journey until its teeth yearned for good wood to cut. It sliced through this wood swiftly and sweetly. Here were his braces. He nailed these into place. He put a shoulder against a corner post and heaved. The framework stood solid. It was not so firm as it would have been if it had been built right from the beginning, but it was much better. He reached for the next board and stopped. The man was making a noise.

"Hey!" the man was saying again and again, each time louder, trying to catch his attention. "Hey, carpenter. What'd you stick me to polish off this thing?"

"Stick?" Hugo Kertchak said. "Polish off?"

"How much to finish it?" the man said. "Do the job up right?"

Hugo Kertchak looked at the framework again. The shed would have no windows. There would be only a door to make. This work was nothing, just nailing boards in place. He tried to estimate a price—one that would not be too low, because this was America, and yet would not be so high that the man would be unwilling to bargain.

"Four dollar," he said.

"Well, now," the man said, rubbing a hand up and down along one side of his chin. "That's a reasonable fair price, I reckon. But cash is mighty scarce in these parts around about now. Tell you what. I'll make it two dollars cash and toss in whatever stuff's left—boards and nails and the like."

Hugo Kertchak's mind worked slowly over the words. "I can do," he said.

"Done," the man said. "Reckon all else you'll need is some hinges and a latch for the door. I'll go rustle some."

The man swung away and Hugo Kertchak stared after him in amazement. There was no arguing back and forth. There was no talk about how much wood he should use and how many nails. There was no talk about how good the work must be for the price or how long he must wait for the money. A man said "done" and it was settled. Hugo Kertchak shed his jacket and began sawing board lengths.

The sun climbed high overhead and the shed sides climbed with it. The man came back with a pair of big hinges and a latch and screws to go with them. He set these down by the lumber.

"Lunchtime," he said. "Better go wrassle yourself some food." He disappeared into the nearby building.

Lunchtime. Suddenly Hugo Kertchak remembered his wife and two children alone on the store platform. Thirty-seven cents would buy bread, if bread could be found in this strange place. He started toward the road. He had not gone ten steps when around the corner of the last building came his wife. She walked proudly with her head high. In one hand she carried two fat sandwiches made of thick slices of bread with meat between them, and in the other hand she carried a tin pitcher of cool water.

"The storeman gives," she said in English, and then she began talking rapidly in their native tongue, but she had no chance to say much because the storeman himself came around the cor-

ner close behind her, and he was talking so loudly that he almost
shouted.

He talked straight at Hugo Kertchak. He was very angry. What
kind of a horned toad was Hugo Kertchak anyway? Why hadn't he
spoken up like a man with a chunk of backbone, and said he had
a family with him and was flat busted and didn't have a place to
stay? What brand of mangy miscreants did he think people in that
state were that they couldn't provide food and shelter for a family
that needed same till they could provide their own? He, the storeman, was going to tell this Hugo what he was going to do, and
he'd better do it. This ring-tailed baboon of a Hugo Crazy-name
was going to set himself and his family down in the extra room of
the living quarters back of the store, and he was going to pay a
stiff price.

How? He was supposed to be a carpenter, wasn't he? So his wife
said, anyway. Well, he was going to prove that. He was going to
slap some decent shelves in the store to take the place of the rickety ones there, and they'd better be good shelves. And maybe he
wasn't such a hollow-head as he looked, because he seemed to
have rustled himself a hammer-and-saw job already, but the shelf
proposition still stood and was he man enough to say would he
do it?

Hugo Kertchak understood only part of the words. But he understood that the storeman's anger was a good anger and that there
was more work for him to do—carpenter's work. He was a good
carpenter, almost as good a carpenter as his father had been.

He looked straight at the storeman. "Done," he said.

The storeman was not angry any more. He chuckled. "Talking
American already," he said. "When you're through here, come on
down to my place."

Hugo Kertchak nailed the last roof board in position. He was
worried about the roof. It should have some other covering to
make it waterproof. He would talk to the man about that. He slid
to the ground and cut and shaped the last side boards to fit up
snugly under the eaves. He ran neat finishing strips down the corners. There was still a nice pile of wood left, and the keg of
nails was only half empty. It was not really fair. All this good wood
and all these nails and two dollars, too, for a little sawing and

hammering, finished, with the afternoon only half gone. There was still a door to make. It should be a good door.

He selected the wood carefully. The door grew under his hands. He cut and mortised the pieces for the outer rim. He planed and fitted the pieces to be set in these and give a paneled effect. The wind of the wide country set the shavings dancing. This was the kind of work that showed what a good carpenter could do. He was so intent on it that he did not hear the hoofs approaching, the sound softened in the dust. He was startled when he looked up and saw a man, a new man, watching him. It was a horseman, and he had a pistol in a leather holder on his hip. Hugo Kertchak saw the horse and the pistol and was afraid. It was an instinctive fear, out of old memories deep in his mind. Then he saw the face of the horseman and he was no longer afraid. It was a young face, serious and sunburned, with many small wrinkles around the eyes from much squinting into the endless wind, and the expression in the eyes and on the face was wide and open like the country around.

"Man, oh, man," the horseman said. He pushed his hat up from his forehead and wiped at the dust there. "You sure can wrangle those tools." He turned his horse and went out of sight around the building.

Hugo Kertchak fastened the hinges to the door. He set the door in the doorway and slipped thin shavings under it for clearance and fastened the hinges to the doorframe. He pulled out the shavings and tried the door. It hung true and swung easily out and back to fit snug and flat in line with the frame. He began work on the latch. This time he heard the hoofs. The horseman appeared around the building. A tied bundle of letters and newspapers hung from his saddle horn. He stopped his horse and leaned forward in the saddle, inspecting the shed.

"Man, oh, man," he said. "That's what I call a door. Kind of like a fancy beaver on a roadside bum, but there ain't no mistaking it's a door." He clucked to the horse and moved on, straight on out into the wide country riding easily and steadily into the far distance.

Hugo Kertchak stood on the small rear platform or porch of the store building and saw the last tinges of almost unbelievable color fading out of the western horizon and the clear clean darkness claiming the land. There were two silver dollars with the thirty-seven cents in the old leather purse in his pocket. Behind him in the lamplit kitchen, his wife and the storeman's wife were clearing dishes from the table. The two voices made a gentle humming. It was remarkable how women did not need to know many of each other's words to talk so much together. But there had been much talk, too, with the storeman himself, who was still sitting by the table reading his newspaper as if he had to cover every word in it. This was only a small town, a very small town, the storeman said, but it would not always be small. Now there were only wide stretches of land around where men raised cattle for meat and leather, and let them wander without fences to hold them. But soon the Government would open the land for farmers and their families. They would come. Whole trainloads of them would be coming. They would settle all around and the town would grow and business would be good.

Hugo Kertchak could hardly believe that what was happening was true. In one day he had new money and some materials for his trade and a friend who could be angry at him for his own good. The people in this country were strange, but theirs was not an alien strangeness. It was only a difference that a man could learn to understand.

His wife was on the porch beside him. "Hugo, think of it. In the cold time, in the winter, they have a school. Free for all people's children." She put a hand on his arm. "We stay here?"

Hugo Kertchak put an arm around his wife's shoulders. "We stay."

Hugo Kertchak was the town carpenter. He helped the town get ready for the coming land boom. He built new shelves in the store and a long new counter and racks for farm tools. He built and polished to a shining finish a bar in the biggest of the buildings, that was a saloon and would be a dance hall. He patched the blacksmith-shop roof and extended it out to form a lean-to addition where wagons could be kept, waiting repairs. He built stalls in the broad shedlike structure that would be a livery stable. These were honest jobs well done, and he could pay the storeman board money and even save a little for the house he would build for himself with the materials he was assembling. But they did not satisfy him. They seemed so small in the bigness of the land.

He sat on the front steps with the storeman and watched the western color fading out of the sky. A man on a horse came along the road, hurrying. It was the young horseman. He stopped and looked down.

"Howdy, Cal," the storeman said. "Climb off that cayuse and sit a spell. Could be there's a bottle of beer hanging to cool in the well out back."

"Man, oh, man," the horseman said. "You would think of that when I ain't got the time." He looked straight at Hugo Kertchak. "Reckon me and the other hands ain't so hot with our hammers. Barn we built's in bad shape. Haymow's collapsed with hardly no hay in it at all. And everybody's pulling out early morning for fall roundup. So I tell the boss how you wrangle those tools. So he sends me to put a rope on you for repairs."

Hugo Kertchak picked out the important words here and there as he had learned to do with these Americans. "Done," he said. "Where is barn?"

It was a big barn, casting a long shadow in the morning sun. Hugo Kertchak drove toward it, perched on the seat of the storeman's light wagon. All the last miles he could see the barn bumping up out of the wide flat land, and he did not like what he saw. It was too high for its width. It leaned a little, as if the bottom timbers on one side had not been set right on a firm foundation. There were no neat slatted windows high up under the pointed eaves to give proper ventilation. The doors sagged and could not be closed.

He stood inside the doors and saw the remains of the haymow and listened to the boss, the ranchman, speak many words about propping it up again and perhaps strengthening it some. He did not listen to catch the important words. He was looking up at the fine big timbers that should have been cut to lap each other and fastened with stout wooden pegs, and instead were simply butted against each other and tortured with long spikes driven in at angles that had already started splitting in the good wood. He did not even wait for the ranchman to stop talking.

"No!" he said in a loud voice. "Sorry is it to me I said 'done.'

This work no." He sought for the words that would say what he meant, and found them, and as always in excitement he forgot the pronouns. "Is America," he said. "Has freedom."

The ranchman's eyes narrowed. "What has freedom got to do with my barn?"

"Freedom," Hugo Kertchak said. "Freedom for work right." He waved his arms at the walls. "You see? Bad work. Not strong. Cold weather come. Snow. On roof. All the time wind blow. One year. Two year. Not no more. Everything down."

The ranchman's eyes were wide open again. "That bad, eh? I know it was slapped together in an awful hurry. Couldn't you fix up some?"

"Fix bad work," Hugo Kertchak said, "makes better. But still bad."

The ranchman remembered that the range would be shrinking as homesteaders came in, and he would have to depend more and more on winter feeding. He couldn't take chances on a rickety barn.

"Maybe," he said, "maybe you could build me a good barn?" He saw Hugo Kertchak's eyes begin to shine. "Whoa, now," he said. "Take it slow. I don't mean the best barn in the country. Just a good, solid, dependable barn. Knocking this one apart and using as much of it as you can for the new one."

Hugo Kertchak no longer said, "I am carpenter." He said, "I am builder." The land boom arrived and the trainloads and wagon-loads of settlers, and they fanned out over the wide land, and with them went word that when it came to building, Hugo Kertchak could do a job right. Most of the homesteaders threw up their own shacks. Many of them simply squatted on their claims in tents and flimsy tar-papered huts, waiting to prove title and sell out for a quick profit. Many others were too shiftless even to do that, and drifted away. But here and there were a few, and those gradually increased, who had capital or the competence to acquire it and could meet the conditions of the new land. They looked forward and they built for the future, and Hugo Kertchak built for them. They paid what and when they could, and sometimes he waited months and a year or longer for the last of the money, but that did not matter, because there was work for every working day and he was building and he had enough.

The town grew and spread out on both sides of the railroad track, and other builders came, men who underbid each other on jobs and hired many men and had the work done rapidly. They built a town hall and a hotel and a jail and a station and some store blocks and some fine-looking houses and other things, and how they built them was their own business. Always there was someone out across the wide land who needed a shed or a barn or a house built as Hugo Kertchak could build it.

Hugo Kertchak's son was a good carpenter. He worked on Saturdays and during vacations with his father, and was paid what a helper would have been paid. But when he graduated from high school, he did not work as a carpenter any more. He worked at many jobs in the town, only a week or two at each. He was restless and irritable in the home. He talked with his father. He wanted to go to the state university and study to be an architect.

"That is right," Hugo Kertchak said. "In America the son should do more and better than the father. Work with me until the school begins again and save the money."

His son did, and when the school began again, what he had with what Hugo had in the town bank was enough.

Hugo Kertchak's daughter was a good cook, like her mother. She was quick with words, too, like her mother and did well in her studies. She won a scholarship to go to the state normal school, but in the first year at the school she met a mining engineer who was leaving soon to work for a mining company in Western Montana. She wanted to marry him and go with him.

Hugo Kertchak comforted his wife. "Is she different than you?" he said. "Is it not she should go where her man goes?" There was only a little money in the bank now, but there was enough for a wedding.

Times were slack. The town was very quiet. The opening of new lands had long since moved farther westward. The population of the town dwindled and dropped to a stable level. There was no more building.

Hugo Kertchak became a maker of barrels. He made them of all sizes for many purposes, from small kegs to big hogsheads. He made them firm and tight. He shaped the staves and fitted them together as he had shaped and fitted the timbers of his barns and houses. He was using his tools on good wood with the skill he had brought with him to this new land. He was building good barrels. But he did not call himself Hugo Kertchak, builder, any more.

Hugo Kertchak's son was home for the summer vacation. After one more school year he would have the parchment that would say he was an architect. Now, during the summer, he worked with his father making barrels. He talked as a young American talked, fast and with much enthusiasm, and his talk was big with his plans for his profession. Hugo Kertchak listened and thought of the time when men who worked with steel and stone and concrete as he worked with wood would build the fine structures his son would design for them. And Hugo Kertchak's wife sat on the small porch in the summer sun and watched the father and the son making barrels together.

Hugo Kertchak's son returned to the university, and the winter was long and hard, and when the spring arrived, Hugo Kertchak's son and other young men at the university were given their degrees early, so that they could enlist and fight in the war with Spain. There would be time enough for him to be an architect when the war was finished. But there was no time. The telegram came, telling that he died in Cuba of the yellow fever.

Hugo Kertchak tried to comfort his wife and she tried to comfort him. He at least had his barrels to make, and she had nothing. Even her daughter was far away in Montana. She sat on the small back porch and watched him. She sat there too often and too late, with no shawl over her shoulders and no scarf around her head. It was pneumonia with complications, the doctor said. Four days after she took to her bed, she died quietly in the night.

Hugo Kertchak stood by the bed a long time in the early-morning light. He cranked the handle on the telephone in the hall and called the undertaker and made the arrangements. He went out to the back yard to his tools, old and worn, but still serviceable like himself. Only with them in his hands did he feel alive now.

Two days after the funeral the letter came from his daughter telling why she herself had not come. Her husband had been hurt in the mine. His left leg was crushed and he would not walk again. The company was paying for the doctor and the hospital, but even so, there was no extra money. Her husband would not be able to do mine work any more, but in time perhaps, with his training, he could do office work of some kind. Meantime they thought of establishing a small store which she could run. The local bank might lend her the money she would need.

Hugo Kertchak sold his house. He kept the workshop and a small bit of land with it bordering on the rear alley, and moved a bed and a table and some chairs and a bureau into the shop. It had a coal stove that gave good heat and on which he could do his small cooking. There was a mortgage on the house, and the price he received was not high, but when the mortgage was paid there was enough. He sent the money to his daughter. He did not need it. He had a workshop and his tools.

Hugo Kertchak made barrels, but they did not sell as they used to sell. They stood in rows and on top of each other along the side of the workshop, and he had no orders for them. Tin and galvanized-iron containers were being used more and more. These were cheaper and more convenient. Hugo Kertchak became a maker of coffins.

The coffins Hugo Kertchak made were good coffins. Always, as he worked on them, he remembered the one he had made for his wife, and worried about the one someone else had made for his son far off in Cuba. He did not make many, most of them only on order from the town undertaker, because good wood was becoming expensive and because working was harder now. He moved more slowly and there was a stiffness at times in his muscles. But the skill was unchanged.

People he had known in the first years died and were buried in Hugo Kertchak's coffins. New people and new generations walked the streets. Electric lights brightened many houses. Horseless carriages began to cough along the roads, and their owners talked about the paving of streets. The new ways of the new century changed old habits. The undertaker came to see Hugo Kertchak. He could use no more of the coffins. People wanted the shiny decorated models that came from the manufacturing places in the cities. And there was a nice profit in them.

Hugo Kertchak puttered around town with any little jobs he could find. Sometimes he built bookcases or pantry shelves or flower trellises when he found people who wanted these. Most of the jobs were tending people's yards, planting bulbs in the spring, cutting grass in the summer, raking leaves in the fall. His daughter wrote to him regularly, once a month. She sent him snapshots of the two grandchildren he had never seen. She wanted him to come and live with her. He could help in the store. There was not much money, but it would be enough. But he could not do that. The thought of living in the mountains frightened him. He could not leave the town and the wide flat country that had welcomed him and the quiet grave in its half of the small plot in the town cemetery.

Regularly he wrote back, laboring hours over his broad, rounded script, careful of his spelling and to put in all the pronouns. He was well. There was plenty of work. Someday soon he would come on a visit, in the fall perhaps, when the rush of summer work was done, or in the spring, when the winter cold was past. And sometimes he managed to put several dollar bills in the envelope for the grandchildren. He did not need much for himself.

Days when there was no work and the weather was pleasant he liked to sit in the sun on one of the benches by the town hall and watch the two morning trains go past on the track across the way—the express that roared through without stopping, and the local that puffed to a stop by the station for a flurry of activity there. Always people were arriving and people were leaving and new faces were around and things were changing, and that was America. He could remember when a train could stop and only a single small family step down from it into a dusty little town that seemed deserted, and yet they would find friendship springing up around them as if from the wide land itself. He sat on the bench and remembered, and people smiled at him as they passed, and sometimes stopped to talk to him because he was a part of the town and of the past that had made the town, and he did not know it, but he was America too.

A woman from one of the county boards came to see Hugo Kertchak in his shop. She talked to him in a self-consciously kind voice. She had a card in her hand that told her facts about him, and she did not know these were not the important facts. He was an old man, living alone, with no regular work. The card told her that.

It would be much better for him if he would turn over to the county any small property he still had and let the county take care of him. The county had a nice old-folks home where he would have companionship and would not have to worry about anything.

The woman saw the tightening of the old muscles of Hugo Kertchak's face, and she hurried to say more. That would not be charity. Oh, good heavens, no. He had been one of the early settlers and he had helped the community grow. The county owed it to him to take care of him.

"Wrong," Hugo Kertchak said. "All wrong. This America owes me no thing at all. It gave what a man needs. A home without fear. Good friends. Freedom to work right. If there is owing, it is for me. To take care of myself." He was indignant, and this made his voice sharp, and the woman flushed and turned to go. Hugo Kertchak was a little ashamed. "I have thanks that you think of me," he said. "It is good that you help people. But for me there is no need."

Hugo Kertchak sat on the bench by the town hall and the tireless wind of the plains country ruffled the dwindling gray hair on his bare head. People nodded at him as they passed, but few people talked to him any more. That was his fault. He talked too much. He wanted to talk about the weather or politics or prospects for the year's crops or anything else another person wanted to talk about. But inevitably his voice rose, shriller and more querulous, and he would be doing most of the talking, telling about the old days when a man said "done" and a thing was settled, and a young horseman remembered a man he saw doing good work and people appreciated work that was done right, not slipshod.

Hugo Kertchak remembered. His old hands remembered the feel of his good tools. He began going home by different and roundabout routes, walking along the roads and alleys and looking for stray pieces of wood. He gathered what he could find—pieces of old shingles, broken boards, crates thrown away. He carried them to his workshop. Two days a week he did gardening, and that paid for his food. The rest of the time he stayed in the shop and worked. When the wife of the man who had bought the house went out to hang her wash, she heard the sounds of old tools in use, the steady striking of a hammer, the soft swish of a plane, the rhythmic stroke of a saw.

The day came when she hung out her wash and heard no sounds in the shop. When she took down the dry clothes in late afternoon, there was no sign of activity. In the evening, when she peered into the darkness, there was no lamplight showing through the shop window. Her husband said, "So what? The old windbag can take care of himself. He's been doing it for years, hasn't he?" But in the morning, after a worrying night, she insisted and her husband went out to investigate. He came in again quickly and went to the telephone and called the coroner's office.

The coroner and a deputy sheriff found the body of Hugo Kertchak on the floor where he had toppled from a chair in the last struggle for breath as his heart failed. The pen he had been using was still tight in his hand. They picked the body up and laid it on the old bed.

The deputy sheriff was looking around the shop. "What d'you know," he said. "Look at these things." On a shelf above the workbench was a row of little buildings, small birdhouses, each delicately made, yet sturdy, with every piece of the old wood shaped and fitted and fastened with skillful care. "I'll be darned," he said. "You never know what these old bums'll do next, fussing around with things like that when anyone's a mind for one can get it for a quarter or maybe fifty cents at a hardware store."

"Shut up," the coroner said. He was holding the unfinished letter that had been lying on the old table. He was reading the last words: "The town people will sell my shop and the land that is left and send the money to you. They are good people. It is for the boy. For help with a school. To study it may be for an architect—"

The coroner folded the paper and put it in his pocket. He moved around the foot of the bed and pulled an old blanket from what lay between the bed and the wall. It was a coffin, firm and strongly built, the once-rough planks cut and fitted and planed smooth and polished to a good finish. On the top lay an old cigar box. In the box were a title form for a small lot in the town cemetery and an old leather purse. In the purse were some crumpled dollar bills and a handful of coins.

"No," the coroner said. "Not this one. He paid his score to the end."

The man filling in the grave finished the job and leaned a moment on the shovel while he took a scrap of paper from his pocket and looked at the name on it.

"Kertchak," he muttered to himself. "Seems like I remember that. Made barrels when I was a kid." He lifted the shovel and went away.

An automobile stopped by the cemetery and two men stepped from it. One was the editor of the local newspaper. The other was tall and erect, with the heaviness of late middle-age beginning to show in a once-lean body. His face, with many wrinkles about the eyes, was wide and open like the country around. Under his arm he carried a cross made of two pieces of wood. "Man, oh, man," he said, "I'd never have known if it wasn't for that article in your paper. Started me remembering things." He went to the mound of dirt and stuck the wooden cross into the ground at the upper end. "Have that matched in stone," he said, "and send the bill to me. I want to pay it." He stood silent a moment, staring at the wooden cross. The upright was a piece of new two-by-four. The crossbar was a board found in the old shop that had once been nailed over the doorway of the house in front of the shop. Carved into it in square solid letters were the words: HUGO KERTCHAK, BUILDER.

The automobile moved away and silence settled over the cemetery. The endless wind blew and whipped some of the dried earth of the mound in tiny dust whirls around the base of the cross and blew in soft whispers on out over the wide land where they stood, strong against weather and time, the sheds and the barns and the houses Hugo Kertchak had built.

YES, YOUR HONESTY

GEORGE AND HELEN PAPASHVILY

Six months in America and already I was a jailbird. Happened this way.

The weeks seemed extra long that first half year I was in New York. No holidays, no feast days, no celebrations to break up the time and then when Saturday came around I had only twelve dollars, at most fourteen dollars in my pay envelope.

The man I met in Central Park on my first day in America gave me a job in his garage like he promised. But after I was there about two months his wife's mother got sick and they closed up and moved to the country. With my poor language, wasn't easy to find another place.

I tried silk mill and after that factory where they made statues—ugly ones—from plaster. I stayed there until head artist gave me camel to cast, only looked like a cow, this camel. I was ashamed to make such a monstrosity animal so I changed shape little bit here and there to give some camel personality to it.

But when artist saw he got mad and told me how many schools he was in—London, Paris, Dresden—(just my point, no camels living in any of those places, certainly) and I'm fired again.

Then I went for house painter but somehow the boss and me didn't suit each other. Finally I met a Georgian, there were only two, three of us in New York this time, who worked in a cleaning factory and he took me for his assistant. It was awful place. I dipped the clothes to take away spots. The gas we used came up in my head and through my throat and out my ears. My every piece of meat whole week long was spiced with that gas.

But no matter how the week went the Sundays were good because then we made all day the holiday and took ourselves in Van Cortlandt Park where there was country and trees and flowers. We could make fires and roast cubed lamb *shashliks* and walk on the grass and forget the factory. For one day anyway we could enjoy to live like human beings.

From six o'clock on, every Sunday morning, subway was packed full. Russians, Syrians, Greeks, Armenians, all kinds of peoples, carrying their grampas and babys and gallon jugs and folding chairs and charcoal sacks and hammocks and samovars and lunch baskets and rugs. Everyone hurrying to their regular place in the park so they could start tea and lay out the lunch, to make the day last a long, long time.

Well, this particular Sunday when all my trouble began was in the late spring. Bright blue day with a high sky and white lamb clouds. The kind of day that's for adventures.

I had my first American-bought suit on and a purple striped tie with a handkerchief to match and a real Yankee Doodle hat from straw. I felt happy and full of prance.

Five or six other fellows and me were visiting around the park. We went from family to family we knew and drank a glass of wine here, tried a piece of cake there, met an uncle just came from Buffalo, saw a new baby first time out and so on.

While we were making shortcut down a quiet path to get on other side of the park we came to a beautiful tree foaming over with white blossoms, how they call in English, dogswood.

"Flowers. Flowers," one Russian fellow, name of Cyrille, said. "I gonna pick. Take bouquet to my lady friend." I don't know who he was, this fellow, he joined us some place we stopped.

"Pick! Pick!" Everybody got the idea. "Pick flowers, take a bouquet to all the lady friends."

"Why spoil a tree?" I said. "Use your brains better. If you want to make friends with a nice young lady, ask her to take a walk. Tell her you gonna show her a bouquet bigger than a house, a bouquet growing right out of the ground. Something interesting. That way you get a chance to be acquainted while you're walking. Maybe you know so good on the way back you can invite for ice cream."

No, no, won't listen. They have to break the tree down. Tear his arms and legs off like wolves. Jumping. Jumping. Who's gonna get the biggest branch? Makes me sick.

"Personally," I said, "I would be ashamed to give a lady flowers that I got for nothing. That I stole. I prefer better to buy. Shows more respect. Or else don't give."

All of a sudden that fellow, Cyrille, who had now the biggest bunch climbed down from the top branches and said to me, "I have to tie my shoelace. Hold my bouquet for a minute, I'll be back." So I held. In that minute a policeman was there.

"Awright. Awright," he said. "Defacing public property. Awright." He asked us our names and started writing them down on a piece of paper.

"What he does?" I asked Sergei.

"Gives us a summons."

"Summons?"

"We have to go in court."

"We're arrested?"

"Something like that. If we pay the fine, everything be O.K. But if we ignore, throw away the summons, they chase us; lock us up."

"What's your name, buddy?" policeman asked me.

I explained the best I can I'm not picking, I'm only holding for the other fellow.

But he doesn't believe me. "Don't argue," he said. "Don't argue or I'll run you in right now."

I explained again. "Boys will tell you," I said. "I wasn't picking."

No, he doesn't believe them neither. "Don't alibi him," he said.

I'd be sorry to be a man like that policeman, suspicious that everybody is a liar. What's the use for a person to live if he can't trust nobody?

So he wrote a ticket for me, too, and went away. And still tying his shoe, that fellow Cyrille wasn't back yet.

"This is an awful, awful thing," I said.

"It's nothing." Sergei could laugh.

"Nothing! I lived my whole life at home and I was never in trouble. Now I'm six months in America and I'm a crook. Nothing, you think? How my father likes to hear such kind of news? Arrested. What will our village say? The first man from Kobiankari ever comes in the U.S.A.—for what? To go in prison!"

"Look," Sergei said. "You don't even have to go in court. Send the money. Plead guilty."

"But I'm not."

"You only say you are. Saves time."

"Then the policeman's right never to believe anybody. Say first, I didn't. Then, next time, change around, say I did."

"If you won't plead guilty, you'll have to go in court and have a trial."

"Then I'll go."

"Lose a day's pay."

"I lose."

"How about we find the policeman," Arkady suggested, "and try once more?"

"No use," Sergei said. "For myself I'm gonna plead guilty, but the best thing we can do for Giorgi Ivanitch, let's we go back in New York and see a Fixer."

"What means vixer?" I said. "Vixer? Kind of a fox, isn't it?"

"Ef. Fixer. It's a man. People pays him for fixing things. He knows how to manage all kinds of permits; he fills out income tax blanks; tears up traffic tickets. Suppose you're refused a license for something, you give the Fixer money, he finds some way around to get it anyway for you."

"Still sounds like a fox."

"That's vixen," Sergei said. "Keep straight the words in your head. You get everybody mixed up. Fixers has big connections. Influences."

So we went and Fixer had big rooms to show up he's a Somebody, but the floor was imitation marbles; the stand lamps some kind of cast-metal golded over to look real and on a veneer table sets a big plated vase full with paper roses. Is plank mahogany, the panels in the wall? I felt them. Nope. Plyboard.

"If he matches his office," I told the boys, "he's not even gonna be a real man. Gonna be a dummy stuffed with straw and a victrola in his mouth."

"Shut up or you'll be twice in jail."

"So what can I do for you, my boys?" Fixer came in. "In trouble?"

I showed the summons.

"Trouble with the police?" The Fixer shook his head very sad. "Trouble with the police is serious business. No doubt you're a foreigner?"

"In the U.S.A. I am, yes," I said.

"Well, give me a retaining fee. Ten dollars is customary, but I'll make you for five and we see what we can do."

I paid him the money over.

"Now let's hear."

My committee explained the whole story.

Fixer thought. Looked through his papers. Made a few notes on a pad. Thought again. "I tell you," he said finally, "only one solution. You go in court tomorrow, plead guilty, is about a two dollar fine and it's all over. I use my connections on the side to fix everything for you."

"Look," I told him, "I didn't pick flowers. So I'm not gonna say I did. Hang me in chains but nobody can make me say I did do what I didn't do."

So that ends that. No more help from the Fixer. He's mad.

Sergei suggested how about we go to see old Mr. Cohen, he was years and years in the U.S.A. Maybe he can think of something.

"Listen," Mr. Cohen said, when we told him everything. "Fixer

Mixer leave alone all. Take my advices. I been a citizen for forty-seven years with full papers. President Hayes signed me in personal. Go in court. When they ask you the first question say, 'Not guilty, Your Honor.'"

"Not guilty, Your Honor. What means 'Your Honor'?"

"Means the judge. All judges in U.S.A. named Your Honor."

"Not guilty, Your Honor. Then?"

"Just tell your story nice way."

"With my broken words?"

"Say the best way you can. Probably judge gonna listen and try to understand you. Of course it can happen you get a mean judge, one that's too tired to pay attention, that don't like foreigners to bother him. But very few those kind. If you get such a one, pay your fine, don't argue. But don't be disgusted with the U.S.A. Just come and tell me."

"What you gonna do?"

"Why, next time, I vote against him, naturally. We don't keep him in office no more, if he don't act nice."

So next morning I went in court. Called the other names, Igor, Arkady, Sergei, Philip. Guilty. Guilty. Guilty. All sent money to pay their fines.

Now my name. I couldn't understand a word they asked me. I was nervous. My English was running out of my head like sand through a sieve. How they told me to call a judge? Your Honorable? No. Your Highness? No, that's Russian. Your—? They were asking me something. I had to answer. I took my courage in my two hands and spoke out. "Not guilty, Your Honesty."

Courtroom went wild. Laughing and laughing. Laughing like hyenas. The judge pounded with the hammer. Bang. Bang. Bang! His face was red like a turkey's. What I done? I was sure I was going in Sing Sing and be thrown in the deepest-down dungeon.

But the judge was giving the audience hell first. "Word honesty—applied by this—cause such mirth—contempt of court."

"Young man." Now he was through with them, it be my turn. "Address the Court as Sir."

"Yes, sir."

"Did I understand you to plead not guilty?"

"Yes, sir. Not guilty."

"This officer says you and your friends were violating an ordinance, destroying a tree. Breaking the limbs."

"Yes, sir. Some was picking. I wasn't."

"Have you any proof of this?"

"No, sir. Friends were with me, but they can't come today. They all pleaded guilty, sent you a fine. Cheaper than to lose a day's pay."

"Why didn't you do that?"

"Because if I'm guilty I admit it, but if I'm not guilty, no man gonna make me say I am. Just as much a lie to say you guilty when you not as to say you innocent if you did wrong."

"Yes, that's correct. How long are you in the United States?"

"Six months."

"In court here before?"

"No, sir."

"Ever in trouble at home? Assault or kill a man?"

"Yes, sir."

"How many?"

"Hundreds. After the first year, I never counted them any more."

"Where was this?"

"In the War. I'm a sniper. It's my job to shoot all the Germans I see. Sometimes Bulgarians, too, but mostly they didn't have much interest to show themselves, poor fellows."

"I see. I mean in civil life. When you were not a soldier, not in the army. Ever hurt or strike anybody?"

"Yes, sir. Once."

"What?"

"Knocked a man's teeths out. Few."

"Why?"

"Catched him giving poisoned meat to my dog to eat."

"Understandable. Only time?"

"Yes, sir."

"Sure?"

"Yes, sir."

"Did you actually see this man," His Honesty asked the policeman, "breaking the tree?"

"No sir. Not exactly, but all the others admitted guilt and he was with them, holding a bunch of flowers."

"I believe he's a truthful man, Officer, and this time you were probably mistaken. Case dismissed."

And then His Honesty, big American judge, leaned over. And what do you think he said to me, ignorant, no speaking language, six months off a boat, greenhorn foreigner? "Young man, I like to shake hands with you."

And in front of that whole court room, he did.

BRUDIE'S PICKLE

BOOTH TARKINGTON

I'm a Forty-Eighter!" said the oldest Mr. Albert Alberger on the morning of his ninetieth birthday.

"I'm a Forty-Eighter, and don't you fergit it, Brudie! Don't you once ever fergit it for one second ever once at all!"

He spoke with vigor, addressing his grandson, the youngest Mr. Albert Alberger. "I got good enough eyesight yet," the old man went on, tapping with his cane upon the little oblong of card-board which had dropped from his grandson's pocket to the floor.

"I got good enough eyesight to see it's a caller's card. So much airs you got to go pudding on!"

"That isn't 'airs.'" Albert protested. "Everybody has their cards."

"Business cards, yes. Caller's cards, no! I got good eyesight—anyway, I got good enough through my spegtickles to see if it ain't a caller's card. Hand it to me, you Brudie."

The youngest Alberger picked up the card and placed it upon the extended palm of his grandfather, whereupon the latter shuffled to the strong light of the open window.

"Caller's card! Didn't I knew it?" he cried. "You got a new name?" he demanded, after a second scrutiny of the card. "You got a double name?"

"It's nothing at all," said the young man. "I don't see what you're so cross about."

"Look!" the grandfather exclaimed. "You read dot card! Speak it out loud, I ask you!"

The grandson, irked but obedient, read aloud what was engraved upon the card:

"'Mr. Albert Alberger, Third.'"

"I hear it!" his grandfather cried fiercely. "What you put on behind you?"

"What?"

"What you put on behind you?"

"You mean 'Third,' gran'pa?"

"What means it—'Third'?"

"Why, that's nothing," said Albert. "It's only so's people can tell you and papa and me apart."

"So!" the old man shouted. "You expect nobody can tell me and your papa from you unless you got a 'Mister' in front of you and a 'Third' stuck on behind you, sittin' on a caller's card? You want to be a aristocracy, I guess so! What you expect I come to America for? To git granchilten born to grow up makin' monkeyshines? No, sir, you're wrong, I'll show you! I marched wit' a *gun* against monkeyshines! I tell you I'm a Forty-Eighter!"

"Well, what you expect me to do?" young Albert inquired plaintively. "I got to have a name of my own, don't I? You're Albert Alberger, aren't you?"

"You bet!"

"And papa's Albert Alberger, Junior?"

"All right."

"Well, I got a right to something, haven't I? I don't know for sure, but I think it's the *law* I got to be Albert Alberger, Third."

"Listen!" said his grandfather. "It's plendy fer you peoble can say, 'He's dot young Alberger fella from "Albergers' Imported Wines, Bowling and Beer Garden."' Ain't it plendy enough you're from Albergers'?"

"No, it certainly is not!" the young man replied with emphasis.

"'Chunior,' dot's all right," the ancient man continued. "'Third,' dot's aristocracy!"

In the grandson's opinion, this ruling was consistent with the unreasonable character of Mr. Albert Alberger, First; and young Albert had learned that, no matter how impulsively the old man spoke, he never afterward confessed a change of view; therefore the only way to deal with him was to reach a deadlock as soon as possible, and allow matters to remain in that state. Accordingly, young Albert said:

"Well, anyhow, I'm going to keep the 'Third' on my name; and I'm going to keep the calling cards, too."

"What you do?" the grandfather cried angrily. "You go pay calls on some silly female monkeys on Maple Street? What else you got 'em for, I bet you! You want to go cut some shines on Maple Street!"

Albert's face had become pink, and his hand shook a little as he extended it in a warning gesture. "Now, you look out!" he cried, with sudden huskiness. "You be careful how you talk! I'm not going to stand everything around here! I got a right to go calling on Maple Street if I want to."

Upon this the countenance of the nonagenarian gave a demonstration of its plasticity. Already remarkable as a bit of eccentric modeling, it ran through a series of such radical alterations in contour that the oldest Alberger seemed to be giving impersonations of a whole gallery of elderly men, none of them much resembling himself, except in the matter of age. Subsequently he chewed with incredible rapidity upon nothing, the process shortening his face appallingly. Then, all at once, he became placid.

"So you want to git mat, iss it?" he said; and sat down in the chair by the open window. "How olt are you, Brudie?"

"I'm twenty years old."

"So? It's a shame!"

"Why is it 'a shame'?"

"Because twendy years olt you ought to know anyhow a little!" replied the exasperating antique.

Certainly his grandson found him exasperating. "*What* don't I know?" he demanded hotly. "Just you tell me anything I don't know!"

That touched a coil of mirth within the breast of Albert the First. He cackled and called upon his God. "'Chust tell me anyt'ing I don't know'!" he echoed in falsetto. "Dot's a putty smart fella, I tell you! One day I ask dot fella if he reads Heine's poems yet, and he t'inks I'm talkin' about dose adwertisement rhymes Heinie Glotz puts in noospapers about his carpet-store!" He laughed again, then abruptly leaned forward and shook his cane at young Albert. "You noodle!" he cried. "All you know iss to spent money on caller's cards and stick some crazy yella chammy gluffs on your hants, and try to be a smart Alecks aristocracy! I know where you go! Me and your papa was out riting in dot surrey-wagon, and didn't we saw you? Aha! we seen you sittin' against a hammick in olt Wilkinses yard—dot olt cheater of a G. B. Wilkins, what I wouldn't wiped my shoe on when he was alife, because I got too much rispect for my shoe—we see you, and we see who sits in dot hammick! All on top she's got yella hair and a hat cost forty dollars, and no sense in her head; only monkeyshines smart Alecks aristocracy and—"

"That'll be enough!" young Albert shouted. "That'll be enough from you!"

"No, it won't! I—"

But the youth's blood was up; it was up so high that his face showed blotches of a color almost carmine against its general flush of pink. "I'll just show you it's enough!" he cried. "You don't get to talk any more like that to me!"

And to make this declaration entirely convincing, he ran out to the street.

The room where he had left his grandfather was the "sitting

room" of the three surviving Albergers. They dwelt in the rear
of the brick building, the forepart of which was the somewhat
Gothic hall, containing the bar, the bowling alleys, the wine tables,
and the cigar cases. The window in the "sitting room" looked forth
upon the neat beer garden; and at this moment Albert Alberger,
Junior, worked therein with trowel and rake; from time to time
giving over his own labor to direct that of an amateur painter, professionally a waiter, who was painting some tubs for plants a pleasant green. The oldest Alberger, again chewing frenziedly upon
nothing, turned his head to blink at these Maytime preparations
for the coming outdoor season.

"You heert dot fella?" he inquired of Albert, Junior, whose cylin-
drical, good-natured head—lifted, after the transplanting of a vine
—was now upon a level with the windowsill. "You heert how dot
fella hollers and goes on?"

Albert, Junior, laughed. "You got to have anyway *some* excitement on your birthday, don't you, Papa!" he said. "If you don't
get it no other way, you got to start a scrap with Brudie."

"He's a noodle!" the ancient asserted with conviction. "Better
for us it been his brudder Herman what got well, when dot
scarlet-feefer was. You know where dot smart Alecks goes to-day,
all dressed up in his yella chammy gluffs wit' a speggle-spotted
silk necktie? Wilkinses! Wilkinses on Maple Street; dot's where he
goes!"

"Oh, well, Papa," said Albert, Junior, "that needn't mean nothing
so much. I wouldn't care if he went there a couple times with some
of the other young fellas his age—maybe to a party, or something
like that—so long he didn't go reg'lar. Once or twice, that's no
harm."

"Once or twice! What about once or twice a day?"

"Well, I wouldn't like it," the son admitted. "Maybe p'raps I'll
talk to him about it, one these days."

"I guess so! What about how he sit by dot hammick we saw
him?"

"I'll have a talk with him, Papa."

"Wilkinses!" the old man cried. "I tell you I wouldn't wipe my
shoes on Wilkinses! You want to know, I'll tell you, I got no use
for dot whole Maple Street fit-out! Kit-gluff show-off peoble!"

"Well, I don't know about that," the younger Alberger said. "There's some pretty good citizens livin' there. Henry Glotz is buildin' a house on Maple Street right now. He goes with them people a good deal."

Albert the First was but the more embittered. "Dot's fine!" he returned. "Glotz, he's gittin' monkeyshines in his noodle, too, is he? You want to know what Maple Street iss?"

"Oh, I guess I know, Papa."

"No, you don't!" the old man said sharply. "You ain't seen it like I haf. You ain't no Forty-Eighter and you ain't no Sixty-Two-er, neither! Listen, Albert, I tell you! I tell you what Maple Street iss."

Albert, Junior, rested his arm upon the windowsill. "Well, go on, Papa," he said, humoring the elder's mood. "*I* got time."

"Maple Street, dot's Wilkinses!" Albert the First declared emphatically. "And Wilkinses iss aristocracy smart Alecks monkeyshines. What you expect I help make so much trouble for, in Chermany in Forty-Eight? Well, I'll tell you, Albert: dot was for freedom. Well, we couldn't git no freedom in Chermany. Instead o' freedom I tell you I hat to light out, quick! So, I come to America —to here where I got already a cousin—and I go to work for him in his beer saloon. He got a little place; right here where I'm sittin', it was. I sticked here when he died, and year by year I builted up dot fine splendit bissness we got here now. Didn't I?"

"Of course you did, Papa."

"Well, how big a popalation was our town when I come here because I can't get no freedom in Chermany? She was fourteen hundut peoble. Yes, sir, chust fourteen hundut. Fine peoble, too; no monkeyshines and noodles, Albert. All peoble what did plendy work; all peoble dot says 'How-dy'-do, good-morning; how's your family?' Nobody tries to be smart Alecks; nobody gits stuck up— everybody goes along good, and everybody iss neighbors. Fine peoble, Albert! Well, sir, she begins to grow; she svells oud. Fifteen hundut? No—! She comes *fifty* hundut; all time svellin' oud pigger; —and here comes Wilkinses!

"Dot olt one, G. B. Wilkins, he's a cheater and a windbag; he's a great kit-gluff fella, and makes speeches. A year after he come here he schwindelt seven, eight hundut dollars from some farmers on a real estate, and putty soon he git in Conguss. Next, he comes back and sits up some more real estating, him and his son, and builted 'em a show-off house on Maple Street. Den dey git some noodles to built some more show-off houses on Maple Street, and rite up and down in carridges, and cut monkeyshines. Well, we got someding else on our hants, dose times, because Abe'aham Lincoln he says America *ain't* got freedom yet. Dot's when you was a baby, Albert, and by Chemminy! I didn't want to go—but I wanted to lif in a country dot hat all freedom, so I went. In sixty-two I went. Yes, sir, I went amarching wit' der boys, and helped let hell into Chonny Rebs.

"Well, when I come home, our town she's still asvellin' oud. Bei Gott, I seen her svell oud from fourteen hundut to sixty-one t'ousand, where she iss now—and all dot time Maple Street gits worse and worse. Wilkinses got some more show-off peoble to built show-off houses on Maple Street. More and more dey got 'em. Soon as a show-off family comes to lif in our town, dey got to go and lif on Maple Street! Dose peoble iss *all* kit-gluff noodles! Olt G. B. Wilkins, he's dead long time; so's his son; but plendy Wilkinses left on Maple Street, and Wilkinses iss head of all dem kit-gluff noodles. Dot yella-hair, ain't she a Wilkinses? Hah! I bet you! You want Brudie turning into a noodle? Fine he'll be arount *Albergers'!*

"Look at dot fine glass o' peoble iss Albergers' customers; fine family trade; peoble wit' good sense and good senses' manners. How long you t'ink dose peoble goin' to haf any respects fer Albergers' if Albergers' cuts up shines wit' yella gluffs and goes chasin' after Maple Streeters? You raised Brudie good, Albert; but I tell you, you let him turn into a Maple Street noodle and he ain't fit to be in Albergers'. No, sir! If he's a Maple Streeter he ain't fit to be a 'Merican citizen!"

The expression of Albert, Junior, had become serious during this discourse. "You're right," he said. "Brudie's got to cut it out. I'll talk to him."

"How long you goin' to wait?" the ancient demanded. "Besites his yella chammy gloves he hat today a yella walkin' cane!"

The brow of Albert, Junior, darkened indeed. "I'll get after him right off," he said. "You bet I'll settle with him before things goes too far!"

He might have felt that things had already gone rather far with young Albert if the latter could have been disclosed to his view at that moment. Young Albert, in fact, had just emerged from the doorway of a corner drugstore at the upper end of Maple Street, and had seized the kid-gloved hand of a passing Wilkins. The manner of Albert was violent; that of Miss Wilkins showed surprise neither at his vehemence nor at the encounter. It was a rendezvous.

She was about Albert's age; not more than a year younger; a fragile, expensive little creature, almost touchingly sweet to look at, and, like spun sugar, not to be handled at all. How well she herself understood this was made plain by the haste of her effort to withdraw her fingers from the bulky enclosure of Albert's chamois glove. However, she had no strength, and could only lift her shoulder and jerk her arm in protest.

"Let go, Albert," she said pettishly, in a charming voice. "Let *go!*"

"All right," he laughed, obeying. "I wasn't trying to hold your hand—not on the street."

"Not anywhere!" she exclaimed, his implication finding little favor with her.

Albert's ample face was tactless enough to exhibit a great deal of mystification. "What's the matter?" he inquired, as they walked slowly on together. "You didn't mind it last Tuesday night when we were sitting out on your porch in the moonli—"

"Hush!" she said crisply. "You mustn't talk like that."

"Why not, when it's the tru—"

"Hush!" she insisted. "Saying things like that isn't *nice!* I don't like it."

"I don't see what *I've* done to make you treat me so different, today, all at once," said Albert, beginning to be offended. "What's the matter, Anita?"

"Nothing at all."

"Well, then, why do you go and get cross when I happen to mention—"

Anita Wilkins uttered a sharp sound of impatience. "If you say any more, Albert," she cried, "I'll turn around, right here on the street, and not walk another step with you!"

After an inner conflict, Albert contained himself in silence.

This was his first sight of Anita since a walk they had taken on the morning after the sentimental Tuesday evening he had thought proper to recall to her mind, and during that previous stroll Anita's mood had been complaisant, even fond. In fact, when they reached the outskirts of the town her small hand had been so friendly as to place itself voluntarily within his own, for a moment or two, without explanation.

Since then, throughout a week which seemed everlasting, he had been looking forward to a repetition of this pleasant event; looking forward also to other repetitions. He thought she would probably be more celestially definite, this time, about how often she thought of him. She had admitted, on their Wednesday walk, that it was "so often, she wondered how much it meant," and a further admission, just as they parted, sent him home by way of the rushing heavens: "Oftener than about anybody else in the world, Albert!"

Now here was a change with a vengeance! She not only jerked her hand away from him, but scolded him; even threatened "to turn around, right here on the street," and make him an ignominious figure to the eyes of any beholder. Albert's breast heaved; the muscles of his large face moved threateningly, and his eyes blinked. These symptoms, ten years earlier, would have indicated to those who knew him that he was about to weep with loud vocal demonstrations; but he never went quite that far now, of course. He was puzzled; more hurt than puzzled; angrier than hurt; and he stalked beside Miss Wilkins in sore dignity, inadequate phrases forming in his mind.

His impulse was to tell her, with all possible bitterness of enunciation, that he wasn't used to being treated like a dog by anybody, and that he didn't propose to get used to it, either! He might have followed the impulse had there not fallen a gentle touch upon his arm; three white-kid fingers rested for a caressing instant upon his sleeve; an appealing whisper fell ineffably upon his ear:

"Don't be cross wif' me, boy?"

And he looked down upon a small, glowing face which almost touched his shoulder and smiled wistfully, asking forgiveness.

"You cross wif' 'Nita, boy?"

He was not. Instantly he was not. This small Anita was the perfect mistress of little enchantments; she was always ready with cunning to compass her desires, and just now her desire was to soothe this bulky lover; for she was tender-hearted, and could never bear to see any animal rage or suffer—not even a big boy. When she did not behold the suffering, it did not matter so much; but Albert's was poignantly visible. For reasons decidedly her own, she had planned to discourage him thoroughly today; but her too gentle heart betrayed her, and she was unable to aggrieve him further while he was yet in her sight and she must be a witness of his distress. So she decided to find another way: Albert was too vivid.

"You're *not* cross, Albert, boy?"

"I was just pretending," he said. "I just thought I'd let you think I was cross."

And he made bold to clasp for an instant the fingers that had touched his sleeve; the which she suffered him, and smiled. "Did you wait long at the drugstore for me?" she asked. "I think it's better, our meeting somewhere like this, than your coming to the house very often; don't you, Albert?"

"Yes, I guess it is," he said; and for a little while they walked without speaking, inwardly preoccupied. What went on in their two minds just then was odd enough; for Anita was remembering how careful she had been that her family did not become too inquisitive about Albert and discover his origin; and Albert was thinking that he would have to bring about no inconsiderable alterations in Anita before she would become acceptable to his father and grandfather. He had not a suspicion that her relatives might have some prejudices against himself, which is further witness to the delicacy of Anita and to that tender heart of hers. It was actually Albert's impression that she had divined the attitude of his own family toward Maple Street noodles.

"She knows when I get home they might ask me where I been," he thought. "Then, if I been to her house, I either have to lie or get in trouble; but if I met her outside and don't have to say I been to her house, then I'll be all right." This was a high compliment to Anita, one of the kind that lovers pay: it invested her with the powers of a seeress, since he had never mentioned the Alberger viewpoint to her. "It's better, meeting like this," he thought. "I can go to her house enough after I teach her to be more the kind of woman *they'd* like. Then they'll think she's fine."

The vision in his mind was of an Anita made over in a fashion suitable to Albergers': an Anita weighing about sixty muscular pounds more than the lady now walking beside him—a saving, industrious Anita, hearty with the customers, anxious to please the family trade, and a capable hand with Swiss-cheese sandwiches, roll'm-ups, and all the wursts. That was the picture which, rather hazily, in his mind's eye, he formed of the intricate little person, Anita Wilkins.

The unfortunate Albert was capable of this vision, even while he beheld before him what she did to her father's four-thousand-dollar income: the New York hat that looked as if some burlesquing boy had made it for a joke on his sister; the misshapen blouse, trimmed with mink; the futurist skirt; the trifling gaiters; the foolishly pretty shoes, twinkling with highlights. The vision of an Alberger Anita was in his mind's eye even when the end of her mink tippet blew into his physical eye; even when she lifted her hand to adjust the tippet, and he saw the crusted miracle of a watch she wore on her white-kid wrist. Albert's visions were somewhat exorbitant; there was poesy in him, evidently.

"I cut something out o' the paper Sunday to show you," he said presently. "I didn't know whether you'd seen it." He handed her the clipping:

"Owing to a business opportunity, Mr. Henry Wilkins, Fifth, has returned from college and will reside with his parents in this city."

"Oh, yes, I saw it," said Anita, tossing the clipping away. "Of course I knew Cousin Henry was home."

"Pretty good joke, isn't it?" said Albert.

"I don't see why."

"Oh, it's all over town he got fired because he couldn't keep up in his studies. That's why there was a 'business opportunity' for Mr. Henry Wilkins, Fifth!"

Anita frowned. "You're entirely mistaken," she said. "Henry's father insisted on his going into business." And as Albert shouted jeeringly, she added, "If you laugh when I tell you things, I'll think you're rather rude."

"Well, I can get along without laughing for a minute; it's nothing to me," he said. "Anyway, we got Henry Wilkins, Fifth, to thank for introducing us to each other. Just a little over four months ago, the night after Christmas; that's when it was."

"Yes, Albert."

"I wasn't thinking much about going to that Charity Ball," he said, plunging, as lovers will, into reminiscences of "how it happened." "And then I says to myself, 'Believe I'll go see if there's any good-lookers there.' So when I got there, I saw *you*. I had to hunt around to find somebody that knew you, so finally I ran across Henry. I traded him a bicycle once, when we were in high school. So he introduced you to me."

"No, he introduced you to me, Albert."

"Yes," said Albert. "That was a pretty important night for you and me, Anita; but I guess he never knew *that*, when he was introducing us! I got something else I want to show you." And he offered for her inspection a card, twin to that which had caused so much emotion within his grandfather.

"'Albert Alberger, Third,'" she read. "But, Albert, it's printed."

"You bet!"

"You ought to've had it engraved."

"What's the difference?" he asked.

"Oh, nobody has cards *printed!*" she informed him. "That isn't a bit nice."

Albert had thought to please her, and he was piqued. He was additionally annoyed when, before he could pursue the subject, the lady he escorted was hailed from the rear, and an exquisite youth appeared, panting.

"I've just been to your house, 'Nita," said Henry Wilkins, Fifth, adjusting his step to his cousin's, but not to Albert's. "Aunt Marjie told me you'd gone walking, and I've been running all over this end of town to find you. Why don't you leave word at the house which way you're going when you know I'm in town?"

Anita looked startled; and a slight agitation became audible in her voice, though all she said was, "Why, Henry *Wilkins!*"

"Well, why don't you?" Henry insisted.

Albert frowned heavily; he was naturally disturbed by the intrusion, and he was annoyed by the high-handed, ignoring way in which it was made. It seemed to him a violation of actual rights which people ought to have sense enough to recognize; and he cast about in his mind for some means to demonstrate that Anita was no longer public property, and that, even for cousins, she did not "leave word," at home, where she was going—not when she was going to walk with Albert Alberger, Third!

Henry paid no attention whatever to him, but continued, to Anita: "You knew I was in town three days ago. Why haven't you called me up? It was your place to do something first, don't you think, after the way you haven't answered my letters lately?"

This had a happy effect upon Albert. His irritation vanished at once; he was delighted, and a merry mood took him. Henry's complaint proved clearly that Anita had something better to think of than answering letters from Maple Street noodles. For, when he looked at Henry Wilkins, Fifth, Albert suddenly agreed with his grandfather, at least about the male population of the pretentious thoroughfare. Henry was a slim youth, as beautiful and cold as the moon. He was fair, with hair of a silver blond; and his expression was infantile in its rapt unconsciousness of all the universe save Henry and what affected him.

"Where you going?" he said. "Let's go back to the house. I want to talk to you."

"Hello, Swink!" said Albert gaily.

"Hellow, Deitsh!" Henry carelessly returned. "Anita, let's go back to—"

"What in the world are those names you're calling each other?" Anita cried; and she managed to add a nervous but placative laugh to the interruption.

"We called him 'Deitsh' at high school," said Henry. "Didn't you hear what I said? How much farther are you—"

"'Swink's' always been his nickname," Albert explained. "I hear you just got fired from college, Swink." And he laughed boisterously, appealing confidently to Anita. "Didn't I tell you it was all over town he got fired because he was so dumb he couldn't keep up?"

Henry was able to ignore this jocular attack, though it rather strained his capacity for ignoring things, especially as Albert had but stated the lamentable fact. Anita, on the contrary, flushed deeper, and suddenly wheeled about, facing homeward.

"All right," she said. "Let's *do* go back!"

"Where can I get a chance to have a talk with you alone?" Henry added, turning with her.

Albert turned also; but he was not quick, and he found himself a step behind them—a step which he took with vigor, placing himself between the cousins, instead of going to Anita's unescorted left. "Well," he said, "I guess I just as soon go back, too. We can't get much more good out o' this walk now."

The cold young Henry seemed not so cold at this. It was with an easily visible amount of heat, in fact, that, after saving himself from a fall (Albert's shoulder having brushed him heavily), he passed to Anita's left. All three faces were flushed: Henry's with indignation; Anita's with anxiety; Albert's with triumph.

"I guess it's all right so far as I'm concerned," Albert said, "if you want to go back to the house. One way or another—go walking or sit in the house and chatter—it hardly makes any difference to *us*, does it, Anita?"

She gave him a dark glance; then she gave her cousin an appealing one. "Oh, it might," she said. "I don't know. I guess so. Yes, it would." For the moment she was disconcerted, and with reason. She had not looked for this encounter. "Cousin Henry," she said, making a pathetic effort, "did you find everybody all well at your house when you got home?"

Henry was not inclined to ease matters; he stalked beside her, furious. "Never mind," he said. "I'll talk to you when we get alone."

Albert laughed a laugh of contempt, not ill-natured, merely triumphant. "Come around some other day then," he said. "Up to then, fall in behind! You're too late to get on the band wagon!"

Anita shuddered.

Henry breathed rapidly, almost audibly, but attempted no retort; and Albert was in high fettle. He laughed loudly again, and, reaching behind Anita, slapped Henry upon the back.

"You're too late for the band wagon!" he cried. "Fall in with the kids behind, old Swinkie!"

"You keep your hands off me!" Mr. Wilkins commanded dangerously.

"You get mad and I'll turn you upside down and spank you!" shouted the uproarious Albert. "If anybody gets mad it ought to be me. Shouldn't it, Anita?"

Scarlet, she made no reply, but hurried the faster toward home, while Albert gaily pressed the question:

"Shouldn't it be me if anybody has to get mad? Here he thinks he ought to get mad while *he's* the one comes spoiling a walk I'm taking with my girl!"

"*Albert!*" she gasped miserably.

"Well, I'm not mad," he laughed; and he stretched forth his hand, offering Henry another good-natured slap; but Henry evaded the gift, muttering savagely. The yellow chamois glove paused in air, then with a second thought rested upon Anita's shoulder. "*We* aren't mad at him, are we, Anita?"

As Anita jerked her shoulder free of that possessive hand, her expression indicated that she considered the moment a tragic one. The two words she spoke, however, lacked every dramatic quality, though the tone was sufficiently emotional.

"Oh, *my!*" she said.

They had reached her gateway. "Come in, Henry," she said, breathlessly. "Albert, I'll write you a note and—"

"Oh, I just as soon come in," he said. "It don't matter so much, once in a while."

She opened her lips to speak, but proved to be incapable. With a blanched face she turned, and followed by the two young men, scampered unhappily to the front door of the house, opened it, and passed within.

The three stood in a broad, old-fashioned hall—a hall with a white-and-black tiled floor, black walnut newel and staircase, dismaying draperies, antlers with hats on them; all haunted by a faint smell of apples.

Anita spoke in haste, and her voice was a tremulous ghost of itself. "Albert," she said, "will you please go in the reception room?"

"I don't care," he responded. "Go and talk with him a while, if Swinkie's got some family stuff he wants to tell you. It's nothing to me, so long as he knows he's too late for the band wagon. Don't take too much time, though: we don't want *all* our afternoon spoiled for us."

And he passed cheerfully through the doorway whither her impatient hand urged him. Henry had already gone into the library on the other side of the hall, and the stricken lady proceeded to follow Henry. Tears twinkled upon her lashes the instant she had closed the door, and she seemed inclined to shed them upon her cousin's shoulder; but he stepped back with convincing haste, avoiding her.

"What did that Dutchman mean?" he demanded. "Nice thing for a man to come back to, isn't it? Find the girl he's engaged to—"

"But we aren't engaged," she protested, moaning softly as she acquiesced in his rejection of a shoulder whereon to weep. "We aren't engaged, Henry."

"Aren't we?"

"No, dear; you know we aren't. We're not exactly engaged," she added, weeping more. "I've never been exactly engaged to anybody in my life."

"Well, that Dutchman thinks you're engaged to *him*, doesn't he?"

"No!" she wailed, sinking into a chair. "Of course he doesn't. He *never* acted such a crazy way before! I don't know what was the matter with him!"

"I do," said Henry. "Nothing could be *much* plainer!"

"What?"

"He thinks you're going to marry him."

The unhappy girl stifled a scream. "No, no, *no!*" she cried. "How could he?"

"Because you've been flirting with him."

"No, no, *no*, Henry!" she protested, huskily. "I haven't ever done anything *like* flirt with him. Sometimes I *have* flirted; I admit that. I did last summer, and told you all about it. Don't you remember?" In the excess of her candor she lifted her wet eyes to his. "But never since this Christmas, when I found out *you* cared. *Never*, Henry!"

"Then what's he mean, calling you his 'girl'?"

"I don't *know*, Henry. It's just his German way, I think. I've hardly seen anything of him at all: he's only been here to call three or four times. I've always been almost *icy* with him. For a while— and you were so far away, Henry—I did think he was rather nice, and sort of big and good-looking and—"

Henry interrupted her violently. "*Aha!*" he cried. "I see!"

"Henry!" she wailed. "I only mean good-looking in his *way*—not a way that appeals to me at all! You've just got to believe me, Henry. Henry, you *do* believe me?" And she seized his hand, clinging to it and leaving tears upon it.

Henry began to be shaken. "You can't fool me," he said. "I know you've been cooin' around that Dutchman; but there's one way you could make me think it didn't amount to much."

"Tell me."

"Go in there and make him understand you never want to see him around the place again."

She dropped his hand and uttered a subdued shriek. "Oh, I couldn't! I couldn't, Henry! It would hurt his feelings awfully, and you know perfectly well I *can't* see people suffer. I *can't*, Henry."

Henry intelligently made for the door.

"Stop!" she cried, running to place herself in his way. "You shan't go, Henry! You *mustn't* be so mean to me!"

"Then do what I say."

She saw that he meant it inexorably; she gulped, shivered, sighed brokenly, and bowed her head in resignation. "You wouldn't mind, Henry," she said feebly, "if I had mamma do it for me?"

"No," said Henry. "I think that would be better. It'd do him lots o' good."

"I won't be long," whispered Anita, and the tender prophecy of a smile might have been seen through the mist of her tears as she tiptoed out of the door.

In the room where Albert waited he discovered the origin of the faint odor noticeable in the hall—a silver bowl of big, polished red apples on a center table. He looked upon these with a pleasant interest, and, seating himself at ease, ate two. He was just finishing the second when a lady of fifty entered the room so quietly that she startled him, and he sat open mouthed, staring, the remnants of the apple in his hand.

She was so gentlewomanly she might have dressed herself in the character of "gentlewoman" for a fancy-dress party. Her delicate head—a religious, elderly replica of Anita's—completed a simple harmony otherwise composed of gray silk, ivory lace, and a cameo. Her voice was almost as quiet and quick as the noiseless step of her invisible feet.

"You are Mr. Alberger," she said, but did not await his confirmation of the statement. "Anita introduced you to me on the porch one evening, but it was dark. I am her mother. I'm very sorry to have something to say which may be a little awkward for both you and myself, Mr. Alberger."

"Ma'am?" he said. "Isn't Anita coming in here pretty soon? I was just waiting for her."

"I'm sorry," she said, quickly. "I came to say that it will be better for you not to wait. Anita is chatting with her cousin."

Albert got heavily to his feet. "What you mean? She isn't going to spend the whole afternoon with Swink, is she?"

"I beg your pardon."

"That Henry Wilkins! She isn't crazy enough about him to spend the whole—"

"She hasn't any such ideas in her head, Mr. Alberger. Both she and her cousin are too young to think of such things yet. I'm afraid I must make it clear," Mrs. Wilkins continued, with an accession of primness. "What I am saying concerns nobody except yourself."

Albert coughed uncomfortably; he was becoming conscious of a destiny overhanging and about to fall upon him ponderously. He felt a strong dislike for this ominous lady. "Well, does something seem to be the matter?" he asked, not knowing what else to say.

"Very much so," she returned. "I think I must be quite frank with you. You see, when Anita met you she had no idea who you were, Mr. Alberger."

"Who I was?" he echoed, utterly puzzled.

"She asked you to call, without knowing who you were," Mrs. Wilkins went on, in her quick, quiet way. "She tells me you came several times before you mentioned definitely who you were. When you did mention it she ought to have told her father and me at once; but Anita is very tender-hearted, and she put off telling us, because she knew that we could take no possible course except to end the acquaintance instantly. I know how sensitive she is to the giving of pain, but I think she was very wrong not to tell us who you were as soon as she found out. She says herself that keeping such a thing secret from us has weighed more and more on her conscience until today, when she felt that she couldn't bear it any longer. She has just come to me in my room and told me who you were, Mr. Alberger."

"Who I *am?*" said Albert. He was dazed; most of what she said amazed and staggered him; he could not discern her meaning. But "end the acquaintance instantly"—*that* stood out with a sinister intelligiblity, and frightened him.

"She felt she must put the matter entirely in my hands," Mrs. Wilkins informed him.

"Look here!" said Albert. "You got me all mixed up. I don't know what you're talking about. Did *she* get you to come in here to tell me she wants to sit in there and talk to Swink Wilkins, now he's got fired and come back to—"

Mrs. Wilkins interrupted him firmly. "I see I shall have to be even painfully frank, Mr. Alberger. You entirely misunderstand your own position. When I heard your name mentioned by Anita, I did not connect it with a place I have often—too often—heard of: the Alberger"— she paused, reluctant to use distasteful words, then compelled herself to go on—"the Alberger saloon!" she said.

"Well," said Albert, "I don't see what's the matter. Albergers' isn't a saloon, though; not as you name saloons. Our place is a wine house and bowling alleys and garden, and it's got the best business in the city. I guess you don't hardly mean Anita thinks she's too good for Albergers'?"

Mrs. Wilkins looked suddenly faint. For a moment she was unable to reply; then she found a voice much louder than she had been using. "Your father is a German saloonkeeper!" she cried.

"All right," said Albert, fiercely. "What comes next?"

"I think you should understand without my saying any more, Mr. Alberger."

"Understand what?"

Mrs. Wilkins looked him full in the eye. "Anita begs me to request you," she said, "that as she was under a misapprehension about you in asking you to call here, you will be good enough not to mention to anybody that you have ever been in this house."

This was, in truth, slightly over-interpreting Anita, but the young man seemed to call for extraordinary clearness of diction; and aside from something which Mrs. Wilkins thought of as "social strata," she had a profound horror of all traffickers in liquor.

"If my husband were here this afternoon," she said, "he would probably insist on your giving your word to grant Anita's request. He would ask you please not to speak to her upon the street—and not to mention her. I hope it will be unnecessary for him ever to have to approach you upon the subject."

She would have said a little more, but Albert's eyes, fixed upon her own, were becoming visibly bloodshot and unbearable. He was slow, but at last he understood her meaning to the full, and he understood Anita's.

Mrs. Wilkins moved backward nervously. "I think your hat—" she began, but decided not to make the suggestion more definite.

There was no need. Albert picked up his hat and stick from the table, where they lay by the bowl of apples; he put his hat on his head, and stamped vehemently out of the house. At the gate he turned.

There was the flicker of a curtain at a window downstairs; and this movement, though inconsiderable and brief, disclosed the fact that Henry Wilkins, Fifth, and Anita, over Henry's shoulder, were watching the passionate departure. They saw that he saw them, and, with a little confusion, decided to become invisible; upon which Albert, discovering that he held the remains of an apple embedded in a clinched palm of chamois, hurled this missive at the window, and departed, swiftly.

He reached the stable behind Albergers' Garden in time to unloose his emotions privately, or at least before a public consisting of no more than the mild horse and introspective cow there enclosed with him. He broke his stick into short pieces; he hurled the yellow gloves into the mire of the stalls, and trampled them down there. He used many words, both whole and broken, and uttered sounds that were not words at all. At last his reddened eyes lifted to a rafter, then slowly descended to the cow's halter of rope.

The combination of materials was gloomily suggestive; but Albert was young, and after a while he went up to the loft, and lay in the hay, brooding, until suppertime.

His father and Albert the First were already seated when young Albert came to the table. They let him begin his meal; then the ancient man nodded sagely to his son, who nodded back, and said:

"Brudie, I got to talk to you."

"Dot's right," said the ancient. "Gif it to him, hot, too!"

But before the son could obey, rebellion flamed from the grandson. He set down his coffee cup, and banged the table with his fist alarmingly. "You better not!" he cried. "I won't stand not one word! I don't have to take it from anybody. I want to get out o' this place."

His two elders stared, incredulous; they looked at each other

blankly, then more blankly at young Albert. Finally the grandfather
seemed to have solved the riddle. He began to nod his fine old head;
he nodded and nodded.

"Yes, sir," he said. "Didn't I knew it? Didn't I tolt you? You put
it off too long, and let him keep goin' wit' Maple Streeters, till it's
happened to him. Dose peoble, you know what dey are?"

"*I'll* tell you what they are!" young Albert shouted. "They're
Americans!"

"*No*, sir!" the old man answered, straining his thin voice with the
emphasis he demanded of it. "It's because you've gone crazy you
say so: nobody can't make Maple Streeters Americans. Maple Streeters iss monkeyshines, and monkeyshines ain't Americans. I'm a
Forty-Eighter and I'm a Sixty-Two-er! I been an American sixty-
eight years; dot's long enough to know who besides me iss Americans, ain't it? You been goin' by Maple Street till you're crazy; you're
spoilt; you're turned into a noodle! It's happened."

"It's a falsehood!" bellowed young Albert.

"Why is it?" his father asked angrily. "Didn't you just say you
want to leave Albergers'?"

"I didn't! I want to leave this blame *town!*"

"Where you want to go, Brudie?" his father inquired, in complete
astonishment.

Albert sat sullen for a moment; then with lowered eyes he said:
"I'd like to go to Germany."

"For a visit?" asked Albert, Junior. "You want to go and study
something maybe?"

"No!" the boy returned fiercely. "I want to go live there!"

The Forty-Eighter hammered the table with knife and spoon; he
burst into uproarious laughter which ran into falsetto and choked
him. "You Brudie!" he said at last. "You go and lif in Chermany—see
how you like it. Why, you can't speak good Cherman!"

"I'd learn it then."

"You better not!" cried the old man. "Pretty quick you'd say
someding if it's understood you git in jail!"

"Why would I?"

"You couldn't *help* it! You got always used to speak what you
want to, ain't you? Here, if you want to cuss somebody, you cuss
him. In Chermany, if you want to cuss der Kaiser, you'd cuss him.

In Chermany you expect a man can open his mout' to speak what he feels like? What am I a Forty-Eighter *for*, you Brudie?"

"I don't know," the youth said sullenly. "I wish you'd stayed there and been a reg'lar German!"

Old Alberger laughed again. "In America you stand up for Chermany; in Chermany you'd stand up for America—"

"You think I would?" Albert interrupted hotly. "It's why I'd like to go and live in Germany—because I hate them damned Americans!"

Again the elder two sat amazed. "You hate *who*, Brudie?" the grandfather asked, leaning toward him, across the table.

"I hate them damned Americans," Albert repeated; and his passion increased.

"You hate *me*? Ain't I an American?"

"You're not!" shouted Albert; and he struck the table again with his fist. "Maple Streeters, *they're* Americans! You're a German! You're a German saloonkeeper!"

"Yes, sir. Go on," said old Alberger, nodding. "What comes next?"

Albert threw down his napkin and leaped to his feet. "*I'm* a German!" he bellowed. "And I wish to God you'd had sense enough to stay in Germany where you belonged, and not come over and get me born here where I got to make myself sick lookin' at *Americans!* That dirty Maple Street ain't nothing *but* Americans!"

. . . He fled, noises of a vehement character marking his path through the farther chambers of the apartment. "Well, sir," said the Forty-Eighter, "he's gone crazy, but I guess we don't got to worry so much. Anyway, he ain't no Maple Streeter!"

And a little later, observing how young Albert rather morosely but efficiently managed the bowling alleys in the somewhat Gothic hall, Albert the First addressed Albert, Junior, again upon the subject. "I guess he don't start for Chermany tonight, not chust yet a while! I expect—well, me and you, we ought—"

He lowered his voice to a whisper as a group of customers jovially approached; and Albert, Junior, was uncertain of his father's words, but he understood the old man's meaning, which was that both of them ought to be very kind to Brudie for a while. The final phrase of the Forty-Eighter was more distinct, however.

"Because Brudie, he's in a hell of a pickle!" his son understood him to say.

YOUNG MAN AXELBROD

SINCLAIR LEWIS

The cottonwood is a tree of a slovenly and plebeian habit. Its woolly wisps turn gray the lawns and engender neighborhood hostilities about our town. Yet it is a mighty tree, a refuge and an inspiration; the sun flickers in its towering foliage, whence the tattoo of locusts enlivens our dusty summer afternoons. From the wheat country out to the sagebrush plains between the buttes and the Yellowstone it is the cottonwood that keeps a little grateful shade for sweating homesteaders.

In Joralemon we call Knute Axelbrod "Old Cottonwood." As a

matter of fact, the name was derived not so much from the quality of the man as from the wide grove about his gaunt white house and red barn. He made a comely row of trees on each side of the country road, so that a humble, daily sort of a man, driving beneath them in his lumber wagon, might fancy himself lord of a private avenue.

And at sixty-five Knute was like one of his own cottonwoods, his roots deep in the soil, his trunk weathered by rain and blizzard and baking August noons, his crown spread to the wide horizon of day and the enormous sky of a prairie night.

This immigrant was an American even in speech. Save for a weakness about his j's and w's, he spoke the twangy Yankee English of the land. He was the more American because in his native Scandinavia he had dreamed of America as a land of light. Always through disillusion and weariness he beheld America as the world's nursery for justice, for broad, fair towns, and eager talk; and always he kept a young soul that dared to desire beauty.

As a lad Knute Axelbrod had wished to be a famous scholar, to learn the ease of foreign tongues, the romance of history, to unfold in the graciousness of wise books. When he first came to America he worked in a sawmill all day and studied all evening. He mastered enough book-learning to teach district school for two terms; then, when he was only eighteen, a great-hearted pity for faded little Lena Wesselius moved him to marry her. Gay enough, doubtless, was their hike by prairie schooner to new farmlands, but Knute was promptly caught in a net of poverty and family. From eighteen to fifty-eight he was always snatching children away from death or the farm away from mortgages.

He had to be content—and generously content he was—with the second-hand glory of his children's success and, for himself, with pilfered hours of reading—that reading of big, thick, dismal volumes of history and economics which the lone mature learner chooses. Without ever losing his desire for strange cities and the dignity of towers he stuck to his farm. He acquired a half-section, free from debt, fertile, well-stocked, adorned with a cement silo, a chicken-run, a new windmill. He became comfortable, secure, and then he was ready, it seemed, to die; for at sixty-three his work was done, and he was unneeded and alone.

His wife was dead. His sons had scattered afar, one a dentist in Fargo, another a farmer in the Golden Valley. He had turned over his farm to his daughter and son-in-law. They had begged him to live with them, but Knute refused.

"No," he said, "you must learn to stand on your own feet. I vill not give you the farm. You pay me four hundred dollars a year rent, and I live on that and vatch you from my hill."

On a rise beside the lone cottonwood which he loved best of all his trees Knute built a tar-paper shack, and here he "bached it"; cooked his meals, made his bed, sometimes sat in the sun, read many books from the Joralemon library, and began to feel that he was free of the yoke of citizenship which he had borne all his life.

For hours at a time he sat on a backless kitchen chair before the shack, a wide-shouldered man, white-bearded, motionless; a seer despite his grotesquely baggy trousers, his collarless shirt. He looked across the miles of stubble to the steeple of the Jackrabbit Forks church and meditated upon the uses of life. At first he could not break the rigidity of habit. He rose at five, found work in cleaning his cabin and cultivating his garden, had dinner exactly at twelve, and went to bed by afterglow. But little by little he discovered that he could be irregular without being arrested. He stayed abed till seven or even eight. He got a large, deliberate, tortoise-shell cat, and played games with it; let it lap milk upon the table, called it the Princess, and confided to it that he had a "sneaking idee" that men were fools to work so hard. Around this coatless old man, his stained waistcoat flapping about a huge torso, in a shanty of rumpled bed and pine table covered with sheets of food-daubed newspaper, hovered all the passionate aspiration of youth and the dreams of ancient beauty.

He began to take long walks by night. In his necessitous life night had ever been a period of heavy slumber in close rooms. Now he discovered the mystery of the dark; saw the prairies wide-flung and misty beneath the moon, heard the voices of grass and cottonwoods and drowsy birds. He tramped for miles. His boots were dew-soaked, but he did not heed. He stopped upon hillocks, shyly threw wide his arms, and stood worshiping the naked, slumbering land.

These excursions he tried to keep secret, but they were bruited abroad. Neighbors, good, decent fellows with no sense about walking in the dew at night, when they were returning late from town, drunk, lashing their horses and flinging whisky bottles from racing democrat wagons, saw him, and they spread the tidings that Old Cottonwood was "getting nutty since he give up his farm to that son-in-law of his and retired. Seen the old codger wandering around at midnight. Wish I had his chance to sleep. Wouldn't catch me out in the night air."

Any rural community from Todd Center to Seringapatam is resentful of any person who varies from its standard, and is morbidly fascinated by any hint of madness. The countryside began to spy on Knute Axelbrod, to ask him questions, and to stare from the road at his shack. He was sensitively aware of it, and inclined to be surly to inquisitive acquaintances. Doubtless that was the beginning of his great pilgrimage.

As a part of the general wild license of his new life—really, he once roared at that startled cat, the Princess: "By gollies! I ain't going to brush my teeth tonight. All my life I've brushed 'em, and alvays wanted to skip a time vunce"—Knute took considerable pleasure in degenerating in his taste in scholarship. He wilfully declined to finish *The Conquest of Mexico*, and began to read light novels borrowed from the Joralemon library. So he rediscovered the lands of dancing and light wines, which all his life he had desired. Some economics and history he did read, but every evening he would stretch out in his buffalo-horn chair, his feet on the cot and the Princess in his lap, and invade Zenda or fall in love with Trilby.

Among the novels he chanced upon a highly optimistic story of Yale in which a worthy young man "earned his way through" college, stroked the crew, won Phi Beta Kappa, and had the most entertaining, yet moral, conversations on or adjacent to "the dear old fence."

As a result of this chronicle, at about three o'clock one morning, when Knute Axelbrod was sixty-four years of age, he decided that he would go to college. All his life he had wanted to. Why not do it?

When he awoke he was not so sure about it as when he had gone to sleep. He saw himself as ridiculous, a ponderous, oldish man among clean-limbed youths, like a dusty cottonwood among silver birches. But for months he wrestled and played with that idea of a great pilgrimage to the Mount of Muses; for he really supposed college to be that sort of place. He believed that all college students, except for the wealthy idlers, burned to acquire learning. He pictured Harvard and Yale and Princeton as ancient groves set with marble temples, before which large groups of Grecian youths talked gently about astronomy and good government. In his picture they never cut classes or ate.

With a longing for music and books and graciousness such as the most ambitious boy could never comprehend, this thick-faced farmer dedicated himself to beauty, and defied the unconquerable power of approaching old age. He sent for college catalogues and school books, and diligently began to prepare himself for college.

He found Latin irregular verbs and the whimsicalities of algebra fiendish. They had nothing to do with actual life as he had lived it. But he mastered them; he studied twelve hours a day, as once he had plodded through eighteen hours a day in the hayfield. With history and English literature he had comparatively little trouble; already he knew much of them from his recreative reading. From German neighbors he had picked up enough Plattdeutsch to make German easy. The trick of study began to come back to him from his small school teaching of forty-five years before. He began to believe that he could really put it through. He kept assuring himself that in college, with rare and sympathetic instructors to help him, there would not be this baffling search, this nervous strain.

But the unreality of the things he studied did disillusion him, and he tired of his new game. He kept it up chiefly because all his life he had kept up onerous labor without any taste for it. Toward the autumn of the second year of his eccentric life he no longer believed that he would ever go to college.

Then a busy little grocer stopped him on the street in Joralemon and quizzed him about his studies, to the delight of the informal club which always loafs at the corner of the hotel.

Knute was silent, but dangerously angry. He remembered just in time how he had once laid wrathful hands upon a hired man, and somehow the man's collarbone had been broken. He turned away and walked home, seven miles, still boiling. He picked up the Princess, and, with her mewing on his shoulder, tramped out again to enjoy the sunset.

He stopped at a reedy slough. He gazed at a hopping plover without seeing it. Suddenly he cried:

"I am going to college. It opens next veek. I t'ink that I can pass the examinations."

Two days later he had moved the Princess and his sticks of furniture to his son-in-law's house, had bought a new slouch hat, a celluloid collar and a solemn suit of black, had wrestled with God in prayer through all of a star-clad night, and had taken the train for Minneapolis, on the way to New Haven.

While he stared out of the car window Knute was warning himself that the millionaires' sons would make fun of him. Perhaps they would haze him. He bade himself avoid all these sons of Belial and cleave to his own people, those who "earned their way through."

At Chicago he was afraid with a great fear of the lightning flashes that the swift crowds made on his retina, the batteries of ranked motor cars that charged at him. He prayed, and ran for his train to New York. He came at last to New Haven.

Not with gibing rudeness, but with politely quizzical eyebrows, Yale received him, led him through entrance examinations, which, after sweaty plowing with the pen, he barely passed, and found for him a roommate. The roommate was a large-browed soft white grub named Ray Gribble, who had been teaching school in New England and seemed chiefly to desire college training so that he might make more money as a teacher. Ray Gribble was a hustler; he instantly got work tutoring the awkward son of a steel man, and for board he waited on table.

He was Knute's chief acquaintance. Knute tried to fool himself into thinking he liked the grub, but Ray couldn't keep his damp hands off the old man's soul. He had the skill of a professional exhorter of young men in finding out Knute's motives, and when he

discovered that Knute had a hidden desire to sip at gay, polite
literature, Ray said in a shocked way:

"Strikes me a man like you, that's getting old, ought to be thinking
more about saving your soul than about all these frills. You leave
this poetry and stuff to these foreigners and artists, and you stick
to Latin and math and the Bible. I tell you, I've taught school, and
I've learned by experience."

With Ray Gribble, Knute lived grubbily, an existence of torn
comforters and smelly lamp, of lexicons and logarithm tables. No
leisurely loafing by fireplaces was theirs. They roomed in West Divinity, where gather the theologues, the lesser sort of law students, a whimsical genius or two, and a horde of unplaced freshmen
and "scrub seniors."

Knute was shockingly disappointed, but he stuck to his room because outside of it he was afraid. He was a grotesque figure, and
he knew it, a white-polled giant squeezed into a small seat in a
classroom, listening to instructors younger than his own sons. Once
he tried to sit on the fence. No one but "ringers" sat on the fence
any more, and at the sight of him trying to look athletic and young,
two upper-class men snickered, and he sneaked away.

He came to hate Ray Gribble and his voluble companions of the
submerged tenth of the class, the hewers of tutorial wood. It is
doubtless safer to mock the flag than to question that best-estab-
lished tradition of our democracy—that those who "earn their way
through" college are necessarily stronger, braver, and more assured
of success than the weaklings who talk by the fire. Every college
story presents such a moral. But tremblingly the historian submits
that Knute discovered that waiting on table did not make lads more
heroic than did football or happy loafing. Fine fellows, cheerful and
fearless, were many of the boys who "earned their way," and able
to talk to richer classmates without fawning; but just as many of
them assumed an abject respectability as the most convenient pose.
They were pickers up of unconsidered trifles; they toadied to the
classmates whom they tutored; they wriggled before the faculty
committee on scholarships; they looked pious at Dwight Hall
prayer meetings to make an impression on the serious minded;
and they drank one glass of beer at Jake's to show the light
minded that they meant nothing offensive by their piety. In revenge

for cringing to the insolent athletes whom they tutored, they would, when safe among their own kind, yammer about the "lack of democracy of college today." Not that they were so indiscreet as to do anything about it. They lacked the stuff of really rebellious souls. Knute listened to them and marveled. They sounded like young hired men talking behind his barn at harvest time.

This submerged tenth hated the dilettantes of the class even more than they hated the bloods. Against one Gilbert Washburn, a rich esthete with more manner than any freshman ought to have, they raged righteously. They spoke of seriousness and industry till Knute, who might once have desired to know lads like Washburn, felt ashamed of himself as a wicked, wasteful old man.

Humbly though he sought, he found no inspiration and no comradeship. He was the freak of the class, and aside from the submerged tenth, his classmates were afraid of being "queered" by being seen with him.

As he was still powerful, one who could take up a barrel of pork on his knees, he tried to find friendship among the athletes. He sat at Yale Field, watching the football tryouts, and tried to get acquainted with the candidates. They stared at him and answered his questions grudgingly—beefy youths who in their simple-hearted way showed that they considered him plain crazy.

The place itself began to lose the haze of magic through which he had first seen it. Earth is earth, whether one sees it in Camelot or Joralemon or on the Yale campus—or possibly even in the Harvard yard! The buildings ceased to be temples to Knute; they became structures of brick or stone, filled with young men who lounged at windows and watched him amusedly as he tried to slip by.

The Gargantuan hall of Commons became a tri-daily horror because at the table where he dined were two youths who, having uncommonly penetrating minds, discerned that Knute had a beard, and courageously told the world about it. One of them, named Atchison, was a superior person, very industrious and scholarly, glib in mathematics and manners. He despised Knute's lack of definite purpose in coming to college. The other was a playboy, a wit and a stealer of street signs, who had a wonderful sense for a subtle jest; and his references to Knute's beard shook the table with jocund mirth three times a day. So these youths of gentle birth drove the shambling, wistful old man away from Commons, and thereafter he ate at the lunch counter at the Black Cat.

Lacking the stimulus of friendship, it was the harder for Knute to keep up the strain of studying the long assignments. What had been a week's pleasant reading in his shack was now thrown at him as a day's task. But he would not have minded the toil if he could have found one as young as himself. They were all so dreadfully old, the money-earners, the serious laborers at athletics, the instructors who worried over their life work of putting marks in class-record books.

Then, on a sore, bruised day, Knute did meet one who was young.

Knute had heard that the professor who was the idol of the college had berated the too-earnest lads in his Browning class, and insisted that they read *Alice in Wonderland*. Knute floundered dustily about in a second-hand bookshop till he found an "Alice," and he brought it home to read over his lunch of a hot-dog sandwich. Something in the grave absurdity of the book appealed to him, and he was chuckling over it when Ray Gribble came into the room and glanced at the reader.

"Huh!" said Mr. Gribble.

"That's a fine, funny book," said Knute.

"Huh! *Alice in Wonderland!* I've heard of it. Silly nonsense. Why don't you read something really fine, like Shakespeare or *Paradise Lost?*"

"Vell—" said Knute, all he could find to say.

With Ray Gribble's glassy eye on him, he could no longer roll and roar with the book. He wondered if indeed he ought not to be reading Milton's pompous anthropological misconceptions. He went unhappily out to an early history class, ably conducted by Blevins, Ph.D.

Knute admired Blevins, Ph.D. He was so tubbed and eyeglassed and terribly right. But most of Blevins' lambs did not like Blevins. They said he was a "crank." They read newspapers in his class and covertly kicked one another.

In the smug, plastered classroom, his arm leaning heavily on the broad tablet-arm of his chair, Knute tried not to miss one of Blevins' sardonic proofs that the correct date of the second marriage of Themistocles was two years and seven days later than the date assigned by that illiterate ass, Frutari of Padua. Knute admired young Blevins' performance, and he felt virtuous in application to these hard, unnonsensical facts.

He became aware that certain lewd fellows of the lesser sort were playing poker just behind him. His prairie-trained ear caught whispers of "Two to dole," and "Raise you two beans." Knute revolved, and frowned upon these mockers of sound learning. As he turned back he was aware that the offenders were chuckling, and continuing their game. He saw that Blevins, Ph.D., perceived that something was wrong; he frowned, but he said nothing. Knute sat in meditation. He saw Blevins as merely a boy. He was sorry for him. He would do the boy a good turn.

When class was over he hung about Blevins' desk till the other students had clattered out. He rumbled:

"Say, Professor, you're a fine fellow. I do something for you. If any of the boys make themselves a nuisance, you yust call on me, and I spank the son of a guns."

Blevins, Ph.D., spake in a manner of culture and nastiness:

"Thanks so much, Axelbrod, but I don't fancy that will ever be necessary. I am supposed to be a reasonably good disciplinarian. Good day. Oh, one moment. There's something I've been wishing to speak to you about. I do wish you wouldn't try quite so hard to show off whenever I call on you during quizzes. You answer at such needless length, and you smile as though there were something highly amusing about me. I'm quite willing to have you regard me as a humorous figure, privately, but there are certain classroom conventions, you know, certain little conventions."

"Why, Professor!" wailed Knute, "I never make fun of you! I didn't know I smile. If I do, I guess it's yust because I am so glad when my stupid old head gets the lesson good."

"Well, well, that's very gratifying, I'm sure. And if you will be a little more careful—"

Blevins, Ph.D., smiled a toothy, frozen smile, and trotted off to the Graduates' Club, to be witty about old Knute and his way of saying "yust," while in the deserted classroom Knute sat chill, an old man and doomed. Through the windows came the light of Indian summer; clean, boyish cries rose from the campus. But the lover of autumn smoothed his baggy sleeve, stared at the black-board, and there saw only the gray of October stubble about his distant shack. As he pictured the college watching him, secretly making fun of him and his smile, he was now faint and ashamed, now bull-angry. He was lonely for his cat, his fine chair of buffalo horns, the sunny doorstep of his shack, and the understanding land. He had been in college for about one month.

Before he left the classroom he stepped behind the instructor's desk and looked at an imaginary class.

"I might have stood there as a prof if I could have come earlier," he said softly to himself.

Calmed by the liquid autumn gold that flowed through the streets, he walked out Whitney Avenue toward the butte-like hill of East Rock. He observed the caress of the light upon the scarped rock, heard the delicate music of leaves, breathed in air pregnant with tales of old New England. He exulted: "'Could write poetry now if I yust—if I yust could write poetry!"

He climbed to the top of East Rock, whence he could see the Yale buildings like the towers of Oxford, and see Long Island Sound, and the white glare of Long Island beyond the water. He marveled that Axelbrod of the cottonwood country was looking across an arm of the Atlantic to New York state. He noticed a fresh-man on a bench at the edge of the rock, and he became irritated. The freshman was Gilbert Washburn, the snob, the dilettante, of whom Ray Gribble had once said: "That guy is the disgrace of the class. He doesn't go out for anything, high stand or Dwight Hall or anything else. Thinks he's so doggone much better than the rest of the fellows that he doesn't associate with anybody. Thinks he's literary, they say, and yet he doesn't even heel the 'Lit,' like the regular literary fellows! Got no time for a loafing, mooning snob like that."

As Knute stared at the unaware Gil, whose profile was fine in outline against the sky, he was terrifically public-spirited and dis-approving and that sort of moral thing. Though Gil was much too well dressed, he seemed moodily discontented.

"What he needs is to vork in a threshing crew and sleep in the hay," grumbled Knute almost in the virtuous manner of Gribble. "Then he vould know when he vas vell off, and not look like he had the earache. Pff!" Gil Washburn rose, trailed toward Knute, glanced at him, sat down on Knute's bench.

"Great view!" he said. His smile was eager.

That smile symbolized to Knute all the art of life he had come to college to find. He tumbled out of his moral attitude with ludicrous haste, and every wrinkle of his weathered face creased deep as he answered:

"Yes: I t'ink the Acropolis must be like this here."

"Say, look here, Axelbrod; I've been thinking about you."

"Yas?"

"We ought to know each other. We two are the class scandal. We came here to dream, and these busy little goats like Atchison and Giblets, or whatever your roommate's name is, think we're fools not to go out for marks. You may not agree with me, but I've decided that you and I are precisely alike."

"What makes you t'ink I come here to dream?" bristled Knute.

"Oh, I used to sit near you at Commons and hear you try to quell old Atchison whenever he got busy discussing the reasons for coming to college. That old, moth-eaten topic! I wonder if Cain and Abel didn't discuss it at the Eden Agricultural College. You know, Abel the mark-grabber, very pious and high stand, and Cain wanting to read poetry."

"Yes," said Knute, "and I guess Prof. Adam say, 'Cain, don't you read this poetry; it von't help you in algebra.'"

"Of course. Say, wonder if you'd like to look at this volume of Musset I was sentimental enough to lug up here today. Picked it up when I was abroad last year."

From his pocket Gil drew such a book as Knute had never seen before, a slender volume, in a strange language, bound in hand-tooled crushed levant, an effeminate bibelot over which the prairie farmer gasped with luxurious pleasure. The book almost vanished in his big hands. With a timid forefinger he stroked the levant, ran through the leaves.

"I can't read it, but that's the kind of book I alvays t'ought there must be some like it," he sighed.

"Listen!" cried Gil. "Ysaÿe is playing up at Hartford tonight. Let's go hear him. We'll trolley up. Tried to get some of the fellows to come, but they thought I was a nut."

What an Ysaÿe was, Knute Axelbrod had no notion; but "Sure!" he boomed.

When they got to Hartford they found that between them they had just enough money to get dinner, hear Ysaÿe from gallery seats, and return only as far as Meriden. At Meriden Gil suggested:

"Let's walk back to New Haven, then. Can you make it?"

Knute had no knowledge as to whether it was four miles or forty back to the campus, but "Sure!" he said. For the last few months he had been noticing that, despite his bulk, he had to be careful, but tonight he could have flown.

In the music of Ysaÿe, the first real musician he had ever heard, Knute had found all the incredible things of which he had slowly been reading in William Morris and "Idylls of the King." Tall knights he had beheld, and slim princesses in white samite, the misty gates of forlorn towns, and the glory of the chivalry that never was.

They did walk, roaring down the road beneath the October moon, stopping to steal apples and to exclaim over silvered hills, taking a puerile and very natural joy in chasing a profane dog. It was Gil who talked, and Knute who listened, for the most part; but Knute was lured into tales of the pioneer days, of blizzards, of harvesting, and of the first flame of the green wheat. Regarding the Atchisons and Gribbles of the class both of them were youthfully bitter and supercilious. But they were not bitter long, for they were atavisms tonight. They were wandering minstrels, Gilbert the troubadour with his man-at-arms.

They reached the campus at about five in the morning. Fumbling for words that would express his feeling, Knute stammered:

"Vell, it vas fine. I go to bed now and I dream about—"

"Bed? Rats! Never believe in winding up a party when it's going strong. Too few good parties. Besides, it's only the shank of the evening. Besides, we're hungry. Besides—oh, besides! Wait here a second. I'm going up to my room to get some money, and we'll have some eats. Wait! Please do!"

Knute would have waited all night. He had lived almost seventy years and traveled fifteen hundred miles and endured Ray Gribble to find Gil Washburn.

Policemen wondered to see the celluloid-collared old man and the expensive-looking boy rolling arm in arm down Chapel Street in search of a restaurant suitable to poets. They were all closed.

"The Ghetto will be awake by now," said Gil. "We'll go buy some eats and take 'em up to my room. I've got some tea there."

Knute shouldered through dark streets beside him as naturally as though he had always been a nighthawk, with an aversion to anything as rustic as beds. Down on Oak Street, a place of low shops, smoky lights and alley mouths, they found the slum already astir. Gil contrived to purchase boxed biscuits, cream cheese, chicken-loaf, a bottle of cream. While Gil was chaffering, Knute stared out into the street milkily lighted by wavering gas and the first feebleness of coming day; he gazed upon Kosher signs and advertisements in Russian letters, shawled women and bearded rabbis; and as he looked he gathered contentment which he could never lose. He had traveled abroad tonight.

The room of Gil Washburn was all the useless, pleasant things Knute wanted it to be. There was more of Gil's Paris days in it than of his freshmanhood: Persian rugs, a silver tea service, etchings, and books. Knute Axelbrod of the tar-paper shack and piggy farm-yards gazed in satisfaction. Vast bearded, sunk in an easy chair, he clucked amiably while Gil lighted a fire.

Over supper they spoke of great men and heroic ideals. It was good talk, and not unspiced with lively references to Gribble and Atchison and Blevins, all asleep now in their correct beds. Gil read snatches of Stevenson and Anatole France; then at last he read his own poetry.

It does not matter whether that poetry was good or bad. To Knute it was a miracle to find one who actually wrote it.

The talk grew slow, and they began to yawn. Knute was sensitive to the lowered key of their Indian-summer madness, and he hastily rose. As he said good-by he felt as though he had but to sleep a little while and return to this unending night of romance.

But he came out of the dormitory upon day. It was six-thirty of the morning, with a still, hard light upon red brick walls.

"I can go to his room plenty times now; I find my friend," Knute said. He held tight the volume of Musset, which Gil had begged him to take.

As he started to walk the few steps to West Divinity Knute felt very tired. By daylight the adventure seemed more and more incredible.

As he entered the dormitory he sighed heavily:

"Age and youth, I guess they can't team together long." As he mounted the stairs he said: "If I saw the boy again, he vould get tired of me. I tell him all I got to say." And as he opened his door, he added: "This is what I come to college for—this one night. I go avay before I spoil it."

He wrote a note to Gil, and began to pack his telescope. He did not even wake Ray Gribble, sonorously sleeping in the stale air.

At five that afternoon, on the day coach of a westbound train, an old man sat smiling. A lasting content was in his eyes, and in his hands a small book in French.

THE AMBASSADOR

EDWARD NEWHOUSE

Henry Applegate liked familiar objects. Although his view of shaving was no different from that of most men, once he got down to it he rather enjoyed the process of working up lather in the meerschaum mug that had served two generations of Applegates before him. With time out for wars and minor trips, the mug had been in constant use since Grant's first year in the White House. It had accompanied Grandfather Applegate through the decades of his lackluster service as a diplomat, and Henry's father had had it even longer. When the boys' turn came— But Mark and Ben, neither of whom was old enough to shave, had already announced that they would use electric razors. The mug, if it remained intact, would then attain the status of an heirloom. Henry liked the feel of it.

He had not got around to shaving until it was almost time for lunch. Gwen must have known how late he had turned in, and she had let him sleep through most of the morning. Nice of Gwen. Nice also of Gwen to have left him alone with Lucy so soon after dinner last night. As always, she had sensed when Lucy wanted to talk. It was not that Lucy talked any less freely to her mother; she had just grown used to trying things out on her father, to begin with. The boys did it the other way around.

Home on her first Easter vacation from college, Lucy had had a lot to say. Her French teacher had a beard, exactly the kind that Frenchmen are supposed to have. The Dean of Women was a sweetie pie. Ancient History was all right, but no more than that —much too superficial. There were saddle horses to be had not too far from campus, but the rates were absolutely criminal. She had been to Boston only four times since Christmas. You were simply strapped without a car. She was in love. The real thing, this time. He was a senior at Harvard, and his parents didn't understand why he should be studying to become an art critic—but Henry would. In fact, Henry would give him a job at the museum next year—yes? Alan was a wonderful-*looking* boy, though he could use an inch or two more in height. Make that three. She wished he'd learn to ride a horse. Didn't Henry think that criticism could be *creative?*

They had spent half the night talking in front of the open fire. Later in the day, Henry thought, he would have to get the boys out of the house and give Gwen a chance to be alone with Lucy, too. He would take the boys down to the old quarry and let them use the .22. They would like that. He dried the meerschaum mug and put it back in the cabinet.

Gwen came in, a little breathless, and handed him a shirt. "Quick, put it on," she said. "Anton's here. Out in the driveway with Lucy and the boys."

"Damn. I thought he'd crossed us off his list for good," Henry said. "How long has it been? Two years? Two and a half? I don't want this kind of shirt. I'm not going anywhere."

"*He's* dressed to the teeth. Including the teeth, in fact. Brand-new set—all white. Brand-new suit—tropical worsted. Brand-new Cadillac—robin's-egg blue. And all paid for. In cash. It was one of the first things he told us. Henry, where would Anton get that kind of money? Something crooked?"

"Not necessarily."

"Smuggling? You remember all those postcards from South America? Smuggling people across the border, you think? I'm sure it's something crooked."

"Not necessarily," Henry said. "If we give him a good enough lunch, perhaps he'll tell us."

"I wish he'd phone ahead before he shows up at mealtime. I asked him to, once, years ago. He said I'd only go to a lot of trouble and prepare something elaborate. I couldn't tell him it's more trouble this way."

"You could have. It wouldn't have made much of an impression."

He went to the bedroom to get a different shirt. Gwen followed him. Through the window they could see the driveway.

"My, that is a car," he said. "Is that what they call robin's-egg blue?"

"Henry, if he's involved in something crooked— Are you still in some way responsible for him?"

"I was never responsible for his morals. All I signed was a document affirming that he would not become a public charge. And even that's run out by now, I think. Does that car look as though he were on the point of becoming a public charge? *Your* cousins may all become public charges. Not mine. Why, at this rate he'll be running around in a Continental soon. Do you remember the times he walked here from the bus stop? Let's go down before the boys take his car apart."

The boys were playing with the knobs and buttons on the dashboard.

"Lucy thinks he's in some kind of awful racket," Gwen said. "She told me so downstairs."

"And she, of course, would know."

"Oh, I'd just hoped he'd never come again."

"So had I," said Henry. "But he's here."

As a child, Henry had loved to hear his grandmother tell stories about Prague, where she had been born and, to some extent, bred. Even then, he had been vaguely aware that the stories did not always hold up (his grandfather had been third, not first, secretary at the American Consulate), but that did not make them any less absorbing. A mettlesome Czech patriot who shared her countrymen's traditional view of their neighbors to the south, she had been the first person Henry heard say, "If you have a Magyar for a friend, you don't need an enemy." After her death, there had been no one who wanted to keep up a correspondence with the brother she had left in Prague, let alone with his issue through the generations. Henry had not known he had a second cousin until a social worker named Mrs. Platt came to see him at his office in the museum. That was a couple of years after the war.

Anton was then in a displaced persons' camp somewhere in the American Zone of Germany. He had left Prague after the Communists took over, and he wanted to come to the United States. Mrs. Platt felt that he was an exceptionally deserving case. For one thing, he had spent most of the war years in German concentration camps. That he had survived at all was due to his skill as a goldsmith and watchmaker; the camp officials had kept him alive and busy, repairing watches and working on gold taken from Jews. It was to his credit, too, that he could not get along under the current regime in Czechoslovakia.

Mrs. Platt's agency had power to act only if Mr. Applegate or some other American citizen was willing to provide a guarantee that Anton would not become a public charge. Just a formality, she said. Red tape. The agency would assume full responsibility. Through its connections, it would have no trouble at all in finding work for a skilled goldsmith and watchmaker. Anton spoke good English; he had been studying it from the time he was a small boy, always with the idea of one day coming to America. It was a matter of giving a man, a young man still under thirty, a chance to start life over again.

Henry sent his affidavit the following day, and received acknowledgment of it at once. Then he heard nothing until, two years later, Mrs. Platt telephoned him at his office. The young man was on Ellis Island, she said. The red tape had all been attended to. There was a job for him with a reputable jewelry firm, one of whose senior partners, a German Jew, had himself lived under Hitler. A furnished room with a fine Czech family, in Yorkville, had been secured, and the rent paid for a month in advance. Mrs. Platt was going out to the Island now. She thought she'd bring Anton back to her office late in the afternoon. Would Mr. Applegate like to meet him there?

Henry said he would indeed. Since it was Friday, he thought it might be pleasant if he drove Anton out to his place for the week-end. Anton could take possession of the furnished room on Monday.

"That would be fine," she said. "That might be just the thing."

When Henry arrived at her office, shortly after five, she came out to meet him in the waiting room. "He's in there," she said. "I wanted a word with you first. He's—not what you'd call communicative. Maybe I haven't found the right approach. He does speak English. He— Good heavens, he looks like you! You could pass for brothers. Twins, if he weren't younger. And you're only cousins."

"Second cousins."

"Remarkable. Well, he's in there. He seems eager to start working. He wants to change his name from Havranek to Byron. Anthony Byron. I guess it's all right. Anybody who's spent four years in places like Neuengamme and Buchenwald is entitled to any name he likes."

"Did he tell you why they put him in a camp in the first place?" Henry asked.

"We haven't talked about it," she said. "Let me see, now. The original arrest was made in Hamburg. Anton—Anthony—was representing his Czech firm there. I think he was accused of arranging to help a Jew escape. Then, once they had him, that was it. They found him useful. He made trinkets for the S.S. men, worked on watches. Maybe you'll find him more willing to talk. Please don't press him."

"I wasn't going to."

"Oh, I'm sorry. You wouldn't, of course. I was just doing my professional duty. Would you like to meet him now?"

They went in. Mrs. Platt had not exaggerated. Anton could easily have passed for Henry's brother. His eyes were on the same level, and for Henry it was like looking into a mirror that made him appear ten or twelve years younger. Somebody, he thought—the great-grandfather they shared, or somebody—must have spawned the mightiest genes on either bank of the Moldau. For all he knew, it gave Anton a turn to catch a glimpse of himself as a man of forty. The resemblance diminished, though, when Anton opened his mouth. He had a full set of teeth made of a dull metal alloy. He wore an ill-fitting, unpressed suit of a material that had begun to fade in irregular patches. Everything he owned was in a cardboard valise not much larger than a briefcase. He would not let Henry carry it.

Downstairs, the combined effect of that suit and that valise made Henry a bit self-conscious about his car, which was an Oldsmobile less than two weeks old. It had never been rained on. Henry still had that Oldsmobile the morning, three years later, when Anton showed up in the blue Cadillac. By then, it had run many thousands of miles and its fenders bore the marks of Lucy's course in driving, but it was in showroom condition the day Anton first saw it, and he took a long look before he got in. He asked, "Are you rich?"

"I'm afraid not," Henry said.

"In Europe, if you owned nothing only this car, you would be."

His accent was just slightly reminiscent of what Henry remembered of his grandmother's. Besides the Czech, there seemed to be a little German in it, and some British. There was no "th" sounds and no w's. And he had a number of expressions that he might have picked up from the Americans who supervised the D.P. camp; "rakeoff" was one.

Driving up Fifth Avenue, Henry made a few attempts to call his cousin's attention to a notable building, a landmark, a store window. Anton barely glanced at each. He did not crane his neck at the Empire State. He uttered a faintly nasal "Mmm" as they passed Radio City. Somewhere Henry had read of the emotional torpor that often settles permanently over people who have spent many years in concentration camps. The writer had compared it to accidie, the sloth that loomed in some monastic theologies as not only the deadliest of the seven deadly sins but the source of all the others. Henry thought of it that afternoon as the possible cause of Anton's apparently total lack of interest in the City of New York.

Later, it seemed more as though Anton were making it a point of honor not to let Henry see he was impressed. "Mmm," he said in response to a comment about the Metropolitan Museum.

Farther uptown, he did incline his head a little as they drove by the museum of which Henry was curator. He even asked what the duties of a curator might be. Henry told him, and, in a burst of relief at this first sign of mild interest, went on to describe how the staff had gone about establishing the authenticity of a Tiepolo etching—rather an involved process. Anton said, "So I suppose part of your income is the rakeoff from the dealers."

Henry turned his head to look at him. Anton was not smiling.

"No," Henry said.

"No?"

"No."

"You buyed this car out from the salary they pay you?"

"Yes."

"Mmm," said Anton.

To reach the Applegates' house, which was in a village called Brandy Point, in the Highlands of the Hudson, they had to cross the river. Henry wondered whether it would be more interesting for his guest to go over by ferry or across the bridge. From the ferry Anton might have got a more leisurely view of Manhattan, but Friday-evening traffic on the George Washington can be something of an experience, too. They took the bridge. Anton did not consider the traffic worthy of remark, but he did ask how much Henry had paid at the tollgate. Then he wanted to know when the bridge had been built and what it had cost. Henry gave him the approximate date and made an estimate in the tens of millions.

"But this means the bridge have been paid for already," Anton said.

"Maybe several times over. I don't know. There's maintenance, of course."

"So where goes all the money?"

Henry gave him a moderately well-informed account of the workings of the Port of New York Authority.

"I mean who gets rich from all the half dollars?" Anton asked.

"Why, I don't believe anyone does, really."

"No?"

"No."

"No rakeoff, you don't think?"

"No."

"Mmm."

Some miles north, on the Palisades across from Yonkers, Henry stopped to give Anton a view of the river, and offered to put a dime into one of the telescopes mounted there, but Anton declined. "How far you live from the city?" he asked.

"A little over twenty miles."

Anton transposed miles into kilometers in half the time it would have taken Henry. "And you are sure that is safe from atom bomb?" he asked.

"No, I'm not sure. I like to think so—hope so, let's say."

"Wind could bring the radioactive up the river between hills."

"Wind could also blow it out to sea. That's what I'm counting on."

"You do not worry?"

"Not often."

"Mmm. You were in the war?"

"Yes."

"Army?"

"Navy."

"You have been bombed?"

"Just once. Off Okinawa."

"Did it hit?"

"No."

"You were on a big ship?"

"Aircraft carrier. Pretty big."

"Those ships are nice and clean," said Anton. "That is the way to fight in the war. You live to tell."

He doesn't feel like staring across at Yonkers any more, Henry thought. And I don't feel like telling him about the *Lexington* and the *Wasp*. All right. I had an easy time in the war. Let it go at that.

They were both quiet during the rest of the drive to Brandy Point. Henry wondered whether that nasal "Mmm" was a noncommittal sound or one of active disbelief.

As they pulled into the Applegates' garage, Anton looked at the station wagon in the other space. "Yours?" he asked.

Henry nodded.

"You do trucking?"

Before Henry could begin explaining the uses of a station wagon, Anton's eyes were fixed on the house. It was a white frame house, well built by Henry's father shortly after Henry's birth. Set on top of a hill that sloped down to the river, it received its shelter from a remarkable group of trees, which enjoyed great local celebrity by reason of size and age. Because of the trees, there was just one other house visible from any of the windows, and only part of its roof, at that. A family of raccoons lived in the large elm behind the garage. The flagstones in the terrace probably had some salt content, because Henry had seen as many as five deer licking them at once. The squirrels and the chipmunks liked them, too.

"In Europe," said Anton, "a man who owned two cars would have a house made from stone. Or brick."

Gwen and Lucy met them at the door. The boys were down in the basement, Gwen said, with a snapping turtle they had caught beside the pond. Lucy offered to take Anton's valise, but he would not hand it over. Lucy was fifteen that year—a tall, slender, awkward, lovely child. She played the piano a lot and wrote poetry. Henry doubted whether any one of the poems could be described as good, but each had a line or two that surprised and delighted him.

At dinner, Anton wanted to know why, in a house supplied with electric lights, candles were used to eat by. Somewhat to Henry's surprise, he accepted Gwen's answer without making the nasal sound. In fact, he made it again only when they settled down to coffee in front of the fire. He said it was foolish to waste wood in a house with central heating.

"He's right," said Lucy, though usually it was she who insisted on having a fire. (She could not take her eyes off Anton. She and Henry had been talking about him only a few weeks before; afterward she had found a book about German concentration camps and had spent an afternoon reading every word of it. Images based on the nightmare photographs had cropped up in two of her poems.) "Now he's going to write his people in Czechoslovakia and tell them how foolish we are."

"I have no people in Czechoslovakia," Anton said.

"No parents?" She had been told not to question him, but the words slipped out.

Anton did not appear to mind. He said, "My father died when I was little boy. My mother was killed when the Russians cannoned the village."

"Oh, I'm sorry," Lucy said.

"Is all right. I did not like her very much."

"You must have," she said. "Everybody does. Most everybody."

"Not most everybody," Anton said. He seemed to be amused. His smile showed the upper row of the dull metal teeth. "Do you remember the Ten Commandments? He tells you must honor your father and your mother. He tells nothing about you must honor your son and your daughter. Why? Because people honor their children without somebody tells they must. To like your father and your mother, this must be Commandment. If most everybody liked his father and his mother, it would not have to be Commandment. You understand?"

"I suppose it's one thing to honor them and another to like them," Lucy said. She kept winding her watch, rather nervously.

"Don't do that, dear," her mother said. "You'll break it."

"Then I will fix," Anton said.

He stared into the fire, and talked a little about how he happened to learn watchmaking. As a trained goldsmith, he had at first been put to work at his own trade in the Neuengamme camp. For the most part, his job consisted of making rings and other negotiable jewelry out of gold taken from the mouths of inmates, dead or alive. This was a private, local enterprise, and Anton remained for a time under the protection of the S.S. man in charge of it. But then the government placed the camp on a sounder bookkeeping basis, and there was a steady fall in the supply of gold that could be held out for local use. So Anton and another young man in the shop decided to learn watch-repair work under an old Jew, whom they kept alive out of their scanty food rations. In due course, Anton and his friend, Otto Pflaum, were transferred to Buchenwald as expert watchmakers. There were thousands of watches to repair at Buchenwald, though their owners no longer had use for them.

"He did a bad thing there, my friend," said Anton. "You see, he was the messenger. He carried the watches from our shop to the office of the *Untersturmführer*. And when he was not sure he had did good job, he changed the tickets. And that put the responsible to somebody else, and so two watchmakers got hanged for sabotage. Fifty with the strap and then hanged."

"Hanged?" Lucy repeated.

"Yes. With rope. And almost I was third, but they let me go with the fifty and some other things. Very trickful man, Herr Otto Pflaum. From all the people I knowed, the first to go to America. Rich now, I hear. Someday I will meet with him."

"What will you say?" Lucy asked.

"To Otto? I will say good morning, how are you, glad to see. Show me how to get rich, I will say."

"That's all? To *him*?"

"What else? What you think, Miss? I am the Graf Monte Cristo? Revenge? No, no. If I responsible Otto, then why not the *Untersturmführer*? Why shall I not responsible the *Hauptsturmführer*? Or the *Obersturmbannführer*? No, no. I live. Otto lives. He has mark like this on his arm, but he lives. So I say him good morning, how are you, glad to see. Show me how to get rich." He pushed his sleeve up, and on his forearm there was a tattooed number so large that it reached from his wrist halfway to his elbow. It was a number in the millions, Henry thought, or at least in the hundreds of thousands. The first two figures were in red, the rest in blue. Henry's eyes turned to Lucy. Her fingernails were dug deep into the flesh of her thin arm. He tried to think of something to say, but Gwen was quicker. In her subject-changing voice, she said, "How could he have got rich in so short a time? With taxes as they are."

"Anybody can make money in this country," Anton said. "What is rich? A million dollar? I will have that."

"That'll be nice," Gwen said.

And so the rest of the talk, that first evening, was devoted mostly to the tax structure. Henry could answer some of Anton's questions easily enough, but many were well beyond a layman's competence. Lucy went upstairs, and after a while Gwen suggested that the adults go, too. Anton was taken to his room and shown where things were. He stopped as he passed the window. "You left the bicycles out," he said.

"It's all right," Gwen said. "It isn't going to rain."

"Will they not be stealed?"

"No."

"That is what I meaned," he said. "One million dollar. Anybody can get rich in this country. You are a country of innocent."

Henry was in his pajamas before he remembered to say good night to Lucy. She was lying awake in bed.

"He looks so much like you," she said. "All those things could have happened to you."

"But they didn't. Go to sleep, girl. It's late."

"Why are his teeth made of metal?" she asked.

"I don't know," he said. "Go to sleep. He'll be all right now. We'll help him."

In the morning, Anton said he wanted to go back to New York. He would not say why, and he insisted. Henry offered to drive him there, but he refused, with finality. All he would accept was a ride to the bus stop. There he took the Applegates' address and phone number. "Soon," he said, "I will give signal of myself."

When Henry got home, Gwen said, "The thing that frightens me about him is that he practically never changes his expression. Did you notice that? He's all twisted up, poor fellow."

"So would I be," Lucy said, almost harshly. "So would you, if you'd been through all that."

"Yes, darling. Yes, of course." Gwen turned to Henry. "Please call him next week and see that he's all right, won't you?"

Henry promised he would call.

On Monday, he got the telephone number from Mrs. Platt, and in the evening he rang up the Czech family in Yorkville. But Anton had already moved away. He had given no reason, the man who answered said, and had left no forwarding address.

On Tuesday morning, Henry called Mrs. Platt.

"Yes, I know," she said. "I just talked to him at the jewelry place. Apparently, he wants to be on his own. I didn't press him for his address, but I told him the immigration people would have to know. He said he would notify them at once. I guess we can always reach him at Wright & Schindler's, where he works. But I think I'd leave him be for a while—wait till he gets his bearings. Funny boy."

Just how much Anton wanted to be on his own, the Applegates found out the following week, when they got his first letter:

Dear Henry:

Here is ten dollar. It will I believe pay for my automobil ride to Brandy Point and for my room and for the meals. It is out from my first salary. So you see I pay my way so I will not be a public charge or your charge. Thank you for lending me this money. I consider it a lending. Mr. Schindler says he likes my work. I will see you in the future.

With highest regards I remain,

ANTHONY BYRON

About a month later, just before lunch on a Sunday, Anton showed up in Brandy Point. He had walked the two miles from the nearest bus stop. He had acquired a new pair of shoes and all sorts of other new clothing. He would not hear of taking his ten dollars back. As a matter of fact, he had brought Lucy a box of candy, as payment, he said, for the lunch he knew the Applegates would want him to eat. Again, all he would accept was a ride back to the bus stop.

These unannounced visits of Anton's, always on Sunday, continued for something less than a year. He never failed to bring a small gift in exchange for his lunch, and he never appeared when the Applegates had guests. Gwen thought he reconnoitered the terrain first and, when he saw a strange car in front of the garage, simply took the bus back to New York. From time to time, she professed to see an improvement in what she called his general attitude. Gwen, who came from Indiana, had great faith, not always shared by Henry, in the healing powers of life in the United States.

She was jubilant when Anton turned up on the day before Christmas and put in several hours helping the children with the tree. After the tree had been trimmed, and the presents (among them were two, originally intended for Henry, that now carried Anton's name) heaped under it, she succeeded in persuading him to spend the night. The gifts were to be opened on Christmas day after dinner.

The next morning, Henry came down late. Everyone else had

had breakfast, and Gwen had started to prepare a turkey for the oven. When Henry had finished eating, she said, "I'm glad you slept well last night. We had trouble. Lucy. I guess you didn't know they stayed up after we turned in."

"Who stayed up?"

"Lucy and Anton. They were up till half past one. About half past three, I thought I heard her crying in bed, and I went in there, and sure enough. She still hadn't had a wink of sleep. He'd been talking about the camps again."

"Damn, I've told him not to," Henry said. "I've told him what it does to her."

"This time, he must have gone on and on. He told her about a boy who was forced to watch while his father— Oh, you can imagine the sort of thing. And he showed her his back. She says it's just a mass of scars from that whipping. She felt them. All rough, up and down his whole back. I had to stay with her most of the night. If he'd only talk to you, instead. Or me. Or even the boys. They've heard him talk, and it doesn't seem to affect them much. They like him. He did a beautiful job of fixing the brakes on Mark's bicycle."

"They're not Lucy. And they haven't read that book or seen those photographs. Is he with her now?"

"They're all down in the basement," Gwen said.

"One of these days, I'll have to tell him to go to hell."

"No, don't," Gwen said. "But I wish he'd do his talking to you or me. Lucy isn't equipped to handle it—not yet. Last night, it just broke her down. She kept wanting to know if anything like that could happen here. To you, mostly. She kept saying how much he looks like you. It was starting to get light when I finally got her off to sleep."

Henry went down to the basement. The boys were playing ping-pong, and Anton was sitting with Lucy on the old porch swing that Henry had rigged up near the hot-water tank. ". . . like a sandwich," Anton was saying. "First the bodies, then the mix of lime, and then more bodies . . ."

"Lucy, your mother wants you up in the kitchen," Henry said. "She thinks it's about time you learned how to stuff a turkey."

"Right this minute?"

"Yes."

She looked at him and saw that he meant it. He waited till she was gone, and then he said, "Anton, remember my asking you not to talk to her about the camps?"

"I remember. I do not understand why not."

"I explained it to you then. She takes it hard. Much too hard, harder than you'd think. She was up most of the night. She cried. She's very fond of you, you know. She imagines all those things being done to you and it's almost more than she can stand. If the—"

"All those things are true. They happened. I saw."

"Of course they're true. And Gwen wants to hear about them, and so do I. But—"

"You want Lucy should live in fairyland? Lucy is not child."

"In some ways she is," Henry said. "In others she's a remarkably intelligent young lady and you can talk to her about anything you like. If you'll just leave the camps out of it. Gwen and I—"

Anton broke in again. "You mean she is young lady, young gentle-lady, and too high"—he stopped for a moment in search of a word —"too high and too good to hear the bad things I say. So. Is easy. I stop talking."

He walked past Henry and up the stairs. Henry followed him slowly part of the way. He heard Anton's voice in the kitchen, and the voices of Lucy and Gwen. They were all casual, even gay; they were discussing the turkey. Fine, Henry thought. We'll wait till after dinner and then soothe such hurt feelings as may show.

The boys called after Henry, begging him to play ping-pong. He went back down, and played for the best part of an hour.

When Henry and the boys went upstairs, Anton was gone. He had taken off without his dinner and without having said goodbye to anyone in the house. Gwen and Lucy had assumed he had returned to the basement.

Henry and Mark drove to the bus stop on the chance of catching him there, but the bus had passed ten minutes before.

"What a goofy thing to do," Mark said.

Several times during the next few days, Gwen asked Henry to call Anton at Wright & Schindler's; they still did not know his home address. Henry decided not to. The truth was, he looked forward to a whole series of Sundays without Anton. And when he got them, he enjoyed them. It took three months for his conscience to catch up with him. Then he called Wright & Schindler's only to find that Anton no longer worked there.

He tried Mrs. Platt.

"I thought you knew," she said. "I'm afraid he lost that job."

"I didn't know."

"Well, it was quite some time ago. Mr. Schindler rated him pretty high, and felt sorry it had to end that way. But it seems the other workers got together and said if your cousin didn't leave, they would, in a body. They threatened to take it to the union. Personally, I don't see what they could have based charges on. All they'd say to Mr. Schindler was they didn't want to work in the same room with him. They said he was surly, wouldn't answer them, made the place unpleasant. That isn't anything for a union to act on. Mr. Schindler tried to tell them about the awful things in Germany, but it didn't help. Did you find him as unpleasant as all that?"

"He's not the jolliest of companions," Henry said.

"So, practically overnight and entirely on his own, he found another job that paid much better," Mrs. Platt said. "But he quit that one, and now he's in business for himself. Just what it is, I don't know. He's on the road a lot. Maybe that's why he hasn't been going to see you. He checks in with the immigration people all right. I wouldn't be too concerned. He seems well able to look after himself."

Whether or not Anton was able to look after himself, he did spend a lot of time on the road. A month or two after the conversation with Mrs. Platt, the Applegates got a card postmarked Rio de Janeiro. It was a view of Sugar Loaf Mountain, and on the back Anton had written, "Grietings, A. Byron." After that, there were cards from Mexico City, Los Angeles, Cleveland, Havana, and Des Moines, always with the same words: "Grietings, A. Byron." The only time Anton varied the formula was when he sent one from Buenos Aires. That one said, "This city is not so inosent. Not enough Americans, too many from Europe. Respectfully yours, A. Byron."

Between the time the card came from Havana and the time the one came from Des Moines, a fat man named Stephen Osička called on Henry at his office. Mr. Osička said he had gone to school with Anton in Prague. Someone, writing from Prague, had mentioned that Anton had finally got to this country, and Mr. Osička was eager to see the boy for old times' sake. He had traced Henry through Mrs. Platt's agency. She no longer worked there, but the other people had given him Henry's address. He was disappointed to find that Henry could not give him Anton's. Henry advised him to try the Bureau of Immigration and Naturalization.

Instead of taking his leave at that point, Mr. Osička leaned back in his chair and lighted up a pipe. "I will do that," he said. "And if they won't tell me, I will hear some other way. Anton is the kind of man you're bound to hear about, don't you think? Now that he's here, I lay money he's going to make good in a big way. He's going to be a big man, like all his teachers said. A big, important man. Mr. Applegate, do you know who wrote the best piece of music about America? A Czech. Anton Dvořak. Do you know the name of the man who could teach you more about the American Indians than anybody? Aleš Hrdlička. A Czech. Anton is going to do something big like that. That's the kind of man he is. Don't you agree?"

"Perhaps," Henry said.

"When we were Sixth Class—that's like maybe second-year high school here—Anton started a club. The Five, he called it. There were only five of us in it, so that was the name. The Five. We were supposed to help poor boys who needed a certain book or a pair of soccer shoes—even a suit of clothes. It was all in secret. The boys never found out where those things came from. Don't you think that's fine? It was all Anton's idea. He did the organizing, too, all of it. The rest of us just went along."

"Did he really do that?" Henry asked.

"He did more. Anton didn't give only things. He gave from himself. Of himself. Which is correct?"

"Of himself."

"Examination time, he stayed up nights after nights to help us through," Mr. Osička said. "Examination is a much more serious thing in Czechoslovakia than it is over here. I can tell. I watch my nephews. In Czechoslovakia, now they have doctors, lawyers, scientists whom Anton helped. He would be one of these, too, if his mother could have sent him to the university. Well. The main thing is, he's here. He'll make good. Don't you agree?"

"Yes," Henry said.

Mr. Osička presented his business card, which identified him as part owner of a printing establishment in Queens. Henry understood him to say that the plant was run by Old World craftsmen, and was equipped to meet the museum's most exacting requirements.

"My sainted grandmother once puzzled me by defining a Magyar as a person who enters a revolving door after you but manages somehow to come out in front," Henry said to Gwen that night. "If that's so, and I doubt it, Mr. Osička must be at least part Magyar. Granted that he had a business reason for wanting to butter me up, how much of what he said about Anton would you say was true?"

"I think it was all true," she said.

"The secret club? The examinations?"

"Yes."

"I wonder if Lucy saw all that. God knows I didn't. Did you?"

"Glimmerings of it, every now and then," she said. "Once, he told me about an old blind teacher he used to visit as a boy. But when I remarked how thoughtful that had been of him, he quickly explained that the man's sister served marvelous pastry. I'm not sure he would have thought it necessary to make that explanation to Lucy. I wish I could have helped him more."

"You tried. We all tried, one way or another."

"My way wasn't good enough," Gwen said. "Nothing would satisfy him but the kind of response he could always get from Lucy. He seemed to find a species of fulfillment in reducing her to tears. I guess I'm not a crying woman, Henry. He probably put it down to callousness. Should we have let him go on talking to her?"

"No."

"Money was the only other thing I've known to give him satisfaction. He used to produce his bankbook the way some men take out snapshots of their first-born. Not that he ever opened it for inspection. Do you think he's really going to make a lot of money?"

"No," Henry said. "How could he?"

"I wish we'd been able to help him more," she said.

Now, at Easter, as Henry and Gwen went out to meet Anton in the driveway, Henry remembered her having said that. She no longer feels so protective, he thought. Gwen had never minded before

when someone stopped in just before a meal. She loved unexpected
guests. But now, by turning up in this preposterous robin's-egg-
blue Cadillac, Anton had proved that, at least financially, he could
look after himself. He had parked his car in the dog-leg of the driveway, right alongside the aging Oldsmobile. "Hello, Anton," Henry
said. "Good to see you again. Mark! Ben! Hop out of that car before it runs away with you."

Anton wore a chocolate-colored suit, impeccably pressed. He
smiled with his new white teeth. "Let them play," he said. "Ben,
please give me the small package from the glove place."

That would be his present, in payment for the lunch to come,
Henry thought. But Anton did not hand it over at once, as he used
to. He carried it into the house and put it on the mantelpiece.

Lunch was uneventful. They talked about air travel, the Spanish
language, hotel accommodations. Anton's English had become
somewhat more idiomatic, but his accent remained much the same.
There was no mention of his running off two Christmases before.
They had their coffee around the fireplace, and he took the occasion to present his gift. It was a gold cigarette box, beautifully
made.

"No," Henry said, "it's much too—"

"Is all right. I made it," Anton said.

"Still, I wish you—"

"Is all right. Please. It is very little to give for your affidavit. It
is nothing."

Then, ostensibly as an afterthought, he pulled a couple of wrist-
watches out of his pocket and gave them to the boys.

"No, Anton," Henry said. "You can't do that."

"Please. They are not good watches. In two, three months, they
stop running. Can't be fixed. That is truth. When they stop running, the boys can take them in parts, see what made them go.
Only toys. Is my guarantee they will stop in two, three months."

"Will they really?" Henry asked.

"I guarantee. That is my business. I import those watches."

"From where?" Lucy asked.

"Not from Switzerland." Anton laughed.

Lucy said, "But if they're really no good, who buys them?"

"Americans," he said, and laughed again. "Americans buys anything. Good watches, bad watches—anything. Long time ago, I tell you you are a country of innocent."

"I'm no innocent." She was eighteen and high up on the Dean's List, and she did not wish to be called an innocent. As Anton continued to laugh, she said, "What's so innocent about buying a watch in good faith? That could happen anywhere. I should think you'd want to import decent watches while you were at it." Then she recalled that she was a hostess, and added, "You know, I've never seen you laugh so much before. Your teeth look very nice, much nicer than those metal ones."

"They look like my own teeth before they get knocked out," he said.

"*Knocked* out?" Lucy said.

"At Buchenwald, when they thought I was sabotage. I did not tell you?"

"No," Lucy said. "Not about that."

"It did not hurt so bad after the first three, because the conscious stopped. So I was without mind for hours. It hurt more the next week, when they put cotton in my ear and lighted it with candle." He smiled at her.

"You never told me that, either," she said.

Henry knew that voice. As a child of five, she had broken her thumb, and the way Henry learned of it, she had walked into his study just after her fall and said, in that same tight voice, "Look, Dad, there's something wrong with my finger."

Anton's laugh was hearty and resonant. "See?" he said. "Little red mark here? Some of it under the hair. That was very painful, more worse than the teeth. I tried to make the conscious stop and I could not. I thought of such many funny things. Someday I will tell, if your father will let. I think is all right, Henry, yes? Lucy is big college girl now. No innocent, she says. Lucy is smart now—smart Yankee. I sell undecent watches to the smart, decent Yankees, like Lucy, and they sell them at higher price to the stupids in Peru, Nicaragua. Everybody happy."

"I didn't mean to hurt your feelings about the watches," Lucy began. Her voice had not changed.

Abruptly, Gwen began to clear the dishes. She made Lucy help her. The boys had gone off with their watches. Anton smiled again.

He *is* happy, Henry thought; for the moment, he *is* happy, the con-
queror left in possession of the field. I've got to get him out of this
house, away from Lucy. "I'm going to take a walk," he said. "Want
to come along?"

"Yes," said Anton. "Is nice out."

The chocolate suit would not have stood up in the woods, so
Henry took him out on the road. They turned north. Anton said
he had never been that way before. Henry said nothing. They had
walked about half a mile when Anton stopped to look at a house.

"Who lives there?" he asked.

"Old lady. Miss Holbrook. Her father made hairpins."

"Now, that is a house. Big. Stone. That is what you should build."

"I like mine."

"You are angry," Anton said. "You are angry because I tell bad
things to Lucy. You wish to keep her still living in fairyland. You
wish to keep her sweet young lady—innocent. But you make mistake. I do not do the harm to her. You do the harm. You do the bad
harm to Lucy."

"What bad harm have I done Lucy?"

"You try to keep her sweet young lady, very high. Must not sell
undecent watches to nice American people. Is all right to know the
life, but only from the books. From museums. Do not listen to the
crazy man tell truth."

"Put it any way you like," said Henry. "I've asked you twice before not to talk to her about the camps, and now I'm asking you
once more."

"I talk to anybody about anything I want."

"Not to her, you don't."

They turned to face each other.

"You damn fool," said Anton. "You know what happened in my
country to the sweet young ladies? When the Russians come, the
smart girls know what to do. They cut their hair crooked. They dirty
up their face. They go to bed, put typhus sign on door. Not the
sweet young ladies. They wait. They put hands in their sweet
young lap and wait. Pretty soon—"

"Shut up now," Henry said. He took hold of the chocolate lapels
and dug his knuckles into his cousin's chest. "Shut up!" he said
again. And he thought, Let him hit me first, and then . . . But Anton

made no move. Impassive, he waited until Henry let go of the lapels. Then he turned and, at his normal pace, walked back toward the house.

He was out of sight around the bend of the road before Henry started back, too. Henry tried hard to imagine what would be said or done when he got home. He could not. By the time he reached the next-door driveway, all his anger was gone. He could not imagine what Gwen would say, or Lucy. He wondered what to do about the gold cigarette box. At the foot of his own driveway, he was nearly struck by the blue Cadillac as it made a sharp turn south and bolted down the road to New York.

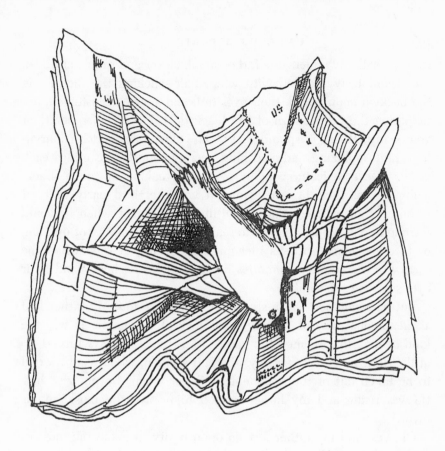

THE DOVE BRINGS PEACE

RICHARD HAGOPIAN

Dai was the man who incurred the deep wrath and maledictions of my father by presenting him with a dead dove. It wasn't so much the dove, as such, that caused my father to suck deeply upon his Turkish cigarettes and exhale smoky pronouncements upon old Dai, the friend of his childhood and his bosom companion through numberless cigarettes, black coffee, and backgammon, which spelled Armenian male old age; it was the circumstances under which it was given.

Since I was old enough to pronounce my first guttural, I can remember the two men—my father small, clever and quick, and Dai, broad and heavy-headed with white hair—clicking the dice along the backgammon board, their eyes dull and smoke-accustomed, anticipating the proper turn of the black dots. I can remember their voices, my father's crisp and witty, Dai's slow and ponderous, arguing, philosophizing, admonishing, ceremoniously insulting each other, with a delicate economy of words, making up again. Backgammon was their favorite game. It was the third party that sat in on all their conversations, awaiting the moment when it would intrude to patch up a quarrel, to seal further a unanimity of opinion, or to offer solace with its meaningless clicking of dice when the sorrow of old-country memories made their hearts heavy and their eyes smart to the smoke.

But backgammon was a sly source of trouble too. My father had a phenomenal way of sustaining his luck at this game. It was the kind of luck that seemed too good to be true. It always turned up at the right time; it was always there, it seemed, when wind needed to be taken out of the opponent's sails, or when the pitch of battle was rising and my father wished to resolve the music in his favor.

Oh, yes, and my father lost no opportunity to make the most of such occasions. The coup was always punctuated with a happy, bland command: "Yeksapert"—that was my mother—"isn't it time for some more coffee? Ach, it is going to be a cold winter this year. Coal will be high." Or to me: "Levon, take your hands out of your pockets; are you cold?"

Dai pondered hard over the board. He glowered at my father, then at me, then at the dice. At this point my mother called, her voice too well-modulated to seem from a distinctly other world: "Levon, go to the store," or "Levon, why don't you bring school books home no more?" or "Levon, the smoky room is not healthy for young lungs."

I left reluctantly, watching the board to see what was happening. No sooner had I left than as though timed by the closing of the portieres, Dai sighed a profound sigh and commenced to utter things in smoldering Armenian—heavy things. When the words finally came out, they were something like this:

"We are not children, you know! We are not playing like bar-

barian Turks, where we have to fight and draw blood at every move!"

"What have I done to deserve this? What words come out of your mouth, my dearest friend?"

This was my father; I was proud of him. He was confused by Dai's words, he was innocent, he was tormented by the words of his best friend. He was being sorry for his partner. Ach, my merciful father!

But old Dai usually had more to say. He started slowly, but when he finished he had covered worlds.

"When we play, we play. We do not flaunt our advantage in the other's face."

"I . . . ?" How incredulous my father's voice sounded!

"What need had we for coffee . . . didn't we just finish? 'It will be a cold winter, coal will be high!' What were you trying to do, impress the boy?"

"Enough, enough." My father's voice was colored with more than a tinge of righteous indignation at this point. "We *are* being children now; we are losing our perspective on things. We have come too far in this world, we have experienced too many of the same tortures at the hands of our mutual enemy to be torn apart now by a mere game. Who cares who wins! Is it not all a game? There is too much sorrow in life already without our adding more to it." Then in a tone that subtly concealed all the qualities of resignation, contempt, utter world-weariness and challenge, he said, "I shall clear the board. Let us leave it to the dust. Better still, my wife will burn it in the morning." But before his hesitant hand could clear the board, Dai caught it mid-air with a word:

"Orator! What has world-suffering to do with a game? What has our friendship to do with a pair of dice? Your *luck* is always an occasion for self-flattery."

"Luck! Ach, Dai, haven't you learned yet that there is little matter of skill involved?"

"Skill! Yes, I know the kind of skill you possess. That is why at the club they don't trust the dice in your hands and make you throw them from a coffee cup. Because of your skill!"

I did not have to see in order to know that the game was over. Dai would be near the window now, looking over the back yard.

My father, crestfallen and insulted, uttering semifinal words through his cigarette.

"*Cheat, liar* . . . so that is what they say about me. All right, Dai, you win. It is enough that the world should have deprived me of a family and country that now you must take from me my good name. Take it, I give it to you." Then near tears: "You have what the Turks could not carve out of us with the knife. You have it, it is in your keeping now, my dearest friend. Take it; take it to the club, put it in a coffee cup, paint my name on it, place it on the tavli table. Let all the friends of my boyhood and suffering point to it. Let them laugh and cry, '*Skill!* His skill has robbed him of what the Turks couldn't get.'" After a dramatic pause my father rose and commenced to clear the board. Dai made the first conversational move:

"I wish for my coat. I don't know where it is. I wish for my coat, then I can go home."

My father (as though talking to the wall) said, "He knows my wife put it away when he came in. He can ask her for it."

"Is it proper that an outsider should command another's wife? Is she my servant? No. If you would please supply my coat I would depart. It is late. My wife and family will be expecting me. I would go without it, but I am young no more. It is cold outside. It is going to be a hard winter."

"*A cold and hard winter!*" My father had not let slip his chance to make the thrust. "Ha, ha, who is trying to impress the boy now? Pretty soon he will be asking for fresh coffee. Wait and see."

At this point my mother bustled by me, bringing in fresh coffee and sugar cakes. Seeing me she scolded:

"What are you doing here? Didn't I tell you to take the dog out for a walk?"

We both had been guilty of the same crime—eavesdropping—but we were happy and contented to go about our jobs, when friendly voices behind the portieres suggested that the crisis had been passed.

Araxy, Dai's little daughter with the deep-colored eyes, knocked on our door about dusk. It was no news to her that her father was at our house, but it gave me something to say when I opened the door.

"Your father's here, Raxy. Do you want to play until they finish the game?"

My mother loved Araxy. She loved to kiss her deep-colored eyes and say, "Some day you will be my daughter."

I loved this time of day best of all. Raxy always came a half hour early so that we could play. Best of all we loved to play bakeshop. She was the doughmaker and I was cook. My mother gave us a slice of soft bread from the pantry. With a little water Raxy molded it into a soft ball. Her clean little hands busily rolled out the dough. Then, after anxiously watching her, my turn came. I cut the dough into squares or circles with the tin covers of cans; then, leaving the dough in the covers, we tucked raisins in the middle or along the edges. After this we put our handiwork on the stove to toast. When the day's cooking was done we played store—I sold and she bought, or she sold and I bought. When we had spent our make-believe money, we ate our wares together, cleaned up the store and waited for my mother to call old Dai.

Everyone was happy at parting time, and again on the next night, the next, and the next.

One day, when Raxy and I had planned to play together after school, she did not come. She told me the next day that her mother had made her stay home to help with the packing.

"What packing?" I asked.

"We are moving," she replied sorrowfully.

"Where, Rax, why?"

"We must go. We are taking the pigeons and everything in boxes. We are going away in a truck to where my sister Vartui lives."

Her deep-colored eyes were dark and sad.

"Then we can't play baker any more!"

But before I could say anything more she commenced to sob and ran away.

Dai did not come to our house for the next three days, so Araxy did not come over after him at dusk. My father acted crosser than ever, and my mother, who loved to sing from time to time, was silent and made an effort to spare her conversations with my father.

I nursed my own feelings by keeping still and out of the way.

My father never left the house, not even to go into the garden. My mother stayed at home most of the time, too.

"Dikran," she occasionally scolded, "why don't you go to the club and play tavli with your friends? I will give you the carfare."

But my father merely sat hunched on the sofa and drew smoke deep into his lungs. He did not go to the club.

It was late in the evening of the fourth day since Dai's last visit when someone knocked timidly on our door. My father looked up excitedly and with an effort sucked on his cigarette. I couldn't move.

"Levon, answer the door," called my mother. When I opened it, it was just whom I had expected—Raxy. But this time I did not say, "Your father's here, Rax," nor did she ask after him, nor did she enter, even after my mother asked her to. In her hand she held a little bundle. She stood on the threshold and offered it to my mother. She spoke haltingly, her deep-colored eyes darker and sadder.

"Papa sends it to Baron Dikran. Good-bye." She turned and fled down the stairs. My mother called after her, but she did not answer or come back. My father didn't even look up.

"What has happened?" my mother asked. "Have you children fought? Levon, answer me."

I told my mother we hadn't fought.

"Then what is wrong with the poor child?" she asked. "This bundle is for you, Dikran. Dai sent it. I'll open it. Do you think they are having trouble at their house?"

By this time my mother had opened the newspaper bundle. In her hands she held a small dead dove.

"Look, Dikran, look what Dai has sent you. Is it a joke?"

No one spoke. Then my mother turned to me. "Ach, Levon, you are too quiet to be innocent. When you act as though the cat has eaten your tongue I know something is wrong. Have you fought with little Araxy and brought shame to our name? Is this a dove of peace? Answer me?"

I told my mother that we had not fought. I told her about the things Raxy had told me, how they had been packing to move away to her sister Vartui's house.

My father looked up at my words. Then he spoke slowly as he

swallowed blue smoke. "Ach, Dai, shameless man . . . he has kept secrets from me."

"But why are they moving?" asked my mother. "Ach, I know," she went on, "it is their landlord, he has raised the rent again. He should be ashamed during these times. He did not want them to keep pigeons on the back porch either. They are going to a strange city to live with a daughter who has married a stranger. Ach, Dikran, we must feel sad for them."

But my father answered with contempt. "No good-bye. Shame upon your white hairs, Dai. Who wants a dove brought by a child! It is an insult to me. We have been friends all our lives. He is going to move away now—maybe he has gone. No good-bye!"

"Maybe he was too sad to say good-bye. . . . That is why he sent the dove with the child. He is an old man, maybe he was ashamed he would cry if he came and said good-bye."

"Poof—old man! Nothing could make him ashamed. He is stubborn. He likes to make me suffer. You are a woman, you cannot understand." Then he muttered a few words in Turkish, the forbidden language, so that I wouldn't understand, but my mother checked him with a few of her own. Then both looked at me self-consciously and all talking stopped.

For many days a calm of mourning descended upon our house. My father ate a bite with us—that was all—and settled in his habitual posture on the sadir, the low homemade couch, legs crossed under him, his shoulders hunched and his head drooped; in his mouth a cigarette. The evenings for me became lonesome, too. Disappointment came every day at dusk. I no longer played games. I felt more grown-up now and a little embarrassed at the thought of baking bread, the raisins, can covers and playing store.

After supper I sat in the kitchen and watched my mother put the supper things away. I noticed that she had commenced to sing at her work again. Each night her voice seemed to grow louder and louder. One night when she was singing full force, my father called out in anger:

"What is the cause of all this joy, woman? One would think there was a wedding around here. You have sung enough. Hush!"

My mother resented this sudden explosion. My father obviously had missed the point of her singing. She answered back angrily:

"If I don't make some happy sounds, who will? I am sick of watching you sulk. Like a death's-head you sit all day and night. And cigarettes! Pretty soon smoke is going to come out of your ears. Ach, it was not like this in my father's house. Always singing, always dancing, always laughter, always . . ."

". . . fight."

"Fight! I will be patient. For a little happiness he insults. Why was I singing? Because my heart was happy, because I feel young again after seeing my white hairs in the looking glass? For you, for you, dumb man; for our home, for our boy." Then pointing to me she lamented, "Look at him. For days nothing has come out of his mouth but *yes* and *no*. He is beginning to look like you. My God! For shame, his shoulders are bending. All he does is sit and look dead. Give him a cigarette, you are his father. That is all he needs. He has looked at you so long that he is an old man before his time."

Now my mother was crying. Poor woman, we had misunderstood her singing. Both my father and I had been so deeply concerned with our own unhappiness that we had forgotten my mother's. Now we had broken her song. Now she was crying. Instinctively I straightened my shoulders and tried to caress her. But she only wept louder and spoke of the undertaker who would very shortly carry her away to bury her next to her mother in an old-country grave.

Early the next morning my father ventured away from the sadir and silently commenced to putter about the kitchen. My mother, long-faced with yesterday's grief, made an effort to remain silent; but after my father had succeeded in knocking down a few pots and pans, she could not refrain from talking.

"He has regained his appetite by breaking my heart. There are stuffed grape leaves in the icebox if you are hungry. Don't put your awkward hands where they don't belong."

My father continued to search, oblivious to her remarks.

My mother's curiosity was piqued now. Finally she called out, "The dead has come to life. What is it looking for?"

Without raising his head, my father mumbled, "The dove."

"Dove? What dove? Is this a poultry house?"

"Dai's dove," said my father tersely. "He sent it to me with little Araxy."

"Aha, so that is it? I threw it away."

For a moment longer my father continued to search, my mother's words not having registered. But when he realized what she had said, he was angry. He looked up and made a terrible face.

"You threw it away? What business was it of yours to tamper with my gift!"

"You did not seem to want it. You said it had been sent to make you suffer."

"Enough! Never mind what I said. You are a woman, you should have kept your place. Dai made a special gift to me. There must have been a reason for it."

"A reason! To make you suffer more?"

"Don't torture me. I will beat you." My father was very angry now. He had taken off his slipper and was brandishing it about in the air, his eyes moist and his lips trembling. My mother, sensing danger, withdrew into her shell and remained silent.

The fury of this sudden outbreak subsided as suddenly as it had come; then shamefaced, his shoulders drooping lower than ever, my father retired once more to his sadir.

"I have had bad dreams. No one can understand."

There he remained. He spoke no word, nor did he eat, nor did he move, except mechanically to put a cigarette in his smoke-weary mouth, light it and reluctantly blow out the flame on the match.

My sorrow for the loss of Araxy was forgotten for the time being. I was frightened by this new behavior on the part of my father. Even my mother looked hopeless now. She had failed to bring sunshine to our home with her singing. Her annoyance with my father for his sudden reaction toward her singing, and his threat to beat her, melted with the morning and from time to time she approached the portieres and cautiously peeked in to see if the old man had varied his position any. I believe she sensed the same kind of fear I did.

"We must mind our own affairs. Men become like this from time to time," she cautioned me in whispers. "We must let him alone.

He was like this once when news came that his sister had been massacred in the old country." Then kissing me, she bade me run off to school and not to worry too much so that I might stay young and not become an old man before my time.

I did not come home for lunch that day, sensing a kind of sad danger at home. When I did return, it was dusk. As I neared our house I noticed that no lights were burning inside. I wondered if my people were away. Then, remembering how my father was, I became frightened and ran madly to the front door. I clambered up the stairs, two at a time, to our floor. But before I could reach out and turn the door knob I was checked by a curious sound coming from within. It sounded like a little boy weeping. Above this I could hear my mother's comforting voice reassuring some-one in soft Armenian. Slowly I opened the door and looked in. The room was dark. I tiptoed over to the portieres. The street-lamps offered enough light for me to see the figures of my father and mother. My father was huddled on the sadir, his head buried in his hands. By him sat my mother, her arm around him.

"No, Dikran," she was saying, "it is not healthy that you should break your heart this way. Come, you have eaten nothing all day. I will make some soup for you, the kind you love, madzoun abour. Come."

But the old man did not look up. He merely responded with hoarse lamentations.

"Ach, Dai, why was I so blind? It is too late, too late. I should have come to you and kissed your hands. I should have wept for you in your loneliness. See, Dai, my old eyes are raining bitter tears for you."

My mother's efforts to comfort him were futile. He went on, his voice old and broken:

"A dove brought to me by a little girl. What more could you have done, what else did you have to offer? Like Noah you sent it to a place of safety—your Ararat—your refuge. Ach, Dai, I dreamed the truth, but I dreamed too, too late."

Gradually his voice died away and only his heavy breathing remained to pulsate faintly in the darkness.

My father was crying and I felt ashamed for having seen him. I turned away and sat down in a far corner of the kitchen.

About an hour later my mother came out.

"Levon, Levon," she called in a voice that did not expect an answer, but was calling to reassure itself in its aloneness. "Levon, why have I forgotten about you?"

"I am here," I whispered. I dared not talk too loud, my throat hurt so.

"Oh, my sweetest," she cried and drew me to her bosom. I clung to her while she stroked my hair.

"Dai is dead," she said. "We heard it this afternoon from Garabed." I clung closer and thought of Araxy; but I didn't dare ask about her, my throat was near bursting.

"Your father's heart is broken," she went on. "I have failed to lessen his sorrow. It is bad for an old man to cry. I don't know what to do, where to go. I must make food for you." Then she got up on a chair and lighted the light.

Once when she looked up at me in the light she saw me trying to hide my tears and, coming to me, she kissed me and told me not to cry.

"We will go and see their family soon. You must not cry. It is different with your father. You must not cry, you will become old before your time."

With the passing of Dai passed my remaining hope of ever seeing Raxy again. Although my mother tried to comfort me from time to time by telling me we would visit Dai's family, I knew she didn't really mean it. I knew we couldn't, because their new home was so far away, and because seeing Dai's family—the little girl who brought the dove—would only further break my father's heart.

So the winter months went on. In our house the note of sadness lingered. Occasionally it let up a bit when my mother tried to sing a few strains from the heroic *Vartan* ballad, or *Alexan Vorti*, the deer boy. But her singing fell on deaf ears. The thrilling account of Vartan's glory, the heart-rending pathos of the Alexan legend, no longer thrilled me. They were completely lost to my father. Gradually sorrow robbed my mother's throat of the last remnants of sound and she became quiet too—quiet like a death's-head.

Things went on this way for a long time. In the mornings I

went off to school, leaving my father hunched on the sadir, my mother before the sink, or on her knees cleaning the floor. At dusk I would return and find them very much the same as when I had left, my father on the sadir, my mother occupied with some menial task.

One Sunday afternoon after church my mother and I were eating in the kitchen. My father was in the other room smoking. He said he wasn't hungry. In the midst of our meal my mother leaned toward me and with a half-happy smile she whispered, "Your father looks brighter today. When you were in Sunday school he took a little walk. A little later, after you have eaten, go in and talk to him; it will cheer him up more." Then she sighed. "Perhaps there is hope for our house yet." She made the sign of the cross on her features and breast and returned to her meal. I hurried through the rest of my food, then, taking courage from my mother's new smile, I passed through the portieres into my father's room.

He was dusting something when I came in. It was the backgammon board. This was the first I had seen of it since . . . When he finally was aware of my presence he looked up quickly, thrusting the board behind him.

"Ah, it is you," he ventured.

"Hello, Papa, are you better?" I asked.

"Ach, little Levon, no man is better. As long as the world is what it is we are all getting worse. Come here, my boy, let me hold you." Then drawing me to him, he placed his arm around me and kissed my eyes. "What a long time it has been since I have loved you, my little boy. But you are a big boy now, Levon."

"Is everything all right now?" I asked. "Maman . . . we have worried about you. Shall I call Maman?"

"No, no, Levon, light of my eyes, not yet. I want to talk to you a little while. Sit here." He motioned for me to sit with him on the sadir. I crossed my legs under me and felt comfortably at home near my father.

"No sorrow can last forever," he went on. "Like our forefathers, we must suffer and be chained; but we must be strong and free again. You are a boy . . . it is different. You were born here. But you have our blood in you, so you must learn to suffer too. Some day you will have friends, and these friends will be your worlds. You will fight in them, find suffering in them; you will laugh and be happy in them; you will be for once contented, your heart and soul at rest in them. You will see your childhood in their eyes when they laugh. You will see the beautiful mountains and lakes of your country in their sad smiles. And when they are angry you will see your old age. You will learn to delight in argument, in wit, cigarettes . . . tavli . . . in being sad, in remembering old things.

"Sometimes these worlds crack, they vanish. They become memories, they die. Then a man needs courage. Sometimes we are weak; we become petty, we do not understand. In our distress we fail to remember the comfort of that God our fathers knew." Then looking at me long and with deep sadness, he said with a sigh, "It is getting toward the close of winter for me. You are the spring. You must learn to be wise and faithful to the friends you will know and love."

I understood my father. I put my arms around his wrinkled neck and comforted him with the love and understanding which had sprung up in my heart through the wisdom of his words. At this point my mother bustled into the room, bearing a tray filled with sugar cakes and small cups of Armenian coffee. Her mouth was twisted into a comical curve by the alternate emotions of her present happiness and the residue of past sorrow. Placing the tray before my father, she burst into tears of exaltation.

"Our happy home is preserved," she wept. "Maybe my song will come back again."

When quiet had come again and our emotions were near normal once more, we sipped heavy, black coffee and ate the little cakes baked by my mother. My father smoked almost with abandon. Even my mother puffed on a cigarette. And we talked of many things: people, the price of food, our garden, and my mother's relatives. When this had gone on for some time my mother rose, saying, "It is time for me to put on the soup." Then with a prodding look in my direction, "Levon, play a game of tavli with your father while I am making dinner."

An awkward moment ensued after she had left. Then, as though obligated by my mother's suggestion, my father reluctantly produced the backgammon board. Reluctantly he opened it and properly distributed the blacks and reds. Then, looking up, he sighed and asked, "Do you know how?"

"Yes," I answered eagerly, "but not very well. But I used to watch all the time when you and . . . I'll learn to play better, then we can play together every night, ha, Papa?"

"All right, my child. You are a good boy, an innocent little boy." For a moment he fingered the dice. "Shall I throw first?" he asked.

"Yes, yes," I answered, thrilled.

But he held the dice; he did not throw them. Then he shook them thoughtfully, and his eyes lighted up for a moment. "I will beat you," he said. But still he did not throw. Then thoughtfully he placed the dice upon the board, and lighting a cigarette, he drew upon it deeply and examined his fingers. Then he called to my mother. "Yeksapert, an empty coffee cup, please." He fingered the dice again, waiting for my mother to bring in the cup so that he could throw from it. He looked at me and smiled. "Maybe you will have a little better chance that way."

EVERY OTHER THURSDAY

EDNA FERBER

From the moment she thrust a swift and practiced arm from beneath the bedclothes to choke the seven-o'clock alarm, Helmi was suffused with the thought that it was Thursday. Not merely Thursday, but *Thursday*. Not only that: it was Every Other Thursday. And Every Other Thursday was Helmi's day out.

She lay there, snug, under the welter of gray blankets, savoring the delicious thought. Her mind leaped at one bound over the dull hours that intervened between 7 A.M. and 2 P.M. From two on and on the day lay before her, sparkling, golden, new-minted, to spend as she liked. She had it planned, down to the ultimate second.

A pioneer April fly buzzed drowsily at her tightly closed bedroom window. Here in America people slept with their windows wide open, but Helmi knew better than that. The night air is poisonous, as anyone can tell you. Helmi never opened her windows until the really hot June nights set in—sometimes not even then. Habit is strong; and there had been no steam heat in the Finland farmhouse of her girlhood, and Finnish nights are cold.

Next Sunday was Easter. At Eastertime, one year ago, she had had no new hat, no new dress, no new coat, no new slippers like the rest of New York. Last Easter she had been thankful just to be here. Lonely and homesick, but thankful. This Easter would be different. This very afternoon would find her on One Hundred and Twenty-fifth Street, East, which is New York's uptown Finland. There she would buy a blue dress and a bright-blue silk hat such as Lempi Parta had worn at the Finnish Progressive Society hall last week; and pale-tan silk stockings, and slippers with bows.

For more than a year a great slice of her wages had gone to pay back her brother, Abel Seppala, and her brother's wife, Anni, for the money they had sent her to buy her passage over—her two passages over. Those terrible two passages, the first unsuccessful, so that she had seen New York's skyline approach and recede; the second dramatically successful. She could laugh now when she thought of that successful second landing. They had fooled them, all right, that time. It had cost one hundred and twenty-five dollars the first time, and one hundred and fifty to bribe the steamship steward the second time. Helmi had been almost a year and a half paying back that money to Abel and Anni.

This afternoon she would go to Anni's in Brooklyn, as usual. But not to stay. From there she would take the subway quickly to One Hundred and Twenty-fifth Street. She had so many things to do. So many lovely things. She ought to start before two, or how could she do all these things that must be done? That must be done today because it would be two weeks before Every Other Thursday came again. Perhaps she would get off at half-past one, or even one, if the work was finished. . . .

The sound of water rushing into the tub in the bathroom off Their Bedroom. Mr. Mawson! He had to have his breakfast at twenty minutes to eight, sharp. It was quarter-past seven! Helmi leaped out of bed, flung off her sturdy cotton nightgown, dived into the knitted union suit, the faded stockings with a run down the seam of one—discarded of Miss Zhoolie—the old sateen petticoat, the blue gingham work dress. Into the stuffy little bathroom off her bedroom. A dab at her face, a splash with her hands, a hasty running of the broken comb through her bobbed pale-yellow hair (that bob had been the first step in her Americanization). Helmi always combed her hair after she was fully dressed. It was interesting to hear Mrs. James G. Mawson on that subject, among others.

Out to the kitchen. Bang! The coffeepot. Rattle! The spoon. Slam! The icebox door. Clash! The silver. Clatter! The china. Whiff-woof! The swinging door. Three breakfasts to get at three different times, and the front room to be tidied in between.

Mr. Mawson had his breakfast in the dining room at twenty minutes to eight. James G. Mawson (the Mawson Optical Company) was a silent, grayish, neat man, behind glasses with special lenses. His breakfast never varied. Half a grapefruit or a glass of orange juice. Two four-minute eggs. Two pieces of whole-wheat bread, toasted. A cup of coffee. Two lumps of sugar. Plenty of cream. Out of the house at five minutes to eight.

In March he had essayed to diet. Mrs. Mawson had said he was getting paunchy, and decreed but one piece of toast, thinly buttered; black coffee with no sugar; one egg. For two mornings he had obediently sipped his coffee, though with a wry face, and had left half of it, a sable pool of bitterness, in his cup. Mrs. Mawson never breakfasted with him. The third morning he broke an oblong of sugar in half and slipped the piece into his coffee. The fourth he just tinged the blackness with one small splash of cream. The fifth Helmi brought him two pieces of toast. He ate them both. The sixth she prepared two eggs as usual, placed the sugar and cream at his hand, and left the room.

These men in America! These husbands! Poor, spineless things, treated like little boys by their wives and daughters. In Finland it was different. The women were independent, yes, like the men. But the men were not bossed by the women. These two women, they ran him. Do this, do that, go here, go there, I want thus, I want so. He hardly ever rebelled. Sometimes, but not often. Usually he just looked at them in silence, and a little line would come into his forehead. Between Helmi, the Finnish maidservant, and Mr. James G. Mawson of the Mawson Optical Company, there existed an unspoken and unsuspected sympathy and understanding. Helmi spoke rarely. She was an almost inspired cook.

Miss Zhoolie always dashed into the dining room just before nine, in a rush, and gulped her orange juice standing, in hat and coat. Mrs. Mawson's voice would be heard from her bedroom. "Zhoolie, you eat something hot before you go out."

"I can't. I've got a nine o'clock. I'm late now."

"I don't care how late you are. . . . Then get up ten minutes earlier. . . . Then don't stay out until one. . . . If it's only a cup of hot coffee. . . ." But Miss Zhoolie had gone to her class at Barnard.

The Mawsons lived in Eighty-sixth Street, West. Those lessons to which Miss Zhoolie dashed each weekday morning were in One Hundred and Sixteenth Street, Helmi knew. Evidently, in this country it made no difference if you reached these classes on time or not.

Mrs. Mawson's tray you brought to her bed every morning at nine, after the others had gone. It was quite a hearty breakfast, considering that Mrs. Mawson Wasn't Strong. She could not rise for breakfast because this brought on one of her headaches. She always spoke of these afflictions in the possessive. One of my headaches. It was as though she cherished them.

It was not hard, once you had got the hang of it. A year ago she could never have done it, but Helmi learned quickly. She had had to work much harder than this on the farm in Finland; had worked in the fields, not only from dawn to dark but far into the bright Northern summer nights. Still, this was hard in a different way. Here they were always changing things, doing things differently after you had learned to do them in one way. In Finland the work had been set, inevitable. Now the cabbages, now the rye, now the potatoes, now the corn, now the oats. The horses the cows the sheep the pigs. But here you never knew. With Mr. Mawson you knew. But not with Her. And not with Miss Zhoolie. Often, after they had told her to do a thing one way and she had learned it that way, they changed their minds and told her to do it another. But Helmi went ahead and did it in the original way, disregarding them. Mrs. Mawson said she didn't understand her.

"I must say I don't understand that girl. Really she's a closed book to me. You can't be friendly with her. She just looks at you. Her face is like a joss-house idol. I honestly think she could come in and find us all murdered and weltering in our blood and she wouldn't turn a hair—especially if it happened to be her Thursday."

The conversation was between Mrs. Mawson and her nineteen-year-old daughter, Zhoolie. Zhoolie had been christened Julia, after the departed distaff grandmamma. This, in her fourteenth year, she had Frenchified to Julie, which she insisted on pronouncing as though it were spelled with a *Zh* and a double *o*. It must even be stated that she frequently even signed herself thus, especially in the tenderer branches of her Barnard educational career.

James G. Mawson spoke up unexpectedly, as he sometimes did when they thought he had not been listening.

"Mighty good girl just the same," he said. "Knows her business and minds it."

"Helmi's a teep," said Zhoolie.

"A what?" inquired James G. Mawson, over the top of his newspaper.

"A teep."

"Spell it."

"T-y-p-e, teep. That's French."

"Well, you," retorted Mr. Mawson, "make me seek. S-i-c-k, seek. That's English."

Sometimes Zhoolie was driven to referring to Helmi as that Hunky. This usually when Helmi had succeeded in making an important (to Zhoolie) telephone message more than usually unsolvable. Her thick tongue and unaccustomed ear made a sorry business of these communications. "W'at? . . . Yeh, iss. . . . Who? . . . Yeh. . . . She ain't here. . . . Wait, I write. . . ."

Mrs. Mawson on her return home, or Zhoolie, would find a scrawl to the effect that someone named U-J-B-D-M had telephoned, and had asked her to call up as soon as she got in. Helmi's own telephone communications were as mysterious as they were private, being carried on in a guttural flood of Finnish, to Mrs. Mawson's bafflement. She always had a helpless feeling that she was being talked about.

Helmi would never make a modish-looking maid. Hers was a trim enough figure, in a broad-hipped ample-bosomed wide-shouldered peasant sort of way. But you always felt that her neat afternoon uniform of black and white confined her against her will, and that someday she would rend these garments from her in a furious burst of Nordic freedom. This irked Mrs. Mawson and Zhoolie.

"Still, if you have only one maid, what can you do? Of course"— hastily—"the Woman comes in to clean one day a week, and the Washwoman. But Zhoolie has so many friends. Half the time Helmi isn't presentable when people come to the door. And her room!" Mrs. Mawson would then gather the subject into a neat bundle and tie it with the sinister generality that they were all alike.

Helmi's bedroom undeniably was not the most exquisitely kept of bowers. Perhaps, after daily scouring, dusting, mopping, and wiping the rest of the Mawson apartment, there was a certain wholesome and nicely balanced defiance shown in the slightly musty disorder of her own private chamber. After all, your chef develops a personal indifference toward food; and walking is no treat for a mail carrier.

Mrs. Mawson had a way of investigating this room on Helmi's Thursday out. This she excused on the ground of housewifeliness. The room was always the same. On the lower shelf of her table reposed last summer's white shoes. There they had been throughout the winter. On her dresser a little mound of spilled talcum, a torn hair net; photographs of bridal couples in cataleptic attitudes, and family groups as stiff as woodcuts; a Sunday rotogravure picture of a motion-picture actress and an actor. Stuck to the sides of the dresser mirror were colored picture postcards that caused both Mrs. Mawson and Zhoolie some merriment. These were, they thought, pictures such as a six-year-old child would cherish. Done in crude greens and reds and pinks, they depicted an old man, white-bearded, got up like a Santa Claus in a pine forest; a white-robed princess-looking female floating on a wave, with stars and sunbursts shooting all about her; a brown-bearded man hammering at a forge like the Village Blacksmith. At the top of these pictures was printed the word *Kalevala*. Underneath, in finer print, unpronounceable words like Wainamoinen and Ilmatar and Joukahaimen.

"Some Finn fairy tale, don't you think?" Zhoolie said. "Poor thing. I'd like to take her up to school for a mental test. Outside her cooking and housework I'll bet she'd turn in an I.Q. of a child of eight."

Certainly Mrs. Mawson and Zhoolie never knew that the *Kalevala* is the national epic of Finland—the *Paradise Lost*, the Shakespeare of that Northern country; and that its rhythms, well known to Helmi and studied by her in her girlhood at the excellent Finnish country school, had been borrowed and stolen and copied by many a versifier included in Zhoolie's English course at Barnard. Zhoolie would have been startled if she could have translated the cadences of the thumbed and greasy volume that lay on the table shelf beside Helmi's last-summer shoes.

> *On his back he bound his quiver,*
> *And his new bow on his shoulder,*
> *In his hands his pole grasped firmly,*
> *On the left shoe glided forward,*
> *And pushed onward with the right one,*
> *And he spoke the words which follow . . .*

"My goodness, why doesn't she open her windows! And look at her lovely bedspread that I took such—why do they always sit on the edge of the bed and never on a chair! And just see this bathroom. I am simply going to tell her that she must bathe oftener than . . . Oh, they're all alike!"

Always capable and energetic in a slapdash, lunging kind of way, Helmi, on this particular Thursday in April, was a tornado. There loomed ahead of her the regular Thursday routine which, on Every Other Thursday, was a rite. The kitchen linoleum must be made spotless. There was some American superstition about the sink faucets being left shining on Thursdays out. On the other hand, it was understood that lunch—if any—was to be most sketchy on Every Other Thursday; that Mrs. Mawson would go out for this meal, if possible. Zhoolie never lunched at home on weekdays. Helmi was free to go when her work was finished.

These things had come to be taken for granted, tacitly. There was little conversation between mistress and maid. Helmi practiced the verbal economy of her race. She spoke rarely, and then in monosyllables: "Yeh, iss. . . . I bake a cake wiss nuts. . . . What you want for eat? . . ." The iceman, the butcher boy, the grocer, the janitor, the service-elevator boy, in person or at the telephone, got short shrift from Helmi in any case. On Thursdays she was curt to the point of insult. Strangely enough—or perhaps not so strangely—this indifference to their advances gave Helmi a certain desirability in their eyes. When occasion presented itself they attempted to woo her in the patois of their kind.

"Say, you're a sketch. You hate the men, don't you? I bet the guy gets you'll have a right to wear a umpire's mask, all right. Listen, baby, don't you never go nowheres? How about a movie? Don't you dance or nothing?"

Did she dance? Did she dance! For what else did she live! To what other purpose was Every Other Thursday planned! Ask the girls and boys at the Finnish Progressive Society hall in One Hundred and Twenty-sixth Street. Especially (alas!) the girls, the girls who swarmed there on a Thursday night with their half dollar clutched tight in their big, capable palms. You went to those dances alone. If you were popular you danced with the boys. Otherwise you danced with the girls. By half-past eight the big dance hall on the top floor was comfortably filled. By half-past nine it was crowded. By half-past ten it was packed. The heavy-handed band boomed and pounded out the fox trot, the waltz, the German polka. Did she dance? Did she dance! These American boys were fools.

This Thursday night she would dance in her new blue dress to be purchased on One Hundred and Twenty-fifth Street. In her new silk stockings and her new kid slippers. And then perhaps Vaino Djerf would dance with her. Helmi danced very well indeed. She knew that. She had been the best dancer in her district in the old country. She had noted how Vaino watched her as she danced at the hall on Thursday nights.

But her clothes! It was not for such as Vaino to dance with her. Vaino, of all the Finnish chauffeurs, drove the finest car. It was big like a railway locomotive. It had great lamps like barrels, and glittering with silver. Often you saw this gorgeous vehicle outside Progressive Hall, where Vaino took his pleasures—had his Finnish steam bath, played pool, danced, boxed in the gymnasium. But when Helmi had her new clothes it would be different. He would dance with her then. She would talk to him (not much—but just enough to let him know that her people in Finland were not common farmers; that she had read the *Kalevala;* had gone to school; could figure; was a superb cook; owed nothing more on her passage money and could save from now on).

There! Mr. Mawson had almost finished his breakfast. Miss Zhoolie's orange juice on ice. A good half-hour in which to start the cleaning. She attacked the living room with fury. Ash trays. Papers. Plump the cushions. The carpet sweeper. Dust.

Usually she accomplished all this almost noiselessly. It was understood that Mrs. Mawson must not be disturbed. But this morning she need not be so careful, for Miss Zhoolie's voice, energetic in argument, and Mrs. Mawson's plaintive tones could be heard in unaccustomed early-morning dialogue. Zhoolie was in her mother's room, and dressing frenziedly as she talked.

"Well, you can *ask* her. . . . Well, Pete's sake, we do enough for her. . . . But I didn't know until last night. Jane asked me if I'd have them tonight instead of Saturday because they're going to Atlantic City on Friday, all of a sudden. And she's been so wonderful to me, and you know what it means on account of Len. Let her go out tomorrow instead of today. My gosh! It isn't as if she really *did* anything! Goes and squats at her sister's or whatever it is, in Brooklyn, and drinks coffee. . . ."

"Sh-sh-sh-sh!" Then Mrs. Mawson's voice, dulcet, plaintive. "Helmi! Helmi, will you come here just a minute?"

Helmi pretended not to hear; made a great to-do with her carpet sweeper. Wasn't it Every Other Thursday? Did not every minute count? Zhoolie opened her mother's bedroom door, poked her head out, called sharply, but with the edge of the sharpness illy concealed in a false sheath of velvet.

"Helmi, Mother wants to speak to you just a minute, please."

Helmi leaned the handle of the carpet sweeper against the table and came. Mrs. Mawson was in bed. She looked very plain and showed her age. Helmi, nineteen, wondered how it must feel to be as old as that; felt a stir of sympathy. In spite of the long period of passage-money payment, she had monthly sent money to her mother in Finland. It was well for Mrs. Mawson's peace of mind and pride that she could not read Helmi's thoughts behind that flat Finnish face. Miss Zhoolie stood in the background. She was fastening her blouse with absent-minded expertness. Little vibratory electric sparks of suspense seemed to dart out from her to Helmi.

Mrs. Mawson cleared her throat ever so slightly, pursed her mouth into the semblance of a placating smile.

"Helmi, Miss Zhoolie just learned last night that the guests she was expecting for dinner on Saturday night—three, you know—Mr. Mawson and I were going out—that makes four, with Miss Zhoolie—"

"Oh, Mother, do come to the point."

"Miss Zhoolie wants to know—they can't possibly come on Saturday—they're leaving town unexpectedly on Friday"—a sound from Zhoolie—"wants to know if you can't stay in today so that they can come to dinner tonight—she's to let them know this morning—and take Friday out instead. Will you do that?"

"No," said Helmi.

The monosyllable was so flat, so final, so direct that it had the effect of stunning her hearers slightly; they appeared not quite to understand. Mrs. Mawson actually repeated, painstakingly, as though Helmi had not grasped her meaning: "You could have tomorrow, Friday, instead of today. You probably have no plans. And it looks a little like rain anyway today, don't you think?"

"No," said Helmi.

"You mean no, you won't? Or—" Then, at the look on Zhoolie's face: "I'll tell you what, Helmi! You could take this Sunday instead. Easter Sunday. It isn't your Sunday, but you could have it—"

"No," said Helmi.

Zhoolie remained in the background no longer. She stamped her foot. Color suffused her pretty face.

"Well, I think you're a mean thing, Helmi! What have you got to do but go and sit at your sister's—"

"Zhoolie!"

"It's true. She hasn't."

Mrs. Mawson fixed her smile again, but not very successfully. It was really only pasted on, and crooked at that. "To tell you the truth, Helmi, one of the young men coming is someone Miss Zhoolie is very—she likes especially, do you see? And that's why she wanted them particularly tonight. This young man—"

This young man. Helmi turned and looked at Zhoolie in her soft girlish beige jersey frock, and her silk stockings, and her smart slippers. Her young man! Well, let her get him, then. Helmi had the getting of a young man to see to. So they stood staring at each other, these two girls: Helmi nineteen, immovable, inscrutable, implacable; Zhoolie nineteen, lovely, tearful, spoiled, furious. Helmi's thoughts, translated, would have read: "Get your young man, if you want him. I have seen your young men, and a poor lot they are, too. I would not exchange my Vaino for a half dozen of them." Zhoolie's flashing eyes and trembling lips meant: "Great clumsy Hunky! To think that you can actually spoil my day for me—maybe my life! Oh, damn! Oh, damn you!"

Aloud she said again, "But, Helmi, it isn't as if you really had anything special to do. What do you do on Thursday out that you couldn't do on Friday!"

What did she do on her Thursday out that she couldn't do on Friday! Within herself Helmi smiled and hugged her golden day to her. The Finnish girls uptown. Lempi Parta. Blue dress. The Finnish steam bath. Swim. Supper. The play at Finnish Hall. The dance. What did she do on Thursday that she couldn't do on Friday! She looked at Zhoolie, unmoved. She looked at Mrs. Mawson, her mistress. Looked at her stubbornly.

"No," said Helmi. Turned, and went back to her work in the living room; went back with redoubled and more furious energy to make up for precious time lost.

"I don't care!" cried Zhoolie, like a child. "She's a nasty, mean thing. What does she do! Nothing! Not a thing. She hasn't the intelligence to plan a holiday. She hasn't a thing to do."

Up the hall came Mr. James G. Mawson on his way to the Mawson Optical Company downtown. He glanced in at the bedroom door. "What's the row?" he asked. "What's the row?"

"Oh, nothing," said Mrs. Mawson wearily. "I can feel one of my headaches coming on."

Zhoolie turned a tearstained face to her father. "I want Helmi to take tomorrow out instead of today, and she won't."

"Don't blame her," said James G. Mawson, maddeningly.

"Oh, you're always like that, Father! Abe Lincoln stuff. It's one of your poses. What difference does it make what day she takes out, anyway!"

"Not any difference to you, Julia; might make a lot of difference to her. . . . Well . . ." The front door slammed behind him.

"I've heard people say 'Cold as a fish,'" observed Mrs. Mawson. "'Cold as a Finn,' I'd say."

Helmi consumed little enough food as a rule, aside from copious and unlimited cups of coffee and hunks of rye bread. Mrs. Mawson bought rye bread studded with caraway, just for Helmi. In citing Helmi's virtues, Mrs. Mawson was wont to include this. "She really doesn't eat a thing, I'll say that for her. I don't know what she lives on. Eating and bathing seem to be two habits that have never got much of a hold on Helmi."

Today Helmi ate even less than usual. She swept through the house like a Juggernaut—living room, bedrooms, dining room, kitchen. By noon she had done the work of three women; had done all the work there was to be done. A cup of coffee taken standing at the kitchen table. By twelve-thirty the smell of burning hair pervaded the Mawson flat. Mrs. Mawson had not yet gone out. She sniffed the air with an expression of extreme distaste. She walked down the hall to the kitchen. Helmi, fully dressed in her street clothes except for her coat and hat, was heating her curling iron at the gas stove.

"Not finished with your work already, are you, Helmi?"

"Yeh."

"Everything?"

"Sure."

"The icebox?"

"Thursday iss no icebox. Saturday iss icebox."

"Oh—well . . ." Mrs. Mawson drifted vaguely away. Helmi made the final trip with her curling iron from the gas stove to her bedroom mirror.

It was not yet one o'clock as she sat stolidly in a subway train marked Brooklyn. Seeing her, you would have known her for a foreign-born servant girl on her Thursday out. High, flat planes of cheekbones; low, full breasts; broad shoulders; pale-blue eyes; frizzed bobbed hair; a pretty good cloth coat; silk stockings; a velvet hat. Certainly you would never have guessed that golden hours filled with high adventure lay ahead of this lumpy creature; and that an exciting and dramatic year lay behind her.

Helmi Seppala was being slowly digested in the maw of New York. Her passage money had been sent her by her brother, Abel Seppala. She had sailed from Åbo. New York reached, she had been turned back at Ellis Island. Her country's quota was already filled. The thing had been overwhelming. Months passed. Again Abel sent money, against the protests of his wife, Anni. This time Helmi bribed the steward on the ship, and sailed as one of the stewardesses. One hundred and fifty dollars that had cost. How sick she had been! She was racked now at the thought of it. The boat reached New York. Unforeseen red tape bound Helmi to the ship. The stewardesses were not allowed to land. Frantic, she managed to get word to Abel.

The boat remained five days in New York. On the day it was due to return to Finland, Abel and Anni came on board, ostensibly to bid farewell to a Finnish friend who was going to his home country. Concealed, they carried on board with them American-made clothes—a dress, a coat, shoes, a hat, powder, rouge, eyeglasses. These had been smuggled to Helmi. Feverishly she had shed her uniform, had put on the American clothes, the rouge, the powder, the eyeglasses. When the call had come for visitors to go ashore, Helmi, with Abel and Anni, had passed down the gang-plank under the very eyes of the chief steward himself—to the dock, to the street, into the amazing spring sunshine of a New York May morning. Spurned as an alien by her stepmotherland, she had disguised herself as a native daughter and achieved a home that way.

At once she had gone to work. At once she had gone to school. Anni had not been very cordial to this sister of her husband. But she had grudgingly helped the girl, nevertheless. She had got her a "place." The wage was small, for Helmi knew no English and was ignorant of American ways, of New York household usages. But from the first, part of that infinitesimal wage went to pay back the passage money loaned her by Abel and Anni. And from the first she had gone to night school, three nights a week. Three nights a week, from eight until ten, after her dinner dishes were washed, she attended the night-school class, sitting hunched over a scarred school desk used by fourth-grade children in the daytime. It was a class in English for both sexes.

Most of the women were servant girls like herself—Swedish, Finnish, Czech, Latvian, Polish, Hungarian. She had the look of the old country. A big-boned girl, with broad shoulders and great capable hands. She had worn her hair pulled away from her forehead and temples, held with side combs, and wound at the back in a bun of neat, slippery braids. In her ears she wore little gold hoops. Her hair was straw-colored, with no glint of gold in it; her eyes were blue, but not a deep blue. She was not pretty, but there had been about her a certain freshness of coloring and expression. Her hair clung in little damp tendrils at the back of her neck. There was great breadth between her cheekbones, her shoulders, her hip-bones. Her legs were sturdy, slim, and quick. She listened earnestly. They read out of a child's reader. The lesson was, perhaps, a nature study.

"What is a frog, Miss Seppala?"

Miss Seppala would look startled, terrified, and uncomprehending, all at once.

Again, articulating painfully with tongue, teeth, palate: "What —is—a—frog, Miss Seppala?"

Much gabbling and hissing from those all about her. Suddenly a great light envelops Miss Seppala. She bounces up.

"A frock iss animal wiss legs iss jumping all the time and iss green." Triumph!

The lesson went on to say, "Dragonflies are called darning needles." Miss Speiser, the good-natured, spectacled teacher, spoke Upper West Side New York English. "Aw dawhning needles hawmful?" she inquired. The result was that Helmi's English accent turned out to be a mixture of early Finnish and late Bronx most mystifying to the hearer. Still it had served.

And now, a year later, her hair was bobbed, and her clothes

were American, and she said, "I'll tell the vorld," and got twenty dollars each week at the Mawsons'. She had paid back her passage money down to the last cent, so now Anni, in one of her tempers, could never again call her a dirty Lapp—that insult of insults to the Finn or Swede. She had learned with amazing swiftness to prepare American dishes, being a naturally gifted cook. She knew how to serve from the left, to keep the water glasses filled, not to remove the service plates until the dinner plates were at hand, to keep thumb marks off glass salad dishes, to mix a pretty good Martini cocktail. She was, in short, an excellent middle-class American servant—spunky, independent, capable, unfriendly.

It was a long trip from West Eighty-sixth Street to Finntown, in Brooklyn, where Abel and Anni lived. Helmi begrudged the time this afternoon, but she went out of a sense of duty and custom and a certain tribal loyalty. Anni's house was a neat two-story brick, new, in West Forty-fourth Street, Brooklyn. The neighborhood was almost solidly Finnish. The houses were well kept, prosperous-looking, owned by Finn carpenters, mechanics, skilled workmen, whose wage was twelve, fourteen, sixteen dollars a day. One of Anni's boys, Otto, aged four, was playing outside in the bit of yard. He eyed his aunt coolly, accepted a small sack of hard candies that she presented to him, followed her into the house, which she entered at the rear.

Anni was busy at her housework. Anni was always busy at her housework. Anni was twenty-seven and looked thirty-five. Between the two women no love was lost, but today their manner toward each other was indefinably changed. Helmi was no longer the debtor. Helmi was an independent and free woman, earning her twenty a week. Anni was a married woman bound, tied, and harried by a hundred household tasks and trials. The two talked in their native tongue.

"Well, how goes it?"

"Always the same. You are lucky. You have your day off, you can run out and have a good time."

"She wanted me to stay home today and go tomorrow instead. I soon showed her and that daughter of hers."

They went into that in detail. Their pale-blue eyes were triumphant.

"You are early today. Did you eat?"

"No. Coffee only."

"I'll fix you some *kaalikääreitä* left over from the children's lunch."

Helmi cast a glance of suspicion at her suddenly suave sister-in-law, but she pulled a chair up to the kitchen table and ate the savory stuffed cabbage with a good appetite. She had had no Finnish food for almost two weeks. It was good.

Well, she must be going. Going? Already? Where was she running? Helmi supped up the last of the gravy on her plate and rose. Oh, she had much to do! "Well, now you are so independent I suppose you will spend all your money." "Yes, and suppose I do? What then?" "Nothing, only Abel is so close with his money. I wish I had a dollar or two of my own to spend. I need so many things." Helmi gave her three dollars, grudgingly. She would do this again and again during the year. She was wild to be gone. She went into the bedroom to look at the baby; powdered her nose; drank a final and hasty cup of coffee, and was off. Anni watched her go, her eyes hard.

A long, long ride this time back to New York. Grand Central. Change. The East Side subway. She was spewed up with the crowd at One Hundred and Twenty-fifth Street; plunged vigorously into its colorful, cheerful hurly-burly. A hundred noises attracted her. A hundred sights lured her. But she knew what she wanted to do. She made straight for the shop where Lempi Parta had bought her dress. Bulging glittering plate-glass windows brilliant with blues and pinks and reds and gold.

Helmi entered. The place was full of girls like herself, with bobbed hair and flat faces and broad shoulders and pale-blue eyes. Upper East Side Finland was buying its Easter finery. A woman came forward—an enormous woman with an incredible bust and a measureless waist and bead trimming and carrot-colored hair. And what can I do for you, Miss? Helmi made known her wants. The woman emitted a vocal sound: a squawk.

"Miss S.! Oh, Miss S.! Step this way. . . . The young lady here wants you should show her something in a blue crepe."

You did not pay for it all at once, of course. You paid in part, and they took your name and address and the name of the people you worked for. (Helmi used to be most demanding about the accent over the *a*'s in Seppala, but she was no longer.) But they obligingly let you take the whole ravishing outfit: blue dress; blue coat lined with sand crepe and trimmed with embroidery; blue silk hat; silk stockings, very sheer; high-heeled slippers. She hung the boxes and bundles about herself, somehow, joyously. Miss S. was most gracious.

Into the five-and-ten-cent store. A mass of people surged up and down the aisles. They buffeted and banged Helmi's boxes, but she clung to them rigidly. A handkerchief, edged with blue lace. A small flask of perfume. A pocket comb that cunningly folded up on itself. An exhausting business, this shopping. More tiring than a day's housework. She stopped at an unspeakable counter and ordered and devoured a sandwich of wieners with mustard (10¢) and a glass of root beer (5¢). Thus refreshed, she fought her way out to the street.

It was midafternoon. She walked placidly up One Hundred and Twenty-fifth Street, enjoying the sights and sounds. Her strong arms made nothing of their burden. Music blared forth from the open door of a radio shop. She stopped to listen, entranced. Her feet could scarcely resist the rhythm. She wandered on, crossed the street. "Heh! Watch it!" yelled a tough taxi driver, just skimming her toes. He grinned back at her. She glared after him, gained the curb. A slim, slick, dark young fellow leaning limply against the corner cigar-store window spoke to her, his cigarette waggling between his lips.

"Watch your step, Swensky."

"Shod op!" retorted Helmi, haughtily.

An open-faced orange-drink bar offered peppermint taffy in ten-cent sacks. Helmi bought a sack and popped one of the sticky confections between her strong yellow teeth. A fake auction, conducted by a swarthy and Oriental-looking auctioneer, held her briefly. He was auctioning a leprous and swollen Chinese vase. A dollar! A dollar! Who offers a dollar? All right. Who says fifty cents! Twenty-five! Step inside. Come inside, lady, won't you? Don't stand like that in the door. She knew better than that; was on her way. Yet the vase would have looked lovely in a parlor. Still, she had no parlor.

Her pale eyes grew dreamy. She walked more quickly now. When she approached the Finnish Progressive Society building in One Hundred and Twenty-sixth Street there was the usual line of surprisingly important-looking cars parked outside. The portion of New York's Finnish chauffeurdom which had Thursday afternoon to itself was inside playing pool, eating in the building's restaurant, or boxing or wrestling in the big gymnasium. The most magnificent car of them all was not there. Helmi knew it would not be. Vaino was free on Thursday nights at ten. Her boxes and bundles in hand, Helmi passed swiftly through the little groups that stood about in the hallway. A flood of Finnish rose to her ears, engulfed her. She drew a long breath. Through the open doorway of the restaurant at the rear. The tables were half filled. Girls eating together. Men, with their hats on, eating together. She ordered a cup of coffee and a plate of Finnish bread—hardtack—*näkki leipä*—with its delicious pungent caraway. This she ate and drank quickly with a relish. The real joy of the day lay still ahead of her.

Into the hallway again and down a short flight of steps to the basement. Through the poolroom, murky with smoke, every table surrounded by pliant, plastic figures intent on the game. The men paid no attention to her, nor she to them. Through the door at the far end of the room. A little office. Down a flight of steps. The steam bath, beloved of every Finn.

All her life Helmi had had her steam bath not only weekly, but often two or three times a week. On the farm in Finland the bathhouse had been built before the farmhouse itself. You used the bathhouse not only for purposes of cleanliness, but for healing: in illness, when depressed. The Finnish women, in the first throes of childbirth, repaired to the soothing, steam-laden atmosphere of the bathhouse. The sick were carried there. In its shelves and on its platforms you lay dreamily for hours, your skin shining and slippery with water. The steam bath was not only an ablution; it was a ceremony, a rite.

On Tuesdays and Thursdays the Finnish Society's steam baths were used only by women. The bath woman, huge, blond, genial, met her, took her fifty cents, gave her a locker. Helmi opened her precious boxes and hung her finery away, carefully, lovingly. The room was full of naked girls. They were as lacking in self-consciousness as so many babies. They crowded round her—her friend Lempi Parta, and, too, Hilja Karbin, Saara Johnson, Matti Eskolin, Aili Juhola.

"Oh, Helmi! How beautiful! How much did you pay! The boys will dance with you tonight, all right!" they cried in Finnish.

She disrobed swiftly, and stood a moment in the moist warmth of that outer room. Her body was strong and astonishingly grace-ful, now rid of its cheap and bungling clothes. Her waist tapered slim and flexible below the breadth of the shoulders. She walked well. Now she went into the steam room. The hot breath of the place met her. She lifted her face to it, enchanted. She loved it. The air was thick, heavy with steam from the hot water that dropped endlessly down on to the hot steam pipes below, sending up a misty cloud. From out of this veil a half-dozen indolent heads were lifted from bunks that lined the walls. On each bunk lay an undraped figure.

Helmi sat a moment on the edge of a bunk. "Hello. Hello, Elli! How goes it, Mari? Oo, this is good!"

She reclined upon the bunk, gratefully, yieldingly. Every nerve, every fiber, every muscle of her being relaxed in the moist heat. This stolid Finn servant girl became a graceful plastic figure in repose, a living Greek statue. The mist enveloped her. Her eyes closed. So she lay for fifteen minutes, twenty, a half-hour. Out, then, with Lempi and a half-dozen others, into the cold green waters of the big pool, stopping first for a moment under a shower in the room adjoining the steam bath.

One after another they stood at the pool's edge, graceful, fear-less, unaffected. This bath, to them, was a sacred institution. It was an important and necessary part of their lives. They dropped then, swiftly, beautifully, flashingly, into the pool's green depths. They swam like mermaids. They had learned to swim in the icy waters of the Finland lakes. Their voices were high and clear and eager, like the voices of children at play. They were relaxed, gay, happy, "Oo, look! Look at me!" they called to each other in Finnish. "Can you do this?"

Back, dripping, into the steam room again. Another half-hour. The shower again. The pool again. Helmi gave herself over to the luxury of a massage at the expert hands of the masseuse. The strong electric human fingers kneaded her flesh, spanked her smartly, anointed her with oils. She felt blissful, alive, newborn. The Mawson kitchen did not exist. Zhoolie Mawson was a bad dream. Mrs. Mawson did not matter—never had mattered. Vaino. Vaino only.

She was so long in donning the beautiful new blue finery that Lempi and the rest became impatient. But at last it was finished. She surveyed herself radiantly. The flat Finnish face glowed back at her from the mirror. Helmi could never be pretty. But she approached it as nearly now as she ever would.

She would not curl her hair now. That she would do after she had had her supper. She was ravenously hungry.

They would not eat at the building restaurant. They were tired of it. They would go to Mokki's, on Madison, just off One Hundred and Twenty-fifth. A real Finnish meal. Here they sat at a table for four and talked and laughed in subdued tones, as does your proper Finnish girl. And they ate! Mrs. Mawson would have opened her eyes. They ate first *marja soppa*, which is an incredible soup of cranberries and cornstarch and sugar. They had *mämmi* and cream. They had salt herrings with potatoes. They had *riisi puuro*, which is, after all, little more than rice pudding, but flavored in the Finnish manner. They drank great scalding cups of coffee. It was superb to see them eat.

It was nearly eight. Helmi must still curl her hair, carefully. This you did in the women's room at the Finnish Society's building. She scanned the line of motors at the curb for the great car—no, it was not there. That was as it should be. The hair-curling business took a half-hour. The room was full of girls changing their shoes; changing their stockings; changing their dresses; combing their hair, curling it; washing.

Helmi and Lempi were going to the play that was to be given in the theater two flights up. Another fifty cents. Helmi did not begrudge it. She loved to dance, but she would wait. She would be fresh for ten o'clock. At ten, though the play would not be finished, she would leave for the dance upstairs. She shut her ears determinedly to the music that could faintly be heard when the door opened to admit late-comers. The play was presented by members of the Finnish Society's theatrical group, made up of girls like Helmi and boys like Vaino. Helmi watched it absorbedly. It was, the program told you in Finnish, *The Second Mrs. Tanqueray*. Helmi and Lempi found it fascinating and true and convincing.

Ten o'clock. They vanished. They deserted Thalia for Terpsichore. They spent another ten minutes before the dressing-room mirrors. The dance hall was crowded. Rows of young men, stolid of face, slim, appraising, stood near the door and grouped at the end of the room, partnerless, watching the dancers. Straight as a shot Helmi's eyes found him. How beautiful he was in his blue suit and his shiny tan shoes! His hair shone like his shoes. His cold blue eyes met hers. Her expression did not change. His expression did not change. Yet she knew he had marked her blue dress, and her sheer silk stockings, and her new, shining slippers.

Wordlessly she and Lempi began to dance together. Lempi took the man's part. She was very strong and expert. She whirled Helmi around and around in the waltz so that her blue skirt billowed out, and one saw her straight, sturdy, slim legs to the knees. Her skirt swished against the line of stolid-faced boys as she whirled past; swished against Vaino's dear blue-serge legs. She did not look at him, yet she saw his every feature. He did not look at her. He saw the dress, the stockings, the slippers, the knees. True Finns.

The waltz was over. Soberly and decorously Helmi and Lempi sought chairs against the wall. They conversed in low tones. Helmi did not look at him. Five minutes. The band struck up again. The polka. He stood there a moment. All about were stolid young men advancing stolidly in search of their equally stolid partners. Helmi's heart sank. She looked away. He came toward her. She looked away. He stood before her. He looked at her. She rose. Wordlessly they danced. One, two, three, and a one, two, three, and turn, and turn, and turn, and turn. She danced very well. His expression did not change. Her expression did not change. She was perfectly, blissfully happy.

At twelve it was over. At twelve-fifteen she had deposited her boxes and bundles—the everyday clothes of Cinderella—in the back of the huge, proud car that had an engine like a locomotive. She was seated in the great proud car beside Vaino. She was driven home. She was properly kissed. She would see him Thursday. Not Thursday, but *Thursday*. He understood. Every Other Thursday.

The day was over. She let herself into the Mawson apartment, almost (but not quite) noiselessly. Mrs. Mawson, sharp-eared, heard her. Zhoolie, herself just returned and not so unhappy as she had been sixteen hours earlier, but still resentful, heard her. Helmi entered her own untidy little room, quickly shut the window which Mrs. Mawson had opened, took off the blue dress, kicked off the bright new slippers, peeled the silk stockings (a hole in each toe), flung her underwear to the winds, dived into the coarse cotton nightgown, and tumbled into her lumpy bed with a weary, satisfied, rapturous grunt.

Zhoolie, in her green enamel bed, thought bitterly: Stupid lump! Went and sat at her sister's or whatever it is, all day, swigging coffee. It isn't as if she had had anything to do, really. She didn't do a thing. Not a thing! And I've given her I don't know how many pairs of my old silk stockings.

Mrs. Mawson, in her walnut bed, thought: They're all alike.

Mr. James G. Mawson slept.

CHINATOWN FAMILY

LIN YUTANG

Tom lay in bed, his limbs tired and all the muscles of his body sweetly relaxed, ready to fall asleep on this memorable first night after his arrival in America. His mother had just clicked off the switch triumphantly, and the light of the globe hanging over the middle of the bed had gone out, leaving for a second a streak of liver red that danced across his eyes. His toes hurt slightly, pleasantly, a new sensation for Tom. He did not often have new shoes, whether leather or cloth, and his father had bought him that day a new pair that cost three dollars and twenty-five cents and had insisted on his putting them on. The nerves across his arches tingled, and his ankles felt stiff, but from the middle of his heel came a sensation that really hurt.

He was drowsy, as a boy of thirteen can be healthily drowsy after a day of excitement. He wanted to sleep. His sister Eva, one year younger, was lying beside him. As he turned on his mattress and let his fingers fall curled on the edge of the bed, he saw the moon above the jagged, square, unfamiliar roofs of the houses across the avenue. For a time, his bed seemed to rock as if he were still on the ship which had docked that morning. He had not been seasick, as Eva had been, but the swaying motion of his bed continued. The moon seemed to swing in the sky, but when he opened his eyes wide, it stood still over the rooftops. Then he knew he was on land in a strange city in a strange country.

He had eaten too much that day, a Chinese lunch followed by a Chinese dinner, after being starved on the freighter for forty-five days. His mind was dim and a little giddy, and only the recollection remained of the swallowing of mouthfuls of inexhaustible rice, oiled by rich gravy and voluptuous hunks of bean curd fried in fat. The sleepy feeling crept over him, dark, sweet, and tender.

But Eva was awake.

"Are you asleep?" she whispered.

"Yes, I am."

"No, you are not."

Eva moved to rise from the bed. The mattress rolled and rocked again.

"What are you doing?" Tom asked.

He saw Eva's shape tiptoe across the room.

Click, click! Click, click! The light over his head went on and off three times.

"Oh, Eva!"

Giggling and triumphant, Eva jumped into bed again and pulled the sheet over her.

From across the room came the old father's voice. "Children, stop playing with the light. It is electricity!" The Cantonese word, *tin,* had a heavy thumping tone—"*Hai tinnn!*"

It was electricity! Momentous word in Tom's mind, symbolic of all that was new and marvelous in this new world of miracles.

The brother and sister had been playing with the switch in the afternoon. Tom had scrutinized the crisscross pattern of the filaments; he had known electric light in Canton and on the ship, but they had not had it at home and the wonder never ceased. He knew he was going to explore that incomprehensible marvel someday; just now he only wanted to understand that nice, neat infallible click. Tom was very impressionable; he liked to puzzle things out for himself, things that didn't puzzle Eva. His father had said, "It is electricity," pronouncing the word with great respect. Electricity was lightning, and he had lightning over his bed. The thought was tremendously exciting.

Out of the silence of the night there had come at regular intervals a mad rushing sound that boomed and rumbled past the bedroom window and rocketed into the dark distance. As the sound approached, the rails wailed like demons in the night, the windowpanes shook, and he saw a succession of bizarre lighted train windows rush by in orderly procession, and then he heard the wheels of the Third Avenue El train screech to a halt at the Eighty-fourth Street station.

A train flying in mid-air before his window! Tom was fully awake now. The noise did not surprise him. He had had a few notions about America before he came to this country. America was a country made all of machines, and machines were of course noisy, and, Tom reasoned, America should be noisy and full of that rushing motion, speeding motion, going somewhere—click—stopping—click—progress—click, click! What puzzled him was something else, something that left him no rest. He got up and peered down from the window. It was unbelievable. How could a flying demon with carloads of people be supported on such thin steel pillars? That was the miracle for Tom. A flying train whizzing in mid-air supported on matchsticks. Tom scratched his head. He wanted so much to know.

As he looked up, he saw men and women in their night-clothes, men with bald heads and women with almost bare bosoms, leaning on cushions and pillows out of the windows across the street.

He went back to bed. It was hot, noisy, strange, and all tremendous and wonderful. Eva was asleep already. His head was heavy, and his stomach was full.

The next thing he knew it was already morning.

"What do you think of Father?" whispered Eva, at the first movement Tom made in his bed. Tom was still in slumber. She shook him. "What do you think of Father?"

"What?" Tom rubbed his eyes. Without thinking, he knew that something good, something wonderful and exciting had happened to him. Then the realization that he was in the United States of America, in famous, fabulous New York, darted into his consciousness. He jumped up. "I am in New York! I am in New York!" It was like saying he was in Wonderland.

"Do you like Father?" asked Eva again.

"I like him," said Tom. "Isn't it strange to have a father?"

"It is not strange. He is our father," protested Eva.

"But it is strange to have a father."

"Don't you like the feeling of it?" Eva always greatly respected Tom's opinions.

"Yes, the feeling is nice. It's like having a double roof. You've got a roof already, and you get another roof. It's nice."

"He works so hard for us," said Eva. "We didn't know."

Of the two, Tom was a little whiter and more slender. Eva, though still a child, had a more prominent jaw and cheekbones and a rather flat bony forehead above her little shining eyes. Her simple, direct smile and her queue made her look like a doll.

Tom had not seen his father since infancy, and Eva had not seen him since she was born. The "father" in their minds was a dream, a legend, a reality so remote that it was unreal.

In good years and bad, the father had sent them money. Family legends told that he had come to the United States with the Alaska gold rush. San Francisco was known to all Cantonese back home as Old Gold Mountain, and to the overseas Chinese in America as the Great Port. Their father had sent home what were called "gold dollars." What Cantonese villager on the south coast—in Toishan, Sunwei, Fanyu—had not heard of the gold country? The plain fact was that villagers whose sons were in America received remittances, had savings and could buy farms, and those who did not could not. Some had built "foreign houses" in Canton.

Twice had Tom Fong, Sr., gone home to China, to stay for little more than a year, and then had returned to America to earn more foreign gold.

But ever since the children had known anything, their father had been in New York. The fact that New York was not Old Gold Mountain did not make any difference—across the fabled Pacific, the two points merged in the distance. There were village legends that the Chinese were mobbed, robbed, killed, and many were driven out of the West Coast, and it was a family legend that their father, Tom Fong, Sr., had escaped to the East Coast after some thrilling adventures. But that was long ago; these stories always sounded like pirate tales. The fact remained that Tom Fong, Sr., survived, and that, year after year, he and the other villagers' sons continued to send gold dollars home to support parents, brothers, and wives and to send their nephews to school. It was a story of survival; it was success; it was struggle triumphant.

On and on the villagers' sons came, and the immigration officials were merely obstacles Heaven placed in the path of men determined to achieve success with patience and persistence. The immigration difficulties were nothing to laugh at, but you laugh at them when you have nothing to lose.

Look at Tom's second elder brother, Yiko. He had come as a seaman at the age of sixteen and jumped ship, and now he was Frederick A. T. Fong, Insurance Agent, representative of Cornelius United States Underwriters! The Department of Justice didn't know. Why it should be the business of the Department of Justice, Washington, D.C., to know his whereabouts, Frederick A. T. Fong never quite figured out. Frederick A. T. Fong always added Washington, D.C., when he mentioned the Department of Justice. He was friendly to everybody, and when he met an American, he always said, "I am Frederick A. T. Fong," without waiting to be introduced.

So while Tom and Eva grew up in their village in Sunwei, their eldest brother Daiko and the second brother Yiko were living with their father in New York. The family was neatly divided into two halves, one earning and the other spending. The mother was one roof, a perfect roof, for Tom and his sister, and the father provided the other roof. Now the two halves were united, and the two roofs overlapped.

To the younger children, the father had been a mystical entity. From all the evidences—the family letters that arrived about once in six months, sometimes at longer intervals; the drafts that usually came with them, especially when the New Year was drawing near; and the trips Tom sometimes made to town with his mother when the letters arrived and the amazing fact that the bank gave them real money when presented with that not too elaborate piece of paper—from all these evidences Tom was willing to conclude that the mystical entity existed, as Christians conclude from the rain and snow and birds and flowers that God exists. His father's letters were always brief and not very communicative. It was either times were good or times were bad, and "enclosed you will find a draft for——"

There were other evidences of the existence of the father. In the first place, the mother believed in him. In the second place, her own brother, Tom's Uncle Chan, was in New York, too. Uncle Chan did not live on Olympian heights, hidden in the clouds; he made his presence felt in their home across the seas; his letters were more frequent and more chatty, even loquacious; real things were happening in New York. It was from one of Uncle Chan's letters that the people at home learned of the dramatic marriage of the eldest son Daiko to an Italian girl named Flora. Tom's father had not thought the fact even worth mentioning. In the third place, there was another old man, also by the name of Fong, now over sixty, who had comfortably settled down in their home village after a lifetime in America and who told Tom, the inquisitive child, about things and customs in the United States, on which the old man was the unquestioned authority.

One of the unforgettable stories old Fong told was that in America there are restaurants without waiters where you put a nickel in a slot and, click, a whole chicken, roasted and brown, sprang into view. Nobody of course questioned such an authority. He would be offended if anybody did. He made a tremendous impression on Tom.

"And turkey?"

"Yes, and turkey. A whole big turkey."

Tom's mouth watered.

"You see what you want through a glass and put in the nickel, and out it jumps. Yes, Amelicans are clever. You go to Amelica when you grow up."

Tom, of course, had wanted to come to "Amelica." He wanted very much to. All the ancient stories about the killings and muggings of the railroad men could not scare him. All the tales about the big bugaboo, the Yiminkeok (Immigration Bureau), and its quiet, absurd tactics stimulated the boy's imagination. What was this Yiminkeok but a lot of officials? By the universally accepted dictum in China officials were a pest to the people anyway. They were no different from the Chinese officials he knew. Why should they be? So long as you have a relative in America you don't have to worry. An official may be an official, but a relative is a relative.

Tom Fong, Sr., had wanted his family to come. For ten long years he had been wanting them. But it was not easy. If his family should come across the continent by railroad, the traveling expense of three people would come close to a thousand dollars. When was he going to earn and save so much money from his laundry? Some years ago, when he thought he had saved enough to send for his family, his bank had failed. Business was bad; fewer people sent their laundry. Those who remained his customers no longer sent their underwear, those who sent shirts seemed to change their shirts once instead of twice a week, and there was much work and little money in sheets. He lowered his prices; he worked long hours (heaven be thanked that there was no law against that!); he stood on his legs and sweated until eleven in the night; and he put all his money in a little cloth parcel inside a steel cabinet locked and hidden in a lower drawer. He had lost faith in all banks. He once prayed for delivery to come from fan-tan and was rewarded with the vision of winning two hundred dollars and then, in the hope of achieving all of his ambition, lost it all again. Thereafter he played moderately, but as a relaxation, not as a means of bringing his family over. But he continued to spend ten dollars systematically every year to take chances on the Irish sweepstakes.

A stroke of good fortune came in the person of his second son, who was beginning to do well as an insurance agent. Generous soul that he was, he handed over one day a check for five hundred dollars, his first savings, and said to his father, "Here, take this and send for Mother and the young children. Tell them Yiko sent the money. I know you want Mother here. It is all in the family."

Something stirred very deep in Tom senior's heart when he heard his son's offer, so deep that it took a long time for his feeling to come to the surface. The armor of patience and strength that he had worn for years had been pierced, and all his muscles relaxed. Slowly a contracted smile found its way to his face, and beads of moisture formed in his eyes. He was so touched that he could not say a word. He merely wiped his eyes. They seemed to say, "I appreciate it, my son. I have wanted very much to have your mother come."

With the money kept severely untouched in the bank, Tom's mother planned to go. For herself, she would rather have remained in China. The arrangement of living as the head of the family back home had been perfect for Mother Fong, and going at her age to America, where the language and customs were so strange, was hardly a pleasant prospect. But she wanted it for Tom and Eva, and there was unanimity of opinion in the family and great excitement among the children. They were not able to go until after the grandmother died. How long this was going to be nobody could tell. Leaving her alone would of course be outrageous, and they were willing to wait. But it could not be very long; Grandmother was in her eighties. Tom secretly wished it would happen soon and then blushed at the thought. But when Tom was thirteen, his grandmother died and was properly buried, and so they came.

No, it was not easy. There were those immigration officials, and there were immigration laws, laws made, it seemed, especially to keep Chinese out of America, or to let in as few as possible. But Chinese are used to officials and know of old that there are ways to get around laws. Yiko's way had been to jump ship. But a mother and her children could not do that. Neither could they be floated ashore in barrels on the California coast or smuggled across the Mexican border. A laundryman certainly could not bring his family into the country legally. But a merchant could if the children were not yet twenty-one years old. And Uncle Chan was a merchant, with a fine busy grocery store in Chinatown. Uncle Chan was glad to help to bring his sister and her children over.

So the legal procedures were taken to make Tom Fong joint owner of the grocery store with Uncle Chan. Thus in the somewhat blinking eyes of the law, Tom Fong became a merchant. Both he and Uncle Chan knew that this was a temporary expedient, to satisfy the law. It was irregular. But the thing was done.

When Tom and Eva saw the Statue of Liberty as the small Panama-registered freighter pulled into New York harbor, the sight of that goddess and of the skyscrapers was not new to them. They had seen these structures on post cards and the screen many times, but now they were in the round. You felt you could reach your fingers behind them, which was not the case with a post-card picture. Yet some of that picture effect still remained. It is like seeing a movie actress in person. She seems to have stepped down bodily from the screen, but she still talks as she does on the screen, and you still don't think her quite real. Eva looked and looked at the skyscrapers, afraid that the dream picture might at any time dissolve and vanish. She turned round several times and looked again, and each time the skyscrapers were still there.

On the wharf to receive them were Father Fong, Daiko and his wife Flora, Yiko (Frederick A. T. Fong), and Uncle Chan. Yiko was the prominent one, in a handsome bright-blue suit with a carnation in his lapel. He was not only the tallest and biggest of them all, he was responsible for producing the cash that brought the family over and was consequently in every sense a "big brother." He had seen the younger brother and sister only seven or eight years ago, whereas Daiko hadn't. He was happy that he was somebody in Chinatown. Out of respect for this great occasion, he had put on a black bow tie.

Without the knowledge of Daiko and his father, Frederick A. T. Fong did something that upset and embarrassed the mother greatly. He had brought a photographer. When the mother walked down the plank, followed by the young children, he went up and planted a kiss on her, while embracing her affectionately. There was a flash. Mother Fong could have swooned.

After the exciting exclamations and bewildering questions and mutual wonderment when the two halves of the family were united after a separation of twelve years, Yiko wanted a group photograph taken of this memorable occasion. The father and mother really should sit down, but there were no chairs on the wharf. Flora, standing beside Daiko on one side, put on a brave smile, but she was still inwardly shy. Uncle Chan, as one of the three elders, was also in the center. He was in his forties. He had put on his best Sunday suit, which was black alpaca, very shiny from use. The surface of his protruded, fat-filled, tensely rounded belly, the most important portion of his anatomy, gleamed like the identical part of a seal. His dark round head, his few thin whiskers, his shining skin, and his swaying motion all contributed to the impression of a seal. Yiko, standing at the other end behind Tom and Eva, putting his hands widespread on the two children's shoulders, with the carnation and his forward-looking smile, seemed to protect his younger brother and sister under his invisible wings.

The mother, a woman of fifty, with a strong, square face, had not yet recovered from the filial but highly unclassical embrace.

"Ah-Tong, whatever you took that picture for?" she said in Cantonese to Frederick, revealing thus the name for which A. T. was the mysterious symbol and which the owner scarcely would care to have discussed. He was Freddy on the amiable social level, Frederick on the legal, professional, check-signing level, and Ah-Tong to his parents.

"Why, it's for the Chinese papers," he replied. Chinatown was going to see how Frederick, the devoted son, welcomed his mother to the New York shore. It was these moments that counted. The American Indians greeting the *Mayflower* were the subject of a historic painting.

"*Sei-lo! Sei-lo!*" sighed the mother. It was not enough that her son should kiss her but that the disgraceful moment should be published and immortalized! It was against all sense of womanly decency.

From that moment there was no peace among the party in the taxi until Daiko intimated that Yiko could keep the picture from being published and all agreed that he should. This was about the time they reached the Tom Fong Hand Laundry.

Things are never what they seem. The little rathole of a shop on a cross street near the corner of Third Avenue was a great disappointment to Tom and Eva and even to the mother. But it was not a rathole. It was a gold mine where the father and Daiko had made enough money for them to buy their farm in Sunwei. Tom had had visions of a spic-and-span shop, all American style, crowded with hundreds of American customers, all talking the gibberish that was English. The basement shop was now closed. Tom tried to read the sign. He recognized the words Tom Fong. The next lines were still beyond his comprehension. They said, "Quick and clean. Try and convince."

Flora had at once taken a fancy to Tom. He pointed at the sign and asked Flora what it said. She merely smiled, for she knew only a few Cantonese words. Yiko answered for her.

"Convince means *seong sun,* like believe."

"What is believe?" asked Tom, gobbling up the new words.

"Believe means *seong sun.*"

"Why not say believe?"

"Oh, convince is a fine word. You say, I convince, much better than I believe."

It was the first English word Tom learned in New York.

The shop was in an antiquated three-story gray house, sandwiched between two red brick four-story buildings. A staircase from the pavement led up to a dark hallway, through a door opened by buzz control. The family's home was on the top floor, consisting of three rooms and a very spacious kitchen overlooking a yard that was empty but for some clotheslines. The two children headed for the roof as soon as they discovered there was a staircase leading up to it. On the left were the backs of the houses on Third Avenue. Through a window Tom saw a woman in pink working in a kitchen and in another house, on the fourth floor, a girl was looking out of a window, her chin cupped in her hands resting on the window sill. Nevertheless, the yard gave a feeling of seclusion and peace. Their section of the yard, like the others, was enclosed by faded, discolored board partitions. A scraggy elm in the neighbor's yard on the right managed to breathe through its few branches of leaves. From the roof, Tom could come within a few feet of the leaves, and the roof was all their own. It was good and peaceful, and the sun was shining in the yard, and Tom was content.

THE ODYSSEY OF A WOP

JOHN FANTE

I

I pick up little bits of information about my grandfather. My grandmother tells me of him. She tells me that when he lived he was a good fellow whose goodness evoked not admiration but pity. He was known as a good little Wop. Of an evening he liked to sit at a table in a saloon sipping a tumbler of anisette, all by himself. He sat there like a little girl nipping an ice-cream cone. The old boy loved that green stuff, that anisette. It was his passion, and when folks saw him sitting alone it tickled them, for he was a good little Wop.

One night, my grandmother tells me, my grandfather was sitting in the saloon, he and his anisette. A drunken teamster stumbled through the swinging doors, braced himself at the bar, and bellowed:

"All right, everybody! Come an' get 'em! They're on me!"

And there sat my grandfather, not moving, his old tongue coquetting with the anisette. Everyone but he stood at the bar and drank the teamster's liquor. The teamster swung round. He saw my grandfather. He was insulted.

"You too, Wop!" said he. "Come up and drink!"

Silence. My grandfather arose. He staggered across the floor, passed the teamster, and then what did he do but go through the swinging doors and down the snowy street! He heard laughter coming after him from the saloon and his chest burned. He went home to my father.

"*Mamma mia!*" he blubbered. "Tummy Murray, he calla me Wopa."

"*Sangue della Madonna!*"

Bareheaded, my father rushed down the street to the saloon. Tommy Murray was not there. He was in another saloon half a block away, and there my father found him. He drew the teamster aside and spoke under his breath. A fight! Immediately blood and hair began to fly. Chairs were drawn back. The customers applauded. The two men fought for an hour. They rolled over the floor, kicking, cursing, biting. They were in a knot in the middle of the floor, their bodies wrapped around each other. My father's head, chest, and arms buried the teamster's face. The teamster screamed. My father growled. His neck was rigid and trembling. The teamster screamed again, and lay still. My father got to his feet and wiped blood from his open mouth with the back of his hand. On the floor the teamster lay with a loose ear hanging from his head. . . . This is the story my grandmother tells me.

I think about the two men, my father and the teamster, and I picture them struggling on the floor. Boy! *Can* my father fight!

I get an idea. My two brothers are playing in another room. I leave my grandmother and go to them. They are sprawled on the rug, bent over crayons and drawing paper. They look up and see my face flaming with my idea.

"What's wrong?" one asks.

"I dare you to do something!"

"Do what?"

"I dare you to call me a Wop!"

My youngest brother, barely six, jumps to his feet, and dancing up and down, screams: "Wop! Wop! Wop! Wop!"

I look at him. Pooh! He's too small. It's that other brother, that bigger brother, I want. He's got ears too, he has.

"I bet *you're* afraid to call me Wop."

But he senses the devil in the woodpile.

"Nah," says he. "I don't wanna."

"Wop! Wop! Wop! Wop!" screams the little brother.

"Shut your mouth, you!"

"I won't, neither. You're a Wop! Wop! Woppedy Wop!"

My older brother's box of crayons lies on the floor in front of his nose. I put my heel upon the box and grind it into the carpet. He yells, seizing my leg. I back away, and he begins to cry.

"Aw, that was sure dirty," he says.

"I dare you to call me a Wop!"

"Wop!"

I charge, seeking his ear. But my grandmother comes into the room flourishing a razor strop.

II

From the beginning, I hear my mother use the words Wop and Dago with such vigor as to denote violent distaste. She spits them out. They leap from her lips. To her, they contain the essence of poverty, squalor, filth. If I don't wash my teeth, or hang up my cap, my mother says: "Don't be like that. Don't be a Wop." Thus, as I begin to acquire her values, Wop and Dago to me become synonymous with things evil. But she's consistent.

My father isn't. He's loose with his tongue. His moods create his judgments. I at once notice that to him Wop and Dago are without any distinct meaning, though if one not an Italian slaps them onto

him, he's instantly insulted. Christopher Columbus was the greatest
Wop who ever lived, says my father. So is Caruso. So is this fellow
and that. But his very good friend Peter Ladonna is not only a
drunken pig, but a Wop on top of it; and of course all his brothers-in-
law are good-for-nothing Wops.

He pretends to hate the Irish. He really doesn't, but he likes to
think so, and he warns us children against them. Our grocer's name
is O'Neil. Frequently and inadvertently he makes errors when my
mother is at his store. She tells my father about short weights in
meats, and now and then of a stale egg.

Straightway my father grows tense, his lower lip curling. "This is
the last time that Irish bum robs me!" And he goes out, goes to the
grocery store, his heels booming.

Soon he returns. He's smiling. His fists bulge with cigars. "From
now on," says he, "everything's gonna be all right."

I don't like the grocer. My mother sends me to his store every
day, and instantly he chokes up my breathing with the greeting:
"Hello, you little Dago! What'll you have?" So I detest him, and
never enter his store if other customers are to be seen, for to be
called a Dago before others is a ghastly, almost a physical, humilia-
tion. My stomach expands and contracts, and I feel naked.

I steal recklessly when the grocer's back is turned. I enjoy stealing from him—candy bars, cookies, fruit. When he goes into his refrigerator I lean on his meat scales, hoping to snap a spring; I press
my toe into egg baskets. Sometimes I pilfer too much. Then, what a
pleasure it is to stand on the curb, my appetite gorged, and heave
his candy bars, *his* cookies, *his* apples into the high yellow weeds
across the street! . . . "Damn you, O'Neil, you can't call me a Dago
and get away with it!"

His daughter is of my age. She's cross-eyed. Twice a week she
passes our house on her way to her music lesson. Above the street,
and high in the branches of an elm tree, I watch her coming down
the sidewalk, swinging her violin case. When she is under me, I
jeer in singsong:

> *Martha's crooooooss-eyed!*
> *Martha's crooooooss-eyed!*
> *Martha's crooooooss-eyed!*

III

As I grow older, I find out that Italians use Wop and Dago much more than Americans. My grandmother, whose vocabulary of English is confined to the commonest of nouns, always employs them in discussing contemporary Italians. The words never come forth quietly, unobtrusively. No; they bolt forth. There is a blatant intonation, and then the sense of someone being scathed, stunned.

I enter the parochial school with an awful fear that I will be called Wop. As soon as I find out why people have such things as surnames, I match my own against such typically Italian cognomens as Bianchi, Borello, Pacelli—the names of other students. I am pleasantly relieved by the comparison. After all, I think, people will say I am French. Doesn't my name sound French? Sure! So thereafter, when people ask me my nationality, I tell them I am French. A few boys begin calling me Frenchy. I like that. It feels fine.

Thus I begin to loathe my heritage. I avoid Italian boys and girls who try to be friendly. I thank God for my light skin and hair, and I choose my companions by the Anglo-Saxon ring of their names. If a boy's name is Whitney, Brown, or Smythe, then he's my pal; but I'm always a little breathless when I am with him; he may find me out. At the lunch hour I huddle over my lunch pail, for my mother doesn't wrap my sandwiches in wax paper, and she makes them too large, and the lettuce leaves protrude. Worse, the bread is homemade; not bakery bread, not "American" bread. I make a great fuss because I can't have mayonnaise and other "American" things.

The parish priest is a good friend of my father's. He comes strolling through the school grounds, watching the children at play. He calls to me and asks about my father, and then he tells me I should be proud to be studying about my great countrymen, Columbus, Vespucci, John Cabot. He speaks in a loud, humorous voice. Students gather around us, listening, and I bite my lips and wish to Jesus he'd shut up and move on.

Occasionally now I hear about a fellow named Dante. But when I find out that he was an Italian I hate him as if he were alive and walking through the classrooms, pointing a finger at me. One day

I find his picture in a dictionary. I look at it and tell myself that never have I seen an uglier man.

We students are at the blackboard one day, and a soft-eyed Italian girl whom I hate but who insists that I am her beau stands beside me. She twitches and shuffles about uneasily, half on tiptoe, smiling queerly at me. I sneer and turn my back, moving as far away from her as I can. The nun sees the wide space separating us and tells me to move nearer the girl. I do so, and the girl draws away, nearer the student on her other side.

Then I look down at my feet, and there I stand in a wet, spreading spot. I look quickly at the girl, and she hangs her head and looks at me in a way that begs me to take the blame for her. We attract the attention of others, and the classroom becomes alive with titters. Here comes the nun. I think I am in for it again, but she embraces me and murmurs that I should have raised two fingers and of course I would have been allowed to leave the room. But, says she, there's no need for that now; the thing for me to do is go out and get the mop. I do so, and amid the hysteria I nurse my conviction that only a Wop girl, right out of a Wop home, would ever do such a thing as this.

Oh, you Wop! Oh, you Dago! You bother me even when I sleep. I dream of defending myself against tormentors. One day I learn from my mother that my father went to the Argentine in his youth, and lived in Buenos Aires for two years. My mother tells me of his experiences there, and all day I think about them, even to the time I go to sleep. That night I come awake with a jerk. In the darkness I grope my way to my mother's room. My father sleeps at her side, and I awaken her gently, so that he won't be aroused.

I whisper: "Are you sure Papa wasn't *born* in Argentina?"

"No. Your father was born in Italy."

I go back to bed, disconsolate and disgusted.

IV

During a ball game on the school grounds, a boy who plays on the opposing team begins to ridicule my playing. It is the ninth inning, and I ignore his taunts. We are losing the game, but if I can knock out a hit our chances of winning are pretty strong. I am determined to come through, and I face the pitcher confidently. The tormentor sees me at the plate.

"Ho! Ho!" he shouts. "Look who's up! The Wop's up. Let's get rid of the Wop!"

This is the first time anyone at school has ever flung the word at me, and I am so angry that I strike out foolishly. We fight after the game, this boy and I, and I make him take it back.

Now school days become fighting days. Nearly every afternoon at 3:15 a crowd gathers to watch me make some guy take it back. This is fun; I am getting somewhere now, so come on, you guys, I dare you to call me a Wop! When at length there are no more boys who challenge me, insults come to me by hearsay, and I seek out the culprits. I strut down the corridors. The smaller boys admire me. "Here he comes!" they say, and they gaze and gaze. My two younger brothers attend the same school, and the smallest, a little squirt seven years old, brings his friends to me and asks me to roll up my sleeve and show them my muscles. Here you are, boys. Look me over.

My brother brings home furious accounts of my battles. My father listens avidly, and I stand by, to clear up any doubtful details. Sadly happy days! My father gives me pointers: how to hold my fist, how to guard my head. My mother, too shocked to hear more, presses her temples and squeezes her eyes and leaves the room.

I am nervous when I bring friends to my house; the place looks so Italian. Here hangs a picture of Victor Emmanuel, and over there is one of the cathedral of Milan, and next to it one of St. Peter's, and on the buffet stands a wine pitcher of medieval design; it's forever brimming, forever red and brilliant with wine. These things are heirlooms belonging to my father, and no matter who may come to our house, he likes to stand under them and brag.

So I begin to shout to him. I tell him to cut out being a Wop and be an American once in a while. Immediately he gets his razor strop and whales hell out of me, clouting me from room to room and finally out the back door. I go into the woodshed and pull down my pants and stretch my neck to examine the blue slices across my rump. A Wop, that's what my father is! Nowhere is there an American father who beats his son this way. Well, he's not going to get away with it; some day I'll get even with him.

I begin to think that my grandmother is hopelessly a Wop. She's a small, stocky peasant who walks with her wrists crisscrossed over her belly, a simple old lady fond of boys. She comes into the room and tries to talk to my friends. She speaks English with a bad accent, her vowels rolling out like hoops. When, in her simple way, she confronts a friend of mine and says, her old eyes smiling: "You lika go the Seester scola?" my heart roars. *Mannaggia!* I'm disgraced; now they all know that I'm an Italian.

My grandmother has taught me to speak her native tongue. By seven, I know it pretty well, and I always address her in it. But when friends are with me, when I am twelve and thirteen, I pretend ignorance of what she says, and smirk stiffly; my friends daren't know that I can speak any language but English. Sometimes this infuriates her. She bristles, the loose skin at her throat knits hard, and she blasphemes with a mighty blasphemy.

V

When I finish in the parochial school my people decide to send me to a Jesuit academy in another city. My father comes with me on the first day. Chiseled into the stone coping that skirts the roof of the main building of the academy is the Latin inscription: *Religioni et Bonis Artibus*. My father and I stand at a distance, and he reads it aloud and tells me what it means.

I look up at him in amazement. Is this man my father? Why, look at him! Listen to him! He reads with an Italian inflection! He's wearing an Italian mustache. I have never realized it until this moment, but he looks exactly like a Wop. His suit hangs carelessly in wrinkles upon him. Why the deuce doesn't he buy a new one? And look at his tie! It's crooked. And his shoes: they need a shine. And, for the Lord's sake, will you look at his pants! They're not even buttoned in front. And oh, damn, damn, damn, you can see those dirty old suspenders that he won't throw away. Say, Mister, are you really my father? You there, why, you're such a little guy, such a runt, such an old-looking fellow! You look exactly like

one of those immigrants carrying a blanket. You can't be *my* father!
Why, I thought . . . I've always thought . . .

I'm crying now, the first time I've ever cried for any reason ex-
cepting a licking, and I'm glad he's not crying too. I'm glad he's as
tough as he is, and we say good-by quickly, and I go down the path
quickly, and I do not turn to look back, for I know he's standing
there and looking at me.

I enter the administration building and stand in line with strange
boys who also wait to register for the autumn term. Some Italian
boys stand among them. I am away from home, and I sense the
Italians. We look at one another and our eyes meet in an irresistible
amalgamation, a suffusive consanguinity; I look away.

A burly Jesuit rises from his chair behind the desk and introduces
himself to me. Such a voice for a man! There are a dozen thunder-
storms in his chest. He asks my name, and writes it down on a little
card.

"Nationality?" he roars.

"American."

"Your father's name?"

I whisper it: "Guido."

"How's that? Spell it out. Talk louder."

I cough. I touch my lips with the back of my hand and spell out
the name.

"Ha!" shouts the registrar. "And still they come! Another Wop!
Well, young man, you'll be at home here! Yes, sir! Lots of Wops
here! We've even got Kikes! And, you know, this place reeks with
shanty Irish!"

Dio! How I hate that priest!

He continues: "Where was your father born?"

"Buenos Aires, Argentina."

"Your mother?"

At last I can shout with the gusto of truth.

"Denver!" Aye, just like a conductor.

Casually, by way of conversation, he asks: "You speak Italian?"

"Nah! Not a word."

"Too bad," he says.

"You're nuts," I think.

VI

That semester I wait on table to defray my tuition fee. Trouble ahead; the chef and his assistants in the kitchen are all Italians. They know at once that I am of the breed. I ignore the chef's friendly overtures, loathing him from the first. He understands why, and we become enemies. Every word he uses has a knife in it. His remarks cut me to pieces. After two months I can stand it no longer in the kitchen, and so I write a long letter to my mother; I am losing weight, I write; if you don't let me quit this job, I'll get sick and flunk my tests. She telegraphs me some money and tells me to quit at once; oh, I feel so sorry for you, my boy; I didn't dream it would be so hard on you.

I decide to work just one more evening, to wait on table for just one more meal. That evening, after the meal, when the kitchen is deserted save for the cook and his assistants, I remove my apron and take my stand across the kitchen from him, staring at him. This is my moment. Two months I have waited for this moment. There is a knife stuck into the chopping block. I pick it up, still staring. I want to hurt the cook, square things up.

He sees me, and he says: "Get out of here, Wop!"

An assistant shouts: "Look out, he's got a knife!"

"You won't throw it, Wop," the cook says. I am not thinking of throwing it, but since he says I won't, I do. It goes over his head and strikes the wall and drops with a clatter to the floor. He picks it up and chases me out of the kitchen. I run, thanking God I didn't hit him.

That year the football team is made up of Irish and Italian boys. The linemen are Irish, and we in the backfield are four Italians. We have a good team and win a lot of games, and my teammates are excellent players who are unselfish and work together as one man. But I hate my three fellow-players in the backfield; because of our nationality we seem ridiculous. The team makes a captain of me, and I call signals and see to it my fellow-Italians in the backfield do as little scoring as possible. I hog the play.

The school journal and the town's sport pages begin to refer to

us as the Wop Wonders. I think it an insult. Late one afternoon, at
the close of an important game, a number of students leave the
main grandstand and group themselves at one end of the field, to
improvise some yells. They give three big ones for the Wop Wonders. It sickens me. I can feel my stomach move; and after that
game I turn in my suit and quit the team.

I am a bad Latinist. Disliking the language, I do not study, and
therefore I flunk my examinations regularly. Now a student comes
to me and tells me that it is possible to drop Latin from my cur-
riculum if I follow his suggestion, which is that I fail deliberately
in the next few examinations, fail hopelessly. If I do this, the student
says, the Jesuits will bow to my stupidity and allow me to abandon
the language.

This is an agreeable suggestion. I follow it out. But it backtracks,
for the Jesuits are wise fellows. They see what I'm doing, and they
laugh and tell me that I am not clever enough to fool them, and
that I must keep on studying Latin, even if it takes me twenty
years to pass. Worse, they double my assignments and I spend my
recreation time with Latin syntax. Before examinations in my junior
year the Jesuit who instructs me calls me to his room and says:

"It is a mystery to me that a thoroughbred Italian like yourself
should have any trouble with Latin. The language is in your blood
and, believe me, you're a darned poor Wop."

Dio! I go upstairs and lock my door and sit down with my book
in front of me, my Latin book, and I study like a wild man, tearing
crazily into the stuff until, lo, what is this? What am I studying
here? Sure enough, it's a lot like the Italian my grandmother taught
me so long ago—this Latin, it isn't so hard, after all. I pass the examination. I pass it with such an incredibly fine grade that my instructor thinks there is knavery somewhere.

Two weeks before graduation I get sick and go to the infirmary
and am quarantined there. I lie in bed and feed my grudges. I
bite my thumbs and ponder old grievances. I am running a high
fever, and I can't sleep. I think about the principal. He was my
close friend during my first two years at the school, but in my third
year, last year, he was transferred to another school. I lie in bed
thinking of the day we met again in this, the last year. We met again
on his return that September, in the principal's room. He said hello

to the boys, this fellow and that, and then he turned to me, and said:

"And you, the Wop! So you're still with us."

Coming from the mouth of the priest, the word had a lumpish sound that shook me all over. I felt the eyes of everyone, and I heard a giggle. So that's how it is! I lie in bed thinking of the priest and now of the fellow who giggled.

All of a sudden I jump out of bed, tear the flyleaf from a book, find a pencil, and write a note to the priest. I write: "Dear Father: I haven't forgotten your insult. You called me a Wop last September. If you don't apologize right away there's going to be trouble." I call the brother in charge of the infirmary and tell him to deliver the note to the priest.

After a while I hear the priest's footsteps rising on the stairs. He comes to the door of my room, opens it, looks at me for a long time, not speaking, but only looking querulously. I wait for him to come in and aplogize, for this is a grand moment for me. But he closes the door quietly and walks away. I am astonished. A double insult!

I am well again on the night of graduation. On the platform the principal makes a speech and then begins to distribute the diplomas. We're supposed to say: "Thank you," when he gives them to us. So thank you, and thank you, and thank you, everyone says in his turn. But when he gives me mine, I look squarely at him, just stand there and look, and I don't say anything, and from that day we never speak to each other again.

The following September I enroll at the university.

"Where was your father born?" asks the registrar.

"Buenos Aires, Argentina."

Sure, that's it. The same theme, with variations.

VII

Time passes, and so do school days. I am sitting on a wall along the plaza in Los Angeles, watching a Mexican *fiesta* across the street. A man comes along and lifts himself to the wall beside me, and asks if I have a cigarette. I have, and, lighting the cigarette, he makes conversation with me, and we talk of casual things until the *fiesta* is over. Then we get down from the wall and, still talking, go walking through the Los Angeles Tenderloin. This man needs a shave and his clothes do not fit him; it's plain that he's a bum. He tells one lie upon another, and not one is well told. But I am lonesome in this town, and a willing listener.

We step into a restaurant for coffee. Now he becomes intimate. He has bummed his way from Chicago to Los Angeles, and has come in search of his sister; he has her address, but she is not at it, and for two weeks he has been looking for her in vain. He talks on and on about this sister, seeming to gyrate like a buzzard over her, hinting to me that I should ask some questions about her. He wants me to touch off the fuse that will release his feelings.

So I ask: "Is she married?"

And then he rips into her, hammer and tongs. Even if he does find her, he will not live with her. What kind of a sister is she to let him walk these streets without a dime in his pocket, and she married to a man who has plenty of money and can give him a job? He thinks she has deliberately given him a false address so that he will not find her, and when he gets his hands on her he's going to wring her neck. In the end, after he has completely demolished her, he does exactly what I think he is going to do.

He asks: "Have *you* got a sister?"

I tell him yes, and he waits for my opinion of her; but he doesn't get it.

We meet again a week later.

He has found his sister. Now he begins to praise her. She has induced her husband to give him a job, and tomorrow he goes to work as a waiter in his brother-in-law's restaurant. He tells me the address, but I do not think more of it beyond the fact that it must be somewhere in the Italian quarter.

And so it is, and by a strange coincidence I know his brother-in-law, Rocco Saccone, an old friend of my people and a *paesano* of my father's. I am in Rocco's place one night a fortnight later. Rocco and I are speaking in Italian when the man I have met on the plaza steps out of the kitchen, an apron over his legs. Rocco calls him and he comes over, and Rocco introduces him as his brother-in-law from Chicago. We shake hands.

"We've met before," I say, but the plaza man doesn't seem to want this known, for he lets go my hand quickly and goes behind the counter, pretending to be busy with something back there. Oh, he's bluffing; you can see that.

In a loud voice, Rocco says to me: "That man is a skunk. He's ashamed of his own flesh and blood." He turns to the plaza man. "Ain't you?"

"Oh, yeah?" the plaza man sneers.

"How do you mean—he's ashamed? How do you mean?"

"Ashamed of being an Italian," Rocco says.

"Oh, yeah?" from the plaza man.

"That's all he knows," Rocco says. "Oh, yeah? That's all he knows. Oh, yeah? Oh, yeah? Oh, yeah? That's all he knows."

"Oh, yeah?" the plaza man says again.

"Yah," Rocco says, his face blue.

The plaza man looks at me with peaked eyebrows, and he doesn't know it, he standing there with his black, liquid eyes, he doesn't know that he's as good as a god in his waiter's apron; for he is indeed a god, a miracle worker; no, he doesn't know; no one knows; just the same, he is that—he, of all people. Standing there and looking at him, I feel like my grandfather and my father and the Jesuit cook and Rocco; I seem to have come home, and I am surprised that this return, which I have somehow always expected, should come so quietly, without trumpets and thunder.

"If I were you, I'd get rid of him," I say to Rocco.

"Oh, yeah?" the plaza man says again.

I'd like to paste him. But that won't do any good. There's no sense in hammering your own corpse.

UNCLE BOSKO

VERN SNEIDER

We had just sat down to supper when the telegram arrived, and right away Mama was so nervous she nearly spilled the borsch all over the new checkered tablecloth Papa had just given her for their twentieth wedding anniversary. "They never send good news in telegrams," she always said, and already I could see her eyes start to get red. Papa, too, was nervous—his hand, holding the telegram, shook. And even we kids, gathered round the kitchen table, were quiet.

But Mama is never one to put things off, even possible bad news.

She slipped a plump arm around my sister Josie, who is only seven, and with her other hand clasped her apron, ready to dab at her eyes. "Louie," she said to Papa, "don't you think we better open it?"

Papa nodded. "Here, Emil." He handed me the telegram. "You read it. I left my glasses down at the plant again. Besides, you're in high school now. You might as well make use of your education."

As I tore open the envelope, Mama started to sniffle, Josie started to sob. Then I started to yell. "Hey, Papa!" I yelled. "Uncle Bosko is coming to America at last!"

"No!" Papa could hardly believe. And I had to put my hands over my ears, because my brothers Stan, Walt, Joe, Steve, and Pete began shouting, "Hurray!" While my sister Sophie, who is sixteen, swooned.

"Quiet!" Papa pulled his napkin from his shirt front and jumped up. "We'll have some manners around here." Papa only comes up to Mama's shoulder and weighs about half as much, but when he says "Quiet!" we shut our mouths. If we don't, he has Mama whale the daylights out of us. "Now." He looked sternly around the table. "Emil, read the telegram. Just what it says on the paper."

So I read. "Bosko Kowalski," it said, "will arrive Willow Run Airport 0215 P.M. Saturday Sept. 21. Please arrange to meet him. Signed: International Society for Displaced Persons."

For a moment Papa just stood there. Then his mustache began to tremble, and he slumped in his chair. "My own brother," he said, the tears coming to his eyes, "and I don't see him for twenty-two years, since I leave Poland."

Right away Mama took her arm from around Josie, went over and put it around him. "Now, Louie. Now don't cry."

"Twenty-two years," Papa went on, "and all the time he is behind the iron curtains . . . starving."

"But, Louie," Mama tried to comfort him, "Bosko is going to be here with us now. Right here in Hamtramck. Here in Detroit."

"For twenty-two years I try to get him from behind the iron curtains—" This time Papa sobbed so loud that Mrs. Dumbroski, next door, looked out of her kitchen window.

Sometimes Papa gets a little mixed up. Actually it had only been during the past ten months that we tried bringing Uncle Bosko to

America. Papa had heard from him in 1939. Then we didn't hear from him again until just last year when he slipped into Western Germany. The Society for Displaced Persons notified us, and Uncle Bosko had someone write a letter for him too.

We could bring Uncle Bosko to America, the Society said, if we found him a home and a job. That made Papa sore. "What's the matter with those guys?" he demanded. "They got holes in their head? What kind of a guy do they think I am? Do they think I bring my own brother over here and let him sit out in the middle of the street? Do they think my home isn't my brother's home?"

Well, when I sat down to write the letter for him, he was still storming around. "You just tell those guys"—he shook his finger—"that this home is Bosko's home. I'm even turning the deed over to him. You just tell those guys—" Papa stopped and pulled his mustache. "Hey, I just remember Bosko wrote he's still a bachelor. Well, tell those guys I'm even going to introduce him to Joe Tomich's widow. Just say she's only forty-nine and a good cook. And that her oldest boy Walter is a welder out at Ford's, and I think they're going to make him a foreman pretty soon, and—"

But I didn't put all that stuff in. I just said, yes, we had a job for Uncle Bosko—even though we didn't, but I figured Papa would probably get him something on the assembly line—and that his home would be with us, and things like that. I knew Papa wouldn't read the letter, because he never brings his glasses home from the plant.

Now the borsch was bubbling, and you could smell the stuffed red cabbage cooking, so my brother Stan said, "Hey, Ma. I'm hungry."

Mama's look made him slip lower in his chair. "Stanislaus, we don't eat when Papa is crying. Now keep still!"

Papa didn't cry much longer, though. Pretty soon he started to smile; then he started to laugh. "So Bosko is coming to America. Well, well . . . Mama, bring on the borsch."

Mama says we should never disturb Papa when he's eating. It might give him indigestion. So we were all pretty quiet, except Stan and Walt got into a little fight over a piece of bread. But tonight Papa didn't seem to notice. He kept smiling and eating, and after his third helping of red cabbage, he patted his stomach and lit his pipe.

"Now," he said, "you kids better polish the car. I want it nice and shiny for when we meet Uncle Bosko tomorrow."

"But, Papa," I said, "we're having a pep meeting at school to-night. Tomorrow Hamtramck Hi is playing—"

"I don't care if you're playing Notre Dame." Papa's face got red. "Do you think Uncle Bosko comes to America every day?"

"But, Pa." Little Josie pouted. "Kukla, Fran, and Ollie are on television in a little while."

Papa pounded the table. "It seems to me somebody around this place is getting pretty smart. Mama, you better get the hairbrush."

Mama pointed. "Shine the car." So we all got up.

Papa had bought the car second-handed down at Smiling Harry's. "Yes, sir, Mr. Kowalski," Smiling Harry said, rubbing his hands. "I have just the thing for you. Now, what you need is a coupe."

"Oh, so I need a coupe," Papa said. "All right. You come around tomorrow night after supper and take us for a ride."

When Smiling Harry came around and saw Mama and us eight kids, he decided that maybe Papa didn't need a coupe after all, even though it was a good buy—the old couple who owned it only having used it on Saturdays to bring in eggs from the country.

But Smiling Harry had just the thing. It was long and black, with folding seats in the rear. Yet the feature Papa liked best was the partition separating the front and back. "It makes driving on Sunday afternoons kinda restful," he always says, looking at Stan, Walt, Joe, Steve, and Pete behind the glass.

Well, the car being so long we always split into two gangs, one starting at each end, to polish it. Still it's a good two hours' job because Papa keeps coming out of the house, saying, "A little more shine on the fenders, please." Or, "The chrome—rub the chrome some more." By the time we finished it was dark, and Papa decided we ought to go to bed. "You'll need a good night's sleep with Uncle Bosko coming tomorrow," he said.

The next afternoon, even though I drove slow, we arrived early at Willow Run Airport. Mama packed a lunch, and for a while we

sat in the waiting room, eating salami sandwiches. But about two
o'clock Papa started getting nervous, so we all went up to the ob-
servation platform, just to make sure we wouldn't miss Uncle
Bosko's plane when it landed. Only Papa got a little mixed up. He
mistook a Cub for a Skyliner, and before we knew it the plane from
New York was in and unloading.

Right away we ran down to where the passengers were coming
in from the south concourse. First came some guy with a brief
case and homburg, then a couple more guys with brief cases and
homburgs, next some fat old lady in a fur coat. Then a little guy
sort of peeked in, and I yelled, "There he is!"

You couldn't miss Uncle Bosko. He looked exactly like Papa,
maybe a little older, but he had the same sandy hair and even the
same shaggy mustache. He was wearing an old sweater and canvas
shoes; and because his pants were too short, I could see that one of
his socks was blue, the other green.

"Bosko!" Papa started running toward him. "Bosko!" Then they
stood there in the entrance way hugging each other, the tears
streaming down their cheeks. Mama sniffled, Josie sobbed, and the
fat old lady in the fur coat gave us a dirty look. When Mama wasn't
looking, I gave her one back.

Papa and Uncle Bosko spoke in Polish. I don't understand
much, but every once in a while I caught something about twenty-
two years, then they would hug each other some more and start
crying again. Finally, Mama tugged Papa's sleeve. Papa looked
around, then said proudly, "Bosko, this is Mama."

Uncle Bosko bowed and kissed Mama's hand, and she hugged him
so tight she lifted him off the floor. "And, Bosko," Papa said, throwing out his chest and switching to English so we kids could understand, "This is Emil, Sophie, Stanislaus, Walter, Joseph, Stephen,
Peter, and Josie."

Uncle Bosko had to go down the line, kissing us all. "Now,"
Papa said, putting his arm around Uncle Bosko, "we go home."

I was going to help Uncle Bosko with his luggage, but he didn't
have any, except a little bundle wrapped in brown paper. As we
walked through the terminal, he looked around, shook his head,
started to speak, and couldn't. It wasn't until he saw the car that
he was able to say anything. "Louie, it's beautiful," he said slowly

in English. "It's . . . it's just like the grand dukes used to have back home. The director must be a good man to let you take his auto like this."

"Yeah," Papa said, "Smiling Harry is all right, even though he sets the mileage back sometimes."

Papa wanted Uncle Bosko to sit in front, so as I drove along I watched him. Mama had given him five or six salami sandwiches, a couple of oranges, and a few bananas. With one hand he gripped a sandwich, but his other hand kept running over the upholstery, and he kept shaking his head. "Emil," he began, "does the director let you take his auto often like this?"

"Who, Uncle Bosko?"

"The director, the big boss. The man who owns the auto."

"But Papa owns it," I told him.

His mouth flew open. "Emil, you mean your Papa owns a car just like the grand dukes used to have?"

"Well, almost. There's only two payments due yet."

"Emil, I can't believe."

"Most everyone owns a car," I said. "Why, the Dumbroskis, next door, have four."

"Four autos! And what does this Mr. Dumbroski do?"

"Well, Benny digs ditches for the city," I said. "But see, he, himself, only has an old jalopy. The rest belong to his sons. They all work on the assembly lines, and since they make the cars, why . . . well, you know how it is. Besides, if they didn't have cars, they'd have a deuce of a time getting back and forth to work."

"They ride to work?" Uncle Bosko's eyes were wide.

"Sure." Then I had to go and open my mouth. "Why, you'll probably have a car of your own just as soon as you get a job."

"Oh, I'm glad you mentioned that, Emil," Uncle Bosko said. "In his letter your Papa told the Society for Displaced Persons that he had work for me. What kind of a job is it?"

I didn't know what to say, because I remembered, then, that Papa didn't mention anything about work when he had me write that letter for him. I just put that in myself, because I didn't think the Society would be interested in hearing about Joe Tomich's widow. But if Papa knew I wrote things he didn't tell me . . . boy, would Mama give me a whaling! I glanced around to see if Papa had heard, but the glass was shut. Besides, Papa was busy bawling Stan out about something, so I just mumbled, "I don't exactly know."

But was I sweating. In fact, I forgot what I was doing. First thing you know, I was hitting it up pretty well, and there was a siren behind us. Uncle Bosko heard it, too, and grew pale. "Emil," he said, "your papers. Get your papers ready."

He was so nervous, I tried to calm him. "Don't worry, Uncle Bosko, I have my driver's license right here."

He didn't hear me. He was opening his bundle, pulling out cards, folders, and I don't know what all. When the squad car came up beside us, the officer called, "Okay, bud, slow it down. Take it easy." So I waved, and Uncle Bosko waved, too, holding up all his cards and folders. Then, as they pulled away, he glanced at me and seemed embarrassed. "By golly, Emil," he said, "I forget. But ever since 1939 . . . ach." He shook his head. "I just forget."

Still he peered uneasily at the squad car, so I turned down a side street, thinking it would make him feel better. Besides, I couldn't see much sense in following them. You never know when they'll change their minds and give you a ticket for speeding.

When we arrived home, Papa said, "Bosko, would you like to clean up? Maybe take a nice hot bath?"

Uncle Bosko nodded. "It would be nice, Louie. But you would have to heat water, and I don't like to use fuel for that."

"You won't be using any fuel," Papa assured him. "The water is heated by electricity."

"Oh, is the electricity on this time of day?"

"I think so." Papa flipped the light switch. "Yep. And it's a good thing, too, or would I tell that Detroit Edison Company."

Then Mama thought of something. "Emil, I just remember we all took baths this morning. Run and get Uncle Bosko a new bar of soap."

Uncle Bosko didn't want to take the soap, but Mama closed his hand around the bar. "We got a lot, Bosko," she assured him. "And be sure to use plenty of hot water. I think that Edison Company gets pretty mad when we don't run up a big bill."

While Uncle Bosko was cleaning up, we laid out all the things we had been saving for him. Papa bought him a nice blue suit, and

some underwear, and some socks. Stan bought him a swell red tie.
I got him a T shirt marked "Hamtramck High School," and everybody had something for him, even little Josie, who saved four
packages of bubble gum for Uncle Bosko. When Uncle Bosko came
out in Papa's bathrobe and saw the things, tears came to his eyes.
"You shouldn't have done it." He shook his head.

"But we want you to have them," Papa said. And little Josie took
Uncle Bosko's hand. "Hurry up and get dressed, Uncle Bosko,"
she told him. "I want to show you how bubble gum works."

Uncle Bosko wanted to save his new clothes, so Papa found him
an old pair of pants, I gave him a pair of saddle shoes, and he
slipped on the T shirt marked "Hamtramck High School." Then
Josie climbed up on his lap and held out the gum. "See, Uncle Bosko,
first you take a stick and chew it up real good."

"Ah, so." Uncle Bosko nodded. "It's sweet, eh?"

"Uh-huh. Then you put your lips like this and blow."

Uncle Bosko blew, but he didn't do so well. "No, no, Bosko,"
Papa said. "Not like that. Josie, give me a stick. I show him."

Papa blew, and Stan yelled, "Aw, Pa, that's not the way."

Papa glared at him. "So you know all about it, eh, Mr. Smarty?
All right. Go ahead. Show us how smart you are."

Stan did pretty well, only Papa shook his head. "No, you don't
hold your lips right. See, like this."

For a while we blew bubbles. Uncle Bosko caught on fast, but
the more Papa tried the worse he did, and his face got red. "All
right, that's enough." He glared at us. "Can't you see you're getting
gum all mixed up in Uncle Bosko's mustache? Besides, Uncle
Bosko and I want to talk." He leaned forward. "Tell me, Bosko, how
are things behind the iron curtains?"

Right away Uncle Bosko looked over his shoulders, but Papa
held up a hand, reassuring him. "You don't have to worry about
microphones here, Bosko. I know all about how they hide those
things behind the wallpaper. I see it in the movies." He pointed.
"Don't let those lumps over there bother you. I papered myself
and those corners always give me trouble."

Uncle Bosko nodded. "I know, Louie, but I keep forgetting. Ever
since 1939 . . . ach!" Then he shook his head slowly. "Things
aren't so good, Louie. Not so good."

"Yeah, that's what I hear the guy on television say. Tell me, Bosko, what did they have you doing over there?"

"Doing? Everything, I guess. One day they come around and say, 'Bosko, we need some salt. Go to Siberia and mine some.' So I mine salt until they say, 'Bosko, go dig some coal now.'"

"And did you do anything else?"

"Oh yes, Louie. After a while they say, 'Bosko, hop on the cattle cars. We're going to cut down trees.' So I cut down trees until one day the director comes around. 'Comrades,' he says, 'I have great news. We start a new five-year plan!'"

"And what did you say?" Papa asked.

"Well, Louie, I say to myself, 'Bosko, I think this means you go back to the salt mines. By golly, you got to get out of this place.'" He waved his hand before him. "Louie, can't we just blow some more bubbles?"

"Well, Bosko, we could." Papa glanced at Stan. "But I was thinking . . . well, I was thinking maybe you would like to see what Emil made in school."

"Aw, Pa," Stan said, "Uncle Bosko wants to blow bubbles. I'll show him how to do it real good."

"Quiet, I'm talking," Papa said quickly. "Emil, run and get what you made in school. Uncle Bosko will like it."

But Uncle Bosko hardly seemed pleased with what I made. "It looks like a bomb," he said nervously.

Papa nodded. "It's an auto bomb. You hook her up to the motor. When somebody starts the car . . . boom!" Papa began to chuckle.

Uncle Bosko edged away. "I didn't know they had revolutionists' school over here, too. Are you studying sabotage, Emil?"

"He studies arithmetic, auto mechanics, and that stuff." Papa beamed. "Do you know, he made that all by himself. The teacher didn't even tell him to do it. Yes, sir, someday I tell those guys down on the assembly line, 'Huh, so you build the cars. Okay. But who figures 'em out? My boy Emil.'"

Uncle Bosko kept staring nervously at the bomb, so I thought I'd better put it away. As I carried it to my bedroom, I saw him smile. Then his arm tightened around little Josie, and he looked at the rest of the kids sitting on the floor. "Ah, Louie," he said, "this is good . . . good. Do you think the director will care if I don't come into work this afternoon any more? I just like to sit here with the children around me, and—"

"Who's this director you talk about, Bosko?" Papa asked.

"The big boss where you get me the job."

"But I don't get you any job."

"No?" Uncle Bosko grew pale. "In your letter to the Society you tell them you got one for me. They got some law that says I can't come over unless I have one."

Looking out from the bedroom, I could see Papa scratch his head, and I felt like crawling under the rug. "Emil," he called, and I didn't know what to do. "Emil, come here." So I walked into the front room. "Emil, when I write that letter, did you say I have a job for Uncle Bosko?"

"Yes, Papa."

"Oh. Did I tell you to put that down?"

What could I say but no? Then Papa exploded. "So you say things I don't tell you to say, huh? Don't you think your Papa knows what he wants to put down when he writes a letter? All right, Mr. Smarty; all right!" He was so mad he couldn't talk for a moment. Then he began shaking his finger at me. "I'll tell you what to do, Mr. Smarty. You just march right over to Confession. And you tell Father Krupinski all about how you write things behind your Papa's back. You just tell him—" He stopped and pulled his mustache. "Hey, by golly, I just think. Maybe if you don't say that, they don't let Bosko come over, huh?"

Mama peeked in from the kitchen; then she came into the front room, wiping her hands on her apron, as if she was getting ready for business. So I decided to get my jacket, but Papa stopped me. "Hey, Emil, wait! You make Father Krupinski trot over from his house when the Notre Dame game is on television, and, by golly, maybe he give you double Penance." He regarded me sternly. "It's not nice for boys to write things their Papas don't tell 'em to." He bowed his head. "But I forgive you this time."

When Mama nodded and went back to the kitchen, I sure felt better. But Uncle Bosko was worried. "Louie, I got to go to work."

Papa regarded him, sitting there in the T shirt, and I'll bet you could count every rib in Uncle Bosko's body. And I'll even bet his wrists weren't any bigger than little Josie's. Papa shook his head.

"Don't worry about a job, Bosko. You just lay around for a while. Get good and rested. Eat a lot of Mama's cooking. Maybe go down and shoot some pool in the afternoon."

"But, Louie," Uncle Bosko said. "I couldn't just stay here and keep taking. It would be like taking from the children."

Papa waved his hand. "Afterwhile we fix you up. But for now, you just take it easy."

Yet Uncle Bosko couldn't forget about work. He talked of it all during supper. And after supper, because he was so tired, he went right to bed. We sat around the table for a long time then, and Mama shook her head. "Poor little fellow. Here he talks of working, and . . . why, I could lift him with one hand."

"Yeah, but we don't let him work," Papa said. "We make him rest. Mama, you cook him lots of things to eat so he gets big and strong like me."

Just then we heard a shuffling as Uncle Bosko came out of the bedroom, and in a minute he stood in the kitchen doorway. Papa had given him a flannel nightshirt. He had on one of Papa's night-caps with a tassel. And his lips were trembling. "Louie," he said, "I been thinking. The law says I got to have a job before I can come over. Maybe if they find out I don't have one, they send me back."

Mama's mouth flew open. Little Josie grew scared and glanced at Papa; and Papa, himself, looked troubled. Then he stood up. "We don't let 'em do that, Bosko." But I could tell that Papa wasn't sure. "You just go and get a good night's sleep."

"Maybe if I get a job real quick, it will be all right, Louie," Uncle Bosko said. "Maybe somebody wants some trees cut down."

Papa led him back to the bedroom, and I could hear him saying, "Now don't you worry, Bosko. I take care of everything." Yet when Papa came back into the kitchen, he was shaking. Then he slumped into his chair and started to sob so loud that Benny Dumbroski, next door, looked out of his kitchen window. "Hey, Louie!" Benny yelled. "What's the matter?"

Papa was crying so hard he couldn't even answer. So little Josie called, "They're going to send Uncle Bosko back."

"No!" Benny threw his window open all the way. "Hey, Louie, wait. I be right over."

Benny is about fifty, smaller than Papa even, and he digs ditches for the city. When he came in and saw everyone crying, he, too, got scared. "Louie, when they going to send him back?" he asked.

Papa could hardly answer. "On the next boat, I guess."

"Aw, Papa," I said, but no one paid any attention to me.

"And he's such a little fellow," Mama managed between sobs. "Why, with one hand I could—"

"Who's sending him back?" Benny wanted to know.

"I don't know," Papa said. "The guys that make the laws, I guess."

Then Benny got mad. "Louie, for two cents I'd go right down to the City Hall and tell those guys. I see 'em walk around all day in their white collars. And, by golly, it's just like 'em to pull such a trick. They don't let him stay, huh?"

"Not unless we get him a job," Papa sobbed.

Benny was puzzled. "Why don't you get him one then, Louie?"

"Could you work after starving for twenty-two years behind the iron curtains?" Papa wanted to know.

"Why, those bums, walking around all day in their white collars!" Benny banged the table. "For two cents I'd . . . Hey, Louie, can't you get him an easy job?"

"Like what?" Papa asked.

"Like maybe on the sanitation department . . . No, that's no good. You got to lift cans." Benny scratched his head. "You don't think of any easy jobs?"

Papa only shook his head, and the tears started again.

Benny sat down. "You don't think he can dig ditches, huh, Louie?"

"How's he going to dig ditches?" Papa wanted to know. "You think he's big and strong like me?"

"Oh." Benny kept scratching his head; then all at once his face lit up. "Hey, Louie, I got it."

"Yeah?"

"Sure. I just remember about that guy Mama and I see the other night in the movies."

"What guy?"

"The one with the mustache that wears his glasses in just one eye. He don't have any money, or any job, or anything either."

"He don't?"

"No. Then this old lady with all kinds of money comes along, so he marries her. And all he does is just ride around on her yacht, and guys are always bringing him stuff to drink, and lighting his cigarettes."

Papa straightened. "And he don't do anything else?"

"Well, sometimes he gets off the boat and goes to this place where he bets a lot of money. Or sometimes he drives like the dickens all over some place called Spain. Or sometimes he plays hockey on horseback."

"Is that all?"

"Yeah. Except he keeps telling this other girl how unhappy he is."

"What's he unhappy for?" Papa wanted to know.

"You know," Benny said, "I been trying to figure that out, Louie. I think maybe he's just nuts. But see, if Bosko marries somebody with a lot of money, he don't have to worry about a job."

"Hey!" Papa's eyes widened. "Then they can't send him back either, huh? Benny, do you know any rich old ladies with yachts?"

Offhand, Benny couldn't think of any. "Don't you know any, Louie?"

Papa didn't know of any either; then he started to beam.

"Say, what's the matter with Joe Tomich's widow?" he asked. "She don't have a yacht, but her oldest boy Walter makes good money out at Ford's, and if they make him a foreman, why—"

"Sure, and somebody tell me the other day that her boy Victor is thinking of starting a bakery."

"No!"

"Yeah."

"By golly." Papa was all smiles. "She's only forty-nine, too, and a good cook. By golly, let's go tell Bosko we got him fixed up." So we all paraded into the bedroom. "Bosko," Papa said, "you don't have to worry any more. We don't let 'em send you back."

Uncle Bosko sat up in bed. "You . . . you got me a job, Louie?" he asked hopefully.

Papa couldn't help but chuckle. "We got you a good job. Now first we get you married to Joe Tomich's widow, then—"

Uncle Bosko seemed frightened. "Louie, do I have to get married?"

"Yeah, you got to do that."

Uncle Bosko turned pale. "Louie, couldn't I just cut down trees?"

"You don't want to do that kind of stuff," Papa said.

Uncle Bosko considered. "But I'd be glad to dig coal even."

"No, Bosko." Papa shook his head. "That's too hard. So we get you married."

"And the beauty of it is," Benny joined in, "that all her kids are grown up and working. It's pretty nice with seven paychecks coming in each week. All you have to do, Bosko, is get a yacht and ride up and down the Detroit River all day. Of course, if Victor starts a bakery, maybe once in a while you might have to go down and tell 'em when to take the bread out of the oven."

"Or maybe take the money to the bank," Papa added. "You don't have to work hard, though."

"But, Louie," Uncle Bosko protested. "I don't think—"

Only Papa didn't hear him; Papa was chuckling too much. "And when those guys come around to send you back," he said, "all you have to do is buy the City Hall and put 'em out of business."

The next evening, as we were eating supper, Benny threw open his kitchen window and yelled, "Hey, Louie, how about taking Bosko over tonight and introducing him to Joe Tomich's widow?"

"That's a good idea!" Papa yelled back.

"Okay. Me and Mama'll be over about seven then."

"Okay." Papa looked around the table. "You kids better get dressed right after supper. I want you to look nice when we go over to the Tomichs' tonight."

"Aw, Papa," little Josie said. "Do I have to go? There's some awful good programs on television Sunday nights."

"Oh, and I suppose you think Uncle Bosko has a date every night in the week?"

"Louie," Uncle Bosko said. "If Josie wants to watch television, I'll be glad to stay home with her."

"She can watch it over there," Papa said. "All she have to do is turn on their set."

Uncle Bosko wilted, and all during supper he had a sick look on his face. But after supper he did put on his new blue suit and red tie. Papa lent him a derby, and by the time Benny and Mrs. Dumbroski came over, we were all set. Then Papa got sore. "All right, Stanislaus. Put the football away!"

"But, Pa." Stan pouted. "How we going to have any fun if we don't play football?"

"So you think you're going to play football in the Tomichs' living room. Well, just remember you're not home, Mr. Smarty. We'll have some manners over there tonight. Now put it away!"

Stan was undecided, so Papa said, "Mama!" And Mama gave him a couple of whacks to help him make up his mind. He threw the ball in a chair, and Papa nodded. "Now we go."

The Tomichs live just down the street, so we walked. Papa, Uncle Bosko, and Benny led the way, with Mama and Mrs. Dumbroski next, and we eight kids followed behind. As we came up on the porch, I guess Walter Tomich didn't know who we were, because he opened the door and said, "All right, you kids. Halloween isn't until next month. Now beat it!" Then he recognized Papa and Benny, and turned on the porch light. "Well, well," he said. "Come in."

Walter is about six four, weighs about two hundred and forty; and until Arthur Godfrey came out with that attachment to make ukulele playing easy, he spent all his spare time lifting weights. Lately, though, he's been practicing up on the ukulele, because he figures if things ever get slow out at Ford's, he might go on television.

"Walter," Papa said, "this is my brother Bosko."

Walter switched the ukulele and held out his hand. "Pleased to meet you, Bosko, I'm sure."

"Bosko just come over from behind the iron curtains," Papa explained, and Walter shook his hand some more. "Well, welcome to America, Bosko."

"Hey, Walter," Stan said. "What you got there?"

"Nothing." Walter put the ukulele up on the mantel. "Mama," he called, "we got company."

Mrs. Tomich came in from the kitchen; and when she saw who it was, she threw her hands up in surprise. Then she had to kiss Mama, and Mrs. Dumbroski, and all of us kids.

"Bosko," Papa said, "this is Lena Tomich."

Mrs. Tomich is about three times as big as Uncle Bosko, and when he bowed and kissed her hand, she giggled all over. "Welcome to America, Bosko," she said. "I hear the neighbors tell that you just arrived. Come in, everybody. We all sit down."

Uncle Bosko smiled and nodded, and Mrs. Tomich said, "Walter, turn on the electric log in the fireplace, and get a pitcher of wine from the cellar, and . . . just sit down, everybody." She went around hitting pillows to puff them up. "Here, Louie, put a couple pillows behind you . . . Bosko, why don't you sit over here in this chair? It's more comfortable."

Uncle Bosko hesitated shyly, but she insisted. Then little Josie climbed up on his lap, and his arm tightened around her. Walter got the electric log going, and Uncle Bosko leaned back, smiling. "You have a nice home here, Mrs. Tomich," he said.

Stan was edging over by the fireplace and looking up at the mantel, so Papa called, "Stanislaus, you let that ukulele alone. I don't tell you again . . . Hey, Lena, where's all the kids tonight?"

Mrs. Tomich threw up her hands. "They all got fellows or girls now—all but Walter—so they're out chasing around. You know how the young people are now'days."

"Yeah, I know," Benny Dumbroski said. "I got nine of my own, and, by gosh, I never see 'em any more."

But Papa didn't seem interested in such talk. Instead, he grew businesslike. "Say, Lena, I hear Victor's starting a bakery."

Mrs. Tomich smiled. "He's opening it next month."

"Is it going to be a big place?"

"He thinks he'll start with about four bakers."

Papa whistled. "Four bakers. Say, that's pretty big. And how is Walter doing?"

"Just fine, Louie. We think he'll be a foreman any day."

Papa considered. "And Sadie?"

"She has her own beauty shop now, Louie."

"Is that right? Things are going okay, huh, Lena?"

Mrs. Tomich nodded. "We're getting along fine."

"That's good," Papa said, and he seemed mighty satisfied.

Walter came in with a pitcher of wine, then; and all at once we heard a loud plunk. Looking around, I saw Stan with the ukulele in his hand, and two of the strings were busted. Walter saw, too, and he was sore as the dickens. He set down the pitcher, walked across the room and turned Stan over his knee.

"Hey, Papa," Stan yelled, "don't let him spank me!"

It was like a morgue around there. Uncle Bosko glanced at Papa. Benny Dumbroski didn't know what to do, and even Mrs. Tomich turned pale. But Papa was smiling. "It serves you right, Mr. Smarty. I tell you to let it alone . . . Go ahead, Walter, give him a good one." And Walter did. "You better give him a couple more," Papa went on. "That'll last him all evening; then we'll play a little pinochle."

It only took Walter a couple minutes to cool off, then he got the card table, and Papa began rubbing his hands. "Come on, Bosko," he said, "me and you'll stand Benny and Walter. We'll show these guys how to play."

Uncle Bosko looked up from the easy chair. "You go ahead, Louie. I'll just sit here by the fireplace and talk with the ladies."

"Aw, come on, Bosko," Benny said.

"But I never play the game," Uncle Bosko protested.

"Don't worry," Papa said. "I'll show you how real good."

Uncle Bosko glanced at the electric log, then lifted little Josie from his lap. "All right, Louie. I might make some mistakes, though."

"That's okay," Papa said and turned. "Hey, Emil, come on. We need somebody to keep score." So I went over by the table. "Now," Papa said, "we cut. Ace high. High card deals."

Well, Papa cut the ace and started to chuckle. "See, Bosko, there's nothing to it. Just like taking candy from the kids."

Papa dealt. Benny passed, and Uncle Bosko was puzzled. But Papa assured him. "You just pass, too, Bosko, and leave it to me." So Uncle Bosko did, and Walter bid twenty-one.

I looked at Papa's cards. He didn't have anything, but he chuckled some more and bid twenty-two. Now the object of pinochle—as Papa plays it—is to run up the other side, get them to bid higher and higher, get them out on a limb, then pass and leave them holding the bag. Only it was Walter who passed; and it was Papa who was holding the bag with the bid.

"Oh," Papa said, glaring around the table, "so that's the way we're going to play. All right. We just show these wise guys, Bosko. This time they don't even take a trick."

I think everything might have been all right, except in playing the hand it was Papa who didn't get a trick, and his face got red. A few hands later, when he again tried to stick Walter, but Walter stuck him instead, he began to get pretty huffy. I guess Mrs. Tomich noticed, because she said, "Wouldn't you men like to watch television? Ed Sullivan is on, Walter, and maybe the boss out at Ford's will get mad if you don't look in."

"It would be nice to watch," Uncle Bosko said, glancing at Papa.

But Papa shook his head. "No, we keep playing."

Uncle Bosko looked at Walter and Benny, but they weren't paying any attention to Papa because they had played pinochle with him before.

The fireworks started, though, about four hands later, when Walter really got Papa over the barrel; and Papa, to get out of it, tried to claim he had double pinochle. "What do you mean you got double pinochle, Louis?" Walter said, looking at Papa's cards face up on the table. "You have to have two queens of spades and two jacks of diamonds for that."

"That's right, Louie," Benny joined in. "And you got one queen of spades and one jack of diamonds. The jack of spades and the queen of diamonds you got with it don't count nothing."

"They don't count nothing!" Papa slapped his forehead. "You mean you guys don't even read about that in the paper? You mean you don't know they changed the rules?"

"Who changed the rules?" Walter wanted to know.

"The guys that write the paper. Yeah, and they even put it right on the front page in great big letters. They say: FROM NOW ON YOU DON'T HAVE TO HAVE TWO QUEENS OF SPADES AND TWO JACKS OF DIAMONDS FOR DOUBLE PINOCHLE."

"Don't give us that stuff, Louie," Walter said.

"Yeah, Louie," Benny said, "don't give us that baloney. You can't read the paper no more than me."

Papa jumped up. "So now I can't read the paper. And you don't even want to play by the new rules."

"Keep your shirt on, Louie," Walter said. "Sit down."

Uncle Bosko was scared stiff. "Please, Louie, please sit—"

"No!" Papa banged the table. "I don't play like that." He considered. "But if you want to call it a misdeal, I'll let it go this time, and we'll start over." He stood there, waiting for them to say okay.

But Walter said, "Louie, we play these cards."

"All right," Papa said. "Then I quit."

Walter shrugged. "Okay. Emil, come on. Take his place."

Well, when they didn't even coax Papa to keep on playing, he sure hit the ceiling. He sulked over to a chair to watch television, and was he ever fuming. And the longer he sat there the more he thought about it, I guess, because he got madder and madder. In fact, by the time we went home, he was so sore he wouldn't talk to anyone.

Uncle Bosko was really worried then. "Walter didn't mean no harm, Louie," he began apologetically after we got in the house. "After all, cards is just cards."

"That's right, Louie," Mama said.

"Yeah." Papa nodded and his mustache began trembling. "But when they don't even let me meld double pinochle, that's going too far."

Right away Mama put her arm around his shoulder. "Now, Louie. Now don't cry."

"And all the time I have two queens of spades and two jacks of diamonds." The tears began to slip down Papa's cheeks.

"Well, Louie, maybe they don't know the rules," Mama said.

"But I tell 'em the rules." Papa started sobbing, and there was no comforting him, so Mama let him cry. Yet after a while he thought of something else, I guess, because all at once he looked up. "Hey, I just remember. Do you know what else that Walter do?"

"What?" Mama asked.

"He even hits little Stanislaus. By golly, that makes my blood boil. And Stanislaus don't even do nothing; he just gives the ukulele a little plunk. Can he help it the strings are no good and bust? By golly, I ought to go back and lick that Walter good."

"Hey, Pa," Stan called. "Come on, I'll go with you. Just because he's a big palooka, he thinks—"

Papa looked at him. "So he's big—so what? I'll just take him by the neck and—"

"Attaboy, Pa." Stan was jumping up and down. "I'll get our coats." But when he ran to the closet, Papa stopped him.

"No, Stanislaus, wait. I give him a break. I let him go this time. But the next time he just better watch out."

Stan pouted. "Aw, nuts! Aren't you even going to take him by the neck, Pa?"

Papa pretended not to hear. "And that Benny Dumbroski, that little shrimp. I ought to fix his wagon, telling me I can't read. Why, one time I read a whole story in a magazine. It was a page long, even."

"Nuts," Stan said.

Papa glared at him. "Oh, so you think I can't read either, eh, Mr. Smarty? Mama!"

Stan glanced at Mama. "I didn't say that. I just said nuts, I bet you don't fix Benny's wagon."

"So you think I'm afraid of that little shrimp, huh? I'll show you, Mr. Smarty. I'm going right over there now, and—"

"Attaboy, Pa." Stan clapped his hands.

Papa started for the door, got halfway, hesitated, then stopped. "You know, I just think. Maybe it wouldn't be nice to fix Benny's wagon. Maybe Uncle Bosko wouldn't like it."

But Uncle Bosko was too scared to speak. He just stood there trembling, and Stan said, "Nuts."

Papa gave him a dirty look. "But I tell you what I do . . . I . . ." He scratched his head. "Hey, I know. I don't fix Benny's wagon. I fix his car. Emil, run and get the auto bomb you made in school."

"Gee, Papa," I said. "I don't think you ought to—"

"Get the bomb!" He pointed. When I brought it, Papa put his finger to his lips. "Now we keep this a secret. See, I'll sneak out in the alley, and tomorrow morning when Benny starts his jalopy . . . bang! But don't tell anyone. We want to surprise Benny."

I guess Benny must have been surprised, because about six o'clock the next morning it sounded as if all of Hamtramck had blown up. I hopped out of bed, ran to the window, and there was Benny, with Stan right behind him, coming across our back yard. Papa was in the kitchen, getting ready for work. And I guess he saw Benny, too, because I heard the lock snap on the back door.

In a minute Benny was pounding like the dickens and yelling, "Hey, Louie, what's the big idea? Stanislaus tell me all about what you do."

Papa didn't say anything, and Stan started pounding on the door too. "Hey, Pa," Stan called, "come out and fix his wagon like you said you were going to."

Benny began hopping around like a bantam rooster. "I dare you to come out, Louie. I dare you!"

But Papa was awful quiet. I even heard him say "sssh" to Mama. And all the time Benny was getting madder. He kept beating on the door and yelling, "So you don't come out, huh, Louie? All right, I fix you. You just wait. I'm going over and see Walter Tomich. And I'm going to tell him all about how you plan to have Bosko marry his Mama for her money."

"Nuts," Stan said. "We'll lick Walter too. Papa will just take that big palooka by the neck and—"

"Shut up, Stanislaus!" Papa yelled.

"I knew you was in there, Louie." Benny brought up his fists and began dancing around. "Open the door!"

"I don't have time," Papa said. "I'm getting ready for work."

Just then Mrs. Dumbroski threw open her kitchen window. "Benny," she called, "it's ten after six. You're going to be late."

"Okay, Mama." Benny gave the door a final bang. "But I'll get you after work tonight, Louie. And you just wait till I tell Walter Tomich on you!" Benny started across the yard toward his jalopy in the alley, and Stan called, "Hey, Pa, let me in."

Then Papa got sore. "You just sit out on that porch, Mr. Smarty. I'll teach you to go shooting off your mouth."

"But, Pa, it's chilly," Stan said.

"I don't care if it's eighty below zero," Papa said. "You just sit there. And don't you dare open any of those milk bottles for breakfast. This time, Mr. Smarty, you go too far!"

Usually, Papa is finished with his shift and home from work by the time I get out of school. But that evening—following the morning that he had attached the auto bomb to Benny Dumbroski's jalopy, and Benny had come over to clean his clock—Papa still hadn't arrived when I came in, even though I stopped to watch football practice. As I put my books down, Mama, who was standing at the window shaking her head, said, "I can't understand it, Emil."

Well, I thought she was worried, so I said, "He probably stopped to get a haircut, Mama, or maybe shoot a game of pool."

Mama waved her hand. "But he's been driving around the block for the past two hours. I just can't understand it."

I couldn't understand it either. But then my brother Stan yelled, "Here he comes again, Ma!" And sure enough, there was Papa, swinging around the corner. When he passed the Dumbroskis', he slowed a little, looked in, then stepped on the gas. As he passed our house, he waved. But when he saw me he began to motion like the dickens. I didn't catch on to what he wanted until the second trip around. Then I hurried out to the curb, and Papa slowed so I could hop in.

"Emil," he said, "how would you like to take a ride?"

"Gee, Papa," I replied. "I'm getting hungry. It's almost time for supper."

"The air will do you good," Papa insisted. "I tell you what. You drive around the block a few times." He took off his hat. "Here, put this on. Your head might get cold. And sit kinda low in the seat and go kinda fast when you pass the Dumbroskis'."

"What for?" I asked.

"When your Papa tells you to drive around the block, you don't ask questions!" He swung around the corner and stopped. "Well, I think I go home," he said, getting out of the car. "I want to go down the alley and see if they pick up the garbage today."

"How many times do you want me to drive around?" I asked.

He considered. "Oh, I wave to you from the front room when it's okay to stop."

Well, I drove around the block. When I passed the Dumbroskis', I saw Benny and Walter Tomich sitting before the windows, looking out. So I waved to them, and Benny stood up and peered closer. Then he seemed to get excited, because he began motioning, and both of them ducked away from the windows. As I turned at the corner, I looked around and saw Benny and Walter Tomich cutting across the back yard.

I was anxious to see what was going on, so instead of going all the way around, I cut down through the alley. Papa was crouched by the Pulaskis' garage and peeking around the corner, while Benny was tiptoeing along our hedge. All at once Benny yelled, "Hey,

Walter, here he is. I got him!" And Walter came out into the alley.

Papa turned pale. And as I stopped the car, Walter walked toward him, and I didn't blame Papa one bit. Walter not only looks like something out of the physical-culture magazines but, besides that, he had a look on his face that made even me start to shake.

"Well, well, Walter," Papa said, smiling. "I'm glad to see you. You're just in time for supper."

I don't think Walter even heard. He had Papa by the shirt front. "Louie, what's the big idea?" he demanded.

"What big idea?" Papa managed.

"You know what I mean. What's the idea trying to get that brother of yours to marry Mama for her little insurance money?"

Papa appeared surprised. "Did I do that?"

"Don't give us that baloney, Louie," Benny cut in. "We know all about your low-down schemes. Go ahead, Walter. Hang one on him."

"I didn't do anything like that," Papa said. "I just remember. Benny did it. And I keep telling him, 'No, that's not nice.'"

"See, Walter," Benny said. "Now he's blaming me. That shows what kind of a bum he is. Bust him good."

"Shut up!" Walter held Papa against the garage. "Louie, I'm warning you. You pull any tricks on Mama, and I'll shove you right through this wall."

"But, Walter—"

"Shut up! Louie, if you do anything to hurt Mama, I'm going to take you apart. Understand?"

Man, I got a look at Walter's face, and the only thing I could think of was to get out of there in a hurry, so I ducked over by the car. For a minute Walter couldn't even talk; then he began again. "And another thing. That brat of yours broke two of my ukulele strings. Louie, you get down to the music store, and you—"

I hopped in the car then, and pulled out fast. I parked in front and had just entered the parlor when Papa came in the back door. For a moment he stood there in the kitchen, trembling.

"What's the matter, Louie?" Uncle Bosko asked.

Papa closed the door. "You know," he said, "someday that Walter Tomich is going too far."

"Hey, Pa, did you take him by the neck?" Stan asked.

"No, I didn't want to hurt him."

Uncle Bosko was upset. "Louie, did he come over because some-one tell him you wanted me to marry his Mama for her money?" And when Papa nodded, Uncle Bosko's face twisted. "But, Louie, I would never do anything like that. Didn't you tell him?"

Papa began marching up and down the kitchen. "I tell him so many things, Bosko, I don't remember what all I say."

"But, Louie, you should have—"

"Don't worry, Bosko." Papa waved his hand. "You just leave that wise guy to me."

"Now, Louie," Mama said. "Now take it easy."

"That wise guy!" Papa pounded the table. "You know what he thinks he's going to do? He thinks he's going to make me pay for the ukulele strings that Stanislaus bust."

"Maybe we ought to," Mama said. And Uncle Bosko nodded.

"No! We don't pay for nothing! So he thinks it's so easy to get money out of me, huh? All right, he can just go down to that de-partment store what sells me the bum refrigerator that time. He can just ask those guys how many times they have to trot out here before I make up my mind to pay."

Uncle Bosko hung his head, and I could tell he was thinking plenty. He was quiet all during supper. And he didn't even pay any attention to television that night, even though he had come to like it a lot. It was just as we were getting ready for bed that he drew me aside. "Emil, how much are ukulele strings?" he asked.

"Maybe thirty-five cents a set of four," I told him.

"Thirty-five cents? Thanks, Emil."

The next noon, as I was getting ready to go back to school, he drew me aside again. "Emil, do you know where I can get a job?"

I didn't know what to say because would Papa burn up if I butted in. "Maybe you ought to take it easy," I hedged.

"But I got to work, Emil. If I don't, they'll send me back."

"They wouldn't do that, Uncle Bosko," I assured him. "Papa just got mixed up."

"Do you think so?" he asked hopefully.

"Sure, but don't tell him I said so."

Uncle Bosko seemed to feel better, yet his face was solemn. "But, Emil, we ought to pay for those ukulele strings."

I had a feeling that Papa probably stopped for them on his way to work. Yet I wasn't sure, because Papa really had that department store running around when they tried to collect on the refrigerator that he thought was no good. Besides, Uncle Bosko was going on, "I don't like to have people mad at us, Emil. It makes me feel bad. Maybe I can find something to do to pay the Tomichs back. Don't you know anyone who wants some trees cut down? I can do that."

Gosh, I didn't have the heart to tell him there was nothing around here like that. But I felt so darned sorry for him, standing there with his face all twisted with worry, that . . . well, I said, "Come on, Uncle Bosko. We'll find something."

The only work I could think of was down at Mike Zachek's bowling alley. That's where we kids always go to earn a little. Yet I knew Uncle Bosko couldn't set pins all by himself. He didn't understand about bowling, so I decided to cut classes.

"Sure, Emil," Mike said, "you can work one and two."

I could work both alleys by myself, but I knew Uncle Bosko wouldn't want it that way. I knew he wanted to earn the money himself. "You take number one, Uncle Bosko," I told him. "I'll tell you what to do. But be sure to keep your legs up so you don't get hit by a ball."

Well, first you have to remember that Uncle Bosko isn't so young any more. Then you have to remember that he went for I don't know how many years over there without a decent meal, and that he couldn't grab a handful of pins like us kids. He couldn't slap them in and bang them down on the alley in a second.

On the first roll someone got a strike, knocking all the pins down. "Roll the ball back, Uncle Bosko," I said, which he did. "Now pick up the pins and put them up there in the rack."

Uncle Bosko picked up a pin, carried it over, then turned around slowly and walked back for another; while up at the far end of the alley some bohunk took a slug from his bottle of beer, flicked the ashes from his cigar, and yelled, "Set 'em up!"

I was busy on my own alley for a second, and before I could hop over and give Uncle Bosko a hand, the bohunk was shouting, "Come on! Come on!"

That's the way it was. It was all new to Uncle Bosko; and he tried, tried his best, but he couldn't help it. Sometimes he'd begin to set up the pins when he wasn't supposed to, or sometimes he'd forget to roll the ball back. Then they'd yell at him. And because they were yelling, he grew nervous and fumbled the pins. I'd jump over to help him then, but with the two of us in there we'd only get in each other's way.

The three other bohunks were taking it up now. If one of them would miss or send a ball into the gutter, it would be Uncle Bosko's fault. And their remarks, shouted down the alley, caused his lips to start trembling.

All I could think of was to get into the fifth game, and then to get it over with. We would have enough money for ukulele strings then. And I wanted to get out of there fast. But in the fifth game, one of those jokers was way off. He had put a couple of balls in the gutter, and I guess he had a couple of dimes bet. At any rate, he started to boil, and he started to blame Uncle Bosko. Along about the seventh frame, this joker got a bad split and hit the ceiling.

As Uncle Bosko got down to pick up the scattered pins, the joker grabbed a ball and let it fly. "Look out, Uncle Bosko!" I yelled. "Look out!"

Uncle Bosko turned. "What did you say, Emil?"

I didn't have time to shout. The ball crashed in among the knocked-over pins. They flew everywhere, and Uncle Bosko was standing there in the middle of them. I saw a look of surprise start to cross his face—then his face went white, and his lips pressed tight, and his eyes closed in pain.

"Oh, God, help." The words escaped me. I scrambled over the partition and saw him sink to one knee. And I thought his leg was broken. I put my arm around him, bracing him. "Let me see, Uncle Bosko." Carefully I raised the trouser leg, fully expecting the jagged end of a bone to be sticking out.

"It's just a little bump, Emil," he managed.

There on his shin the skin was broken, and the blood was trickling down. As gently as I could, I felt for a break. I felt, and probed, and felt. And never in my whole life have I ever been so thankful, for it was only a bump, though a painful bump.

Then he managed a little smile. "It will be all right, Emil. It just stings."

Looking around, I saw the bohunk who had thrown the ball. He was standing up by the foul line. I don't exactly know what happened then, except I had a bowling pin in my hand and I was charging up the alley.

"Now take it easy, kid," the bohunk said. He had a scared look on his face, as if he thought he might have to pay a hospital bill. And Mike Zachek, who owns the place, came hurrying over. Just as I was working into position to get a good swing at the guy, Mike made a grab for me. "All right, Emil, that's enough of that!"

But I broke loose and jumped up onto the seats. There were some empty beer bottles there on the floor. I picked one up and circled, so that I could get a clear shot at the bohunk. And Mike moved in front of him. "Don't throw it, Emil," he warned.

"Get out of the way!" I yelled. But he wouldn't move, so I swung my arm, feinting, pretending I was throwing. Both Mike and the bohunk ducked then. And with Mike out of the way, I had a wide-open shot. I brought my arm back and was just set to let the bottle go when Uncle Bosko limped between us. "Don't throw it, Emil," he said. "That's not nice."

For a second I hesitated. Mike Zachek began edging over, and I knew what he was going to do. He was going to grab Uncle Bosko. "Mike," I warned, "keep your hands off him! If you touch him, I'm going to start throwing. The first bottle goes through your plate-glass window. Then I'm going to bust every glass on your bar."

Now that's the kind of talk Mike understands. He reached into his pocket. "Here's a couple dollars, Emil. Come down, and we'll forget it."

"Please come down, Emil," Uncle Bosko begged.

When Uncle Bosko said that . . . well, I nodded. But I knew those jokers. The minute they got the upper hand, they'd rough me up, and probably Uncle Bosko too. "I don't want your money," I said. "Just give me the dollar we earned. Don't come near me! Put it on the seat over there." I edged along and picked it up. "Uncle Bosko, you go up by the door." I backed away.

Reaching the door, I threw the beer bottle and bowling pin on the floor. "Emil," Mike said, "don't you ever come back in here."

"Nuts," I said, and slammed the door.

As we walked down the street, I was still burning. But Uncle

Bosko was so upset that I forced a smile. "We'll get the ukulele strings now," I told him. And I tried to give him the whole dollar, but he wouldn't take it.

"No, Emil," he said. "We worked together. Half is yours."

The strings came to thirty-six cents, with tax; and as we started toward the Tomichs', Uncle Bosko carefully counted the dime and four pennies in his hand. "Emil," he said, "is there a store near here where we could get perfume?" He flushed a bit. "It might be nice to take Mrs. Tomich a little bottle."

The only thing I know about perfume is that you can't get much for fourteen cents. I looked at him, limping along, and I was still burning because of those jokers at the bowling alley. And I didn't want to have him laughed at now because of a bottle of cheap perfume. Yet his face was so solemn that I couldn't help but say, "Sure, we'll go over to the dime store and pick something up."

The girl acted as if she was doing us a favor by waiting on us. She stood there chewing her gum. And when Uncle Bosko took so much time looking over the bottles, she began to get disgusted. I guess Uncle Bosko noticed it, too, for he seemed embarrassed. "I'll take this one," he said quickly, smiling at her.

She didn't even look at him. Instead, she slipped the bottle into a sack and yawned. "Ten cents."

Uncle Bosko handed her a dime. And then, as if trying to make up for keeping her waiting, he carefully took a penny from his hand, handed it to her and smiled shyly. "That's for you."

She glared at him. "Gee, buster, thanks." And that's the way I was afraid it would be with Mrs. Tomich when Uncle Bosko came in with the perfume.

"Did I do something wrong, Emil?" Uncle Bosko whispered.

"Naw," I said in a loud voice. "Some dames have just got holes in their head." I took his arm. "Let's get out of this firetrap."

His lips were working. He was puzzled and hurt, and I didn't know what to say. Anyway, we went over to the Tomichs' and rang the front doorbell. There was no answer, so we went around to the back door, rapped, and Mrs. Tomich looked out of the kitchen window. To tell the truth, I had a chip on my shoulder. I guess I expected a dirty look. So I was taken by surprise when she smiled and began straightening her hair.

She was baking bread, and when we walked into the kitchen, that warm smell came up and hit me and my mouth started to water. "Come right in," she said. Then she became a little flustered. "I was baking, Bosko, and I'm afraid I'm not dressed up very much, and—" She straightened her apron. "Come right in."

Uncle Bosko held out the ukulele strings. "Mrs. Tomich, we just brought these over to replace those Stanislaus broke the other night. Stanislaus didn't mean any harm. He's just a little fellow, and you know how boys are."

"I know he didn't mean it, Bosko. But you shouldn't have bothered."

"But we owe you for them," Uncle Bosko said. "And we don't like Walter to be mad."

You could see the worry on Uncle Bosko's face, and Mrs. Tomich said quickly, "But Walter breaks strings all the time, Bosko."

"He does?"

"Oh, yes. Why, sometimes when the orchestra plays kind of fast on television, and Walter sits there playing along with them, he'll break eight or nine in an evening."

"Is that right?" Uncle Bosko seemed to feel a little better.

"That's right. Walter just can't seem to learn that playing the ukulele isn't like exercising with dumbbells."

"I didn't know that, Mrs. Tomich. I thought maybe he never broke a string before," Uncle Bosko said, then looked down at the floor. "And we bring you a little something too."

"You did?"

Mrs. Tomich took the package from Uncle Bosko, and I held my breath. As she took the little bottle of perfume from the sack, I watched her face. For a moment she just looked at the bottle; then her lips began to quiver, and I thought she was going to cry. "It's— it's lovely, Bosko," she said. "I don't think I can ever remember anyone bringing me such a nice present."

Sometimes people just say things, but I knew this wasn't baloney. I knew Mrs. Tomich meant it. Then she blinked a couple of times and said quickly, "Excuse me a minute, I want to put it in my room."

But Mrs. Tomich was gone for more than a minute. In fact, she was gone for quite a while. And when she came back into the kitchen, her eyes were awfully red. Then she threw her hands in the air. "My goodness, I forgot all about the bread!"

"It sure smells good," I told her. "Doesn't it, Uncle Bosko?"

"Oh, yes, Emil. By golly, I don't think I smell anything so good since I was just a little fellow and Mama used to bake."

Right away Mrs. Tomich asked, "Would you like some bread, Bosko?"

"Oh, that would be too much trouble, Mrs. Tomich."

"No it wouldn't. You just sit down. You know, I bet you like the heel of the bread, don't you?"

Uncle Bosko grinned. "Yeah, I like that."

"With a lot of butter?"

Uncle Bosko nodded shyly.

"I just knew you did," Mrs. Tomich said. "And I bet when you were just a little fellow, your Mama used to call you into the kitchen every time she baked, didn't she?"

The smile was all over Uncle Bosko's face. "Mama always used to do that. We had a little farm outside Pinsk, and, by golly, I can still remember how Mama used to—" He shook his head.

"Well, we'll just have some good old Polish bread then," Mrs. Tomich said. "Now you sit there, Bosko, and I'll just cut the heels off, and—" She put five thick heels of the warm bread on Uncle Bosko's plate and five on mine.

Uncle Bosko took a big bite and the butter oozed out. "Oh, this is good," he said. "Even Mama couldn't bake like this."

Mrs. Tomich flushed with pleasure. "I think it might have gotten a little heavy."

"Oh, no, Mrs. Tomich," Uncle Bosko said. "Oh, no. But aren't you going to eat any?"

Mrs. Tomich considered. "Well, I don't think so, Bosko. Sadie —that's my daughter who has the beauty shop—has been saying, 'Mama, you ought to go on a diet.'" She sort of glanced at Uncle Bosko. "So . . . well, I think I might start."

"But this is so good."

Mrs. Tomich beamed, then grew apologetic. "I hope you'll pardon the butter, though, Bosko," she said. "It's just store butter. It's not like the old kind."

Uncle Bosko assured her it was fine. Yet she shook her head. "It's not like the kind we used to have in the old days. My Papa had a little farm, too—near Baranovich—and I can still remember how that butter tasted when it came from the churn." She pulled up a chair. "And do you remember that buttermilk, Bosko? Remember how it would have big pieces of butter in it, and . . ."

". . . and we used to keep it in the well," Uncle Bosko added between bites. "And remember how we used to come in from the hayfields in the summertime, and we used to be just about burning up from swinging the scythes? Then we used to go to the well, and that buttermilk was so cool in our throats." He shook his head in remembrance. "Oh, that was good."

"And what about the herb butters?" Mrs. Tomich asked. "Did your Mama ever mix rosemary, or chervil, or thyme in with the unsalted butter?"

"Oh, yes. Mama always had a big herb garden."

Mrs. Tomich shook her head sadly. "I miss those herb gardens, Bosko. I don't think there's anything so nice as fresh green herbs."

"They are nice," Uncle Bosko agreed.

"Do you know, Bosko, I always wanted a herb garden over here."

"Is that right? By golly, it is nice to have something like that. It makes a person feel good to get out in the evening among the growing things. It makes you feel good just to . . . well, just to be there."

Mrs. Tomich nodded. "That's what I always said. But Joe—that was my husband—had to go and cement up the whole back yard and build garages all over the place so he could rent them. Sometimes he used to make me so mad." She waved a hand, as if to dismiss it.

I looked at Uncle Bosko. He was sitting there with his elbows on the table, a heel of warm bread in his hand and a little melted butter on his chin. I thought of those jokers down at the bowling alley and that dumb dame at the dime store. And all at once I felt good, because I knew where he belonged—here in this kitchen.

But I was curious about something, so I asked, "Uncle Bosko, how come Papa came to America?"

Uncle Bosko considered. "I think, Emil, it was as Mama always used to say—that your Papa and his Papa were two of a kind. By golly, I'll never forget. We'd all get out to cut hay in the morning, and Papa would say, 'Well, I think we better start at this end of the field.' Then Louie would shake his head. 'No, Papa, I think we better start at the other end.'

"Or sometimes in the fall," Uncle Bosko went on, "Louie would say, 'Well, Papa, I think we better take the geese to market.' Then Papa would say, 'No, Louie, they're not ready yet.' But Papa always missed Louie something terrible; he used to get so lonesome with no one to argue with."

Mrs. Tomich nodded. "I know how those things are, Bosko." And the clock struck four-thirty then.

"I think we better go now, Mrs. Tomich," Uncle Bosko said.

"Oh, stay awhile, Bosko. It's early."

But Uncle Bosko thought we better be getting home. Mrs. Tomich started to say something, then smiled. "You know, Bosko, I just remembered. I have to bake bread tomorrow afternoon again."

I took a look at the table and wondered what the Tomichs were going to do with all the loaves piled there, plus the bread Mrs. Tomich intended baking tomorrow. She caught me looking and flushed a little. "We eat a lot," she said quickly. "So if you happen to be going by, Bosko, why, maybe—"

Uncle Bosko nodded. "Yeah, I might have to go to the store or something, Mrs. Tomich, and so—"

So I decided to walk on ahead. But I got to thinking. I got to thinking about some of those girls over at high school. And I got to thinking it would be pretty nice to have someone wait for you after classes. Someone who wouldn't care if you were a little late. Someone who would be interested in . . . well, mechanical drawing and auto mechanics, and things like that.

Right after supper the phone rang, and Walter Tomich was on the line. "Emil, let me talk to Bosko," he said.

I called Uncle Bosko, but Uncle Bosko had never used a phone before. "Emil, I can't understand over those things," he said. "Will you listen for me?" So I explained to Walter.

"That's okay, Emil," Walter said. "I just called to tell him thanks for the ukulele strings. And tell him thanks for bringing Mama that perfume."

"Did she really like it, Walter?" I asked.

"She sure did. All during supper she kept saying, 'Imagine some-one bringing a present for a fat old lady like me.' It sure pleased her. By the way, I dropped into Mike Zachek's bowling alley after I got off shift. Someone told me you blew your top down there this afternoon. What was the trouble?"

So I explained to Walter how we were setting pins to earn some money, and I told him about the joker who threw the ball.

"Is that how Bosko earned the money for the perfume and strings?" he asked.

"Yeah."

Walter didn't say anything for a moment. "I didn't mean that Bosko should . . . Well, tell him thanks, Emil. I sure appreciate it. Do you know who rolled the ball?"

"No, but Mike Zachek could tell you."

"Thanks, Emil. I think I better drop in and have a talk with a couple of guys. Let me speak to your Papa."

"Okay." So I yelled, "Papa, Walter Tomich wants to speak with you."

Papa was sitting in his easy chair, cleaning his pipe. "Who?"

"Walter Tomich."

Papa hopped up like a jet taking off. "Tell him I'm not here. Tell him I had to go downtown for something."

"He knows you're here, Papa. And he says if you're going down to pick up ukulele strings, you shouldn't bother."

Papa was already taking his hat out of the closet. "He does?"

"Yeah. And he says he's sorry for blowing his top the other eve-ning. He didn't mean to get sore."

"You mean he wants to apologize?"

"Sure. Come on and talk to him."

Papa glanced at Stan, then slammed his hat down in a chair. "No! I won't do that!"

"But, Louie," Uncle Bosko said. "Walter is sorry."

"I don't care. That wise guy. See, Stanislaus, he knows I was just getting ready to go over there and lick him good. Now he wants to get out of it. Well, I'll show him."

"I don't think he'll talk, Walter," I said.

"Well, just tell him, Emil, we'd like him to come over to the house some night; tell him to bring the family along, and—"

"I don't ever go over to that house!" Papa began strutting up and down the living room.

"Walter, maybe you better catch him some other time," I said.

"Okay, Emil. But tell Bosko I said thanks again."

I hung up. "See Stanislaus," Papa was saying. "See how he's afraid of me." Papa was all chest. "Those wise guys know that when I get sore, they better not monkey around. Just feel that muscle." He flexed his arm.

"Boy, Pa," Stan said. And Steve, Walt, Joe, and Pete had to feel Papa's muscle too.

"Emil." Uncle Bosko's face was lined with worry. "Do you think your Papa means it when he says he's never going over to the Tomichs' again?"

I knew what was bothering him. He was thinking that maybe Papa wouldn't want any of us to go over to the Tomichs' either. I wanted to assure him then; I wanted to tell him that it would blow over. But you never know about Papa. At the moment, Papa was kneeling with the kids gathered around him. "All right, you guys," he was saying. "Come on. I Indian-wrestle any one of you."

When the kids backed away and Papa started to chuckle, I became pretty upset. Papa was enjoying himself too much; and if there's anything Papa likes, it's to have the kids stand around him with their mouths open.

"What do you think, Emil?" Uncle Bosko asked.

And all I could say was, "I don't know."

The next noon I said, "Uncle Bosko, aren't you going over to see Mrs. Tomich? Remember, she said she's going to bake bread."

Uncle Bosko was staring vacantly out of the window. "I don't think so, Emil."

"Oh, come on," I coaxed. Papa was at work. And I wasn't going to take no for an answer, because I knew Uncle Bosko wanted to go, so I got his coat. "Come on," I said, "I'll walk over with you. It's on the way to school."

He regarded me. "I shouldn't, Emil."

"Papa won't know," I told him, and realized that I had said the wrong thing, so I went on quickly, "but she asked you, Uncle Bosko. We can't snub people just because Papa is mad at them."

"That's right." He nodded. "Maybe I should go this once."

I expected him to be smiling as we walked down the street, but he wasn't. And as I left him at the Tomichs', I got to thinking of that kitchen with the warm-bread smell, and the way Mrs. Tomich piled the heels of bread on his plate; and I'll have to admit, I started to get pretty sore at Papa.

Uncle Bosko didn't get home until just as Mama was putting the things on the table for supper. I tried to catch his eye, but couldn't. And all during supper he kept looking down at the tablecloth. It worried me, and I wanted to talk for him. "Gosh, Papa," I wanted to say, "why can't you get him some sort of a job? Maybe he has some plans of his own." But I didn't say it. In the first place, even I could see that Uncle Bosko wasn't able to work, though he wanted to. After those years over there . . . well, that's the way it was. But I couldn't understand why he shouldn't be able to go down and visit Mrs. Tomich in the afternoon without feeling that he was going against Papa. So I said, "Hey, Papa, why don't we invite Walter Tomich over here for a game of pinochle tonight? He's a good guy."

"Since when?" Papa said.

"Yeah, since when?" Stan joined in.

What's the use of arguing? First thing you know, I'd have Papa all riled, and I'd really get things mixed up. So I just shut my mouth, but I was thinking plenty.

Along about seven o'clock the phone rang and Walter was on the line. "Emil, let me talk to your old man," he said. And right away I knew something was wrong; and I didn't know what to do, because I didn't want Walter jimmying up the works either. "Emil, get him on the phone!" Walter said. He wasn't fooling, so I called Papa.

Papa threw out his chest. "Oh, so he wants to apologize some more, huh? Well, tell him to go soak his head."

"Attaboy, Pa," Stan said. But I wasn't going to tell Walter that. Besides, he was going on, "Emil, I'll give him ten seconds to get on the line or I'm coming over and knock his block off."

"What's the matter, Walter?" I asked.

"Plenty. Mama's been crying all evening."

"What for?"

"None of your business."

Just then Papa called, "Emil, tell that big palooka—"

I couldn't get my hand over the phone in time. "Emil, did he call me a palooka? That settles it. I'm on my way over!"

"Wait a minute, Walter." Brother, was I sweating!

"What do you want?"

"Where you at?"

"Melenkovich's Tavern. Why?"

"Look, could I talk to you a second? I mean before you come over?"

Walter finally agreed to buy me a boilermaker before coming over to knock Papa's block off. But I'm too young for boilermakers, so he said he'd make it a milkshake instead.

When I walked into the drugstore, Walter looked at me. "Now, Emil," he said, "what do you want to see me about?"

To tell the truth, I didn't want to see him about anything; I just wanted to keep him away from the house. But I couldn't tell him that, so I said, "Walter, will you do me a favor? Will you tell me why your mother was crying?" I held my breath, because I didn't know what he was going to do.

For a minute he was undecided; then he said, "It was something Bosko told her this afternoon."

"You mean Uncle Bosko said something wrong?"

"No, Emil. He said because of the way things were, he thought he better not come over to the house any more. You know, Mama never had a very easy time of it, Emil. My old man was all right sometimes, but most of the time he was an awful krauthead. And I've been worried about Mama."

"In what way?"

"Well, pretty soon Victor, and Sadie, and the rest will be getting married and leaving home, and what's left for Mama any more? So when she laughed all during supper after you and Bosko had come over . . . and when she seemed so happy, why—Emil, if your old man don't keep his snoot out of this—"

"Now wait a minute, Walter." I didn't think it was a good idea to let him get talking about Papa. "All of you think quite a bit of Uncle Bosko, don't you?"

"Why shouldn't we? Imagine a little guy like that getting himself busted with a bowling ball so he can buy me ukulele strings and Mama perfume. I'd give my right arm for a guy like that, but your old man—"

"I know," I said quickly. "But do you want to give Uncle Bosko a break?"

"You think I wouldn't?" Walter said, and I thought he was going to hang one on me. So I thought I'd better explain.

I explained how Uncle Bosko hadn't had a very easy time of it either. And I told him about what the real krautheads, over there, had done to Uncle Bosko. "Gee, Walter," I said, "when we were setting pins that day, he could hardly lift the bowling balls."

Walter shook his head. "Is that right?"

"Sure. And so far as his ever being able to work again—"

"You don't think he'll ever be able to do anything?"

"I doubt it. So why should we put him on the spot?" I said. "Why should we make him feel he has to make a choice between Papa and going over to your house? Why even bother him with it?"

Walter nodded. "Yeah, I guess you're right."

"How about working together then?" I asked. "How about us patching up this business with Papa?"

Walter considered. "Well, to tell you the truth, Emil, I'd like to take just one poke at your old man, but—" He held out his hand. "I'm with you. Shake. What do we do?"

The next evening when the doorbell rang, I made sure I got to the door first. "Well, well! Come in!" I said, trying to act surprised. Then I called, "Hey, Papa, you got company."

Papa was relaxing in his easy chair. "Yeah? Who?" He looked around and saw Walter and Victor Tomich and Benny Dumbroski standing in the hall, looking like a couple of tackles out of the Notre Dame line with the water boy in between them. I guess Papa thought they were going to mob him, because he turned white.

"Hello, Louie," everybody said, and Benny added, "We just come over to play a little pinochle."

Papa was scared stiff. "Okay, I'll get the table." He edged away, and I could see he was heading for the back door.

"I'll get it, Papa," I said quickly—and did he give me a dirty look! He gave me another one, too, because before he could think of any more excuses to get out of the room, I said, "Josie, get the cards and score pad. Steve, run down to the cellar and draw a pitcher of wine." And I even sent Pete into the bathroom to wash his hands, so Papa was stuck.

"Hey, Louie, where's Bosko?" Walter asked.

Papa wiped his forehead. "Helping Mama with the dishes."

Just then Uncle Bosko peeked in from the kitchen. When he saw Walter, he started to smile. But I guess he remembered something, for he looked at Papa and didn't seem to know what to do.

Walter put his arm around Uncle Bosko's shoulder then, and introduced him to Victor. "How's your leg, Bosko?" Victor asked. The two of them towered over him, and he looked up at them.

"It was just a little bump," he said.

Papa was surprised. "Did you get a bump, Bosko?"

"Yeah," Victor said. "We had to do a little pulverizing, but we took care of it . . . By the way, Emil, any time you want to set pins, why, Mike Zachek says you should come right in and make yourself at home."

Before I could say thanks, Walter was yelling, "Ouch!"

Looking down, I saw Stan kicking away at Walter's shins, and my heart was in my mouth, because Walter's face was getting red. "Stan, cut it out!" I yelled. But Stan wouldn't pay any attention. And Papa looked as if he was about to jump through the window, figuring, I guess, that Walter would blow his stack and start to clean house.

But Walter gritted his teeth and took his arm from around Uncle Bosko. "Stanislaus," he said, forcing a smile, "that's no way to fight."

"Who said so?"

"I did." Walter stooped, turned Stan around and took him by the wrists. "Come on, I'll show you how to box. Now see, here's a left jab." And Walter put him through the motion.

"What's a left hook, Walter?" Stan asked.

"Like this. And here's a right cross."

I wiped the perspiration from my forehead. "Don't you think we ought to play pinochle?" I asked.

"No!" Stan said. "Walter's showing me how to fight."

It took me a good twenty minutes to get the game under way, because Stan didn't want to quit. But finally I got Papa and Benny paired off against Walter and Victor Tomich. "Hey, Stan," the kids yelled then, "come on, we're going to wrestle in the parlor."

But Stan shook his head. "No. I want to sit by Walter."

I hadn't counted on Stan taking a kick at Walter. Yet I was glad it happened because now Stan was sitting there, counting the cards to make sure that Benny, who was dealing, gave Walter enough. So I had one down. But I had one to go and glanced at Papa.

Papa was pretty doubtful about this pinochle business. He still looked as if he would head for the back door at any moment. But when Walter opened with twenty-one, Papa bid twenty-two, even though he didn't have anything.

Well, when Papa stuck Walter with the bid—as we had agreed should happen—Papa started to chuckle. And when Walter was set, mainly because Victor—his partner—kept throwing all his counters to Papa and Benny, Papa started to laugh. "Hey, Benny." He laughed. "We got 'em down already. We show these guys how to play. Hey, everybody, how about a little glass of wine?"

Well. After Papa and Benny set them a couple more times, there was no holding Papa. First thing you know, he was flipping the cards behind him and over his shoulders, and saying, "Attaboy, Benny." And most of the time he had to hold his sides, because he was laughing so much.

After he and Benny took six straight games, Walter looked at me as if to say, "Emil, enough is enough." So I nodded, and Walter pushed his chair back. "What say we quit?"

"Aw, come on," Papa coaxed. "I'm just getting warmed up."

Walter shook his head. "Nope, you're too good, Louie." And did Papa ever beam!

"Let's just talk awhile," Victor said. "Bosko, I was wondering if you might not like a job."

That caught me by surprise. It caught Uncle Bosko too. His face lit up and he began nodding. "Yeah, Victor, I would like that."

But Papa cut in. "What kind of a job is it?"

Victor glanced at Papa, and I thought he was going to say, "Louie, mind your own business." Instead, though, he said,

"Well, you know I was thinking of starting that bakery here in Hamtramck, Louie. But it takes more money than I thought, and I just don't have it. So last night we talked it over at home."

"Yeah, Louie," Walter said. "And Mama couldn't see why Victor should let this chance get away. So we're all pitching in to help out. We're making it a family affair with Victor managing it."

"That's right." Victor nodded. "Mama says what good is a family if it don't stick together? So that's what we're doing. Together we have plenty of money to get started. In fact, we're even opening a branch store down in Wyandotte."

Papa's eyes widened. "You ought to make some dough, huh?"

"Sure," Walter said. "And we want Bosko to come in with us. We'll need someone to take care of the Wyandotte store—someone who isn't going to get into the cash every time our backs are turned —so right away we thought of him."

"And you just want Bosko to run the place?" Papa asked.

"Yeah," Victor said. "We won't have to worry then. We know he'll see that the place is kept clean, and that he'll be nice to customers, instead of driving them away, like these snooty clerks."

"That's right, Louie," Walter said. "And Victor can teach him about managing the store, and—"

"And I'll help him, too," Papa added. "If he wants to know anything, all he has to do is just come and ask me."

Victor glanced at Walter. Walter glanced at Victor. And I wanted to say, "Papa, keep out of this."

But Papa was going on. "Now first of all," he said, "I think we ought to buy a cash register."

I could tell that Victor and Walter were getting sore. And I didn't know what to do, because I didn't want Papa ruining Uncle Bosko's chances. Then I remembered something Uncle Bosko told me about Papa and his Papa over in Poland, so I gave Walter the high sign. "Hey, Papa," I said. "You're wrong."

"Who's wrong?" Papa demanded.

"You are. They'll need at least two cash registers. Maybe three."

"You got holes in your head?" Papa said. "What they need three for?"

"I just think it's a good idea."

"Well, it ain't!"

"And another thing," I said, winking at Victor, "I don't think it's a good idea for Uncle Bosko to take this job."

"Oh, so you don't think so, eh, Mr. Smarty? Well, I think it is!"

"You think I should take the job then, huh, Louie?" Uncle Bosko asked.

"Yeah, you take it," Papa said. "And don't you let any of these wise guys talk you into buying cash registers."

Victor and Walter glanced at me and nodded. And I knew it was going to be quite a job, but I felt sure that between us we would be able to keep Papa from butting in. Then we looked at Uncle Bosko. He was like a kid with a new cowboy outfit. Then for a moment I thought he was going to cry. He sort of looked up at Walter and Victor, and they grinned at him. And I sure felt good, because now he had plenty of muscle on his side.

But I was curious about something, so I asked, "Walter, if Uncle Bosko is going to run the place in Wyandotte, does it mean he has to move down there?"

Papa banged the card table. "Emil, what's the matter with you? Uncle Bosko is going to live here in Hamtramck."

Walter's face was solemn. "I don't think he ought to move out of Hamtramck, Emil. It'd be pretty lonesome for him down there. We didn't mean that. We just thought this would give him a chance to earn some money, and . . . Well, maybe he has some plans of his own."

I looked at Uncle Bosko. His eyes met mine, then sank to the floor, and he began to grin. And I had the feeling that one of these days I was going to be having some new cousins.

"You know, Uncle Bosko," I said, "maybe you ought to buy yourself a car."

Uncle Bosko's mouth flew open. But Benny and Walter and Victor, and even Papa, joined in then. "Sure, Bosko, that's just what you need," they said.

And I got to wondering. I wondered if, maybe, Smiling Harry might not have a coupe on hand. After all, Uncle Bosko wouldn't need a big car. Just something to get back and forth to work. And something for him and Aunt Lena in case they wanted to go driving on Sunday afternoons.